CEDAR

PRESS

Printed in Australia

First Printing: July 2023

Paperback ISBN 978-1-7638384-0-6

eBook ISBN 978-1-7638384-1-3

A catalogue record for this work is available from the National Library of Australia

CEDAR

KIM WINTER

<u>In Memoriam</u>
Richard 'Dekenai' Crispin
Aviator
Larrikin
Poet
Horseman
Gentleman
Mate

Dedication
For
Jasmine, Samuel, Brodie and Cora
All my love

To my mother, Elsie, who always believed in me.
I did it, Mum.

*'They suffered wounds, thirst, hunger and weariness almost
beyond endurance but never failed. They did not come home.
We will never forget them.'*
Inscription on a Desert Corp War Memorial
Macquarie Street, Sydney

*'…Most obediently and often most painfully, they died.
Faithful unto death…'*
St Jude's
Hampstead, England

THE STATION AND SURROUNDING AREA

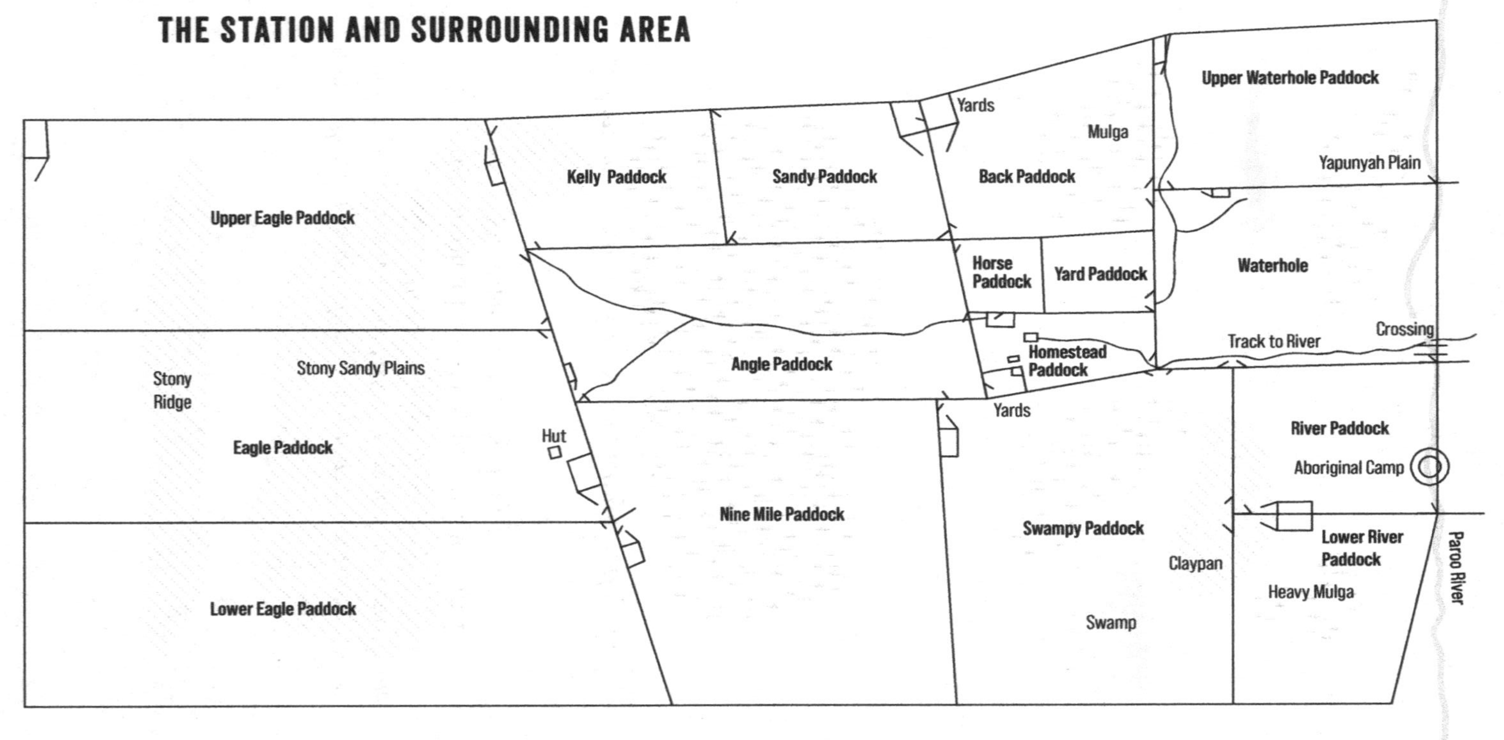

HOMESTEAD

Yards
Acacia
Windmill
Harness Shed
Kennels
Kitchen
Homestead
Stores
Scrub
Sheep Yards
Shearing Shed
Shearer's Quarters
Scrub

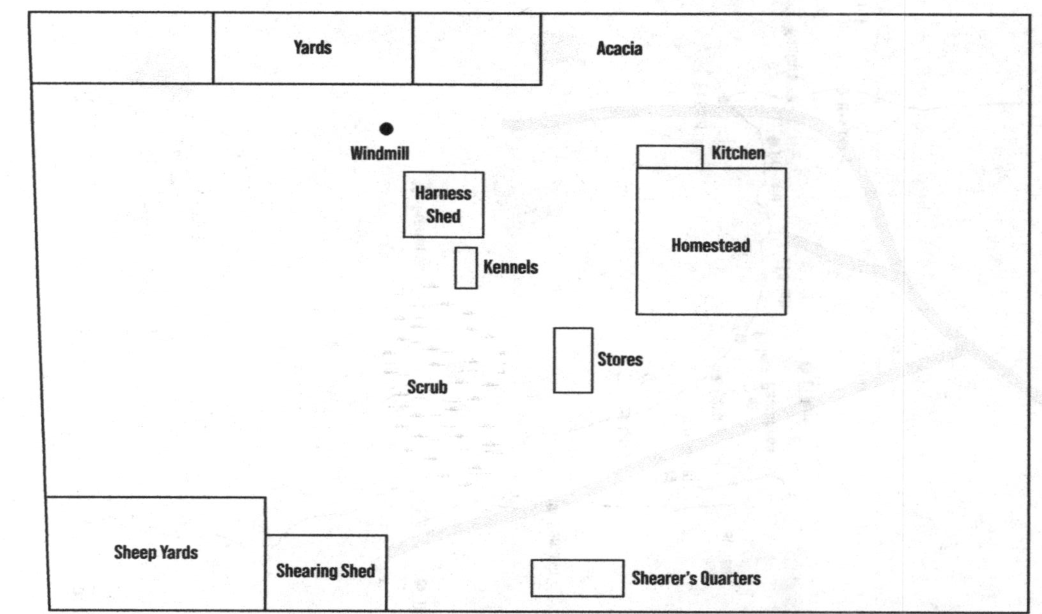

THE MIDDLE EAST, WW1

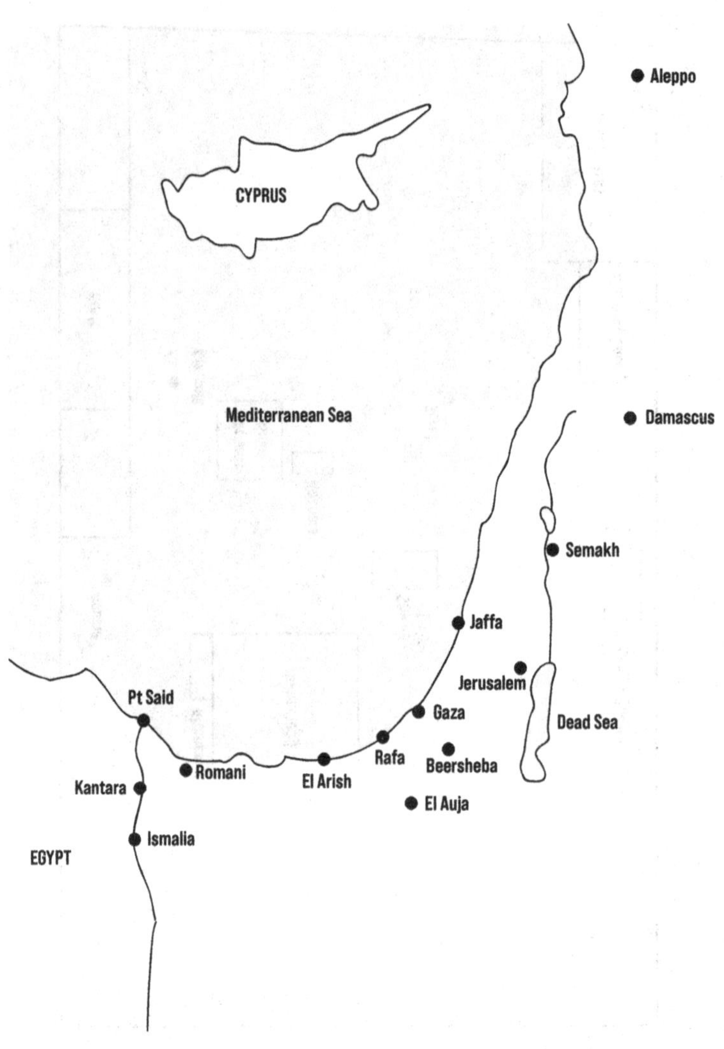

FRANCE / BELGIUM, WW1

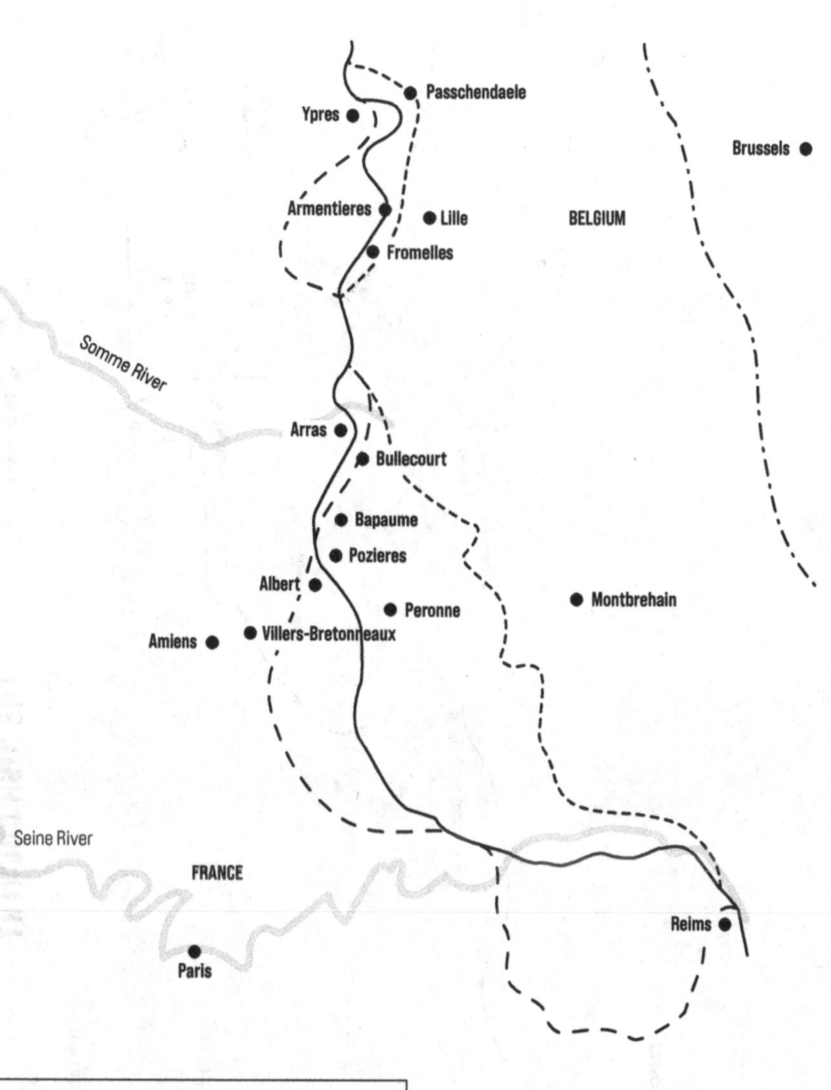

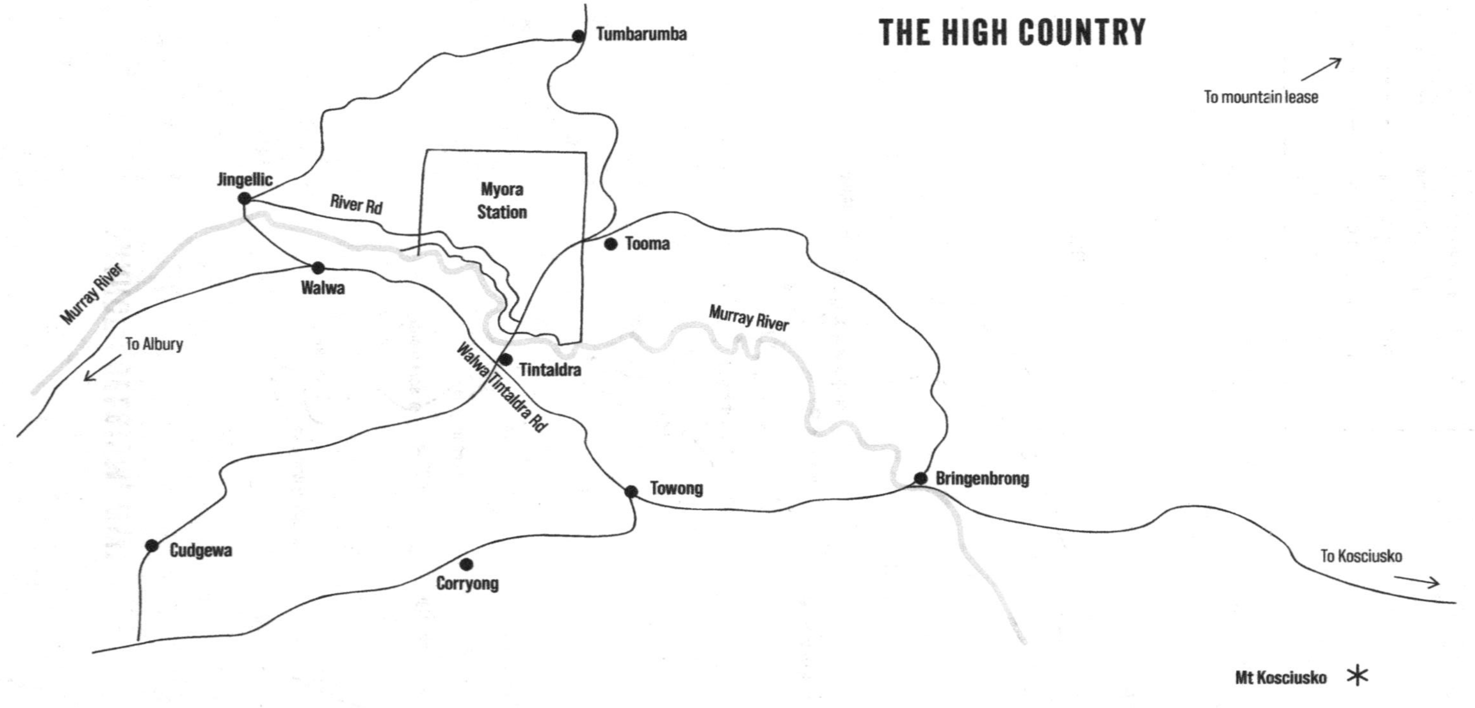

THE HIGH COUNTRY
Tumbarumba
To mountain lease
Jingellic
River Rd
Myora Station
Tooma
Murray River
Walwa
Murray River
To Albury
Walwa/Tintaldra Rd
Tintaldra
Towong
Bringenbrong
Cudgewa
Corryong
To Kosciusko
Mt Kosciusko

ONE

It rained. Not gentle spring rain or gusty winter rain; instead, drops the size of shillings plummeted to the ground. The water soaked the parched red sand until it could absorb no more. Sheeting across the land, running in angry rivulets, growing larger and stronger until it was a torrent cascading over dead mulga branches, through the spinifex mounds, it surged towards the dry riverbed.

Eight-year-old Matty was entranced; he could not remember rain like this. He'd felt mist on his face and seen brief soft showers, but never had he seen such a deluge. He stared up at the huge gunmetal grey clouds, his eyes squinting to keep the raindrops from splashing in his eyes. He felt as though the clouds would press him into the earth. He reached up, thinking he might touch them, but only felt the large drops hitting his hands and running down his arms.

He turned around and round, his face held up to the pelting rain. He thought that the rain was spiralling to him as he spun faster and faster until dizzy, he stumbled and fell. He giggled, slashing at the water, watching the droplets rise and mingle with the falling rain. He lay in the puddling water and reckoned his mother would be happier now that her plants would not die after all. And Father, well, Father could smile and take him riding again and Dave, Bert and George might come back now there could be work. Father would be able to pay them again. Matty smiled as he imagined how days would get back to the way they were when he was little; maybe now he could get the horse his father had promised him. With this thought, he got up from the swirling red slush and ran, leaping the mulga stumps and scaring the few remaining sheep as he jumped and yelled, 'It'll be all right now, it's raining, it's raining.'

* * * *

Eliza was searching everywhere for Matty, knowing that sudden downpours could cause flash flooding. Her heart steadied as she watched him coming from the yard paddock, kicking the water in front of him, stopping to scoop it up and throw it high, laughing as it fell back on him. This was to be their only child, the one that Minnie had saved from snakebite, the one who constantly scraped his knees, fell out of trees, and brought home all manner of pets. The house had been home to a sand goanna and shingle back lizards, wounded birds, bush mice, and even a bat for a while. Then there was the python. Eliza hadn't known that pythons were non-venomous. Her heart stopped when Matty came in the back door to show her his new friend.

'Charlie found him for me, Mother. He's not poisonous – he's a carpet snake. Charlie calls him a *yabaa*. I'll keep him in the wood box and feed him mice and… what else?' He paused, thinking of something a snake might eat in a drought, while his hands gently controlled the writhing beautifully-marked reptile.

Eliza reeled in her wits, which had fled screaming, at the sight of the snake.

'You… will… not… young… man!' she enunciated each word. 'You will take him back to Charlie. You will say to Charlie, that the Missus has forbidden any snakes as pets. Do you understand, Matthew?'

Being called Matthew made him realise she was serious, so he turned without argument and took the snake down to the river to let it go. There were no more pet snakes after that.

* * * *

For seven years, the land had been without decent rain, life-giving, resuscitating rain. The signs of drought were all around him. Bleached bones of sheep and cattle lay where they had fallen, too weak to make the long walk from the few dry remnants of spinifex to the bore at the homestead. Most of the birds and native animals had either moved on or perished like the stock. In the homestead paddock, the bore trickled water into an old tin trough, and at dawn and dusk, the few remaining animals and birds would gather to take their fill. It was Matty's job to fill the water tank at the back door by redirecting the pipe at the bore to the homestead every day. He thought of his mother looking up at the burning sky.

'The garden is not going so well, Matthew. I fear there will be few vegetables this year,' she would say.

Matty watched his mother help Tan carry the water to the vegetable patch every day and pour it onto the struggling plants. It wasn't enough that the plants battled the hot drying winds, or that the sandy soil did not retain moisture, but they also had to rely on his mother and Tan watering two, sometimes three times a day.

At night, Matty listened from his bed as his parents talked about the prospect of rain, their voices low, despair underlying every word. For months, Matty's father had been silent and brooding, whereas before he'd been laughing and full of fun. Now his face, lined and burnt brown, never smiled. Cutting mulga to feed their remaining sheep and cattle often kept him away for days, as he went further and further out with the wagons. Keeping the windmills from breaking down was a bigger problem. The hard work and sleepless nights had worn him out.

His mother often had accompanied Matty on his adventures into the paddocks or played with him on the verandah but now she was always weary, too tired to keep him amused. The drought had dragged on for years, banks crashed, and people were being foreclosed on all over the country. Thankfully, they owned their property and had no overdraft. They could no longer afford to keep on the governess, and so Matty's mother took over his lessons. The Aboriginal women helped her with housework, but Eliza was not a stern mistress and the girls usually made games out of simple chores, their work haphazard. The Aboriginal stockmen stayed on; Charlie, the horse-breaker; Big Jim, who was now Thomas's head stockman; Billy and Ned. They received tea, flour, and tobacco but the credit at the store was running out. Matty's father would not be able to provide even that soon. He was trying to get through without using the last of his invested money.

Thomas could not afford to kill any meat from the remnants of their sheep flock. If he were to build up numbers to make an income, he had to hang on to the remainder of his cows and ewes. He had also lost several good horses including the stallion he had bought from Bourke. The Aboriginals brought kangaroo meat to the house and Minnie showed Eliza how to cook the game meat on the fire. In return, Eliza made pigeon pies for Minnie, who had developed a liking for them. Eliza knew they would have given up and left the property if it was not for Minnie and her people.

Matty was too young to realise that this harsh, burnt, brutal land had made his parents old in thirteen years.

* * * *

Matty caught sight of his mother. Running and jumping, laughing all the way, he raced towards her and hugged her waist.

'Mother, it's raining, it's raining. Do you think I'll get my horse now?'

'We'll see, Matthew. You will have to ask your father,' she answered, as she brushed his wet blond hair out of his eyes.

He ran to the kennels where his father was repairing the mulga covering that served as a roof over their remaining sheepdogs.

'Father, it's raining! Can I have a horse of my own now?'

Thomas straightened up and smiled at his son's naivety. 'It will take a bit more rain than this to get things back to normal, Matty; well, as normal as what can be out here. But we shall see, will we? Maybe, if we get follow-up rain, we might manage a horse for you in a while.'

Matty jumped and yelled with joy. To his eight-year-old mind, he was getting a horse and that was enough.

As Thomas watched Matty run to his mother to tell her about the horse, Charlie came galloping up the track leading from the river.

Charlie drew rein, his horse blowing heavily. 'Boss, fella big trouble downriver. River risin' fas' an' him git catched crossin'. Big Jim, him gone to help, we need rope.'

Thomas wasted no time. Running to the horse yard, he grabbed a bridle from the gate and eased through the gap in the rails into the yard. He walked up to the big grey gelding in the corner, having already weighed up which horse would be the best to take. Moon was half Percheron, strong enough to pull loads, if needed. Thomas put the bridle on the gelding, mounted bareback, and pushed the horse into a canter from a standing start. He guided the horse at the fence and with a boot in the ribs; the horse cleared the rails easily. Turning on landing, Thomas headed the horse to the house.

'Get me the rope from the back step. Now!'

Matty had been watching his father since he heard Charlie gallop up, and now he ran to do his bidding. He had never seen his father ride bareback before and realised that the matter must be urgent.

'Eliza, there's a bloke in trouble at the river. Put old Bess in the dray and follow us down but stop at the gully. The gully may well flood too if this rain keeps up,' Thomas explained. 'Bring some tea and food and blankets. We may have to stay out. Get Matty to help you throw a canvas in, too.'

Thomas reached down for the rope Matty had brought and spun his horse away, Charlie following at the gallop. As they raced towards the river, thoughts ran logically through Thomas's head. He hoped that the bloke had been closer to this side of the river when the water hit, as it would now be too wide to help if he were on the other side. Some years ago, Thomas witnessed his first flash flood when the Paroo was nearly dry and rain had fallen heavily upstream. The water rose seven feet in two hours after the initial wave of water and getting cattle across had been too risky. The water spread out and took two weeks to drop.

Thomas pulled the horse back to a trot; it would do no good to kill it trying to get there. He trotted for five minutes then walked for two, then cantered again. It was eight miles to the crossing from the homestead and it would take a good twenty minutes there. Passing through the gully, Thomas thought of Eliza. If the water kept rising in the river then the gully would fill as the river broke its low banks. Charlie's horse was blowing heavily, and he pulled her up, telling the Boss that he would run and catch up with him at the river. Thomas had grown used to Charlie's extraordinary talents, one of which was to get off his horse and after loosening the girth, run beside the mare to give her a rest. As Charlie rode barefoot, he did not have the added burden of running in boots. Although the sand was deep in places, Charlie could run for miles in it.

Thomas pushed his horse into a canter again, ever mindful of the sharp mulga sticks that could open a nasty wound in the horse's leg. Looking ahead he could see the last bend in the track before the river and slowed, knowing that the water could be just around that corner. The true riverbed was another quarter of a mile away but the land was flat, and by now, the river would have spread out, its main bed deep and running a strong current. The Percheron's ears pricked as it heard men yelling and the frantic nickering of a horse. Thomas held him in check and as they trotted the last corner, Thomas saw what he had only heard.

A young boy hanging tightly onto a rope attached to a fine-looking thoroughbred stallion, which was rearing and pawing at the water that lapped at his hocks. The boy had taken a turn of the rope around a red gum sapling to help him hold the frightened horse. Big Jim and two other stockmen were pushing their horses into the water, calling loudly. Jim reined his horse up the bank as he saw Thomas ride up.

'Boy's father in there, Boss. Boy reckons his father with him, then the horse roll over and him, him not come up,' he said, shaking his head. The water spilled from the crown of his hat. 'We bin lookin', no sign of him. That water plenty wild.'

Big Jim pointed to the middle of the brown river where the currents swirled, dragging leaves and branches down, only to let them pop up a few feet further along.

'Get the men to ride downstream, Jim. Check the riverbank down as far as you can. Take this rope,' said Thomas, throwing it to him. 'I'll help the boy get that stallion under control and come after you.'

Big Jim called the men and, urging their horses into the edge of the rising river, they moved off slowly, the men's eyes searching every part of the bank. calling out, hoping for an answer as the water eddied around and under the turkey bush and lignum.

Thomas rode the grey over to the boy and sidling the gelding up to the stallion, spoke quietly to the frightened horse.

'Whoa then, old fella. What's this all about?'

The stallion stopped his rearing, his ears flickering back and forth, sniffing the scents of this strange man and horse. Taking a tentative step towards the grey, who remained quiet, the stallion calmed, taking courage from the other horse.

Charlie had quietly come up and tied his mount to a sapling.

'I take him now, Boss,' he said, as he moved to take the stallion's rope from the lad's hands.

The boy passed the rope to Charlie, who unwound it from the tree branch. Speaking softly to the stallion in language, Charlie led him up the bank to higher ground.

The young fellow stood looking up at Thomas, squinting his eyes to keep out the large raindrops.

'Come out of there, boy,' called Thomas, as he slid from the Percheron and stood holding the reins, waiting for the boy to come to him.

Blue eyes stared back at him from under a jagged black fringe, as the boy waded out of the river. His clothes were sodden and worn, the holes in them stitched crudely. His limbs were thin and wiry, and he trembled as he held his hands under his armpits.

'What's your name, boy?' Thomas asked.

'Jack Henderson, sir,' he replied, his lips quivering.

'How old are you?'

'I'm nine, I think.'

Thomas took his oilskin off and wrapped it around the boy.

'Can you tell me what happened, Jack?'

'Me da an' me, we was goin' to Gumbo to work for Mr Phillips and we was behind time. That's why Da tried to cross the river. He said it wouldn't be deep yet, so he put me up on Longman, the stallion, there, see, and he was holdin' the stirrup on the offside upriver, but the horse, he hit somethin' an' rolled under. I held the saddle an' come back up but Da… Da didn't, an' I couldn't see him.'

His body shaking, tears dropping down his white cheeks, Jack's eyelids fluttered and he slid down to the red sand.

'Charlie, the young fellow's all-in!' Thomas called. 'Tie that stallion up and come help me, will you?'

Thomas knelt and raised the unconscious boy's head, noting the rope burns on Jack's hands as he did so.

'Looks like he was trying to hold that stallion for a while, poor kid,' he said, as Charlie came up to him. 'We'll put him up on the grey and you can take him back along the track till you see the Missus. She and Matty are bringing the dray. Get a fire going and ask the Missus to put on some tea. This boy will need it and so will the men. I'll take your horse and see how they're going with the search.'

Between them, they lifted Jack onto the horse and while Thomas held him steady, Charlie swung up behind him. Taking the reins, Charlie said, 'We find him by-an'-by, Boss. Water go down, we find him.'

'That's what I am afraid of, Charlie. We are too late.'

Thomas walked up the bank and mounted Charlie's mare. Reaching over, he untied the stallion and, leading him, went to search with the men.

TWO

'Charlie, Charlie!' Matty's voice called. 'Come'n see, Charlie!'

Charlie put down the bridle he'd been repairing and walked out of the slab shed into the harsh sunlight. He looked about for the boys and spotted them sitting on the tank stand near the shearing shed.

'Why you fellas no school?'

'Mother had to salt the meat, Charlie!' Matty called back. 'But see, Charlie, look at Longman. He's makin' babies with Dusty!'

Charlie stepped around the side of the shed to where he could see the horse yards. He grinned at the sight of the stallion mating with his mare.

'Baby horse by-an'-by, Matty. See the Boss, meybe, you have horse?'

Jumping off the tank stand, Matty ran to Charlie and threw his arms around him.

'You mean it? Can I have the foal?'

'We ask him Boss. He say.'

Matty turned to Jack. 'Hey, your stallion, he was a racehorse, wasn't he?'

'Yeah, that's what Da said. Got him off a fella at Bourke races. Da was gonna put Longman out for service. The fella was broke and needed money quick, so, Da gave him all our money, knowin' his was goin' to work for Mr Phillips...' Jack's voice lowered as he turned and walked towards the shearing shed.

Matty realised his friend was going into one of his quiet moods; Jack did that whenever anyone mentioned his father. They never found his father's body and so Jack stayed on with Matty's family. He helped around the place and shared lessons with Matty when Eliza had time. The boys became good friends in a short while. Eliza had written to Bourke to inform the local constabulary of the tragedy, and after questioning Jack as to his family, of which there was none as far as he knew, she offered him a home with them.

Matty followed Jack, staying a little way behind. He felt his friend's pain. He bit his lip and screwed up his nose in his effort to think of something to take Jack's mind off his father.

'Hey Jack, remember I was telling you about Sammy? He should be back soon.'

The only other boy Matty's age on the property had been Sammy, a black child who had gone on 'pfella bus'ness' with his father and uncle, to their people further upriver. Matty had told Jack how he and Sammy had grown up together, and how he was looking forward to Jack and Sammy meeting.

'Yeah,' was all Jack said.

A soft growling drew Matty's attention.

'Hey, Jack. How about gettin' Brownie here to go away, so as we can look at the pups.'

'You'll cop it from your da if he finds you messin' with her pups.'

'Na, we're only lookin'. You get a lump of that roo that's hanging in the shed for the dogs and throw it to her. While she's eatin' it, we'll have a look at the pups,' Matty said. 'I'll keep a look out.'

'All right, let's do it.'

Jack went into the shearing shed and took the knife that was wedged into the batten on the wall. He stretched as high as he could. Grabbing what was left of the tail, he sliced off a slab of meat from the roo's rump and after carefully putting the knife back where he found it, he returned to where Matty was keeping watch.

'Here, Shorty,' Jack said as he threw the meat to Matty, 'you wouldn't have reached it.'

The boys slunk towards the back of the shearing shed. Thomas had constructed a shade over the den Brownie had dug in the red soil, away from the other dogs. When they got to the corner of the shed, Jack whistled and Matty threw the meat as far as he could. The bitch, with her full dugs swinging, ran to the meat and settled down to eat. It had rolled under a stand of turkey bush, blocking Brownie's line of sight to her pups.

'Now,' Matty whispered and crept towards the pups.

Jack followed, looking over his shoulder with every step he took.

Crouching down, the boys stared at the pudgy, wrinkled pups, their eyes still tightly shut.

'They are so small,' Matty whispered in wonder. 'You'd reckon they'd never get as big as Brownie.'

Jack agreed, 'Yeah, but I heard Charlie say these pups'll grow bigger, 'cause that blue-speckled dog of Big Jim's is the father.'

A low rumbling snarl from behind the boys alerted them to their danger. Jack had forgotten, in his fascination with the pups, to keep an eye on the turkey bush. The boys did not move a muscle. Jack very softly said, in as deep a voice as his tightened throat would allow, 'Brownie, old girl. Get behind, girl, get behind. Now, sit down, girl, sit.'

The dog went in quickly, hackles raised. After giving Jack a quick nip on his heel, she swung her head sideways and grabbed Matty's trousers, growling savagely as she shook her head, pulling the cloth back and forth.

Jack scurried backward through the sand, away from the bitch, away from Matty. When he considered it safe, he jumped up and ran for an old limb that had fallen from the tree overhead. Keeping his eyes on the dog, he picked the branch up and immediately felt a burning sensation in the soft skin between his fingers. Jack looked at his hand gripping the decaying limb and swore. Large orange bull ants were climbing out of the bark, racing towards his hand, where one ant was trapped in between his fingers. Jack threw the branch down, and with his other hand, swiped wildly, trying to dislodge the bull ants that had crawled up it.

'Jack, get her off me. Jack?' Matty yelled.

'I'm trying, I'm trying,' Jack yelled back, rubbing his hand up and down his trouser leg, trying to watch both the dog and the raging ants.

Sssrrrr-ack.

Things happened in quick succession. Brownie let go of Matty and slunk over to her pups, Matty rolled away from the den, pulling his trousers up to inspect the damage and Jack limped slowly towards the corner of the shed, shaking his swollen hand.

'Boys 'n plenty trouble, eh?' Charlie's white teeth showed in a grin as he rolled his stockwhip over his shoulder. 'Missus fin' out, b-i-g trouble.' Charlie's grin got bigger. 'Him, Boss, him gonna plenty boot 'em boys!'

Charlie's arm moved swiftly, snaking the long rawhide stockwhip softly around Jack's middle as he backed away.

'Git back here, gimme look'um hand,' he demanded, reaching out for Jack's arm. 'Ol' *Gabiyan* give you fire stick, eh? Give me look. Ol' Minnie, she fix 'em up.'

Matty, judging he had crawled far enough from the den, stood up and took a wide circular path to where Jack stood.

'Charlie, we can't tell Mother. We won't be allowed out for ages and ages,' he said, appealing to Charlie's easy nature.

Charlie studied the two boys, weighing up the consequences.

'Him Boss, him be plenty mad. You two fella worry dog,' he said sternly. 'You fellas, you go river… Minnie. I talk to Missus.'

Matty sighed with relief but Jack poked his finger into Matty's ribs.

'We're not out of the woods yet, Shorty. We gotta get down to the river without no one seeing us,' he said.

'Go long way, way 'round stockyards tank, back of mulga,' Charlie suggested as he turned to go to the big house.

A growl came from the shade of the bitch's den and, without the protection of Charlie, the boys wasted no time in getting away.

They ran, their injuries forgotten. Passing behind the shearing quarters, the boys crossed the sandy track and entered the dense mulga shrub. Here they pulled up and sat together in the sand to get their breath.

'What's it like at the blackfella's camp, Shorty? They're different,' Jack asked.

'Nah, they're like us but they don't live in a house. They eat really different but the food's good.' Matty smiled, watching Jack's face. 'They eat roo and snake and flowers!'

'Flowers?' Jack glanced at him suspiciously.

'Yeah, they dig 'em up and the bottom's really crunchy but nice. In the waterhole, they pull up reeds and they're the same, juicy and crunchy.'

Jack shook his head. 'Nah, you're having a lend, mate.'

'You wait, you'll see,' said Matty. 'C'mon, Charlie'll beat us there. It's on the bend of the river and it's a long way.'

The boys stood, brushed the fine, red sand off their pants then headed east for the Aboriginal camp.

'Hey, Matty! How do you know which way it is?'

Matty stopped and looked at Jack's bewildered expression. He gazed around, taking in the mulga scrub, the mounds of silvery green spinifex, stared at the ground where his bare feet sunk into the sand and then, cocking his head to the side, squinted at Jack. 'I dunno, just do.'

'Whad'ya mean?' Jack pressed.

'Well, our shadows are pointing that way.' Matty indicated east by a throw of his hand. 'The sun rises in the east and sets in the west. It's afternoon, so the sun is headin' west, so it throws a shadow to the east. The camp's by the river and I know that is east of the homestead, so we go the way of the shadow.'

Jack looked at him in awe.

'Shorty, how do you know that?'

'Charlie.'

'What, Charlie taught you that?' Jack asked.

'Well, sort of. The way he says things, you just get to know.'

Jack shrugged his shoulders and kept walking, his mind trying to sort out this new and interesting information. Stopping, he turned and jumped, stepping sideways, always watching the ground.

'What you doin', Jack?'

'I'm trying to trick my shadow.'

Matty giggled. 'You can't do it. Your shadow is always there unless it's cloudy.'

'Well, how do you tell where you're goin' when the sun's not out?' Jack's face lit up. Now he would stump Matty.

'I dunno, you just know.'

Jack gave up and walked beside Matty, looking at the surrounding country with new eyes.

'Charlie showed me where the *Thuli* hides, that's a sand goanna. You see his tracks, like a bit of rope dragged in the sand but with footprints on both sides, and he burrows under the spinifex if you scare him. He waits real still and then comes out. He's fun to chase but quick, real quick,' Matty explained. 'You just got to look and you see where everything goes.'

He ran ahead of Jack; his eyes had picked up a track.

'Look, this is where an emu has been an' he's got young uns.' Matty pointed to the ground. 'See, the big middle claw and two littler ones outside and a bit of a heel at the back. And there's one left and one right and he takes big steps. Then there's lots of little ones, same shape but little. The father emu, he brings up the babies, the mother leaves. Different, eh?'

Jack bent down and traced his finger in the sand, following the depressions left by the passing birds. He began to think that maybe there was a lot more to learn than just listening to the Missus on the back verandah school.

'I've never really thought about stuff like this before, Matty. This is dinky-di stuff?'

His mate looked at Jack, direct. ''Course it is. I'm not joshin' you, Jack. C'mon, let's go, see what Charlie said to Mother.'

The boys started at a slow trot, twisting in and out of the spinifex mounds, their unshod feet padding softly through the sand, slowing only to pass through the thicker mulga stands. They covered the ground easily.

Ten minutes later Jack pulled up.

'Matty, slow up. I got to get me wind. Me hand's hurtin' bad too.'

Turning back, Matty went to Jack, sinking down beside him.

'Show me your hand,' he said.

Jack showed him the hand that the bull ants had attacked. It was swollen, little blue marks surrounded by reddened patches of raised skin, covered his arm.

'Ooh, that looks sore, mate. Is it hurtin' bad?'

'It's throbbin' an' burnin',' Jack replied, staring at his hand in fascination. 'For a little animal they do some damage, don't they?'

'Yeh, we'd better keep goin'. Minnie'll have something to fix it; she's good at that sort of thing. She saved my life when I was little.'

'What happened?'

'I don't remember all of it but Mother said my cat was playing with a snake, a mulga grey, and I tried to stop it 'cause I thought the snake was attackin' the cat. Anyway, I got bit and the poison was killin' me but Minnie came an' did things and I lived.'

'What'd she do?'

'Mother doesn't know cos Minnie sent her out, but I got a little scar where it bit me. Mother says Minnie is a very special person 'cause Minnie helped Mother too. I think Mother lost my brothers and sisters somehow…'

'What do yer mean lost 'em?'

Matty looked at the sky. 'You know, like, had trouble havin' 'em. You know, like when the lambs are born an' some's too early and they die. Anyway, Minnie helped and Mother says Minnie is better than a doctor! So she'll fix your hand.'

Jack did not know what to say, so he stood and started off again, more purposefully this time.

'Hey, Jack, this way,' Matty chided, pointing to the east.

Jack shrugged and turned following his friend, mumbling, 'I'm gonna have to ask Charlie about all this.

THREE

On the riverbank, a small fire gave off a slip of smoke and several bark humpies were scattered about the area. A river red gum, with its low spreading branches and pendulous leaves, gave deep shade to the people who sat beneath it, all women. They sat in a circle, bare-chested, wearing only Eliza's cast-off skirts. Their hands were busy with reeds pulled from the water.

A raised arm beckoned the boys and they went to join the gathering.

'Why you here for, young fella?' Minnie asked.

Matty did not look at Minnie; he watched the women's fingers as they wove strips of reed into dilly bags. He thrust his hands deep into his pockets.

'Must be plenty trouble? Young fella?' Minnie had helped raise Matty; she understood him like her own. She waited, silently, her hands stripping the reed she held into thinner pieces, which she then laid in front of a younger woman at her side.

'Well, sort of,' Matty replied slowly.

Matty's eyes roamed everywhere, anywhere other than Minnie's face. Finding an object that could not look back at him, they locked onto the finished bag that hung from a snag in the tree.

'We was lookin' at Brownie's pups an' she caught us. She bit Jack on the heel and me, she grabbed me trousers! And then Jack picked up a branch to get her off me and there were bull ants on it and they bit him bad…'

'Yeah?' Minnie asked and waited. She knew Matty to be truthful and that the story would come out.

'Well, then Charlie found us and cracked the whip and Brownie let go of me, but the ants, they were hurting Jack, and Charlie said that we should come to the camp, and you would know how to fix Jack's hand.'

'Missus, she know you here?'

'Charlie was gonna see her.'

Minnie nodded her head and said something in her language to the other women who laughed.

Jack leaned towards Matty. 'What'd she say, Matty?'

'Dunno.'

'Well, why are they laughin'?'

'Dunno.'

Jack shrugged his shoulders and watched as the women quietened and returned to their work.

Minnie waved at Jack. 'Young Jack, come here, me have a look.'

Having not yet met Minnie, he hesitated. She looked very old to him, but though unsure, he moved deliberately forward when Matty muttered, 'She won't eat you.'

Minnie gestured for Jack to sit beside her, one of the women rising to make way for him. She gestured with bent fingers then opened her palm. Jack put the injured hand in Minnie's for her evaluation. She gently turned his hand over, making clicking noises with her tongue. Looking sideways at Matty from under her wisps of grey, frizzy hair, she spoke firmly.

'The Boss, he no be happy fella, Matty. Ol' Brownie, she jus' lookin out for her babies. You bad fellas, botherin' her. Them ants, they get you for it.'

'Yes, Minnie,' Matty answered.

'Now, we get somethin' for burnin', eh, Jack?'

'Yes, please.'

'Bess, you go git hop bush,' Minnie directed her daughter. 'Daisy, you git billy boilin'.'

The women rose to their allotted tasks while Minnie stretched her stiffened limbs. She grimaced, making her wrinkled features even more distorted.

'What's wrong, Minnie?' asked Matty.

'Ol' legs, dey tired, get stiff.'

Distracted by a loud call from behind them, they turned and saw Charlie, standing a little way off.

Jack called to him, 'What are yer doin' over there, Charlie? Come over here.'

'No, he can't. We got to go to him,' Matty said as he laid a hand on Jack's shoulder and pulled himself up.

'Why can't he come over here?'

'It's somethin' to do with Minnie bein' his relation. Charlie married Minnie's daughter, Annie. It's blackfella law,' Matty explained. 'Mother tried to tell me about it and I don't really know but that's what they do.'

Charlie saw the boys walking to him and moved into some shade further upriver from the women. He stretched his lean frame against the butt of the tree and, waiting for them to get closer, he gestured for the boys to sit with him.

Jack looked over to where Minnie sat, then back at Charlie.

'Why can't you talk to Minnie?' he asked.

'She *garrimaay*, no talk to her. Must, um, respect her. Is our people's law.'

Jack's face showed no sign of understanding.

'Do you have lots of laws?' he asked.

'Our people, they come from the dreamtime, make the laws. When you boys growed bit more, me tell you.'

Matty told Charlie how he had shown Jack the emu tracks.

'Can you teach me, Charlie? Can you show me how to tell where we're goin' by the sun as well?' Jack asked, his face excited, his bites forgotten.

'You boys, you bin bad. You'—Charlie glanced at Matty—'you not annoy Brownie. Boss tol' you dat.'

Matty nodded his head. 'I'm sorry, Charlie.'

'Me no told Missus. Me tell 'em, go to the waterhole, take boys. Few days, camp, hunt.' Charlie grinned in anticipation.

'Oh, Charlie! What did Mother say? Did you hear that, Jack?' Matty jumped up, bouncing up and down, his feet throwing up puffs of fine sand.

Jack leaned back, spitting out the dust. 'Cut it out. Yer don't know what yer ma said yet.'

Matty stood still, his eyes locked on Charlie's. 'Tell us she said yes, Charlie?'

Charlie looked towards the river and sighed. Above their heads, a willie wagtail landed on a branch not far from them. Bobbing and weaving, he scolded these humans. Charlie pointed at the bird and said to the boys, '*Thirithiri*, he sayin' go way. Him must have nest close up. He say, "Go way".'

Jack looked towards where Charlie pointed. 'What'd yer call him, Charlie?'

'Willie wagtail, *Thirithiri*. Now, Charlie, are we goin' to the waterhole?' Matty broke in, impatient to know if they were allowed to go.

Charlie smiled. 'You always in plenty hurry, Matty. You go see if Minnie got med'cine ready.'

'But, Charlie...'

'Me tell you by-an'-by, you go.'

Getting to his feet, Matty headed to the tree that Minnie sat under. As he left, he heard Charlie say to Jack, 'You town boy, eh? You look, listen, you be station boy soon.'

The women, after gathering some hop bush leaves and bark, had torn some of it and placed it in the billy of boiling water over the fire. After the brew had simmered for a few minutes, they took the billy from the fire and poured the contents into a metal pannikin. One of the girls said something to Minnie, who then said to Matty, 'Tell young fella come here, med'cine ready now.'

Matty jogged over to where Charlie and Jack sat talking.

'Minnie's got the stuff ready to fix your hand, Jack,' he said, keeping his eyes firmly on Charlie. 'Charlie, are we going to the waterhole or what? Are you havin' a lend?'

Charlie shrugged and grinned while Jack swiped away a fly trying to settle on his upper lip. Jack stared at the women across the way and mumbled, 'Come with me, Matty.'

'You'll be right, Jack. Minnie's all right. I want to find out what Mother said,' Matty said, dismissing his friend's fears, eager to find out if they were indeed going to the waterhole.

Jack got to his feet and, dragging them through the sand, went slowly to the group of women. He was wary, not having had much to do with Aboriginals before coming to the station. In the city, Jack heard stories of mayhem and murder. He had thought all Aboriginals savages. Watching the life of the station over the last month, he realised that maybe there was more to Aboriginals than he knew. He had met all the stockmen and some of the women that helped at the station, but Minnie had been away visiting country while he had been at the station. She was a little scary, a black version of what he imagined a witch to be, her skin all lined and folded, a mole on her cheek and wild grey hair standing around her head like fine wire, completed his picture. He breathed deeply through his nose and went to Minnie.

Matty flopped down in the sand, frustration all over his face.

'Charlie, please tell me what happened! What did you say to Mother?'

Charlie sat up from his resting place against the rough bark of the tree, flicking a wandering ant off his leg.

'You all time hurry like little ant. Always, run here, run there. Things happen by-an'-by,' he said, looking out over the brown water of the river. He turned his head and smiled at Matty. 'Missus say, boys stay with Charlie. I say Missus, you busy, Missus, Charlie take boys to waterhole. We fish, we hunt, few days. She say yes.'

Matty's eyes widened and his arms went up in the air. 'Wa-hoo! Oh, Charlie we're gonna have so much fun!' He jumped up and jiggled in a circle. 'We're goin' huntin', woo hoo!'

'Missus say no snakes. She no like snakes, eh, young fella?'

Matty stopped his hopping and looked at Charlie. 'We can still hunt them, Charlie, just don't tell Mother.'

'Missus say no snake, Charlie not hunt snake.'

'All right, but we can hunt goanna an' cook it up like we did when I went with you and Jim last year?'

'Annie come too. Missus give me plenty flour, plenty tea. Annie cook up damper like Minnie teached her, dig yams, we have plenty tucka.'

Jack came over to them, waving his hand at Matty.

'Look, she wrapped it up in leaves. Minnie put my hand in the pannikin. It was a bit hot but I stood it,' Jack said proudly. 'She smeared honey on it, called the honey sugarbag. Then she wrapped all these leaves around it. Minnie said it will take out the hurtin'. It feels better already.'

'Minnie plenty good, she fix plenty people,' Charlie said. 'C'mon, we go now.'

Jack looked a bit dubious and asked Matty, 'Are we really goin' campin'? What are we goin' to eat?'

'Charlie will hunt and we'll eat goanna and echidna and all sorts of things.' Seeing Jack's face register alarm, Matty added, 'It's good stuff, even Mother had some. Minnie cooked it up for us. Mother said we would have been poorer in food if Minnie and her people hadn't helped us. Anyways, when I went with Charlie and Jim'—Matty drew himself up proudly—'I ate all sorts of things and it was really good.'

Not to be outdone, Jack said, 'Well if you can eat it, I'll be blowed if I can't too!'

Charlie smiled at the two boys and called to Annie, '*Biliirr, thaay yanaya.*'

'What'd you say, Charlie?' Jack asked.

'I call Annie *Biliirr*, her *koori* name.'

'Why does she have two names?'

Charlie shrugged his shoulders. 'White fella boss, he name my father when he go to station to work. White fella gives us all white names, we call black fella name and white fella names. Black fella have many names. One secret one, never call it.'

Jack looked at Matty and raised his eyebrows; it was a little too much for him.

'Come on, let's get crackin', Charlie. We're going huntin',' Matty insisted.

They left the river with its cool shade and walked out onto the claypans, hot and solid under the sun. Charlie walked ahead, carrying a few spears and answering the boys' constant questions, while Annie cast her eyes about, and when spying something they could eat later, took herself off to dig it up or pick it, putting it in her woven dilly bag. They passed from the claypans onto the open sandy spinifex clearing. When they spotted a goanna resting in the shade, the boys took after it, running in and out of the mounds, leaping over fallen mulga until they pulled up winded. Charlie and Annie had stopped and were laughing at their antics.

'You fellas!' Annie said as she calmed her heaving sides. 'You no get tucka dat way. Charlie show you how.'

Charlie motioned to the boys to come behind him.

'You two fellas, follow, watch.'

The boys watched as Charlie bent low, walking gently, one foot in front of the other, lifting one then pausing before the other foot went down. His head moved slightly from side to side. Charlie went on like this for some ten minutes before he stopped, not suddenly, but seemed to flow from movement into stillness. He squatted down, beckoning the boys with a flick of his wrist.

'See tracks, one foot, two foot, both sides. Long bit where goanna drag him tail. Now, goanna, he go west, where sun go down. We follow very quietly, very slowly.'

Jack, awed by the change in Charlie, whispered, 'How do you know they're not old tracks?'

'Me bin hunting long time, piccaninny time. Uncle, father, ole men taught me. It like when you book learn with the Missus, you know,' Charlie explained. 'We walk quietly, ole goanna, he hide in grass, he sit in sun, no move. We look all around, we see him. When he run, we run, see where he hide, we hit him on head.'

Charlie looked up as Annie called to him, and following the direction of her arm, saw three men and a boy, walking towards them.

Matty shaded his eyes trying to pick out who they might be. As the group came closer, Matty recognised his friend Sammy.

'Here's a go, Jack. This is Sammy come back,' he explained. 'C'mon, I'll introduce you.'

The two parties greeted each other, the adults moving into the shade of the mulga, squatting to talk, while Matty excitedly introduced Sammy to Jack. He quickly explained the events that had brought Jack to the station. Sammy eyed Jack warily then broke into a big grin. 'You Matty's friend, you my friend.'

Jack nodded in agreement and put his hand out. Sammy took Jack's hand and shook it vigorously, as though to accentuate his words.

'We're going camping at the water hole. Charlie's taking us,' Matty explained. 'Go ask your uncle can you come too!'

'Why doesn't he ask his father? Why his uncle?' Jack asked.

Matty watched as Sammy ran over to the group of adults. He tried to think of how to explain tribal ways to Jack.

'Blackfellas do things different to us. His uncle sort of becomes his dad and tells him all about the tribe and things. He has to ask the uncle, not his father.'

Like before Sammy was born, everyone in the tribe knew that his uncle would be responsible for him. Aboriginal tribal laws were complex and Matty had only the barest grasp of them. Intensely curious, he often pestered Charlie or Jim to explain why they did or did not do certain things, but being young, Matty usually understood only a small portion of what he was told. The Aboriginals saw Matty as an enigma; he did not fall under their laws but was treated both as the son of the Boss and as a child to be taught whatever they could teach him. Both benefited from the relationship.

Sammy came back to the boys at the run, leaping over the mounds, laughing.

'Uncle say I go with you mob.' He grinned.

While the boys waited impatiently for the adults to finish talking, they began a game of chasing which quickly turned into a game of bushrangers. They squatted behind the lignum bushes and, using sticks, fired at each other, calling out when they were shot. Running and firing at each other, they took turns to be the bush ranger and the police.

The boys' game took them further than they had intended to go and they found themselves at a bore tank, its towering windmill standing lonely and out of place in the red sandy landscape. Sammy was the first to reach the trough that was fed by the tank. He dunked his head in the water, then shook it, drops spraying everywhere. Jack and Matty did the same, laughing at each other when the water ran in rivulets down their faces, leaving clean wet tracks on their dusty skin. Jack's eyes wandered over to the ladder that led up to the head of the windmill and, grinning, he ran over and grabbed the rungs. Climbing rapidly to the platform below the sails, he sang out to those below, 'I'm the king of the castle, you must be the rascals.'

Sammy and Matty both reached for the ladder, Sammy being first by a small margin. He started up the steel rungs, but when he looked down at Matty, his eyes glimpsed something else. He leaned out from the ladder as far as he dared and gripping it tightly with one hand, he looked down into the bore tank.

'Hey, you fellas, there's a plenty cheeky fella snake in the tank an' he's wrigglin'!'

Matty shaded his eyes to look up at Sammy. 'Can't be. How would a snake get in there?'

Jack got down on his hands and knees and peered cautiously over the edge of the narrow platform. 'Jeez, Matty, there is! It's a brown. How'd he have got in there?'

Sammy swung back against the ladder, pointing up at the platform. 'Maybe kookaburra catch him. Drop him up there when he eatin' him.'

'Well, we'd better get him out or he'll foul the water,' Matty said. 'How we gonna do that?'

Sammy and Jack climbed down, joining Matty on the ground.

Sammy had an idea. 'We get a stick or bit of wire, we put under him, lift him up. Throw him out.'

'Good idea, Sammy!' Matty said, immediately looking around. Not far from the tank was a small yard, put there for when the men were mustering. It consisted of boxwood post and rails, but also had strands of wire between the rails. Getting the wire untwisted from the strainer posts took some effort and the boys' hands were scratched from the sharp ends. Taking it back to the tank, Jack bent the wire into a hook at one end then looked at Matty and Sammy. 'Who's gonna do it?'

'We'll do one potato, two potato. That'll be a fair way to do it,' replied Matty. They put their fists out and began to count. Sammy was out first, then Matty. Jack nervously clenched the wire between his lips and turned to the ladder. He climbed far enough up to where he could lean his belly against the tank and reach down into it with the wire. He guided the hooked end slowly under the snake.

'Get out of the way, fellas, here it comes!' he yelled, getting excited.

His excitement interfered with his judgement and the snake slipped back through the hook, splashing into the water. The reptile swam around the edge of the tank, its head held high out of the water, tail thrashing wildly, thrusting it forward. A small bow wave rippled out until the water looked like a wind-chopped lake.

'Bloody hell,' Jack swore. 'I've dropped him. I'll have another go.'

'Take it slow,' the boys on the ground called out in encouragement. 'You'll get him, Jack.'

Jack took a deep breath and lowered the wire again. The snake had slowed its race around the tank and Jack guided the hook very slowly, deep in the water, under the snake. This time he aimed for its middle. When he thought that he had achieved this, he lifted the wire clear of the water. The snake hung suspended, its muscular body writhing and twisting, trying to escape the metal hook.

Hand over hand, Jack raised the wire until he decided that the snake was as close to him as was safe, but clear enough of the tank for him to fling it over the edge. He swung the wire back a little, then with all his strength, he heaved it over the edge, wire and snake together. It glided through the air, a curved shape descending rapidly towards the two boys on the ground.

Sammy and Matty's faces registered alarm, quickly turning to horror as the snake landed not far from their feet. The snake, angry and fierce, reared the front half of its body from the ground, its head flat and with a flick of its tail, swiftly headed for the boys.

Sammy took two steps and leapt for the top of the tank, just grasping its edge, drawing his legs up to his waist. Matty headed for the ladder.

Being shorter, he instantly worked out that he would not make the tank edge and that the ladder was the best option. From three foot away he jumped as high and as far as he could, his nose slamming into the ladder at the fourth rung. He kept climbing, tears of pain blurring his vision.

'You bloody idiot, Jack. You was supposed to throw it out the other side!' Matty yelled.

Sammy nodded his head in agreement. 'We lucky fellas. That one plenty cheeky fella. He cheeky, cheeky.'

'You're right there! He's stirred up bad, Sammy. He's also a bloody taipan, not a brown!'

They heard the air whoosh out of Jack's lungs. He had held his breath when he realised what he had done. He squirmed in embarrassment.

'I'm sorry, fellas. I thought it would land further away.'

The boys sat quietly on the ladder talking, waiting while the snake calmed down and slid off into the scrub. Climbing down, they all swore each other to secrecy. Matty's life would be hell if his mother found out about what had just taken place, and the other boys would suffer the strap as well.

They skirted the bush that the snake had disappeared into and made their way back to where the men and Annie were still talking.

FOUR

For Matty, time dragged slowly as he watched Dusty's stomach grow larger. Indiscernibly at first, the mare's flanks slowly rounded out and Matty drove everyone to distraction with his excited talk of the mare. His parents eventually barred horse conversation from the dinner table and Matty quietened on the subject of the mare's pregnancy. It didn't stop him from going out to the Angle paddock whenever he could sneak away. He would sit and watch the mare graze, dreaming of the horse that would be his. Jack and Sammy, quickly growing bored with watching a stomach fatten, stayed at the homestead to help Charlie with the horses or learn to plait with Jim.

The stockmen had told him of the signs to look for when the mare was ready to foal and when he saw Dusty's udder swelling, he raced home to ask Charlie if it would be all right to bring the mare in.

'We ask the Boss, eh,' Charlie said.

Skipping in excitement, Matty took Charlie's hand and pulled him over to the house, where his father sat on the verandah, reading the mail.

'Father,' he called, 'Dusty's ready to foal. Can we go get her?'

Thomas smiled. He could remember when he was Matty's age; he too had been excited at the arrival of newborns on the farm. This was a little different though. He had given Charlie the mare to own, and Charlie in turn had promised Matty the foal. Charlie could have sold the foal or kept it as he pleased.

'We don't usually bring in horses just because they're foaling, Matty,' he said, winking at Charlie.

'But Father! This is special. She's gonna have my foal!'

'Well, what do you think, Charlie? Should we go to the trouble of getting your mare in, just to watch another foal born?'

Spinning around to Charlie, Matty's eyes pleaded with him.

'Boss, him bin out dere many days, all the time look at dat mare. He too worn out to go get mare,' Charlie replied, his face straight. But he couldn't keep the laughter from his eyes.

Leaping up the stairs, Matty appealed to his father, 'You're just joshin' me, aren't you, Father? Can I get Jack and Sammy and go bring the mare in?'

Thomas sat back down, casually crossing his legs. He looked up at Matty. 'You will have to ask Charlie. It's his mare.'

'Ohhhh!' Matty leant over the verandah rail, his face full of frustration. 'Please, Charlie, can we go get Dusty?'

Charlie laughed. 'Go on, bring her in.'

Matty whooped and raced to the harness shed to fetch a halter, calling for Sammy and Jack as he ran. The boys arrived in a hurry.

'The mare's ready to foal,' Matty explained, shouldering the halter. 'Comin' to get her in with me?'

Catching Matty's enthusiasm, the boys nodded their heads and they set off for the paddock at a jog. This was getting exciting now; no staring at a fat mare but the opportunity to watch a new animal being born, always an interesting diversion.

The mare had not wandered far from the bore where Matty had last seen her and allowed Matty to put the halter on her without any trouble. He stroked her between the ears, telling her, 'You're gonna have the best foal, aren't you, Dusty?'

Snorting gently, the mare rubbed her head against Matty's shoulder.

'See, she agrees with me!' He laughed.

Sammy gave a wry grin, while Jack said, 'Yeah, Matty. She knows what you're sayin'.'

'Well, maybe she does. Charlie reckons she understands everything he says!'

Laughing, Jack replied, 'If you don't git a move on, she'll have the foal here.'

Matty started walking, leading the mare at a gentle walk back to the homestead. Charlie met them at the gate and ran an experienced eye over the mare.

'You right, young fella. Foal come by-an'-by, maybe tomorrow, maybe next day.'

'Will I put her in the sheep yards?' Matty asked. 'There's a good bit of feed in there and nothing to bother her. And I can keep an eye on her.'

Charlie nodded and watched as Matty walked beside the mare towards the paddock gate.

'Him no sleep till foal come,' he said to Jack and Sammy, shaking his head, smiling.

Sitting on the hard rails of the fence, Matty watched the grazing mare wander the yards until Eliza sent Jack to fetch him for dinner. Eating hurriedly, he sat waiting impatiently for the others to finish and then, after he was excused, he ran down to the fence again, a little disappointed that Jack did not join him.

Jack sat on the verandah step, plaiting strands of leather that he had cut from an old hide.

'That's a nice bit of work, Jack,' Thomas remarked, as he came to sit in his usual chair for his after-dinner pipe.

'Jim's been teachin' me. He said I could try a stockwhip next, but first I got to get the eight-strand plaitin' right.'

Sitting back in his chair, Thomas gazed at Jack as he bent his head over his work.

'It's about time you had your own horse too, Jack,' he said thoughtfully.

His leather strands forgotten, Jack turned to look at Thomas. 'Really, Boss?'

'I appreciate that you have allowed me to use Longman. After all, he is still your horse, even though he can't be ridden.'

'Yeah, it was a shame that he cut his legs bad like that,' Jack agreed. 'It's a mystery how he got out of those yards. Jim put up extra rails so that he couldn't. The honey Minnie used on his cuts worked like a miracle.'

'I dare say he jumped the rails, high as they are. When a mare's in season, a stallion will do anything to get to her,' Thomas replied. 'I was thinking that the black horse Charlie broke in last year would suit you.'

'Thank you, Boss!'

'You've been a big help around here, Jack, and the Missus and I think you deserve something,' Thomas said, pleased at Jack's reply. 'Well, it's getting late. You had better go and find Matty and get yourselves to bed.'

Jack put his plaiting away and went down to where Matty sat with his back to the gate post.

'Your da said it's time for us to get to bed,' Jack said, startling Matty. 'You was day dreamin' again, eh?'

'Yeh, I can't wait, Jack. My own horse…'

'The Boss said I could have Nugget, that black horse that Charlie broke last year.'

'Hey, that's great. I'll have to wait a bit before I can ride mine, but I can still ride Moon till the foal grows up. I reckon you and I are like brothers, Jack, so Father should treat you same as me. That's why he probably gave you the horse. You let him use Longman for the mares, too.'

Jack ran his sleeve across his eyes, glad that in the dying light of dusk, Matty couldn't see the tears.

'Come on, Shorty, let's get to bed before the Boss gets mad and takes our horses away,' he said gruffly.

* * * *

Groaning, the mare lay on her side, her belly distended and rippling with contractions; sweat darkened her chestnut coat. She raised her head and bringing her forelegs underneath her chest, rested for a moment.

Matty sat shivering in the pre-dawn light, unable to leave to get a warmer coat. The mare's body heaved again, her groans sounding loud in the stillness. He watched as she put out her forelegs and gathering her hocks under her, hauled her heavy body up to a standing position. She walked forward and Matty gave a small gasp. Under her raised tail, he could see two small dark hooves. The mare turned to look at her flanks then she lay down again, stretched out on her side. Matty held his breath as with one great grunt the mare heaved again, and the shiny silvery-blue placenta, full of dark wet foal, slid out and lay still. The covering shuddered as the foal shook its head, its little ears flapping. A wet mucousy snort came from within the pearly covering as the foal took its first breath, moving its spindly legs, causing the sharp hooves to break the shroud that enclosed it.

Matty let out his breath slowly, entranced by the delicate form taking its first breaths in the cool air, steam rising from its coat, still warm from the womb. The foal nickered very faintly, and the mare answered, her head stretched out as she lay recovering from the strain.

Dusty took her time, but eventually she rose and after smelling her foal, began to lick its coat with her large tongue. Matty laughed as she pushed the foal this way and that, in her determination to clean it. In its hurry to get going, the foal tentatively put out one leg, then the other. With a lurch, the foal pushed itself up, only to land on its nose. As Matty watched, laughing again while the foal attempted to stand once more, a voice spoke softly to him from behind.

'You've got yourself a filly, Matty. I thought I would find you here,' Thomas said. 'Your mother worried when she found you gone.'

Matty stood up slowly, not wanting to startle Dusty, his eyes not leaving the foal.

'Isn't she beautiful, Father? She's so little!'

His father agreed with him. 'It'll grow quickly, though. In about an hour it will be racing around the paddock. Herd animals have to get up quickly after they're born, so dogs or other animals don't get them,' Thomas told his son.

The two stood watching for a while as the foal tried to get up again. This time she managed to stand, wobbling on her stalk-like legs for a few seconds before taking a step. Tangling her unresponsive legs, she crashed in a heap and was content to sit for a moment, gazing about, her small ears twitching, listening to the sounds of her new world.

'Let's go and have breakfast, then you can bring your mother to see your new foal,' Thomas said.

Matty ran ahead, eager to tell his mother and Jack the news. He thumped up the verandah stairs, cheering loudly, waking Jack.

'Mother, where are you?' he yelled as he hurtled down the wooden verandah. 'Dusty's had her foal.'

The noise had brought Eliza from the kitchen and, turning the corner, she collided with her son.

'It's a filly! And she's beautiful!'

Pushing her fingers through his sun-bleached hair, she smiled. 'Oh, so that's what all the noise is about. You've been down at the sheep yards!'

'Yes, Mother. Father has seen her, now you've got to come see.'

'I'll go with you after breakfast. You go and get Jack and wash yourselves. There's water in the dish. Then come and sit down.'

Matty called out to Jack, who by now had already dressed and was washing the sleep out of his eyes.

'Did you hear, Jack—'

'I heard, I heard! You made enough noise to wake ten dead people,' he said grumpily. Realising that his words had taken away Matty's excitement, Jack thumped him on the shoulder and added, 'That's really good, Shorty. I'm glad it's finally here. Now, come on, hurry up, I'm starving!'

In his hurry to show Jack and Eliza the new foal, Matty jumped up and cleared the table, then taking their hands, he dragged them to the shearing shed.

Eliza watched her son climb the rails and point at the foal, who by now was steady on her feet and sucking greedily at the mare's udder.

'I told you she was a beauty,' he said proudly.

She gazed at the filly. The foal's coat was drying rapidly, showing dark liver chestnut with paler fuzzy patches around her belly and neck. A narrow white blaze ran down her face and white stockings on all four legs made a pretty picture. The foal's colour made Eliza think of her old cedar chest that she had to leave behind at Welaregang. In it, her first ball dress lay folded with the dried roses of her corsage, along with favourite things she had collected in her childhood.

She sighed and said to Matty, 'Your filly is the same colour as a cedar chest I had when I was a girl.'

* * * *

Matty spent every waking moment that he could with Dusty and Cedar. He would stand beside Dusty until the foal, curious and playful would walk up to him, allowing him to scratch her soft woolly coat.

Thomas allowed this for some days but eventually he told Matty that the mare and foal would be turned out into the Waterhole paddock. Matty was devastated and pleaded with his father to let him keep her closer to the house.

'No, it's distracting you from your lessons and your jobs,' Thomas replied sternly. 'You've been ignoring Jack and Sammy, and although they probably understand, it still doesn't make it right.'

Matty hung his head, tears in his eyes. 'Yes, sir.'

'You will end up spoiling it and anyway, we haven't got the feed to keep a horse in this close till she weans the foal,' he said, his voice softening a little. 'You can ride out and check it every now and then with Charlie.'

This didn't make Matty much happier. His father had spoken and that's the way it would be.

FIVE

Winter had passed and the dry sandy land lay burning in the height of another hot season. The boys were again on the way to the waterhole, older and taller. Matty was excited at the prospect of seeing Cedar. Charlie had checked on the mare and foal six weeks ago and reported all was well with them. Matty had been disappointed at not being able to go with him to see his foal but lessons came first, and he'd learnt many more, both from the Aborigines and from the Missus on the verandah school.

Eliza had asked Sammy's uncle if Sammy could join the boys in learning to read and write. Sammy fought through the difficulties of differences in white man's talk and his own, and he enjoyed the lessons. Aboriginal language had no words for numbers; something was either big fella mob or little fella mob with a few variations. Eliza, after years of talking with the women and the stockmen, had come to understand the differences and put the lessons in a way that Sammy understood, and all three boys could enjoy.

Charlie's work would not start until the men returned with the horses, so Thomas let the boys have time off from the constant full days of work and school lessons and sent them out with Charlie.

The boys walked ahead of Charlie and Annie, practising their tracking skills, Sammy carrying a spear that he had made with his uncle's help.

He had been through tribal initiation and while learning the white man's way under Eliza's guidance, he was also expected to learn his people's ways. He was sometimes confused, as the two ways often clashed, but he shrugged his shoulders and went along with the way of whoever he was with at the time. He was happy that Uncle had allowed him to go with Charlie and the boys. Uncle had said, 'Them fellas, they no spear roo, they no catch goanna. You help Charlie, you feed the camp.'

This made Sammy pleased. He knew that Matty and Jack could catch goanna and snare rabbits and birds, but Sammy would be the one to hunt kangaroo.

Now he said, 'I go hunt roo. I be back by-an'-by.'

Matty and Jack stepped forward to go with Sammy, but Charlie called them back. He knew that they were not ready to go on a hunt for an animal that took skill to get close enough to spear.

'You two fellas come with me, we go find tracks, you two fellas get echidna.'

It wasn't as exciting as going with Sammy. The two boys realised that Charlie was offering them another tracking lesson and they grudgingly turned back to him. Annie, taking her digging stick, had wandered off, looking for goanna.

'We eat plenty tucka dinnertime.' Charlie grinned, looking sideways at Jack. 'Big smoke boy eat bush tucka now, eh?'

Jack smiled back. 'You bet, Charlie. Bush tucker, good tucker.'

'We go that way. Echidna, he like the shade when sun high up.'

Charlie led off, explaining the various animal tracks that crossed their path.

'How come we don't see all these animals?' Jack asked.

'Them night fellas. Dey camp in the day,' Charlie replied. He told them which animals slept by day and came out at night and of others who buried in the sand in the heat of the day. He squatted down and with his fingers, made tracks in the sand.

'What tracks him be?' he asked the boys.

The boys answered as one; they had been paying attention.

'Bandicoot!'

'This?' Charlie made more imprints.

'Dingo!'

Charlie nodded and swept the sand clean again. He drew curves one after the other, either side of a soft drag mark.

'What him?'

Matty knew but he let Jack have a guess.

'Don't know, Charlie,' Jack admitted.

'Him echidna. You look for them tracks and we find echidna.'

Charlie straightened up, fluid in his motions. He was about to step forward, he stopped, nostrils flaring, he turned his head from side to side.

'What is it?' Matty asked.

'Bad smell, animal properly finish up.' Charlie pointed to where a large clump of mulga stood.

Jack looked puzzled and asked Matty what Charlie meant.

'Properly finish up means something's dead,' Matty explained, having seen a lot of death while growing up.

Charlie moved forward with the boys close to his heels. As they drew closer, crows rose from amongst the mulga, cawing loudly, letting their displeasure at this interruption be known. The boys could smell the sickly-sweet smell of decaying flesh. A strange bustling wet noise came from the direction of the mulga.

They soon saw what he was talking about as they pushed through the hop bush.

Charlie's chestnut mare, Dusty, lay with her rump in the sand, her right foreleg trapped, broken, in the fork of a fallen branch. Around her, bushes lay crushed, and gouges in the sand showed her struggle to live. Dingoes and crows had feasted, and now maggots had hatched in the putrefied flesh and were slowly reducing the mare to bone covered by a drying hide.

The black man fell to his knees, arms outstretched, wailing loudly, startling the boys. His wailing slowly turned to a soft lament as he mourned the loss of his horse. Jack and Matty, sickened by the stench, sought the comfort of the open clearing.

Matty gave a gasp and looked about wildly. He turned to Jack, fear contorting his face.

'Where's Cedar? She must be around here somewhere!'

The boys looked about, unable to see the foal, living or dead.

Jack tried to console Matty. 'She'll be alright, we'll find her.'

Annie wasn't with them but on hearing her husband's lamenting, came quickly. 'What he cry for?' she asked the boys.

'His mare, she's dead. He's over there,' Matty said quietly, pointing to the mulga.

Annie patted Matty on the head. 'Him grew-up horse from baby. That horse, that horse close fella.'

It was as close as Annie could come to explaining Charlie's loss. She knew that he had a special way with horses, but she did not have the words to explain her husband's grief.

'Horse bin good fella dog. Charlie plenty unhappy horse finish up,' she said.

Matty and Jack now understood; they had lost pets before.

The lamenting had stopped and Charlie came out, his shoulders hunched, his spears trailing in the dirt. Annie went back to collect their swags and rations, leaving Charlie to the boys.

'That's bad luck, Charlie,' Matty mumbled, not knowing what else to say. Jack nodded in agreement.

Charlie squatted, and laying his spears at his side, stared into the distance. The boys sank to the ground beside him, waiting for him to speak. Matty was impatient to find out what had happened to the foal, but he understood now was not the time to ask.

Charlie put aside his grief and started to speak, softly, slowly.

'Dusty, I break long time ago, Matty not here yet. She one plenty wild horse, put her down with rope, put saddle on, let go. She fight dat saddle long time. We catch her again, Boss threw me up, them boys held her, let go. She buck, she buck an' buck plenty all time.' Charlie shook his head, remembering. 'By-an'-by she stop. I take off saddle an' wipe all over with flour bag. Worked that horse long time, we gallop, we chase cattle. Dusty, she come to me when I go to yards, follow me all time. Strong, work day, night, all time. Dat mare number one, Boss gave me her.'

There was quiet, a quiet that can only be heard in the outback. It settled on them. The boys began to fidget and squirm. They felt his sorrow, they heard it in his voice but they did not know how to comfort him. A circling hawk whistled, breaking the silence.

Taking Charlie's hand in his, Matty stared at the calloused hand with its long bony fingers. 'She was special, Charlie?'

Nodding, he looked at Matty, and slipping his hand out of Matty's grasp, he patted him on the head. 'That foal, she somewhere, tracks all round. We go look, eh?'

Glad that he did not have to ask, Matty jumped up, full of questions.

'Which way did Cedar go? How long ago do you reckon?'

Jack stood up, wiping the sand from his behind.

'Do we walk around the trees until we find a track, Charlie?' he asked. 'The foal would have to find water, so maybe it went from that side of the trees to the waterhole.'

'Young fella bin hearin' Charlie. We go look between trees and water hole, find tracks.'

'What do you think happened to the mare, Charlie?' Jack asked.

'Maybe dingoes chase foal and they gallop. Mare, she get leg stuck, broke. Not get up.' Charlie shrugged his shoulders. 'No water, by-an'-by all finish up.'

A shout made them look around. Shading their eyes against the glare of the sun, they saw Sammy. Draped over his shoulders was a kangaroo, not quite full grown, but big enough to make him stagger under the weight of it, as he walked over and proudly dropped the roo at their feet.

'Good fella, Sammy. Plenty meat on that ol' roo.'

Sammy pushed his chest out, a wide grin showing a slash of teeth. His smile faded as he felt the sad air around Charlie. 'What's wrong?'

'Charlie's mare broke her leg. She's dead,' Jack answered. 'Matty's filly must be around and we're goin' ter look for it.'

Matty pointed to the mulga. 'We're gonna start over there. It would've headed for water.'

Charlie leant over and swung the kangaroo over his shoulders. Reaching out with his foot, he grasped his spear between his bare toes and lifted it to his hand. Steadying the roo with his other hand, he started walking, the boys having to jog to keep up.

'What about Annie?' Jack enquired. 'How will she know where we've gone?'

Sammy pointed at Charlie's track. 'All woman know their husband's tracks. All people know their tribe's tracks. No worries.'

Jack jogged after Charlie.

Starting at the edge of the mulga stand, they slowly worked outwards. Charlie showed them which tracks were old ones, racing wildly as Cedar went back and forth, unable to understand why her mother would not come. He showed them where fresher tracks had overlaid the older ones, as the filly went to the water hole to drink and returned to graze near its mother. They cast out wider, looking for hoof prints that led away from the mulga stand, in any direction but to the waterhole. Finding none, they followed her tracks to the waterhole, searching for where Cedar may have cut off and gone in a different direction. At the edge of the waterhole – a large body of water five miles long, two miles wide – they found where she had come to the same place to drink each time.

Charlie reached up and grabbed the kangaroo by its hind legs, swinging it down to the ground from around his shoulders.

'We sit down here. You fellas get wood, I make fire, cook roo. No good if we no cook him now.'

Matty bit his lip.

Catching the look, Charlie said, 'We look again soon.'

The boys searched around, bringing back various thicknesses of branches. Jack dragged a large branch that had fallen from a tall red gum and dropped it near the kangaroo. Charlie directed Sammy to get some dry grass, saying to the other boys.

'You fellas learn 'nother way makin' fire.'

Matty had often seen the men light a fire, as Charlie was about to do, when they had run out of matches. Matty had tried to show Jack but had not succeeded and had given up with tired arms. They watched now as Charlie broke the spinifex into very small pieces, rubbing it between his fingers until it was nearly powder. Then he broke more grass, this time leaving the stems a little longer. The rest of the spinifex was crumpled together in a ball. Charlie reached into the side pocket of his trousers and drew out an old tobacco tin.

'Dis here, dis goanna fat. Put little bit on the wood.'

He picked up the piece of wood; it was hard on the outside, and the pith, soft on the inside. He smeared a dollop of the fat in the centre. Taking a long straight smooth stick that he carried with him, he pressed it into the centre of this and began to twirl it between the palms of his hands, running them down to the base of the stick, then moving back to the top. His hands moved quickly, making the faintest wisp of smoke drift up. He kept up his efforts and a stronger slip of smoke rose. Stopping and discarding the fire stick, he carefully lifted the base wood to level with his lips, while his other hand reached for the smaller stripped grass. Blowing very softly on to the smouldering wood, he sprinkled on the grass. As a small flicker of flame emerged, Charlie gently lowered the wood to the ground. Reaching for the ball of grass, he put it onto the growing flame and then fed it small twigs. He worked the fire up, gradually putting larger branches on as it the flames caught. All this had taken him less than fifteen minutes.

'You boys, you hands soft, get sore,' he told them, opening his hands to them. They looked at the pale palms, covered in calluses, scarred and thorny. 'My hands tough, no blisters.'

Charlie smiled, knowing that the boys' hands were toughened but not quite tough enough for what he had just done. When Charlie was happy with the fire's heat, he threw the kangaroo on, where it slowly swelled as the fur burnt and the skin charred. Once cooked, the charred skin would peel off, leaving tender juicy meat to be sliced from the carcass.

Annie called to them, holding up two goannas, a big smile on her face. Walking to them, she dropped the dead reptiles on the sand near the fire. They would be put on the coals when the roo was nearly cooked. She lifted the blankets from her back and pulled the dilly bag off her shoulder. Jack had asked if he could help carry this load when they first set out but Charlie had said, 'Blackfella woman strong, that her job, not man's job.' Annie accepted this: it had been the female role since time began, amongst other things, that the boys had yet to learn.

Searching in a large hessian bag, Annie pulled out a smaller calico bag containing flour with a little salt added. This she carried to the edge of the waterhole and scooped water into it. Putting her hands in, she mixed the flour and water together until she was happy with the consistency. She walked back to the fire where Sammy had cleared away the burning wood and scraped a hole in the hot sand. Annie turned the damper mixture out of the bag and after patting it into a round ball, dropped it in the hole, quickly covering it with hot coals. When Jack had first tasted damper cooked this way, he thought he would be eating sand, but was surprised when the cooked damper's crust, after being brushed off, was relatively free of grit. With a bit of sugarbag drizzled on it, it was a simple but delicious bread.

'Kangaroo take long time cook. We go look for horse, eh?' he said to the boys.

The three boys jumped up from where they had been lying in the shade, watching Annie. Charlie walked to where the filly had drunk from the water hole. Slowly he walked a wide circle until he found tracks leading in a different direction to the dead mare. He beckoned to the boys who were standing back watching him.

'Here, she give up mother, she head off to find other horses. Dis way,' he said, pointing to a pile of dung. He bent down, picked up a pellet and broke it open. 'Bin few days. See, dry but not plenty dry.'

Matty, copying Charlie, picked up a piece of manure, and broke it open, finding it still slightly damp inside. He looked at Charlie, many thoughts racing through his head.

'Do you think she'll live, Charlie? Where would she head?'

'Foal drinking water, eat grass, mare milk finis'. She be old enough,' Charlie replied as he stood up. 'Gotta stay near water, maybe she follow the bores, gates open this side, by-an'-by find other horses.'

'She might have met up with that mob that Jim and Father were going to muster,' Matty said hopefully. 'We won't have time to follow her too far. Mother expects us home tomorrow by dinner time.'

Jack added, 'This paddock's too big anyways, we could spend all day in just this half.'

'He right,' Charlie acknowledged. 'We get back to homestead. That filly bin long time gone. Me ride out to the muster, see if dey find her.'

All three boys babbled with excitement, asking could they go too. He answered them with, 'Ask the Missus.'

They set off back to the waterhole, stopping on the way when Charlie spotted a wild bee's nest. Tearing a small limb from a tree, Charlie took the matches from his pocket, winking at the boys. It took a few moments for the green leaves to catch, but when they did, smoke issued forth in clouds.

With great care and agility, he climbed into the tree, holding the smoking branch under the hive and removed a piece of honeycomb.

They returned to the camp, where Annie retrieved the cooked damper and had hot pannikins of tea waiting. They feasted on the kangaroo meat, goanna and damper dripping with honey until they could eat no more, then laid back on their blankets. Watching Charlie's face in the flaring light of the fire, his voice low, they listened to him tell stories of the horses he had broken in, and how he had been taught to hunt by his uncle.

Out in the darkness that surrounded them, the bush held its secrets, not to be seen, only heard. The nocturnal animals, whose waking life carried on after the sun had given way to the night, scurried about with soft rustlings, finding food, continually alert, listening for an owl or a dingo. The birds, roosting in the trees, had an occasional squabble, and a mopoke sang its lonely melody. Frogs of different species had gathered at the water's edge, all with the same motive, to attract a mate. When Charlie fell quiet, their voices echoed across the water, *brrfffing* and *krreggning*.

The boys drifted off to sleep, lulled by the rhythm of the dark hours.

SIX

As dawn lightened the eastern sky, small pink clouds layered beneath pale blue, and birds greeted the rising sun with song. It rose and roused the bigger, louder birds, adding to the chorus. The smoke from the last remaining coals blended with the mist that swayed in wispy fragments over the water, as a soft breeze played with it. Matty wakened slowly, rubbing his eyes, looking around. He watched as cockatoos flew in to drink, tipping from side to side in flight, as they came down and landed on a branch jutting out of the water. One stayed behind, high up in the branches of a coolibah, watching, looking. The others, ten or so, bobbed up and down as they drank, their yellow combs standing out against the stark white of their plumage.

After taking their fill they rose and flew into the surrounding trees, squawking and squabbling. Picking off young leaves, hanging upside down and chasing each other up and down the branches.

Charlie crouched on his haunches, feeding the fire with wood to make coals in which Annie could cook johnnycakes for their breakfast. Matty called to Jack and Sammy, waking them.

'C'mon you fellas, let's go for a swim. We won't have a chance again for ages!'

He ran to the edge of the waterhole, stripped off his clothes and waded into the tepid water. Underfoot, the bottom was smooth and sandy; the water deepened slowly, so that Matty was a hundred yards from the shore before it reached his shoulders. He heard a splash and turned to see Sammy and Jack having a race to him. He struck out, swimming as fast as he could, but the bigger boys hauled him in quickly. They sprayed and dunked each other, at home in the water as if they had gills and a tail.

By the time Annie had breakfast ready, the sun was hot enough to dry the boys quickly, as they stood naked and unconcerned, eating their johnnycakes.

'Better git movin',' Charlie said. 'We be home by dinnertime, we hurry up.'

* * * *

Eliza heard Matty calling and, leaving her sewing, she walked along the verandah until she could see the group of travellers arriving at the gate.

'Mother, we found Charlie's mare! She was dead and we don't know where Cedar is! Can we ride out to Father to see if she's with the other horses? Please, Mother?' Matty ran out of breath.

'Oh, that is not good, Charlie,' Eliza said. Turning back to Matty, she continued, 'Firstly, you had better thank Charlie and Annie for taking you to the waterhole. Then you three boys can go wash up before lunch. I will talk to Charlie about this.'

'But Mother…'

Eliza looked at Matty with a gimlet eye; Matty shut his open mouth.

The boys thanked Charlie and Annie and jumped up the verandah steps, racing each other for the wash-house.

'Dem boys, always hurry.' Charlie laughed. 'Never slowly.'

'Yes, I wish I had their energy,' Eliza agreed, watching them running, their bare feet slapping the floorboards. She turned back to Charlie.

'What is this about Cedar, Charlie? And mustering?'

The sparkle went from Charlie's eyes as he replied, 'Dat mare the Boss give me, she all finish up.'

'Oh, Charlie, that is a shame,' Eliza sympathised.

'It all right, Missus. But Cedar, she gone. Maybe find other horses? Maybe dead, maybe not.'

'You think it may have ended up with the mob that the Boss is mustering?'

'Yes, Missus. Maybe.'

'And you want to take the boys with you to see?'

'If that all right, Missus?'

Eliza sighed. Matty was growing beyond her. She felt he was safe when he was on hunting trips with Charlie, as they walked instead of riding. Even though Matty could ride well, she didn't like to think of what could happen in the wild chase of a horse muster. He was twelve now, and she would have to accept that she could not protect him all the time. Thomas complied with her wishes, knowing how fearful she was of losing her only child. Eliza looked at Charlie thoughtfully, not realising that her direct look worried him.

'I bin done nothing wrong, Missus?'

Eliza gasped and shook her head. 'No, Charlie, no! I have been trying to decide whether or not to let Matty go with you to the muster.'

'I get him on ol' grey horse, he slow, we no go fast, Missus. Matty, him like to find foal.'

'Yes, Charlie, I know. He may go with you, but promise me you won't let him chase the horses. And tell the Boss that I have said the same.'

'Yes, Missus.'

'Now, you had better go out to the kitchen and get Bess to feed you before you go. Annie, you needn't work this afternoon.'

Annie smiled. 'Yes, Missus. I go see Minnie. We maybe catch fish, bring back here?'

'That would be nice, Annie,' Eliza replied.

She returned Annie's wave, then walked into the house, rubbing her hands down her dress. It had been a hard decision for her. Eliza was not sure that she wanted to go through with it, but her word had been given, and so she went to find Matty to give him the news that would make him happy. Eliza walked down the long hallway, passing out onto the verandah, where she turned and headed for the kitchen.

Looking in, she could see the three boys eating the mutton stew that Bess had prepared that morning. She leant against the door jam and thought about how close the boys had grown. Matty was a lucky child to lead the life he led. He had the Aboriginals, who cared for him as their own; his father, a generous and dependable man; the bush to roam in and two boys to call his friends. Yes, it was time to let him go with the men. She couldn't keep him at her side forever.

Stepping through the door, she waved her hand at Bess, who had reached for another plate to serve her.

'No, thank you, Bess. I just want to have a word to the boys.'

Drawing a chair out from the table, she sat down where she could look at the three of them face to face.

Matty asked, 'Can we go? Please, say yes, Mother.'

Eliza sat taller, her back straight, her face stern. She met the eyes of each boy, aware of the eagerness in each face.

'Yes, you may go—' Her words were interrupted by yelling, as three excited youngsters scraped back their chairs and danced around the table.

Bess laughed, throwing the tea towel at them. 'You fellas, don't be noisy. Listen up to the Missus.'

Jack settled down quickly. Matty was about to speak but thought better of it when he saw his mother looking at him with raised eyebrows. Sammy stepped back, unsure if he was included in what Eliza was about to say.

'Sammy, you sit down too,' Eliza said, noticing his hesitation.

He stepped forward and sat down in front of his plate.

'Sammy, you are the eldest and you're a good boy. You have been a good friend to Matty and the Boss and I think you will do well. You have been lucky. On other stations, most other Aboriginal boys your age would have been working for a long time, not having lessons with the Boss's son.' She paused, letting her words take effect.

Sammy stared at the table, shy at the Missus's words.

'When you ride out to the men with Charlie, you are to do as Charlie tells you until you get to the Boss. Then he will let you know what you should do. You are not to encourage Matty to join in with the rough and...'

'Ow, Mother!' Matty butted in. 'I'm not a baby any more. I can ride good. Father said I could start helping him.'

'Yes, I know you're not a little boy anymore, Matty. I just don't want to see you get hurt,' Eliza replied. 'And do not interrupt me when I am speaking.'

Matty hung his head, embarrassed.

Eliza turned her attention back to Sammy. 'Now, Sammy, I expect you to do as I ask.'

'Yes, Missus,' came the quiet reply.

She turned to Jack, who coloured slightly, wondering what was to come.

'No racing, no getting on wild horses. I don't want any of you brought back with broken limbs!'

This was all too much for Matty. Wiping angry tears from his eyes, he pushed back from the table and stood facing his mother.

'You're making me sound like a baby, Mother. I can ride and I can do what you say without havin' Sammy or Jack keepin' an eye on me!'

He rushed past Eliza, stopping short when she reached out and caught his shirt tails.

'Oh, Matty. I don't mean to treat you as a baby.' She reached her arms around him, hugging him to her.

Matty stood still, his body stiff, and unable to look at the other boys, who quietly made themselves scarce, leaving the table and retreating to the verandah.

'Matty, look at me,' Eliza said, lifting his head gently.

Wiping away the tears from his cheeks, Matty looked his mother in the eye.

'I suppose I am a bit of a baby, cryin' like that, aren't I?'

'No, you have your heart set on growing up too quickly, riding with the men and doing cattle work. I lost my little brother when he was twelve. I haven't told you that, have I?'

He shook his head. 'How?'

Eliza looked out the door, her face slackening with memory. 'He went mustering up on the lease in the snow country. His horse's front legs went down a wombat hole and the horse rolled on him. Daniel was twelve and he lived only long enough to say goodbye to our mother when they carried him down from the mountain. He must have had very bad injuries inside. Daniel wasn't a baby; he was very brave and he knew what he was doing. Accidents happen and that is why I am afraid for you.'

Matty flung his arms around his mother and Eliza held him tightly, her wet cheek resting on his thick blond hair.

'I shall have to let you grow up, won't I?' she said, her pain back down in her gut where she stored it.

'Yes, Mother, but I understand now why you worry,' he replied, his seriousness bringing a small smile to Eliza's eyes.

'Well, if you can keep your word, you had better go. I'll pack some food for your little riding party. You had better go and help Charlie saddle up.'

He ran through the door and caught the door jamb with his hand.

He spun around and came back to his mother. Matty reached out and put his arms around her neck.

'I promise I'll be careful.'

Kissing her cheek, he turned and walked out of the kitchen, breaking into a run along the verandah.

Eliza rose from the table, wiping her tears away with her apron. She leaned out the door watching, as her boy ran to Charlie, excitement in his step.

SEVEN

The horses jogged, feeling the excitement of their riders, while the boys talked about what they might find at the yards out in Eagle Paddock. Charlie rode along behind, his reins loose on the horse's neck. He looked around, instinctively taking in the changes in the country since the drought had broken. Rabbits had ravaged large tracts of country; so far, Mulga Plains had been lucky. Tales of rabbits in their thousands had drifted up from down south but it was only in the last couple of months that they had begun to make their way in greater numbers onto this property. All the stockmen carried guns and shot them on sight. The Boss had put in an order for an extra case of .22 rounds and these would be on the next supply wagon. The boys had been pestering Charlie to let them have a shot; Charlie had to say no. That was the Boss's department. He looked up ahead and, noticing that the boys were drawing away, pushed his horse into a trot, closing the distance.

Puffs of fine red dust rose as the horses' hooves sank into the bull dust, the boys' legs gripping the horses' sides, slowly applying more pressure till Jack's horse broke into a canter. Matty pushed the old grey, but remembering his mother's words, allowed his leg muscles to slacken, being satisfied with a slow canter.

Jack looked across at Matty, his eyebrows raised. Matty shook his head and stared ahead; it was a canter, not a flat-out gallop.

'Not long, fellas. We be there,' Charlie said, watching Matty. He was rewarded, for Matty's face lit up and his smile was huge at the thought of seeing his filly again.

Dust hung over the mulga scrub in the distance and the noise of the muster came to them. The horses pricked their ears and pulled at the bit, anxious to join the others.

The yards were beside a windmill that was barely discernible in the red haze rising from the constant movement of men and horses. Matty's eyes scanned the yard for his filly but could not see her. He saw his father leaning against the rails and rode over to him.

'Father, have you seen Cedar?' he shouted.

His father turned, surprised to see Matty. 'What are you doing here, young man?'

Jumping off his horse, Matty told his father of finding Cedar's mother dead in the paddock, and of how they had looked for Cedar.

'Your mother gave you permission to come out here?' His father raised an eyebrow.

'Yes, sir. She explained that I must do as I'm told, though.' He smiled. 'I'm not allowed to race or ride any wild horses.'

His smile disappeared as his father said, 'No, we haven't seen your filly, but we haven't got all the horses in yet.'

'When can we get the others?'

'I was going to send Jim and the boys out in the morning. Did your mother say you could camp?'

'Yes, and she packed some more tucker for us. What can we do to help?'

'Not much at the moment. We were just about to call it a day. The boys will be in for tea soon. Let's go see what Tan's cooked up?'

* * * *

The sun hovered below the horizon, giving a luminosity to the surrounding country. The soil seemed paler and the spinifex silver, in the stillness of dawn.

Matty listened to the quietness, broken now and then by the birds waking, and the muffled hooves of the restless horses in the bulldust of the yards. Occasionally a horse would snort or shake itself and Matty felt a contented happiness to be out here.

He threw off the coarse woollen blanket and pulled on his pants and boots. Looking around, he saw that Tan was already at the fire and the men were washing at the bore. He searched for his father but could not find him. Jack mumbled incoherently when Matty prodded the blanket with his toe.

'Hey, sleepy head, everyone's up. Sammy's gone with his father.'

Jack rolled over and pulled the blanket over his head. Matty walked to where Jack's toes were just visible at the end of his blanket and, reaching down, tickled them. Jack grumbled and drew his knees up, so Matty grabbed two handfuls of blanket and pulled backwards, falling over himself in the process. His mate was on him in a trice, lightly pummelling him with his fists.

'You bleedin' little rat. Won't let a bloke sleep, will you, Shorty?'

Giggles came from under the blanket that Matty had managed to entangle himself in. He poked his head out and Jack tousled his hair.

'All right. I'm up, Shorty. Let's get some breakfast.'

The boys dusted themselves off and went to the bore to wash up before joining the men at the fire. They all ate quietly, intent on getting their fill before the long day's work.

Thomas rode up, his horse already covered in a layer of fine dust.

'Ned's found another mob of horses out near the Ridge, over in the west corner,' he said to the men. 'You boys go help him bring them in. Charlie, there's a filly in the yard, a flea-bitten grey. I want you to start on her. She'll make the Missus a nice pony for Christmas. Get the rough out of her before we get back to the homestead.'

'Filly no rough, Boss. She out of ol' Daisy. She be fine,' answered Charlie.

Thomas smiled and shook his head. Charlie had already cast an eye over the horses and likely as not, knew which would be easy to break and which would prove troublesome.

'I swear you know every horse on this property, Charlie.'

Charlie nodded. 'Yes, Boss. I broke 'em.'

Thomas turned his attention to Matty and Jack, who were hurriedly finishing their stew, wiping their plates with johnnycakes.

'You two fill your water bottles and saddle up. I'll meet you at the Eighteen bore,' he said, jerking his thumb in the opposite direction to which the men had ridden out. 'Stay on that fence and you will come to it.'

The boys rinsed the plates in the kerosene tin and stacked them for the cook. They had learnt the hard way that Tan's temper was not to be pushed. They walked out to their horses and, after taking off the hobbles, led them to the yard and saddled up.

'Whad'ya reckon we'll be doin', Shorty?'

Matty shrugged his shoulders. 'Don't know. Father'll have something in mind.'

Mounting, the boys rode at a slow trot, their eyes following the tracks of the cattle, keeping the fence in sight. After two miles, they reached the bore. Thomas had not shown up yet, so the boys allowed their horses a small drink while they wiped water over their faces and necks. Already, it was hot and yet it was still early. The sun was only just over the horizon.

'Today's gonna be a scorcher, eh, Jack?'

'I'll say. I reckon we'll be wishin' we were at the waterhole by lunchtime.'

Hearing muffled hoof beats, the boys turned and saw Thomas riding towards them through the hop bush scrub.

'You didn't let those horses drink too much, did you? They'll get the gripes if we have any fast work.'

'No, Father. Just a little bit, like Charlie taught us,' answered Matty.

'You boys are very lucky to have Charlie to teach you, you know. I don't know where we would have been without Charlie… and the other boys for that matter,' Thomas mused. 'Well, we won't find your filly standing here!'

Thomas's last comment jolted Matty into action. He mounted his horse quickly and gestured for Jack to do the same.

'C'mon Jack, hurry up! Father, where will we start lookin'?'

'Well, I had a word with Charlie and he seems to think that she would have headed into Upper Waterhole then through into Back Paddock. She may even be in Sandy Plain – all the gates in those paddocks are open. But she would have had to stay near water, so we'll start at the second bore in Sandy Paddock and work up.'

Thomas rode off, leading, while the two boys followed. Matty was tense with excitement and his horse responded. The grey jig jogged. Matty realised his body had tightened and so he relaxed, causing Moon to slow his pace to a walk. The grey was an experienced old gelding, used to responding to the body movements of its rider, a quality invaluable in a stock horse.

A large male rust-coloured kangaroo sat up on its haunches, watching the approaching group of horses and riders, its nose raised, smelling the slight breeze that played over the spinifex. The roo leant forward onto its fore paws and after spinning around, took off with bounding leaps that covered the earth easily.

Matty pointed to the fast-moving animal. 'We scared him out of his layup, Father. He must be the biggest roo I ever saw.'

Thomas nodded before his head turned suddenly in the opposite direction. His hands tightened on the reins, halting the horse. Leaning his forearm on the pommel of the saddle, he stared towards the west. The sudden halt caused the boys to pull up and they looked in the same direction.

In the distance, a thin dusty haze hung in the air. What was causing the dust to rise was hidden from their sight by a line of scrub.

'What do you think it is, Father?'

Shaking his head, Thomas answered, 'It could be some bulls stirred up, having a fight. I don't know, but how about we go and have a look?'

'But what about Cedar?' Matty cried.

Thomas turned his horse around and rode up beside Matty. He looked down at his son and the anguish he saw tempered his tongue.

'Son, you should know that looking after the stock on this property takes priority over everything else. They're our only income – the drought took all our savings. Now let's go and have a look at what's going on.'

Matty bowed his head and, stung by his father's words, apologised.

Thomas drew his horse's head around and pushed it into a slow, loping canter. Jack's horse was fresh and resisted his hand, giving a pig root and throwing his head around. Jack sat calmly, both hands on the reins, talking quietly, gradually steadying his mount into a canter. Matty rode at the rear, Moon quite happy to follow along gently.

Thomas looked about to get his bearings. Fifteen minutes later brought them to a barb wire fence, at which Thomas turned westward. He pulled his horse back to a walk and lifted his arm.

'See how the dust is Nor' west… Whatever is causing it will be on the other side of the fence in Kelly Paddock. But it's not as thick as it was.'

Jack and Matty looked to where Thomas was pointing. The cloud of dust had thinned, just a ghost of it hung in the air.

'There's a gate in the corner on this fence line,' Thomas explained. 'We'll be able to go through there.'

As the boys rode mutely, looking about for the cause of the dust, the sound of bleating sheep came to their ears. Passing through yet another clump of trees, the cause of the noise became evident. Bunched in the corner of the next paddock, a mob of sheep was circling, tightly packed and calling to each other. Raising his hand, Thomas motioned the boys to halt and dropping his reins, drew the .303 from his rifle bucket. He thumbed off the safety and gently pulled back the bolt to load a round into the chamber.

Matty and Jack sat motionless, their eyes scanning the scrub for what Thomas had seen. Very carefully, Matty lifted his hand an inch off his saddle and pointed towards a cluster of turpentine bushes. Following Matty's finger, Jack could pick out the shape of a dog lying in the shade of the bushes. He looked at Matty with raised eyebrows. If this was a wild dog, it was uncommon to see it in the daylight, let alone remaining around when humans were about.

Matty watched his father raise the rifle and take aim. The horses started at the loud report but they were used to rifle fire and quickly settled. The boys took no notice of the horses' movements but intently watched the dog. As the bullet hit, the dog rolled backwards and did not move.

Dismounting, Thomas handed the reins of his horse to Jack, saying, 'I'll make sure it's dead. You two bring the horses.'

He opened the bolt of the rifle and climbed through the fence while Matty and Jack rode down the fence line to the gate, Jack leading the Boss's horse. The panicked sheep stood watching this new threat and refused to move out of the way. Matty had to jump off and by waving his hands around and yelling, he managed to push them back far enough to let Jack and the horses through. The boys trotted up to where Thomas stood looking down at the dog. They pulled up, their eyes taking in the scene. A sheep with its stomach ripped open lay a few feet away from the dog.

'Why didn't the dog run, Boss?' Jack asked.

'Hop down and have a look,' Thomas replied, gesturing towards the dog.

The dog was mangy and grey around the muzzle. It was missing its front paw, probably from a dingo trap.

'It tried to hide rather than run. Probably knew it couldn't outrun us,' Thomas told them.

The dog had not long killed as the dead sheep was still warm. Thomas skilfully skun it and bound the hide onto his saddle.

They mounted again and rode towards the windmill in the next paddock. Moon lifted his head and pricked his ears. Thomas's horse did the same and Matty sat taller in the saddle, his eyes scanning the bush for what the horses heard. Moon tossed his head and nickered, and Matty, hearing a faint reply, reined in his horse.

A dull thudding sound announced the arrival of another horse as Cedar galloped around the edge of a clump of bushes.

'It's her. She survived!' Matty cried out.

The filly pranced up to the other horses, her neck arched, her legs lifting high in the air. She snorted and tentatively reached her muzzle out to smell the other horses.

'Oh, Father, she has grown! Isn't she a beauty?'

The filly reared playfully. She had lost the fuzziness of a foal and her liver chestnut coat shone in the hot sun. The other horses, after a snort and a sniff, settled and disregarded this young upstart.

'She'll follow our horses, so we'll head back to the gate and then to the yards,' Thomas said.

They reined their horses around, Cedar trotting alongside, occasionally breaking into a canter and kicking up her heels.

Matty turned in the saddle, his eyes not leaving his filly.

'She's happy to see other horses, look at her carrying on.' Matty laughed.

The filly hung back, wary as Thomas reached down and opened the gate. The three of them rode through, continuing on a little way, trying to entice Cedar to follow. She ran wildly up and down the fence nickering until, with a burst of speed, she raced through the gate and far out into the next paddock.

'She's going away. How will I get her?' Matty cried.

Thomas looked away and said, 'Well, I don't know, son. What do you think, Jack?'

Jack caught Thomas's wink and, turning in the saddle, looked at Matty.

'I don't know, Shorty. She might run all the way back to the waterhole!'

Matty stared at Jack. Then he saw the lines of his father's eyes crinkle and burst out, 'Ohhh, don't joke about this. How am I going to catch her?'

His answer came with the beat of hooves as Cedar came galloping back, snaking her head and slowing to a trot as she reached them. Snorting, and blowing heavily from her gallop, she settled in behind the group of riders as they trotted across the paddock towards the yards. Matty kept turning in the saddle, talking to his filly, telling her what he planned to do with her.

'Looks like we'll have to ban horse talk at the dinner table again, Jack.' Thomas laughed.

'Talking of dinner, I think we've missed it, Boss,' Jack replied as he wiped the sweat from his face with his sleeve and nodded towards the sun.

'Tan will have kept something for us. He's worth his weight in gold, that man.'

The mention of food drew Matty's attention. 'Where did Tan come from, Father?' he asked.

Easing his horse back to a walk, Thomas replied, 'We'll walk for a while and spell the horses, boys. It'll do no good to knock them up in this heat.'

The boys slowed their horses and Matty checked that the filly was still close behind.

'Now, I'm not sure where Tan came from before here, but he is from China and came to work in the gold fields. He had family in China and sent money home to them, but there was a big flood near his home town and his family died.'

'How did he end up here at the station?' asked Jack.

'On Turon Gates Field, he was badly beaten and robbed, so he went to work in a store, but the men in town also gave him trouble, so he left. I think he may have been a shearers' cook for a while, before he turned up here. I wouldn't part with him for anything. I only hope he will stay on.'

'Too right, Boss. He's the best cook, ever!' Jack agreed, then his face reddened.

Thomas caught on quickly. 'You mean after the Missus? No, Jack, even the Missus reckons he's the best ever.'

Jack's lips turned up in an embarrassed smile and he nodded at Thomas.

'Is that why him and Bess argue in the kitchen?' Matty put in. 'They're always yellin' at each other, aren't they, Jack?'

Thomas laughed as he remembered some of the antics that went on in the cookhouse.

'Remember when Bess chased him out of the kitchen for throwing out her rusty old knife? And then, Bess was upset when she discovered Minnie and Tan swapping remedies. Those pair are a trial to the Missus.'

His eyes still on Cedar, Matty asked, 'How old is Tan?'

'He came out to the goldfields a young man, and that was back in the sixties so he'd have to be near sixty.'

Their conversation was interrupted by a whistle as Sammy and Jim rode towards them, Sammy's smile wide as he showed his pleasure in Matty finding his filly. They halted and Matty's excitement made his speech quick as he told of Thomas shooting the dingo and finding Cedar.

Jim couldn't resist needling Matty. 'Boss, I reckon filly get lotta money. That fella hawker, he buy her.'

Not taken in, Matty laughed with the others. 'Nobody's gonna buy this horse, Jim. Charlie gave her to me and he's gonna help me break her in.'

'I is gonna be sit down on the fence, you get on her, you gonna fly like a bird, Matty.' Sammy laughed, his body shaking. 'She gonna buck, buck big. Look at her.'

Their eyes all turned to watch Cedar as she came close to the new arrivals, then danced away, bucking and twisting. Sweat darkened her neck and flanks as she raced around the group.

'That's just spirit,' Matty said hesitantly. Then he added more confidently, 'Anyway, like I said, Charlie'll help me with her.'

The group rode on, Jack and Sammy catching up on what each had done during the day, while Thomas and Jim talked about the growing dog problem.

Cedar announced herself at camp by galloping up to the yards, where her curiosity about the other horses trapped her. Charlie had seen her coming and opened the gate at the end of the wing and, although she had been wary, it was too late. With a hoo-haa, Charlie waved his arms and Cedar trotted through into the yards. With arched necks and tails held high, the other horses came to smell her. A few squeals and kicks sorted out the pecking order and the horses soon settled down.

Charlie stood by the rails, smoking a pipe. It wasn't long before Matty rode up calling, 'Did you look at her, Charlie? Isn't she bonzer?'

Nodding, Charlie said quietly, 'We talk by-an'-by. What you do now?'

Matty looked down at Moon, seeing the dark sweat on the horse's neck, then he jumped off.

'I'll unsaddle and rub him down, then I'll be back.'

He led Moon over to another yard where Sammy and Jack had already taken care of their horses. Matty felt ashamed that he had not thought of his mount first. His excitement in catching Cedar had made him break a rule that Charlie had taught him for as long as he could remember.

'Look after your horse and he will look after you,' Matty said to himself. He thought back to when he had climbed the rails to watch Charlie break in a horse. The gaps in the rails seemed enormous to his small legs, and he could only just reach his arms over the top rail. Charlie had seen him but did not take his concentration from the horse he was working. After about twenty minutes, the horse in the yard was leading quietly and Charlie gently rubbed him all over with an old hessian bag, then took the halter off. The horse promptly folded its legs underneath and sank to the ground to have a good roll in the red sand.

Walking over to the fence, Charlie had looked up at Matty and said, 'Him good horse. Work well. Rub him down, take care of him.'

Matty nodded his head, taking it in.

'You treat horse properly, horse come when him called. Him properly work. Him look after you.'

Charlie had turned and left the yard, leaving Matty to think about his words.

A hand on his shoulder startled Matty as he rubbed the saddle marks from Moon's back.

'Come and eat before you start on that filly, son,' Thomas said.

'But…'

'No, I reckon you're going to need a bit in your belly before you tackle Cedar. Anyway, Tan's kept back some of his stew for you.'

* * * *

The filly stood square, facing Matty, her head lifting slightly as he took a step towards her, talking to her.

'Remember when you were little, I'd rub you and give you sugar I'd pinched from the pantry? Now you are grown, do you remember?'

He put his hand in his pocket and drew out a brown paper packet.

'Look, I brought you this. I got it when we came lookin' for you.'

Cedar turned her head from side to side; her ears pricked at the sound of crinkling paper.

'Here, I'll put it in my hand and you can lick it like you used to.'

Matty took another step towards the filly. 'You can't have forgotten. Charlie says horses never forget.'

Taking another step forward, Matty held out his hand, the sugar white against it.

The filly stretched her neck out, sniffing, her body tense. Slowly Matty put one foot in front of the other.

Cedar snorted and, dropping her shoulder, spun sideways, trotting around the edge of the yard, tail up, head in the air.

Matty's shoulders slumped in disappointment. He returned to the middle of the yard, while the filly pranced along the rails. He glanced to where his father, Charlie and his two friends were watching him from under their hats.

He shrugged. 'I thought she would remember.'

Charlie walked slowly to the fence, but Cedar swerved away. As the filly slowed to a walk and then halted, keeping the two humans in full view, Charlie said quietly, 'Baby horse, she know you. She bin alone. Horses bit stirry like that. You go quietly, slow. She come.'

Matty started over again, talking softly, saying what ever came into his head, his tone soothing. Cedar pricked her ears, and just when he thought he was close enough for her to reach out to take the sugar, she spun away. After fifteen minutes, he tried another tactic. Dropping his hands to his side, he turned his back on her and walked to the rails. He leant against them, looking out over the paddock. His ears strained to hear every move the filly made, his body strained, as his nerves reached out, feeling her movements.

Slowly, curiosity got the better of Cedar and she took one hesitant step at a time towards Matty's still form.

By twisting his wrist and reaching his hand out behind him, Matty managed to offer the sugar. He could hear her sniffing and feel her slowly moving up behind him.

Then it happened. He felt the lightest touch as her whiskers moved over his fingers and then her soft lips gathered the sugar. He did not move.

'There you are. Do you remember the sugar?' he whispered.

The filly's lips played with his hand, searching for more.

A little louder, he said, 'If you don't run away, I'll find you some more.'

Slowly he reached into his pocket again and drew out more sugar, turning as he did so that he could see her and reached out his hand.

Cedar stretched out her nose, her well-muscled body taut. The taste of the sugar was in her mouth and that overtook her readiness to run. She nibbled at the white powder and then licked Matty's hand.

Everything in Matty wanted to reach out and pat his filly, but Charlie's lessons came back to him.

'You git the horse to do somethin', that enough.'

Matty walked backwards towards the gate, the filly following him slowly. He turned, unlatched the gate and passed through it, locking it. Cedar stood looking at him through the rails.

'I'll have to get more sugar from Tan. I'll come back in a while,' he promised her.

He felt proud as Charlie smiled at him and then said to Thomas, 'Young fella, he listen to Charlie. He did good.'

By tea time, Cedar was walking up to Matty freely, allowing him to rub her face and neck. After bolting down his meal, Matty returned to the yards where Cedar was a dark shape in the starlight but still, he rubbed her and told her of his plans for the two of them. It was only when his father called to him that he said good night to his horse and went to bed.

EIGHT

Eliza hugged her son tightly and then tipped his head back gently with her hand. She looked into his eyes.

'I did as you asked, Mother. I didn't take risks.'

She hugged him again and allowed herself to be led quickly by the hand down to the yards.

'It'll be another two years before I can ride her but Charlie said I can halter break her and lift her legs and things,' he said, his hands moving in motion to his words.

'Well, Matty, she is going to be a beautiful mare. Her colour is extraordinary, and her mane is lovely and fine, not thick like the other horses.'

'Charlie reckons that's because of Longman being a thoroughbred.'

Eliza glanced around and, leaning down, said in a conspiratorial tone, 'That Charlie is a magician with the horses, isn't he?'

'Wait till you see… Oh… um… you just wait and see, Mother.' Matty blushed, horrified to have nearly given away the secret of Eliza's Christmas present.

She smiled and changed the subject. 'Your Uncle Robert is coming for Christmas. He is my eldest brother. He wrote saying he would like to see how we do things up here.'

Eliza stared out over the red soil dotted with clumps of scrub, so different from the property she had grown up on with its green river flats and steep hills. She had made her home here and was proud of what Thomas and she had achieved. She straightened her shoulders and said to Matty, 'One day you will be able to go to Welaregang and meet the rest of my family.'

Looking up at his mother's face, he said earnestly, 'Don't be sad, Mother. We have a good time here, don't we?'

'I still miss the mountains, and the snow in winter was just so beautiful. But this land has its own beauty.'

Matty's blond head nodded. 'Minnie says that you belong to country – that your country always in you.'

Eliza smiled at her son parroting the old woman. 'Minnie and her people know a lot more than we do about the land; it's good for you to listen and learn. And, young man, speaking of learning, you three boys have a lot of schoolwork to catch up on!'

'Ohhh, Mother, I've just got Cedar back.'

'You can work on her after lessons. Your schooling is important. If you are going to run this place one day, you will have to be able to do the accounts and write to people. So go and get Jack and Sammy for your French lessons.'

Matty exploded. 'Why do we have to learn blanky French?'

'Matty! Please do not use that tone with me. All well-educated young men speak French. What if you want to travel overseas when you are older? French will come in very useful. Your father learnt Latin, as well as French.'

Matty's face showed his astonishment. 'Did he?'

'Yes, and he writes with a beautiful hand, something that you need a lot of work on!'

Matty tried to sort these new facts out in his head and came to the conclusion that if Father had studied these things, well, they couldn't be that bad. Then a thought came to him.

'But, Mother, I am already learning a new language.'

Eliza looked at him with an enquiring lift of the eyebrow. 'Mmmm?'

'I'm learning Charlie's language!' he said triumphantly.

'That will be useful for you here, Matty, but I think you will find in different parts of Australia, the blacks speak different languages.'

'Oh, well, at least I can learn to speak like Minnie and them.'

'You go and get the boys and we will start on your French this afternoon.'

* * *

The weeks passed quickly and the days grew hotter and longer. Secret talks went on behind closed doors and letters went with the mailman who now called twice a month.

The three boys looked on wistfully as Thomas and Big Jim harnessed up the draught horse team for a trip to Bourke. They pleaded to be allowed to go but Thomas replied that someone had to stay and look after the property and Mother. The boys felt very important for a while but soon realised that Mother ran the house, Charlie looked after the animals and Tan ruled the kitchen.

Eliza gave them lessons early in the morning before the heat became stifling. After morning tea, they packed their saddlebags with damper and corned meat and rode out to the waterhole. Over the days, Matty and Jack became deeply tanned, as the three of them spent hours fishing for yellow-belly from the canoe that Big Jim and Billy had made for them. They would return with fish for Tan to cook, making a change from salted beef and mutton. Sometimes they went to the river and caught yabbies with pieces of meat on a string. Tying semi-rotten meat to the string, they cast it out and then sat patiently under a shady tree. When they felt a tugging on the other end, they very carefully started to pull the string in towards the bank. Sometimes the meat was nearly to the edge of the bank when the yabby would let go and with its tail flapping, rapidly backing off into the deeper holes. Minnie made them a net to scoop up the yabbies that got close enough. It took great patience to slide the net behind the yabby before it took off. It was a great competition between them as to who caught the most.

Returning to the homestead one evening after a trip to the river, they saw two strange horses in the yards. They unsaddled, rubbed down their horses and raced to the house, each carrying a net holding yabbies.

'Missus,' Jack called. 'Yabbies for tea, Missus.'

Running up the steps, they pulled up short as Eliza came out the door followed by a visitor. The stranger was tall, with dark hair and dressed in moleskins and a pale blue shirt. He looked crisp and clean in the stifling heat. Matty stepped forward, taking a closer look.

'These are the boys. Matty, our son,' she explained to the stranger as she held out her hand towards Matty.

'Hello, sir. Are you my Uncle Robert?'

Robert nodded his head, his look stern as he stared at the three boys with their wind-tossed hair and bare feet.

'Ahem, yes. I am your Uncle Robert. And who is this?' he asked, looking at Jack.

Eliza put her arm around Jack's shoulders and playfully ruffled his hair.

'Jack came into this family in rather unfortunate circumstances, but he belongs here now with us, don't you, Jack?'

A shadow of sadness flickered briefly on Jack's face, but he straightened his shoulders and returned Eliza's smile.

'Yes, Missus.'

Robert's glance fell on Sammy and he looked questioningly at Eliza. Before she could say anything, Sammy put out his hand and shyly introduced himself.

'Sammy, sir. Me and Matty and Jack, we mates.'

Robert hesitantly put out his hand and shook Sammy's stiffly, dropping his hand quickly. The boy stepped back, bewildered.

Eliza noticed her brother's disdain, and said tightly, 'Well, I see at least one of you three boys has manners!'

Jack and Matty hurriedly put out their hands to shake Robert's, both murmuring in embarrassment. 'How do you do?'

'You three go and get cleaned up. Give those yabbies to Tan. They will be lovely for tea.'

The boys headed off towards the kitchen, while Eliza led her brother to the coolest side of the house and invited him to sit. Robert pulled at his trousers and, sitting down, studied the country before him.

'It's nothing like home, I've got to say, Eliza,' he said, refraining from commenting on how she had aged. 'Has it been hard?'

Eliza sat back and thought for a moment. She brushed a stray lock of greying hair from her eyes and rubbed her hands down her dress. Starting to say something, she stopped, thinking again. It would be disloyal of her to moan about all she had been through when Thomas had worked so hard to build up the property. Her eyes fixed on some long strands of hair from a horse's tail that had been caught in the fence and hung lifeless and still in the heat.

She drew in a breath and let it out slowly, her face hardening.

'Well,' she started. 'If you call losing two children at birth, one in its sleep at six months, having your only remaining child bitten by a deadly snake when he was four and living through a drought where we nearly lost everything hard? Yes, it has been very hard.'

She glanced at Robert, taking in the look of horror on his face.

'Father didn't raise you for this, Eliza!' he burst out. 'Your letters gave no hint that it was that bad.'

'I saw no reason to bother you with my troubles.' Sitting a little straighter, Eliza held up her hand and continued in a strong voice. 'But, it has been rewarding to build up something of our own. When we first came here, we lived in a bark humpy that the blacks helped us build. The stockmen that Thomas brought with him from Mossvale left when we could not afford to pay them, because of the drought. None of the governesses would stay more than a month. Thank God for the blacks. Minnie saved Matty's life when he was bitten by that snake. They brought us food when we couldn't kill any more stock or we would not have had anything to build on after the drought broke. The gins helped in the house and the men are invaluable hands on the property.'

At that moment, Tan appeared, carrying a tray set with Eliza's best china and a lace doily. Dressed in an exquisitely embroidered yellow smock and with his hair pulled back in a shining plait, he placed the tray on the table beside Eliza.

'Missy pour or Tan?' he asked Eliza, his countenance solemn.

Eliza had to try very hard to keep the surprise from her face. Her eyes shone in gratitude to this small Chinese man, who had taken such care for her visitor.

'Please, Tan, would you pour?' she said softly.

'Yes, Missy.'

He lifted the delicate cup, and slowly and with great care, poured the tea. Eliza's nose twitched as she smelt the aroma of it and realised that Tan had delved into his personal supply of fine tea.

'Sugar, Mista?'

Robert nodded his head.

'Milk, Mista?'

At this point, Eliza could not help herself.

'Oh, Tan! Where did you get the milk? We haven't had any for ages.'

'Dat old black cow, she have calf little while ago. I milk,' Tan stated simply, bowing his head in Eliza's direction. He didn't mention that it had taken him four days to break her in to being milked nor the countless kicks he had avoided.

He poured Eliza's tea and then withdrew, again bowing slightly.

Eliza waited for Robert's questions, which she knew were coming.

'Well, he seems to be a good servant. Well-mannered. Where did you find him?'

'He found us. Tan arrived one day, carrying a blanket and a bag full of his possessions. Gradually, Thomas got out of him that he had had a rough time on the goldfields and became a shearer's cook. Thankfully, he has stayed on here. He is a very good cook and he grows the most amazing vegetables. He has a way with—'

The sound of running feet and screeching in Chinese caused her to pause. The three boys came tearing around the corner and, seeing the adults, thrust their hands behind their backs as they stopped in front of Eliza. Matty peered up at his mother from under his fringe, waiting for her to speak.

Sitting back in her chair, after half rising, Eliza said, 'Will you not steal Tan's bread before he is ready to serve it! How many times have I told you not to annoy him? Now go and apologise.'

Sammy gazed up in astonishment, wondering how the Missus knew what they had done. The boys turned and in single file walked back down the verandah, their precious stolen goods not tasting quite so good, as they stuffed the rest in their mouths before facing the irate Tan.

Eliza turned back to Robert, smoothing down her dress with her roughened hands.

'It must appear to you that we are a bit scruffy, but they are good children and we do live very comfortably now,' she said. 'We have just added on two new bedrooms and widened the drawing room. Thomas has a man coming to put a wash room inside. Think of that, way out here, a wash room inside.'

'My dear sister, I think you have done admirably, given the circumstances. I can see that Thomas has provided well for you, especially now that you are back on your feet. Why didn't you tell us? Why didn't Thomas's father help you?'

'Thomas wouldn't take any help from his father, no matter what. He is a mean and arrogant person. Did you know that Thomas had slept in the workers' quarters until we arrived at Mossvale, married? He was a very cold man and when we left, he disowned Thomas. Thomas had worked for no money and was treated like a lackey. Admittedly, the old man put him through a very fine school, but he had no mother and was miserable. The stockmen were his only friends. I find it amazing that he is such an even-tempered and gentle person, given his upbringing.'

Looking uncomfortable, Robert rubbed his chin. 'You have certainly kept a lot to yourself, sister.'

'What good would it have done to tell you of my woes? You were all too far away and there was the matter of proving that we could do it on our own. And we have survived.'

Shaking his head in wonder, Robert replied, 'What I can't understand is why you let your son run around with blacks. He should be in school.'

Taking a deep breath, she answered him as calmly as she could. 'That black child was my son's only companion until Jack joined us. His grandmother saved Matty's life! These people have accepted us with open arms. They were badly treated by their last Boss. Indeed, when they left his property, he came here looking for them with the police. Thomas had to write to the magistrate in Bourke and put in a claim for them. We don't pay them, but we don't beat them. Some of the stories I have heard would break your heart. We give them clothing and food. The blacks stay willingly. This is their country and they are happy here.'

'What do you mean, their country?' Robert said derisively.

Eliza spread her arms towards the open paddocks where the heat shimmered above the dry vegetation.

'Look about you, Robert. They were here before us and they survived!' she answered. 'Country is something that they belong to and it is part of them. I suppose the nearest I can explain it is... well, if you are religious you feel God in you. These people have a different religion and country is a big part of it. That is why they are happy here. They enjoy working with the horses and the cattle, but they are free to live their own ways. In the quiet seasons, they can have their ceremonies and do what they want. It is an amazing sight, to see all their relations come to the river for a corroboree. Anyway, I have grown used to their ways, and they to ours and we do very nicely, thank you! Once you have been here a while, you may begin to understand.'

Once again, their conversation was interrupted as Matty, Jack and Sammy returned. Jack and Matty were wearing shoes, had changed into clean clothes and combed their hair.

'Much better, boys. Now, I think you can show Uncle Robert around while I go and see Tan about tea,' Eliza said.

The first stop was the yards where Cedar stood, flicking her tail lazily at the flies. Robert agreed that Cedar was a fine filly. He was given a tour of the new corrugated iron shearing shed, the shearers' quarters and the harness room, and shown how the bore worked. He declared to the boys that it was very different where he came from and told them of the mountains and the green pastures, of the forests of eucalypts and the clear running streams fed by the melting snows. Matty and Sammy gaped at him wide-eyed, not being able to imagine such things. Eliza had told Matty when he was little, but she seemed to have put it all behind her and did not talk about it much now.

'Tomorrow, we will take you to the waterhole, Uncle Robert. We fish and hunt there,' Matty said proudly.

Robert wondered what there would be to hunt in this empty land but he refrained from saying anything and decided to wait for the morning.

* * * *

For Christmas, the boys decided to give a concert for the adults. Matty and Jack sat on the verandah, trying hard to memorise the poem they had chosen. Sammy was in the shed, sorting through some old clothing for them to dress up in.

A faint 'Git alonga' came from far away to the east and Matty's head snapped up. He shaded his eyes, scanning the track that led to the river. A faint dusty haze moved slowly, heading for the homestead.

Jumping to his feet, he slapped Jack's shoulder.

'Father's home. Let's go meet him,' he yelled, jumping off the step and racing for the yards. Jack followed, calling for Sammy to come.

They jumped on bareback, kicking the horses into a canter before Matty, remembering his promise, pulled his horse up and rode back to the house, scattering Tan's chooks.

He walked the horse through the garden gate and up to the verandah.

'Mother, they're back. Jim and Father are back,' he called.

Eliza came to the door, smiling, wiping her hands on her apron. The smile quickly turned to a frown when she saw him riding bareback.

Matty saw her face and got in quickly. 'We won't gallop, we'll go steady. Anyways, they're not that far!'

'All right, but just go steady,' Eliza agreed. 'Tell your father that Robert is here.'

Matty wheeled his horse around, its hooves cutting up Eliza's precious grass. He trotted out to where the boys waited, then, breaking into a gentle canter, they rode along the track to meet the wagon.

The team had their heads down, pulling hard into their collars, sweat lathered white under the harness as they hauled the load through the sand. Thomas and Jim sat perched on boxes, the dray piled high with goods.

'Well, look at this, Jim. A welcoming party,' Thomas said as the boys reined in their horses alongside.

'We have a visitor, Father,' Matty said. 'Uncle Robert has come from Welaregang.'

'Ah, we must have missed him. We stopped at Ford's Bridge, at David William's place for two days to fix a wheel.'

'We're having a concert – Sammy, me and Matty,' Jack broke in. 'We read about it in an old newspaper and we're gonna perform.'

Thomas pushed back his hat and smiled. 'Well, is that so? And when will this be?'

'Christmas Eve,' Matty said.

'Dress up an' all, Boss,' added Sammy.

Thomas pushed back his hat and glanced at Jim. 'This will be something to look forward to, eh, Jim?'

'My word, Boss, him be plenty funny.' Jim's smile softened his words.

The word spread quickly of the arrival of the supplies and the station hands came in to help unload the dray. The boys unhitched the team and after removing the harness, they gave the big gentle Clydesdales a rub down before watering them. As keen as they were to see what came off the wagon, the boys cleaned the sweat from the harness first before hanging it up. Their jobs finished, they ran over to the shed.

The arrival of stores was always a big event at the homestead. Besides the staples of flour, salt, tea and sugar, there would be tobacco, jam and golden syrup. Eliza would go through it all with Tan and sort out the rations for the stockmen and their families, then they would pack the rest away for the homestead. There were some knowing glances between Thomas, Eliza and Tan as one big box was carried into the house.

'What's in that box, Mother? Is it Christmas gifts?'

'Nothing for you to worry about, son. Just some things I asked your father to get me.'

Matty scowled and, turning to Sammy, asked, 'Did you tell your mob about our concert?'

'Yeah, them coming. They reckon it gonna be funny, like Big Jim said.'

* * * *

Christmas Eve, Minnie and the other women came up from the river, while the station hands all came in from where they had been working. Eliza, Tan and Bess spent all day in the kitchen preparing food for that evening and Christmas day.

Robert sat on the verandah and gazed about at the gathering of people. The thought went through his mind that this was a little village, with a mix of humanity and with laws unto itself. From his talks with Thomas and Eliza, he had now realised that without the Aborigines, Thomas and his family could not have stayed here. Old Minnie, as black skinned as he had ever seen a human, Sammy and Tan; they were all contributing. He remembered watching Charlie working on Eliza's horse, wondering at the skill and gentleness that the man possessed.

'How do you get on living so far from the police and town?'

'All the blacks have their own laws,' Thomas replied. 'They can be pretty complicated and often a lot tougher than ours. They manage their own kind. All our people are good people, so we never really have any problems. They take care of any other blacks that come onto the property. If anyone turns up, they are fed and given a bed for the night, anyone what does the wrong thing gets short shift and is run off the place. Sometimes we get swaggies through; again, same thing applies. We had a missionary turn up once but he didn't stay long. He reckoned our blacks had been tamed. He went off somewhere else to save souls. Tame! If you'd have seen a corroboree, you wouldn't call them tame! And the didgeridoo is so haunting, it sends shivers down your spine. No, we are lucky. We haven't had any of the problems that others have had, but then, I believe we treat our blacks a lot better as well.'

Thinking back over what he had seen in the past few weeks, Robert knew that Thomas and Eliza did take care of their people and he had begun to see what Eliza had spoken to him about on the first day he arrived. It was a rare but good relationship, and probably only existed because of the remoteness of the property and the natures of Thomas and Eliza.

Robert watched as Thomas and Eliza handed out tobacco and clothing to the Aboriginals as Christmas presents. He laughed when Minnie said, 'Missus, you tellum Jesus, he good fella for givin' 'bacca.'

Over dinner one night, Eliza had told Robert of her difficulties in trying to explain white man's religion to the Aboriginals, and how she had laughed at some of the conclusions they had drawn. In the end, she gave up and began to listen to their stories of creation, full of rich detail.

Being a special occasion, Thomas had killed and dressed a steer, some of which Tan roasted in the big wood oven. Weeks ago, Eliza had made plum puddings that had hung in their calico cloths until now. Milk from the black cow meant that she was able to make custard, a rare treat. Eliza sat in a chair that Charlie brought down from the verandah, while the others sat cross-legged, or sprawled out on the sparse lawn in the shade of the white cedar and Kurrajong trees that Eliza had planted when they first arrived on the property. A few giggles were heard as Sammy, Matty and Jack mounted the stairs, dressed in some of Thomas's cast offs, far too large for the boys. Standing on the edge of the steps, the boys recited 'A Bush Christmas'. Matty turned to his uncle and explained that the next one was for him, but on account of it being so long, they would read it, and so in unison three of them read 'The Man from Snowy River.' The Aborigines paid close attention, story-telling being part of their culture and they listened to the white man's words carefully. After the boys had finished, there was general agreement that the stories were good ones.

The boys picked up wooden rifles and Jack told of the Kelly gang who, over twenty years ago, filled the newspapers with their deeds. Jack played the part of Ned, Matty was Dan and Sammy the policeman. After being shot by Ned, Sammy fell to the ground and laid prone. Matty and Jack waited, the audience tittering at the lull in proceedings. Trying to prompt him, Matty lent over and whispered loudly, 'Quick, Sammy, now you gotta be Joe Byrne,' to which Sammy replied, 'I can't, I dead, remember. Jack shot me.'

As the sun began to throw its dying colours against the clouds, turning them orange and magenta, the people made their way back to the river, carrying their gifts and talking about white man's Christmas being good time. Eliza and the men retired to the verandah, where the men smoked and spoke of the differences between the outback and the mountains, the cricket and other topics that Thomas had not kept up to date on. Matty and Jack went to bed early, eager for the morning.

* * * *

They were up early, anxious to see what gifts would be under the tree. Running into the drawing room, they stared in disappointment under the branch of a redgum that Eliza had decorated. It was bare of presents for them. Only their carefully wrapped gifts for the adults sat there, five objects mocking them. They sat on the verandah steps, watching the day come to life, waiting for the adults to rise.

'Why do you suppose there are no presents?' Matty asked, swatting at an early fly.

Jack shrugged his shoulders. 'Dunno. We've been good, haven't we?'

Noises came from the kitchen as Tan lit the fire for breakfast but Jack and Matty took no notice.

They watched as Charlie brushed the grey filly that was Eliza's present. A soft whistling made them look over to the track where Sammy came striding along, his hand dragging a stick. He was surprised when he saw them sitting on the step.

'You fellas up early. Why you fellas look like that for?'

'No presents under the tree,' Jack replied.

'You mean like the Missus give us las' night?'

'Sort of,' came the short reply.

Sammy saw the confusion in their eyes and sat beside his mates. He knew from the school room that white man gave each other presents, and that these were usually under a tree in the drawing room.

Matty sighed, and unconsciously the other two sighed. They sat listening for movement from inside the house that would alert them to the adults having risen. Finally, Jack started to fidget and, getting up, said he was going to help Charlie. Sammy went to follow him but when Matty stayed seated, staring into the distance, he sat back down.

Eventually, Matty heard footsteps along the hallway and, turning, saw his parents, dressed in their town clothes, ready for Christmas Day. Eliza's eyes were bright and his father's mouth struggled to hide a grin. They stood in the doorway, waiting for Matty to speak. He looked, first at his father then at Eliza. Slowly, comprehension came to his face and he jumped up, shouting, 'Jack, Jack, they've played a trick on us!'

Jack came running from the shed where Charlie had hurriedly taken the filly.

'What do you mean?' he asked as he ran up the stairs.

Pointing at his parents, Matty exclaimed. 'Look, they're trying not to laugh!'

Jack laughed and Sammy stood, looking a little confused.

Thomas took pity on the boys. 'After breakfast we will see what Christmas brought, shall we?' he said. Pointing at Jack and Matty, he added, 'You two, go and get dressed properly for the occasion,' noticing their bare feet and work clothes.

Turning to Sammy, he pointed towards the kitchen and winked, careful not to let Eliza see.

'You get along and see Tan. Tell him I said you could have some breakfast, then go and help Charlie. We'll be out after breakfast.'

Sammy nodded, understanding the subtle message, and scampered up the verandah to the kitchen, his mouth watering at the thought of warm damper loaded with dripping.

When Matty and Jack returned, dressed in Sunday best clothes, the family went into the dining room where Tan had laid out Eliza's best crockery. He then brought in steaming plates of eggs, fresh bread, jam, butter and best of all, thick slices of bacon. Salted and cured back in October when they had last killed a pig, it had hung in the small cellar dug into the floor of the kitchen, saved for this occasion and now it lay on their plates, crisp and brown. The boys ate hurriedly until a clearing of the throat from Eliza slowed them down. Robert pushed his plate away and sat back.

'Well, boys, what did you want for Christmas?'

Jack glanced up at him and, seeing the corners of his eyes crease, realised he too was in on the joke. He hung his head and sadly said, 'We must have been bad. Father Christmas didn't come last night.'

Matty opened his mouth to say something but shut it promptly after Jack pinched him on the thigh under the table.

He too, hung his head and wiped away an imaginary tear. Playing along with Jack, he said, 'Yeah, we must've been bad.'

Robert laughed. 'So what did you ask for?'

Jack answered first, picking up the knife from his plate and staring at it. 'Well, maybe a new knife. The blade on my old one snapped when I tried to cut some of that leather Jim gave me for plaiting.'

Robert nodded and turned to Matty. 'How about you, nephew?'

'I was hoping for a halter for Cedar. You know, those fancy ones with the brass buckles.'

Tan came through the door and spoke quietly. 'Boss, that Charlie, he says he ready for you.'

Pushing back his chair, Thomas rose and thanked Tan for breakfast. Tan inclined his head slightly and started to back out of the room. Thomas held up his hand.

'No, Tan, I think you should come with us. I know you don't celebrate Christmas like us, but I would be pleased if you would share in this with us.'

Tan nodded again and stood waiting. Matty and Jack caught on to what Thomas was alluding to and, scrapping their chairs back, came and stood each side of Eliza.

She looked at Robert and then at each of the two boys in turn, finally resting her eyes on her husband.

'What is all this about, then?'

With a nod from Thomas, Matty said excitedly, 'We're gonna show you your Christmas present. Come on!'

He put his hand under her elbow and helped her rise, then with the boys each taking one of her hands, dragged her up the hallway and out onto the verandah. Thomas and Robert followed the procession and stood beside them. Tan stood to one side where he could watch the Missus's face.

'Charlie, you can bring it out now,' Matty yelled, peering anxiously towards the shed.

From around the corner of the shed, the horse breaker proudly led the filly he had broken in for Eliza. The filly stepped daintily, her mane and tail flowing from the brushing Charlie had given them. Sammy walked alongside of Charlie, smiling when he saw the look of amazement on the Missus's face.

Matty pulled his mother down the stairs, nearly causing her to trip over her long skirt.

'She's for you from us,' he explained, casting his hand around to indicate everyone present. 'Father picked her out and Charlie broke her.'

Reaching out her hand slowly, Eliza stroked the filly's nose, turning her hand over to let the horse smell her scent. She slowly moved her hand up and stroked the filly's neck, saying, 'Thank you, everyone. She's beautiful. I haven't had a horse of my own since, well, since a long time.'

She put her hand to her face and wiped away the tears of joy. Catching Thomas's eye, she mouthed the words 'thank you' and stepped back to admire her present.

'What will you call her, Mother?'

'Mmmm. Snowy…? Princess…? No, I have it – Lady!'

Eliza thanked Charlie and asked him to put the filly in the yard, that she might ride her later. As Sammy turned to go with Charlie, Thomas called to him.

'Sammy, you come with us.'

Sammy stared in amazement at the Boss and after receiving a reassuring nod, walked up the stairs with the others, though hung back a little when he reached the verandah.

This is white man's business, this Christmas business, he thought.

The adults all stepped back and motioned the three boys to walk ahead of them to the kitchen. Their pace quickened and by the time they got to the kitchen door, they were running. They entered the doorway and stood, peering about, trying to spy what could be hidden in here. Tan appeared quietly in through the back doorway holding a key, which he presented to Thomas, who in turn, went to a long cupboard in the corner.

Thomas drew out the moment by giving the boys a talk on how they had been helpful around the property, and he expected them to try hard at their studies. He watched them carefully and when he saw Matty start to clench his hands with impatience, he unlocked the cupboard and threw open the door. Three .22 rifles sat side by side, their wooden stocks gleaming richly.

Jack's mouth fell open and Matty glanced quickly at his mother. Eliza gave a little nod, and Matty broke the silence that had fallen.

'For us? Our own rifles?' he yelled. Taking a step forward, he stopped suddenly and looked at his father.

He glanced at Sammy, then at his father. He did not know how he knew but slowly the thought crystallised. It may have been his uncle's first reaction to Sammy or maybe he had picked it up from conversations past, but he knew with certainty that this was a very generous gift from his father to Sammy. Jack was part of the family, an adopted son, but Sammy? He turned away from the cupboard and hugged Thomas.

'Thank you, Father, for giving Sammy a gun. Now we can all go hunting together, all of us with our own gun.'

He ruffled Matty's hair and smiled. *We are doing something right with our boy,* he thought proudly. *He realises that we value our people.*

Sammy reached out and lifted one of the rifles from the cupboard. He stroked the dark polished wood and ran his fingers, feather-light, up the barrel.

His dark eyes were wide as he turned to Thomas and asked, 'Mucka me! Him, Boss, him give me a rifle?'

The adults smiled at the incredulous look on his face and the slip in his pronunciation.

'Yes, Sammy, it is yours.'

The Boss said sternly, 'Now, you three. No shooting anything but rabbits and dingoes, all right?'

He received violent nods as Matty and Jack took their rifles from their hiding place.

'We'll have some target practice later. I think we might go and see what's under the tree for the rest of us,' Thomas said as he winked at Eliza. 'After all, Uncle Robert and I haven't got anything yet.'

Matty had conspired with his father to give his mother a new hat from Bourke and for his father, he had asked Jim to make a stockwhip. Jack shyly gave Thomas a belt and hat band he had plaited from a kangaroo skin. After Eliza had opened her present of a beautifully worked leather bookmark, she hugged Jack and complimented him on his growing skill with leatherwork. The two boys then presented Uncle

Robert with his gift. Unwrapping the brown paper parcel, Robert was astounded to find a bridle, plaited and woven.

'See, Uncle.' Matty pointed out the woven strands of dry spinifex and the white horse hair that Jack had carefully worked into the bridle as he plaited. 'The leather's from an old stud bull that Father bought ages ago. This is for you to remember us.'

Jack reddened when Robert thanked him and complimented him on his craft. 'Matty helped.'

'He got the hair from Moon's tail and the grass and wove it like Minnie showed him,' Matty added.

'It is a very fine present, boys. Thank you.'

Robert put his presents to the side and drew out a large box from behind the chair. He held it out and said, 'You two might get some fun out of these.'

Jack pushed Matty forward and after taking the box, Matty opened it. Nestled in amongst green paper were two pairs of boxing gloves.

'Crikey, Uncle Robert, these are bonza.' Matty grinned.

'Thanks, sir,' said Jack.

'That's all right. I'll give you some lessons before I leave.'

Thomas stood and the boys jumped up excitedly, each holding their gloves.

'Come on, Robert, how about we give these boys some gun practice?'

Out on the verandah, where Sammy sat waiting, admiring his gift, Thomas and Robert showed the boys how to carry their rifles, then how to clean them.

'A dirty rifle can kill you,' Thomas said. He sat back in the chair and eyed the boys sitting cross-legged in front of him. 'How can a dirty rifle kill you?'

Jack stared at the lawn; suddenly, his head jerked up. 'If it's clogged up, it won't fire?' he asked.

'Nearly right. If the barrel is blocked because, say, you've put it down barrel first and got dirt in it, well, when you fire it, the barrel will explode. If it doesn't kill you, it will certainly maim you,' Thomas explained. 'You must always remember that a gun is a weapon and treat it as if it is always loaded.'

Robert nodded. 'There have been many people that have been injured or killed because they thought the gun was empty.'

'Now, a gun is a big responsibility. Sammy and his people hunt with spears. It takes a great deal of skill and patience. He has been taught for years to do this. With a gun, you point and fire and if your aim is good, you will hit what you are aiming at. This is where being responsible comes in. If you shoot an animal, do it as cleanly as possible – a headshot or at least a shot through the heart. Never leave an animal injured.' Thomas looked at each boy in turn, his eyes boring into theirs. 'Is this understood?'

All the boys nodded fiercely.

'After today's practice, you will get a certain amount of ammunition. This is to last till the next load of supplies arrives. You may only shoot injured stock, rabbits and dingoes.'

'What about crows when the ewes are lambing?' Matty interrupted.

'Yes, and crows. You are to leave the roos for Sammy's people. Sammy, it will be up to your uncle to say if you can shoot roos. Now, let's have some practice.'

Being in on the surprise, Tan had saved up empty jam tins from the kitchen and now the boys set them out along the rails on the horse yards.

'Always look beyond your target. What can run into your field of fire or behind your target? What will you hit if you miss what you are aiming for?' Robert instructed. 'Now, each of you load and fire one at a time.'

The sound of shots broke the stillness and continued through the morning, their aim steadily improving. They cleaned their rifles and reluctantly put them away with Thomas's guns. The Boss had promised a ride the next day to have some more practice on rabbits.

Matty handled Cedar for a while and then left her in the yards while they had lunch. A commotion in the horse yards made him come to the verandah where he could see Cedar snorting, her head tossing from side to side as she stood in the middle of the yard, striking at something with her forelegs. She struck out again then raced around the yard, her head sideways, watching whatever it was that had stirred her up. Charlie ran from the shed carrying a shovel. He climbed the fence one-handed and then stopped, sitting on the top rail.

Matty jumped over the verandah rail, landing heavily. He rolled and got up, running flat out to the yards, his heart pounding, calling out to Charlie, 'What's wrong with her, Charlie?'

Charlie turned and seeing Matty, raised his hand.

'Slow down. Cheeky fella, him all finish up.'

Matty's face went pale and he stared through the rails to the centre of the yards. A twitching grey snake lay in the dust, its body torn and bleeding. Matty quickly bent and squeezed through the rails ignoring Charlie's calls of 'no, she plenty wild'.

He slowly walked towards Cedar, his hand outstretched. She stood, head high, snorting and showing the whites of her eyes. Every muscle in her body was taut, ready to run, her flanks heaving and sweating from her exertions.

He spoke slowly and quietly, 'Calm down now, girl. That snake's not goin' to hurt you now.'

Desperately, he examined her legs, looking for drops of blood. The filly watched him intently as he slowly got closer. She stretched her neck out and sniffed his hand, her dilated nostrils blowing in and out. Matty very carefully ran his hand up the side of her face and stepping closer, ran his hand down her neck. Gradually her muscles relaxed, although she kept an eye on the battered mess lying in the dust of the yards.

Seeing the filly had quietened, Charlie lowered himself into the yard and picked up the snake by the tail. Cedar's head jerked up and she snorted heavily. Matty stroked her but she spun away, racing around the yard.

Charlie turned and flung the reptile over the rails, then motioned for Matty to follow him out the gate. 'Out here, young fella.'

Matty stood, watching Cedar. His father's stern voice got his attention. 'Do what Charlie said. Now!'

Matty turned at the sound of his father's anger and left the yard quickly. Thomas met him at the gate.

'I've just left your mother in a state of shock,' he said, keeping his anger down. 'Go and tell her you're not hurt.'

'Cedar wouldn't have hurt me, Father!'

'Do as I said.'

Thomas watched as his son walked towards the house, Matty's head turning now and then to look at his mare. The anger that had come quickly left. He beckoned to Charlie to follow him to the house. The other boys stood at the rail, mute; it was not often that they had seen Thomas so angry.

Going to Eliza, Matty bent down and hugged her.

'I'm sorry for scaring you, but I thought she was bit and had to see. The snake was dead.'

Returning his embrace, Eliza said, 'I am over it now, Matty, but you did give me a turn. Now, sit down. We had better ask Charlie what happened.'

Matty went and sat on the bottom step. Jack and Sammy joined him, eager to hear how the ruckus had started.

Looking up at his father, Matty apologised. 'I'm sorry, Father, for worrying you and Mother. But I thought Cedar was hurt and I had to see. She really wouldn't have hurt me.'

His father glanced at Eliza, then back at his son. 'You scared your mother and you disobeyed Charlie. You didn't think before you went in there.'

Matty hung his head. 'Yes, Father.'

Thomas reached out and patted Matty's shoulder, his anger having dissipated. He was just thankful that his son had not been hurt. Turning to Charlie, he asked if he had seen what happened.

Leaning against the verandah rail, Charlie pointed to the harness shed. 'Me sittin' in shed, makin' bridle. Filly come drink at tank. Horse, she blow loud, look up and I see snake, him in tree over tank. Him after bird eggs. Snake, he on little branch, it break. Him fall on her head.'

Drawing in his breath, Matty jumped to his feet but his mother caught his arm.

'Wait a minute, let Charlie tell the rest,' she said, nodding at Charlie.

The horse breaker squatted down, pushing his hat back on his head. 'Dat mare, she shake her head. Snake, he on ground, under tank and him headin' for filly. Maybe she step on tail, him plenty angry. He up, strikin',' Charlie explained, his hand mimicking the snake's actions. 'She rearin' and jumpin' at snake. She muckka him bad.'

'No wonder she put on a performance,' said Thomas, shaking his head. 'You'd never think of such a thing happening!'

'Charlie, do you think that she got bitten?' asked Eliza.

'I dunno, Missus. I look soon, when she settle down.'

His fear showing on his face, Matty pleaded with Eliza. 'Can I go see now, please, Mother? I've got to see if she's hurt.'

Eliza sighed and glanced at Thomas as if he would provide the answer for her. She knew that her son loved this filly and had not thought of himself in his bid to take care of her. The muscles in her stomach tightened again as the image of the frightened horse came to her again. She knew she had to let him go to Cedar – he would not calm down until he had. Thomas gave a slight nod and Eliza reached out her hand, patting his shoulder.

'Go on.'

Matty ran to the kitchen, begged Tan for some carrots, and then after grabbing a halter from the shed, he entered the yard. Calming himself, he held out the carrots to Cedar. She walked up to him, interested in what he was offering her, seeming to have forgotten about the snake. Matty put the halter on her and held her, stroking her, as Charlie ran his hands over her head and neck, then her legs.

'No see bite on animals. We wait, see,' Charlie said. 'We watch, see if she get sick.'

Charlie gave the filly a pat, then leaned against the rails and rolled a smoke. Matty let the mare go and she snuffled his pockets, then wandered around the yard. When she reached the spot where the snake had left blood in the dirt, she shied away at the smell and snorted. Trotting back to Matty, she stood beside him, and after a while closed her eyes to the flies and the heat. Jack and Sammy had climbed up and sat on the rails to watch but grew bored after half an hour, and wandered back up to the house.

The sun poured down on them and Charlie suggested that they sit in the shed. He could keep plaiting and they could watch Cedar at the same time.

After a couple of anxious hours, Charlie finally said that he didn't think the filly had been bitten. Matty was relieved as they went back to the yard.

'How much longer before we can start breaking her in, Charlie?'

'Longa time, she not grown 'nough now.'

Matty gave Cedar a final pat and let her out into the horse paddock.

NINE

The drought deepened. The red soil baked in the heat and plants curled their leaves, trying to retain any moisture left in them. As the Paroo dried up to become stagnant pools, the waterhole shrunk with the river no longer feeding into it.

There was no time for lessons as they were too busy keeping the bores going to water the stock. While the three boys rode from bore to bore, checking the windmills and camping out for weeks at a time, the stockmen rode the boundaries checking on stock, pushing them onto better grazing.

Thomas and Eliza glanced at each other over the dinner table and remembered the last time. The previous three years had been good ones. They had built up the stock numbers again, but they knew if the drought dragged on, the small amount of money would dwindle. One hundred bales of wool sat in the woolshed waiting to be taken to Bourke. The bales would sit there until the Darling rose enough to let the paddle steamers back up the river. The alternative was to pay for transport to Sydney by train, a very expensive proposition.

Supplies were low and they would have to go to Bourke soon. Travellers reported that the government bores along the Yantabulla Road were holding up so Thomas made the decision to leave the wool in the shed and do a quick run to Bourke for supplies.

He sent Ernie and Billy out to bring the boys in; the stockmen would travel the property's bores. He needed the boys to stay around the house while he took Charlie and Jim to Bourke. If the bores had stopped along the track, the Aboriginals would still hopefully be able to find water. Thomas never gave up marvelling at their knowledge of the land, even when it was at its most inhospitable.

The boys came in and Eliza stared at them in surprise. They had been out for six weeks and she had forgotten how quickly they were growing. Taller than Thomas now, Jack's once skinny frame had filled out with the hard work on the property and he could no longer wear Thomas's cast-offs. He was fifteen; Matty, at fourteen, was only just beginning to develop but he was wiry and now looked down on his mother while Sammy was still as thin as a whip but long and tall, his grin as cheeky as ever against his dark face. She regretted that they had not been able to stay on the verandah, learning their lessons. Instead, this savage land had forced her to let them go, go to where they were needed – boys, doing men's work.

The dray was pulled from the shed and its axles greased, the harness oiled. The draught horse team were brought in and shod as they made their preparations.

Thomas had watched as travellers arrived in the new invention, the automobile, but he could not see the point in owning something that needed fuel to run. Where would he get the fuel? The boys always examined these strange contraptions when they arrived, loaded with tins of petrol and not much else. The driver would usually spend time repairing tyres or engines. The outback took a hard toll on these machines.

Tan showed great patience as Eliza tried to help him pack supplies for the trip. Eliza could not concentrate, thinking of the tough going ahead for Thomas. She put in the tea and then pulled it out, saying it was not enough, ordered the boys to fill up more water bags, then tried to do it herself. Stoically, Tan carefully wrapped eggs in dried grass, measured out quantities of flour and salt and placed them in the tin trunk holding the supplies. Eventually, he tactfully suggested that Eliza had best pack Thomas's clothes and things calmed in the kitchen.

With a full moon rising over the distant scrub, the men set off, taking advantage of the coolness of the night. This would be their pattern until Bourke, resting in the heat of the day in whatever shade they could find, and travelling in the cooler hours.

* * * *

Sammy and Jack went hunting early in the morning, while Matty worked with Cedar. He had missed the filly while they were out on the bore run but now he made up time with her. He called her in every morning from the twenty-acre horse paddock and she came galloping, eager for the handful of oats that he had made last from the previous supply run. Charlie had taught the boys to shoe the horses and although it wasn't time for Cedar to be shod, Matty would lift her feet and tap them with a hammer, getting her used to the feeling. Her hooves were hard and never needed much filing, unusual for white hooves.

He would put on the halter and lead her for miles, talking to her constantly. Once back in the yards, he would tie her to the rail. He rubbed her over with hessian sacks and cracked the stockwhip around her, preparing her for the day he would ride her. Cedar grew used to all this and Matty grew bolder. He would place his hands on her back and slowly put more and more weight on her. She side-stepped nervously to start with but gradually she learned to stay still under the weight. Soon Matty was lying across her back. He kept this knowledge to himself. His mother would be horrified if she knew what he was doing; she thought that fourteen was too young for horse breaking.

Jack surprised him one morning and caught him on Cedar's back. Matty swore him to secrecy and enlisted his help.

'I want to surprise Charlie when he gets back. She's nearly three now, she's old enough,' he said. 'Will you hold her while I try and sit up on her?'

'The Missus will go spare if she catches you!'

'Well, we won't get caught. We'll tell her we're going hunting. You get your rifle and we'll get Tan some rabbits for a stew. I lead Cedar everywhere now, so it won't seem strange if we take her with us.'

'If we get caught, we will get a bollocking.'

Matty shook his head and smiled. 'We won't get caught.'

Jack went in to tell Eliza that they were going out to get rabbits, but the smell of fresh baked biscuits drew him to the kitchen. He left a message with Tan about going shooting. He thought that Eliza might see through the story and then the game would be up. Grabbing a handful of biscuits, he tucked the rifle under his arm and re-joined Matty, who sat impatiently under the acacia tree by the yards.

Jack handed his mate some of the biscuits and they headed out towards number two bore, Cedar nosing at Matty for a share of biscuit.

'It's a shame Sammy's not here to see this,' Jack said, a smile spreading on his lips. 'This could be funny, if she acts up!' He dug Matty in the ribs. 'Hey, Shorty.'

Matty ignored Jack and wished that Sammy hadn't had to take supplies out to Billy and Ernie. The day before, a message had come in that there was trouble with a bore out in the furthest western paddock, and so Eliza sent Sammy out. Matty and Jack had mustered the Back Paddock and put the sheep into the Upper Waterhole paddock where there was still a bit of feed. After checking the cattle in another paddock and making sure the bore was running, they looked forward to a day off.

Turning to Jack, he said, 'Sammy'll be back later tonight. He'll be on his way by now.'

They walked through the red sand, the heat making mirages in the distance. Matty kept glancing back and when they were well away from the house, he stopped.

'Put the rifle down,' he told Jack. 'Then you hold her for me.'

Jack walked over and laid the rifle against a stump, careful to keep the barrel out of the sand. Walking back to Matty, he tried one last time. 'What am I goin' to tell the Missus if you get hurt?'

'Tell her something scared Cedar and she dragged me 'cause I wouldn't let go,' he answered, thinking quickly.

Jack shrugged his shoulders and, taking a tighter grip of the soft plaited rope, nodded to show he was ready. Cedar stood placidly, waiting for the boys to move off again, her tail swishing at the constant flies. Matty rubbed his hands over her back and cautiously put weight on her back. The filly did not react so he pushed harder. Jack stood to the side of her in case she jumped forward.

'Give us a leg up, will you?' asked Matty, lifting one leg off the ground.

Taking the rope up a little so that the filly's head turned in towards him, Jack bent forward and grasped Matty's leg, giving him a push up.

Slowly, Matty lay all the way over Cedar's back. When the filly stood quietly and did not move, Matty carefully swung his leg over her back. The filly stepped forward, her ears twitching back and forth, unsure at this movement. Matty stopped. He stroked her neck, talking to her, while his mate held the lead rope tightly, waiting. Cedar relaxed again when nothing awful happened, Matty continued to let his leg down her side. Staying down along her neck, he rubbed her shoulders and down her sides before, very slowly, sitting up.

Jack watched her head nervously, waiting for any sign that she would buck. When she did not move after Matty had sat up straight he whispered, 'Will I lead her forward?'

'No, this'll do for today. I'll get off now,' Matty whispered back.

Slowly, he reversed his movements and slid softly to the ground, giving Cedar a pat.

The two mates eyed each other as they realised how well it had gone.

'I won't have to go and tell the Missus anything, eh, Shorty?'

'She's great, isn't she? Did you see how she took it?' Matty said, full of pride.

He led Cedar back along the dusty track while Jack ranged out, searching for rabbits. A crack echoed over the plains, and the galahs resting in a nearby tree to flew up, squawking their alarm.

There go the rabbits, thought Matty as he walked along slowly, his eyes now instinctively checking the ground as he walked. He could see where a snake had crossed the track and where a mob of kangaroos had passed. Now and then he glanced about, taking in the stillness of the day. The heat had driven the birds and animals to shade and rest.

Another crack came from further away and he knew that Jack was heading back to the house, around behind the shearing shed. He led Cedar to the horse paddock and let her go, happy with what he had achieved that morning. As he walked to the shed to put away her halter, Matty heard strange voices. Quickly putting the halter on a peg, he ran around to the front of the house.

Matty took in the sight of two bearded men, sitting astride horses in poor condition. A packhorse stood behind them, its head drooping, sores showing where the pack had been ill-fitted. The fact that these men had not been invited to share a cup of tea on the verandah came to him as he heard his mother's tone when she spoke.

'You can keep riding. There are no gins here. They've gone up country.'

He let himself through the house yard gate and strode up the path to the verandah steps. The men only glanced at him, turning their attention back to Eliza.

The larger of the two men scowled and glanced about, a sly smile coming to his face.

'Where be the Boss man, Missus?'

Matty could see his mother's hands grasping her dress, her knuckles white against the red of her work-roughened hands. Taking the steps two at time, he stood beside her and studied the two men carefully. One was deeply tanned, a long black beard covering most of his lower face. Strands of hair draggled out from beneath his hat where they lay, dark and greasy against his shoulders. Big fists bunched the reins tightly between his fingers as he rested them on the pommel of the saddle. His clothes were filthy, stained with red dust and his boots worn.

The man riding with him was slight and sat hunched over in the saddle. He was pale in contrast to his friend and his clothes appeared too large for him. Matty took in the stock of a gun protruding from the rifle bucket on the offside of his saddle.

He heard his mother reply and her answer proved the feeling that had been growing in him.

'He's up at the bore, not two miles away. Now I'll thank you to be on your way.'

His mother had lied. He drew in his breath; these men gave him a feeling of revulsion he had never felt before. He heard soft footsteps in the hall but he kept his eyes on the men. Feeling more than seeing, he knew Jack had stepped out of the hall and was standing to his mother's other side. The sound of the bolt of a rifle sliding home caused him to flick his eyes towards Jack.

The boy stood with the rifle over his arm, cocked and ready to fire.

'You heard the Missus. The blacks have gone up country past Yantabulla,' he stated, indicating a northerly direction with the barrel of his rifle.

The larger man laughed at the sight of Jack with the rifle.

Jack stood calmly, his eyes boring straight at the men. 'Mister, I can shoot the eye out of a rabbit at fifty yards. Your head would be no problem.'

Listening to Jack's mastery of the situation, Matty felt ashamed that he had not thought to get his rifle to protect his mother. He knew he could not move, as any movement might start something.

A voice said from the corner of the verandah, 'If he miss, I not.'

Tan stood there, a twelve-gauge shotgun appearing large against his small frame.

'Well, well, the Missus got a chinee boy and two kids to look after her. I'm tired of mucking around here. These people aren't friendly, are they, Jimmy?'

His partner shook his head and jerked his horse around. He spoke for the first time in a deep voice, unexpected given his size.

'We got money to make. Com'n, let's go git these gins.'

As the two men turned and rode off in the direction that Jack had indicated, Eliza reached for a chair, collapsing into it.

Matty rushed to her side, anxious that she might faint.

'No, no, I'm all right. It just gave me a bit of a shock. We haven't had any men like that here before.'

Unloading his gun, Jack took the shotgun from Tan and broke it open. It was empty. They looked at him in admiration at his bluff. Tan appeared embarrassed as he mumbled something about not being able to find the shells for it.

They all laughed and the tension lessened.

'My brave knights,' Eliza said. Her hand flew to her mouth and her eyes opened wide. 'No!'

The other three stared at her in alarm.

'You told them north, Jack,' she said. 'What if they swing back to the river? You boys will have to ride to the camp and warn the women. All the men are out on the property, and we don't have a hope of getting them back in time.'

Jack and Matty stood staring at Eliza, not understanding.

Sizing up their bewilderment, Tan explained.

'Bad men, they git girlies and take 'em way. They sell them up north, on coast. Pearlers, sugar cane.'

The boys had read of these things in the newspapers, but it was always far away from them. To think that it could happen to Sammy's mother or Annie galvanised them into action.

Running into the drawing room, Matty took his rifle from the gun cupboard, grabbed a handful of bullets and followed Jack to the yards. Tan took a bucket of grain and stood at the horse paddock gate rattling it, yelling, 'Gee up, gee up, horseys.'

As the boys dragged the saddles from the shed, they heard the muffled sound of galloping horses. In these times of dry sparse grass, the horses would come immediately for the promise of a feed of grain. Tan shut the gate behind them as they ran into the yard. Matty pushed Cedar away as she came to him, expecting a treat.

'Not now, girl. No time.'

Quickly they saddled up and, flinging themselves onto their horses' backs, they galloped out the gate that Tan held open. As he shut it, Eliza came to stand beside him, fear in her eyes.

'They good boys. They nealy grown now, Missy. They be wight.' He tried to allay her worry.

Eliza wiped at her face with the bottom of her apron, nodding at Tan.

'I know, Tan. I only hope those men keep going north.'

The boys headed southeast, leaving the track and cutting through the scrub. They slowed when they came to open ground, not wanting to kick up too much dust on the dry sandy plain. They trotted, giving the horses a short break, then when they rode back into scrubby country, they galloped again. The distance to the river shortened quickly and they rode into the camp, scattering the dogs. Matty flung himself off the horse before it had quite pulled up and after getting his balance, ran to where he could see Minnie sitting in the shade of a redgum.

'Minnie, men are looking for the women,' the words spilled out. 'Mother says they will take them away. We've got to get you all back to the homestead.'

The younger women started to wail. Minnie reached out for Matty to help her stand. Leaning on his arm, she spoke sharply to the women. They quietened and some ran to get their babies. The others went to the riverbank and tore off large pieces of brush.

Minnie hobbled over to her humpy and gathering her bag of things, she turned to Matty.

'You take girls to house. I too old, too slow. Me go back way.'

Leading his horse to Minnie, Matty shook his head violently. He stared at Minnie, noticing how old she had become. This was his second mother and her ancient, withered frame appeared as though it would snap if a storm blew up.

'Jack, Bess, come here!' he called, a plan forming in his mind.

Jack gave Annie his horse to hold and he and Bess went over to Matty. They caught on quickly and each stepped up beside Minnie. She looked at each of them and then the horse. She stepped back, shaking her head.

'No, no, me no ride horse. I walk, always walk, long time, I walk,' she said, her head wobbling from side to side as she spoke.

'Come on, please, Minnie. If you don't get on the horse, I'll stay here with you,' Matty threatened.

The old black woman stared at Matty, her knowing look raking his face. As much as Eliza had tried to protect this boy, he had not been raised a coward. She knew how cruel the white man could be, her younger years bore the scars and if Eliza had sent her son to help the women, Minnie knew that these men were a bad crew. She relaxed and nodded her head.

Jack got down on his hands and knees, while Bess and Matty half-dragged, half-lifted Minnie onto Jack's back. Wobbling on her thin legs, Minnie reached up and grabbed the saddle. Bess pushed her backside up and slowly, in a very undignified manner, Minnie sat on a horse for the first time in her life.

Three of the women carrying babies had already started out, heading through the scrub towards the homestead. Jack rode out to the north, flanking the straggled party, his eyes scanning the distance for any sight of the two men. The other women with older children walked in a single file ahead of Matty's horse, the camp dogs sniffing the ground and following. Matty walked along beside the horse, one hand on Minnie's leg. He would tighten his hold when he felt her sway a bit, but she soon got used to the swinging gait of the horse and although she never let go of the pommel, she managed a little laugh.

'I bin' ride like longa time, eh, young fella?'

Matty squinted up at Minnie and saw the look of pride in her accomplishment, unwelcome as it had been. 'You'll be able to come ridin' with Sammy and me and Jack now!' he answered.

This caused another guffaw from the old woman and she turned in the saddle to give Bess instructions, nearly losing her balance. Matty grabbed her leg and after he was sure she was steady again, released it.

'You bin brush those tracks properly. No leave no tracks,' she called over her shoulder.

Matty glanced over his shoulder to see Bess and Annie bent over sweeping the ground with the branches they had taken from the edge of the river. He clicked to the horse to hurry him up and cursed under his breath at the length of time it would take to get to the homestead.

Jack rode back in every mile or so to let Matty know that there was nothing to be seen of the men, then he rode out again.

The women ahead had scared a flock of cockatoos and they flew up screeching. Matty gritted his teeth. As he trudged through the sand, the thought came to him that he had never felt fear like this before. There was the time when Cedar killed the snake, but this was different. It was a fear that twisted his insides, made him jump at every sound. These men were after women, their women, and he did not quite know what would happen if they caught up with this small group, but he knew it could get nasty. He could not imagine life without Minnie or Bess, or any of them. He put his hand in his pocket and fingered the bullets that were in there and turned to check that his rifle was in its bucket. Could he fire at another human?

Of course you can, he thought. *It would be like shooting a dingo!*

A small thought grew until he could not push it away. *You've never fired at a person before, how do you know?*

He straightened up and staring straight ahead, said loudly, 'If you had to, you could, so there.'

'What you say, young fella?' Minnie asked from her perch on the horse.

'Nothin' Minnie, just thinkin'.'

They reached the homestead paddock and Matty could see his mother on the verandah, talking to the women who had gone on ahead. Jack dismounted and helped Matty get Minnie down off the horse.

'Whoa, Minnie!' Matty said, supporting her, as Minnie's legs buckled underneath her. 'Your legs will feel funny for a while.'

She gratefully held on to his arm until the other women came down to help her up the steps.

Eliza asked Tan to make a big pot of tea, while she thought about where everyone would sleep. She sighed as she heard Bess and Tan already arguing on their way to the kitchen. She gazed around at the women sitting around on the grass in the shade of the trees, some holding babies, others watching that the other children didn't stray too far. These were her people and she had to take care of them, come what may. She felt a weight settle on her as she wondered how long it would be until Thomas returned. Matty broke into her thoughts.

'Mother, should Jack and me ride out and get the boys?'

'Not me, Matty. *I*. It is Jack and *I*,' she muttered. She shook her head, trying to clear her thoughts. 'No, we'll manage.'

When would there be gentleness again? she thought.

Eliza leant against the verandah post and wept.

As Matty and Jack dropped their reins to run to her, Minnie waved them away.

'You fella's, go fix'em horses,' she said. 'Missus, she tired, dat's all.'

Bewildered by Eliza's tears, the boys did as Minnie asked and led the horses to the yards.

Minnie hobbled over to Eliza and gently rubbed her shoulder. She opened her thin arms as Eliza turned into them and lay her head on Minnie's shoulder. The black woman mumbled words that Eliza neither understood or heard as she sobbed her anguish. Taking her by the hand, Minnie led Eliza inside to the drawing room and settled her on the new leather chaise. Grasping her back as she straightened up, she smoothed down Eliza's skirts and shut the door behind her.

'Missus, she not good. She need quiet. Annie, you take dem kids out da back, keep 'em quiet,' she said, waving her arm along the verandah. 'You girls, git out in the shed, make places to sleep.'

As the others rose and went along to do Minnie's bidding, she sat down into a chair and waited for Jack and Matty.

They came slowly up the path carrying their rifles, their clothes dusty, their expressions confused. Minnie beckoned to them, and they sat beside her, silent.

She looked at each in turn and spoke quietly.

'You fellas, you not like our people. Our boys, dey go off for pfella bus'ness. They come back, they grew up. You white fellas, you belong Missus, all time. Missus, she always look after all us, now she tired. She be right soon. She need sleep. Me look after her.'

It was enough to convince the boys that nothing major was wrong with Eliza. She sat back and closed her eyes. The last few hours had taken a toll on her as well.

Jack and Matty got up and, taking their rifles, went back to yards. Climbing up onto the windmill, they settled down to keep watch out for the return of the men. Late in the evening as the sun spread its last red glow over the plains, their attention was drawn to a horse and rider coming towards the homestead from the west. They climbed down and went to meet Sammy as he rode into the yards.

'We've had a bit of a do, here today,' Matty explained as he saw Sammy glancing over at the house and the women sitting around the lawn. 'Come and we'll get a feed and tell you what happened.'

They helped him unsaddle and, after letting the horse go, they headed for the kitchen where Tan had left a large pot of stew simmering on the wood stove.

Over the last mouthfuls of food, they decided to take turns to keep watch during the night. In their old way of working out who would go first, they put out their fists until it was Matty who would take the first watch, Sammy, the second, and Jack the last.

Minnie told them that the Missus had taken some tea and was now in bed. Matty wanted to see her, but Minnie told him to let her sleep. He could see her in the morning.

He sat on the verandah, the knowledge that his rifle lay behind him giving him courage. The country at night held no fear for him. He knew of nothing out there that could hurt him, except those men. His mind played tricks on him as he stared out into the darkness. A quarter moon was rising, casting shadows, and he caught himself imagining movement where there was none. The horses moved around out in the paddock, a dog rattled its chain in the kennels and the sleeping noises of the Aboriginal women and children all slipped into the background as Matty strained to hear anything unusual. With the station dogs and the Aboriginals' camp dogs lying about, he was confident that no one could ride up unannounced, but a niggle of worry still caused him to scan the paddocks wide-eyed, while watching the Southern Cross slowly change direction, remembering the stories that Charlie told about how the constellations were made, the time of year, and how you could navigate by them.

A hand touched his shoulder.

'Bloody hell, Sammy,' he whispered, spinning around. 'You move so damn quiet.'

The dim light showed a flash of white teeth against the darkness of his face, letting Matty see that Sammy was pleased with himself for putting the wind-up Matty.

'I learn me lessons well, mate. My turn to watch. You go sleep.'

'Do you think that maybe they've rode on? That they're not comin' back?'

'I dunno. But we keep an eye out, eh?'

As he stood up, Matty looked at the boy who had always been there, a shadow in his life. Sammy was his friend and when Robert had dropped Sammy's hand as though it were a hot coal, he had felt a hurt in him. He had been confused when Jack first reacted to the people on the station with caution. *How could they not like our people?* he thought. As Sammy sat down on the step to take his turn at the watch, Matty reached out and shook his shoulder.

With laughter in his voice, he said, 'You stay awake, won't ya mate?'

Sammy grunted and stared out over the land. 'Hmmp, you go bed. A man's in charge now!'

Matty laughed quietly as he walked down the verandah towards his room.

* * * *

Waking just as the sun threw out its first weak glow, Matty went out to see if Jack had any news. Tan was sitting in a chair on the verandah, snoring softly. Not seeing Jack, Matty headed for the kitchen. There, he found Jack spreading golden syrup onto a freshly baked slice of damper. Getting another knife from the drawer, Matty cut a piece of the soft bread and dribbled syrup over it.

Between mouthfuls, Jack told Matty of Tan scaring the daylights out of him, just after dawn, when he came rushing out of the kitchen, waving a knife and muttering in Chinese. It turned out that Tan had had a bad dream and still half asleep, had gone to the kitchen, grabbed a knife and was going to attack the 'bad men'.

'His hair was out, flying everywhere. He was only in his pants and he looked wild!' Jack said, wiping runs of syrup off his chin. 'He calmed down when I asked him what he was doin'. Then he cooked this damper and said he'd take watch.'

The two boys turned as Sammy came through the back door of the kitchen.

'You buggers left any for me?'

Jack pointed at the mound under a linen cover. 'You'd better not let the Missus hear you talk like that, Sammy. She'll have your hide.'

'Is the Missus up yet?'

Matty shrugged. 'Don't know. I thought I'd leave her alone like Minnie said. Should we go see?'

'We'll take her some breakfast,' said Jack, as he rose and went to the water fountain on the stove. He stoked the wood box to get the heat up. Rinsing a teapot, he placed tea leaves in it and sat back down to wait for the fountain to boil.

Matty cut a slice of damper and laid it on one of Eliza's fine bone china plates, smothering it with syrup. He searched around for a tray and placed the damper, sugar bowl, milk jug and teacup on it before sitting down to wait with Jack. At last, the soft bubbling of boiling water could be heard in the silent kitchen. After filling the teapot and letting it brew a moment, Jack poured a cup for Tan and gave it to Sammy to take out to him. Matty carried the tray with Jack following him up the hallway. They glanced at each other before Jack raised his hand and knocked gently on the door.

A quietly spoken 'come in' encouraged them to open the door and enter Eliza's room.

Still in bed, she turned from staring out the window, surprise showing in the raising of her eyebrows.

'Well, what a treat. Breakfast in my room. And what a breakfast it is,' she said, indicating to Matty to put the tray on a little drop-sided table beside her.

'Do you feel better this morning, Mother? Jack and me and Sammy, we were worried about you.'

Eliza's face was pale, her eyes smudged with darkness. 'I don't know what came over me, boys. I just became very weary, but I will be alright. Minnie gave me one of her drinks that made me sleep.'

After giving his mother a hug, the boys left the bedroom. Sammy met them at the front door. 'We betta git them steers outta Lower River and move 'em over to Swampy.'

'Good idea, they'll be nearly out of feed,' agreed Matty. 'I'll let Tan know what we're doing, and he can keep an eye on things here.'

Leaving Jack and Sammy to get the horses in, Matty went in search of Tan who had woken and was now in his vegetable garden at the back of the kitchen. He was piling dead leaves on the soil around the plants and Matty watched him for a while, trying to understand why. Peering up, Tan saw him standing there, and noting the curious expression on his face, explained.

'The sun, he burn up the water I put on. This help keep water in soil. I cart water from yards, want it to stay as long as can in the ground.'

'Oh,' Matty responded. He knew the family ate well because of the work Tan put into the garden. 'I remember when the last drought was here and Mother tried to grow things. She said the soil was too sandy to hold the water.'

'Dat's why I put vege'ble scraps, horse dung and leaves. Dig it in. It changes the soil. Helps hold water.'

Tan had belted in posts around his garden and tied sacking over them to protect the vegetables from the worst of the heat during the day. Matty inclined his head in understanding. Tan's vegetables grew in neat rows and were strong and healthy, so his methods must be working, Matty reasoned to himself.

'We're goin' to muster down near the river. Can you keep an eye on things here?' he asked.

Laying down his shovel, Tan walked up to Matty. 'Alwight, you go get cattle. I lookee station.' He smiled, thinking of how much the boys had grown in the last year. 'I make tucka quick for you.'

The sound of horses and an excited yipping of the dogs at the front gate let Matty know the others were waiting for him. Carrying out the food that Tan prepared for them, Matty packed it into his saddlebags and mounted the horse that the boys saddled for him. The three mates turned their horses together and three abreast, walked them out along the track that led to the lower southeast paddocks. They all sat straight-backed, one hand on the reins while the other hand rested along a thigh or dropped beside a leg. They did not talk but enjoyed the silence of mates who knew each other so well. The dogs trotted along behind the horses, happy to be off the chain and working. The scrub opened up onto a claypan with small ridges of rocky ground. When it rained, the claypan became a wetland full of water birds and fresh growth. Now its hard surface lay shimmering in the early morning sun, and the boys, pushing their horses into a trot, heard the clay crunching under the horses' hooves. Half an hour later, they reached Lower River Paddock. They spread out, and rode up the eastern side, hoping to catch most of the cattle still near the bore. Sammy pulled up and sat waiting for Jack and Matty to travel further up. When Matty had reached the end of the paddock, he used the whip to let the others know to start pushing towards the bore. They rode, cracking their whips and urging the dogs into the scrubby patches. In twos and threes, cattle moved in front of them. When one would try to turn back, the dogs would be on to it, turning it in the direction the muster was headed. Gradually, one and twos became twenty and thirty and the bellowing of the cattle mingled with the barking of the dogs, split now and then by the crack of a whip. The dust rose and swirled, choking the riders. When Sammy judged he was near the bore, he hung back letting his mob of cattle settle in the shade. He would wait out on the wing until Matty wheeled his cattle down the fence, then Jack would push his mob into Matty's. Jack rode out on the wing with Matty pushing them from behind. Gradually the larger mob came closer and mingled with Sammy's. Sammy held them against the fence. The dogs running to and fro kept stragglers up, turning back the cattle that tried to make a break into scrub. The cattle grew tired and the heat caused them to balk, trying to remain in the shade, but the horse riders and dogs pushed them on, until finally they ran into wing of the holding yard at the bore and Matty shut the gate behind them.

The boys laughed at the dogs as they jumped up and lay in the trough, lapping at the water. Dismounting, they loosened the girths and gave the horses a small drink before tying them up in the shade of a box tree on the fence. While Sammy got a small fire going, Jack filled the billy from the tank and put it on the coals. Taking the saddlebag from his horse, Matty unwrapped the corned beef and bread and shared them with Jack and Sammy. They sat back in the shade, slowly sipping their mugs of tea, the dogs lying about in the shade, taking advantage of this rest stop by stretching out. Some slept with one ear up, waiting for the first sign of movement, which would signal work starting again.

Jack scratched a drawing of the paddock in the sand. 'I reckon if we ride up the west fence and spread out at the top, we'll be able to push the rest back to the yards. There can't be too many away from the water in this heat.'

'We got most of 'em,' Sammy agreed. 'Never get a clean muster, just us three.'

'But the main thing is to move most of them onto more feed,' Matty said, swatting at the flies that made nuisances of themselves in his face. 'So, we'll do what we can, eh?'

They rose and stretched, their muscles having tightened while they rested. Pulling up the girths and mounting, they rode towards the back fence, the dogs eager again for work after the rest. A blue-speckled dog propped and stared intently at a patch of low scrub, then with a furious barking he set off through it, the other dogs setting up a chorus and following.

'Bloody hell, they've flushed some roos,' Matty yelled, standing in his stirrups.

'C'mon, they'll go for miles.'

The boys put their horses to the gallop and went after the baying dogs. Dodging stumps and brush, the horses flung up their heads and enjoyed the race, while the boys, cracking their whips, yelled at the dogs, trying to bring them back under control. Finally, the dogs baled up a large red buck on the fence. The boys rode in, letting their whips fly. The dogs pulled out of the melee, yelping when they caught the end of a whip. The kangaroo sniffed at the group and realising he had been let off, sped away, his bounds long in his escape. One red thin dog was limping badly and Sammy pulled him up over his pommel by the collar.

'If Father was here, they would never have run off like that. Bloody dogs would lie down and die for him, never disobey him.'

Jack laughed. 'They reckon we haven't earned our stripes yet. The Boss has always been their Boss.'

As they rode Jack watched the pack of dogs that followed behind, their tongues hanging out. He pulled his horse up for a better look at one in particular.

'Oh, no. Shorty,' he called, as he swung down off his horse. 'That bitch out of old Brownie, she's been gutted.'

Matty turned in horror. This was Trudy, one of his father's favourite dogs. He jumped from his horse and ran to the dog, who immediately sank to the ground. He rolled her over and saw a long gaping wound beneath her ribs.

'Ol' roo, he's got her good,' Sammy noted. 'We take her to Minnie. She stitch up sheep at shearin' time, she fix her. Bit of tar, she be right.'

Matty looked at his mate dubiously. True, Minnie did work wonders with injured animals, so did Charlie, but this was a bad gash. He could see the flesh ripped open and the bare bone of the ribs, but surprisingly little blood. Taking off his shirt, he bound it around the dog's torso, drawing it tight and tying the sleeves to hold the wound together.

He stared at the dog, torn between riding straight back to the homestead or finishing the muster. The cattle won. They were their livelihood and could not be left in a paddock without feed. He lifted the dog up across the horse's rump where she lay limply, seeming to know that this was the best way. Matty mounted and squeezed his horse into a walk.

'I'll stay here on the fence. You two go through and push everything to me.'

Sammy and Jack rode off, calling some of the dogs to follow. Matty rode slowly, stopping now and then to listen to the other's movements. Soon, he could hear the sound of beasts on the move and the barking of the dogs. The bitch behind his saddle whined and struggled to get down.

'No, you stay right there. You've done enough for today,' Matty said as he put his hand behind and stroked her ears. She relaxed under his comforting touch.

'How am I ever goin' to tell Father what happened?' he asked. The horse flicked his ears back, but quickly put them forward, listening to the sounds coming from the middle of the paddock. Matty shrugged and, still stroking the dog, rode on along the fence.

Two hours later found them all back at the yards, having found another twenty head of cattle. They opened the gate of the yard and pushed them along the fence and through into Swampy Paddock. As the last few were about to step through, a steer broke from the mob and raced back towards the bore. Sammy pulled his horse's head around and, booting it hard, raced after the runaway with the dogs following. He veered to the left, pushing his horse into a flat gallop, trying to cut the beast off and turn it back towards the yards. The steer propped and stopped dead, then broke into a gallop heading back the other way. The dogs caught up with it and ringed the panicked beast. It shook its head and bellowed, kicking out at the barking pack that surrounded him. He menaced them with his long horns and snorted, bellowing again when one dog raced in and nipped him on the nose. Another had latched onto his tail and swung there, hanging on tightly. The steer leapt forward, over the dogs and propped again. He swung his head around, searching for something to take his anger out on. A horse and rider came into his field of sight and the beast lowered his head, raised his tail and charged.

Sammy saw the giveaway movement and spurred his horse out of the way. His mare had just come back into work and was slow responding. The steer bore down on her; Sammy knew that he was in trouble. Digging his left spur into her ribs, he pulled her head around. She leapt sideways, thus receiving only a blow from the steer's shoulder as he missed his target. It was enough to put the mare off balance and she fell heavily, trapping Sammy under her. Matty and Jack watched in horror as the drama unfolded and now they raced over to the fallen horse, the steer having re-joined the herd, leaving bedlam in his wake.

Not wanting to spook the mare, the boys stared down at Sammy. They heard a faint groaning from under his battered hat, his hand holding the mare's head down by the rein.

'Sammy?'

'Me leg's a bit squished, but I'm alright.'

Jack sighed with relief. 'Sammy, old mate. It's not time for laying about.'

'I just laying like lizard in the sun, maybe lucky, not like roo full of spear holes.'

The boys shuddered at the thought of the steer's long dangerous horns having pierced Sammy's hide.

'C'mon Sammy, you're all right, aren't you?' Matty asked anxiously.

In answer, Sammy released the mare's bridle. She gathered her legs under her and stood up, narrowly missing treading on Sammy, who scrambled on his backside out of her way. He dusted himself off, and limped over to the mare. A scrape on her rump showed the closeness of the passing horn. Leading her forward, he could not detect a limp and so mounted again.

'Take more than that get rid of this fella,' he said, still grinning.

Jack shook his head. 'I think we've had enough for today. Let's get this dog back to Minnie.'

The sun was a memory as they finally turned up the track to the homestead, the way lit by starlight. The lights shone from the homestead and Eliza met them at the gate. Her worry was evident in the torrent of words that lashed them.

'Where have you been? I've been worried so! Are you all right? Matty, where's your shirt?'

The boys said nothing of Sammy's escape from injury, instead imploring Eliza to help with the dog. Matty carried it to the verandah, calling for Minnie to come see.

She came hobbling from the kitchen and, untying the shirt, clucked and muttered over the dog. Under the kerosene lantern, Matty's already tanned skin glowed a deep red and Eliza berated him for his thoughtlessness in getting sunburnt.

'You'll pay for it later, son. You will be very sore. Make some tea to use to bathe it later when it has cooled down.'

Leaving the bitch to Minnie and Eliza, Matty put the kettle on the fire and then joined the other two to put the horses away. Tan appeared from the back gate and, calling the dogs, took them to the kennels to be chained up and fed.

TEN

Huge, cumulus clouds gathered and rose from the horizon every afternoon, the air becoming heavy and oppressive but by sunset; the clouds crumbled to tiny patches of thin white wafers, lit by the dying sun. The thermometer near the door of the kitchen reached 119 degrees Fahrenheit at afternoon teatime. Tan lay under the shade of a tree on the lawn. Constantly wiping her brow with a handkerchief, Eliza sat at her small desk in the drawing room, trying to concentrate on writing a letter to Robert. The boys had risen early to fish at the river and were not expected back until late that evening. Everything was quiet, the sort of quiet that the heat brought, even the most robust animal, too lethargic to move about. The birds did not argue in the branches of the trees nor did the dogs move about, they just lay in the shade, sleeping. The only sign of life were the ants, racing to and fro, unheeding of the heat, their frenzied scurrying, minute against the larger stillness that lay over the homestead.

Eliza rose and went down the hallway to the kitchen, looking for Tan. She felt an unusual coolness in the kitchen and realised that Tan had let the fire go out in the stove. Murmuring to herself, she stepped out the back door and saw him lying in the shade of the white cedar tree in the corner of the lawn. Not wishing to disturb him, she turned up the verandah but halted when she looked out over the horse yards.

Instead of the usual shining snowy billowing skuds that had been building every afternoon, low black heavy clouds stretched across the horizon. She breathed a sigh of relief; these looked like rain. Her relief was short-lived, as she saw a streak of lightning stab out of the cloud and spread into a jagged spear that aimed itself at the earth. She ducked as a massive roll of thunder erupted over her head. Turning abruptly, she ran down the verandah towards Tan, nearly colliding with him as he raced up the stairs.

'Missy, storm come!'

'Lightening, Tan, no rain yet!' she said, pointing at the sky that suddenly let loose another bolt. 'Buckets, we've got to fill the buckets and put them around the house.'

Running awkwardly in his slippers, Tan raced over the lawn to the shed. Grabbing as many buckets as he could carry, he went to the trough at the windmill and started to fill them. After he filled them, he carried two at a time to the yard, where he placed them around the house.

Eliza dashed over to the harness shed and stopped just inside the door, waiting for her eyes to adjust to the dim light. In the corner of the shed, folded and stacked, lay a pile of hessian sacks. Dragging them outside, Eliza dunked them in the horse trough. The water made them too heavy, so she ran and got Tan's wheelbarrow from the garden. The wind rose and tore at her skirts. She tripped. Eliza paused and taking one side of the long skirt up, she tucked it into her waistband, giving her legs more freedom.

Tan saw what Eliza was doing and went to get the wash tub. He placed it on the lawn, helped her put the sacks in it, emptied a couple of buckets of water into it and went to refill the buckets.

'Get the horses in, Tan,' she yelled, her voice lost as about them, the thunder roiled, crashing seconds behind the lightning that grew larger and more violent. She pointed at the horse yards and Tan caught her meaning. He could not be heard as he called to them and the paddock was too big for him to round them up on foot. All he could do was leave the gate into the yards open and hope they would come in.

Scanning the horizon, Eliza wiped the perspiration from her face with the back of her hand. She walked the verandah, around and around, looking for the first wisp of smoke. Leaves tossed by the wind, brushed at her and a corner of the iron roof banged as it gradually loosened in the tempest. Her breath caught in her throat and she grabbed at the verandah post as she saw a haze over the track. A flash of lightning stunned her eyes and when they cleared, she saw that it was dust, dust from the hooves of the horses as the boys galloped home.

'Thank God,' she cried. 'Tan, the boys are back!'

She ran over to the yards and opened the gate for them as they came past the homestead. The horses' bodies were dark with sweat, their necks white, where the reins had rubbed the sweat to lather. Nostrils were wide, drawing in hot air as their sides heaved.

'I told the camp to stay at the river. It'll be safer for them,' Matty yelled to his mother. 'The stockmen should be on their way in. They'll open the gates as they come. We've opened them along the track.'

Nodding her agreement, she pointed at the horse paddock. 'Don't get off, you'll have to get the horses in. We may need them.'

Eliza thought the storm could not get any louder, but as Matty tried to speak, the wind shrieked, only to be drowned out by the thunder that rolled on and on.

The boys rode out into the horse paddock searching for the horses. They found them, their rumps to the wind, behind a stand of box trees in the far corner. With a yell and cracking of the whips, they set them galloping towards the yards. Once there, the boys saddled the quieter horses and put halters on the rest. As they joined Eliza and Tan at the house, they watched the lightning grow in intensity until the dark sky was ablaze with flashing light. A blinding streak quickly followed by a deafening crack, blasted them as they stood watching. The smell of ozone came sharply, and they ran to the front of the house where smoke drifted up from a patch of spinifex just outside the front gate. Within seconds, a tongue of fire flicked up from its centre, the wind whipping at it, sparks leaping out to start new fires.

The boys jumped off the verandah, grabbing buckets as they ran towards the gate. The fire was already throwing out a fierce heat and they threw the water from as close as they could get. Tan appeared behind them holding some of the dripping sacks, thrusting them at the boys then taking the buckets to be filled. Their flailing arms grew tired as they beat at the flames, which the wind made dance from mound to mound. Matty paused, looking up to see where the wind was pushing the fire. It was swinging around toward the shearing shed. He put his head down and beat at the burning spinifex with all his might, glancing behind now and then to make sure that he had not flung any sparks behind him.

A sudden lull in the wind allowed him to yell at the others. 'The wool! We can't let it get to the shed.'

The boys bent over the flames again, choking in the smoke, working along the edge trying to turn the fire away from the shed.

Eliza and Tan heard Matty and grabbing as many wet sacks as they could carry, raced over towards the shearing shed, watching for falling embers, damping them out as they landed.

A yelling from their right made them look up and break into grim smiles. Ernie and four other stockmen were racing towards the gate out of Angle Paddock. The men didn't stop to open the gate, but set their horses at it, all of them jumping the four barred wooden gate. Flinging themselves off, they put their mounts into the sheep yards and ran to take over from Tan and Eliza.

As fast as his slippers would allow, Tan ran back to the house to get more wet sacks for the firefighters. He loaded them into the wheelbarrow, grunting, and cursing in Chinese, he struggled to push the barrow through the red sand back to the shearing shed.

The wind shifted and dropped a little as it turned towards the track. The group fighting the fire did not let up. Knowing the wind could swing back at any time, they fought on, determination on their faces.

As they beat out the last flames, raindrops began to fall, getting heavier until they were a deluge. The firefighters threw down their sacks and raised their faces to the sky, letting the downpour drench them, washing away the soot from their bodies. The three boys danced about like children, enjoying the coolness of the rain. The stockmen put away the horses and dried the saddles.

Tan waved at them from the kitchen as they all trooped up onto the verandah, leaving puddles of water on the boards, as they walked along it.

Tan muttered, 'Dis country always wild,' as he brought out cups of tea and some biscuits.

The rain pounded the iron roof above them and fell in sheets from the edge of it. They all sat silent, watching the storm dump its load on the parched ground, removing the risk of more fires. When the noise abated and the downpour had turned to a light drizzle, the oldest stockman told the boys stories of helping to light grass fires when he was younger.

'We burn country, the country live after,' Ernie said, his eyes watching the parched ground swallowing the rain. 'No more... too many sheep, too many fences.'

The stockmen drifted away and Sammy went with them, back to the camp to see his people. A whine from the back step interrupted the quietness that had settled on those left. Trudy walked gingerly up the steps from under the verandah where she had been hiding. Her wound was healing but it still had the raw stitching that Minnie and Eliza had put in. She came and sat by Matty, pushing her nose into his hand.

'You're a lucky girl,' he said, stroking her. He looked up at his mother. 'We're lucky to have Minnie, aren't we, Mother?'

'Yes, we are. There are white people who are gifted in healing, but the blacks seem to inherit it, in their way of life. They learn from the elders when they are young and I suppose in all the time they've been here, they have come to know so much more than us, about living in this land.'

'How long do you think that they've been here?' Jack asked.

'People that have studied the blacks say that they have been here for thousands of years. I read an article in the newspaper that said that they have many different languages in Australia. Some out in the desert still live like they did before Captain Cook discovered this land.'

Jack shook his head. 'A thousand years is a long time, isn't it? Why don't the blacks live in the towns like other people?'

'They aren't allowed. People don't understand them; some even say that they are animals. They are put in missions and the government looks after them. You boys are old enough now to understand,' Eliza answered. She clasped her hands together and lent forward. 'There have been many cruel things done to the blacks. When they fought to keep their land, they were hunted down and shot. We lease this land from the government. They own all this side of the Paroo. The blacks are not allowed to own land; they can't even vote. When you leave this property, as one day you will, you will find that we live very differently to most people.'

Matty interrupted his mother. 'What do you mean we live differently?'

'Well, for a start, we don't make them live in houses. If they wanted to, we would give them the shearing quarters, but they live how they want. We have to let the government know how many we have here. Some stations have fifty or sixty blacks and don't let them have their women with them. We only have twenty or so. When we first came here, I thought that the gins would make fine housemaids, but they don't. It's not in their nature to be restricted to doing things at certain times. It took me a few years to realise that it is easier to say sometime tomorrow, than seven in the morning. Between us, we still get the work done and everyone is happy. They go off to do what they need to do and that leaves me with some peace and quiet. The stockmen love their work and horses. Sometimes one will go away for a while. Generally, they turn up whenever needed, as they did today.'

The two boys listened, nodding their heads in agreement. 'But why are we different?' Matty asked again.

Eliza sighed, realising that Matty had not left the boundary of their small world; in fact, she herself had been off the property only three times since Matty was born. She had left him in the care of Minnie and Tan, as he had been too young to take on the long trips.

'On other stations, the blacks wear uniforms and stay at the homestead. They work seven days a week and go to church. If they don't, they're taken away and put on missions. Some are unlucky enough to get a boss that beats them, amongst other things.' Eliza's face flushed as she thought of the half-caste children on other properties. 'About two years after you were born, we went to visit at Wanaaring. There was a race meeting, and it was then I realised just how different we are here. Some would say we're too lenient. Others were appalled at how much we let our blacks live their own lives. The older blacks were badly treated before they came here. We have grown into a big family; they have their ways and we have ours. We are happy.'

Matty sat listening, stroking the dog. As he heard his mother's words, he realised that her tone did not match what she was saying. He remembered when she had been put to bed by Minnie when the men came to get the gins. He thought of the visitors that dropped in now and then, and how eagerly she listened to them. There were rarely any women visitors. He had never experienced loneliness – his world was made up of people he knew and loved; the station his playground.

He pulled himself up by the post and went to his mother. Kneeling down in front of her, he said, 'I never realised how lonely you were, Mother.'

Eliza closed her eyes, and when she opened them, tears ran slowly down her face. She sighed, wiped at her eyes with the edge of her sleeve and reached out with her hand to cup his chin.

'I'm usually too busy to be lonely, son, but I do miss other white women to talk to. We'll be getting the telephone soon, that may help. I'll be able to talk to our neighbours whenever I want. Hopefully, this rain will improve things and we may be able to go visiting. It is about time you boys saw something else other than this property.'

Her words opened up a new world for Matty. With all that happened on the station, they had been too busy to go anywhere; they had been needed here.

'I can sort of remember living in town,' Jack said. 'But mostly we travelled around, camped wherever we stayed.'

'Well, I think a trip is just what we all deserve. How about you, Tan? A trip to Bourke?' Eliza asked.

'No, Missy. Thankee, I stay here. Here is very good. Maybe get some things. Maybe Matty and Jack buy for me?' he said, glancing at the boys.

'Why don't you come?' Matty asked.

'Not a nice place out there. Missy right when she say other people different. They no like Chinee, they treat bad. Bourke all right mostly, some Chinee live there, garden, sell vegetables. I stay here, read my books, do my garden.'

Jack swung his legs around and leant against the railing. 'Is that why you came here, Tan?'

'I leave China, I peasant. My parents work the land but give most to the Empress,' he said sadly. 'My uncle, he say that Tan go to Australia, dig gold, send money to China. He give me money for boat and I come. I hear that big flood in China take away all my family, so I have no one in China. Old Chinee man taught me to read and I move about, make money cooking for shearers but then it happen again. Bad men come and have big fight in shearing sheds. I hear in Bourke, Missy look for cook. I come here before you born. White men, stockmen, they leave when drought comes but I stay. It is good here. I happy here.'

The others listened in amazement. Tan had never spoken about his previous life to them before; he never said more than two or three sentences at any one time.

'Well, you're part of our family. Isn't he, Mother?' Matty said emphatically.

Eliza nodded. 'Yes.'

'You told Father about this, didn't you?'

'He Boss, he need to know. He Boss.'

Matty stared at the floor, thinking. 'How come you're telling us now?'

'I sit here, listen to Missy. She right. You need to know about things. Missus and Boss very different from all other people, very kind, very good.'

Eliza blushed at Tan's compliment and said, 'Maybe if you ask Tan, he might teach you about China. The Chinese had fireworks and writing before anyone else, didn't they, Tan?'

'Really? What are fireworks?' Jack asked.

'Still raining tomorrow, we sit down, talk about China, eh? I go put tea on now,' Tan said, getting up from his chair.

As he left, Matty got up and ran after him. Catching Tan's smock, he hugged the old man. 'Tan, we are very glad that you came here.'

His actions touched Tan deeply. He bowed his head to hide his face, on which emotion was showing too strongly.

'Thank you. You good boys. Family good people,' he said, patting Matty on the shoulder as he walked on towards the kitchen.

As he lay in bed that night, Matty's head was full of new thoughts. He wondered why he had never questioned their way of life here, why he had never really understood what his parents' hushed voices meant when they spoke of the goings on in the outside world. It came to him as he finally drifted into sleep. He was getting older, old enough to be told the truth. His parents had never lied to him, just omitted certain facts; they let him keep his innocence. With the truth came responsibility.

* * * *

Dogs barking woke the homestead before dawn. Through their open window, the muffled hoof beats and jingling harness sounded the arrival of a wagon. Jack and Matty stumbled from their bedroom, half-dressed, with their eyes trying to open as they belted along the hallway. The Boss and his men were home. With them were the women and other stockmen. They had heard the wagon splashing through the crossing in the dark and walked alongside the dray to the homestead. The muted whispers gave way to joyous shouting when a light shone from the Missus' bedroom.

Stepping down stiffly from the seat, Thomas looked about in the early dawn. The clouds had cleared but raindrops rested on the plants, making everything appear fresh and revitalised.

'I see you had a fire!' he said to the boys.

'Yes, sir. Mother and Tan had everything ready. It happened just as we got back from the river. Ernie and the men rode in to help,' Matty said solemnly. 'We also had some unwelcome visitors.'

Thomas looked sharply at his son, wondering why he wasn't bursting with excitement with his news.

'How did you go, Boss?' Jack asked, he too looking strangely at Matty.

'Dry, Jack, dry. The country was tinder dry. The Warrago at Ford's Bridge was only puddles. Youngerina Camp had water, but we had to go without until Kelly's. Kerrilee had pump trouble. There were some blokes fixing it as we went past.'

'Did you get caught in the storm, Father?'

Casting his hand at the wagon covered with a canvas, Thomas

explained. 'It hit us yesterday as we were coming past Yantabulla. We had to pull up and cover the load. We sat it out. Started again when the storm passed.'

'You're safely home, Thomas. Thank goodness. I expect the boys have filled you in on what's been happening here?' said Eliza as she joined the group after having dressed. Thomas nodded, taking another look at Matty.

'How about you two get the horses out of the wagon?' he said. 'I want to speak with the Missus.'

He stepped over to Eliza, kissing her cheek. He took her arm and walked her towards the house.

'What is wrong with Matty? He would usually be jumping out of his skin with all that's happened while we were away?'

Eliza smiled up at Thomas. 'Your son is growing up.'

'I'm missing something here,' Thomas replied, confusion on his face.

'Yesterday, after the stockmen had left, we talked about what goes on off the property. What people are like, especially the way they treat the blacks. Tan opened up and told the boys a bit as well.'

'I see. It has given him a bit to think about.'

'Yes. I also told them that it was about time we went visiting. If the drought breaks, I thought we might plan a trip to Bourke. We can call in on our neighbours and introduce the boys.'

'Mmmm, we have been remiss in not doing so before, but with one thing and another.' Thomas spread his hands and shrugged his shoulders. 'I...'

By the look on her husband's face, Eliza sensed he had something else to say, something she feared she did not want to hear.

'Yes?'

'While I was in Bourke, John Peters caught up with me. He wanted to know why the boys weren't coming in for training.'

'Training?'

Thomas looked at the ground, then slowly raised his eyes to Eliza's face.

He spoke slowly, repeating what John had told him. 'All boys between the ages of twelve and twenty-four are required by the government to undertake military training, in the Cadets.'

Eliza stared at Thomas, her emotions playing over her face. First fear widened her eyes, then anger caused them to narrow.

'No, not our boys. They can't, they live too far away!'

'Matty would be in the Juniors and Jack, the Seniors,' Thomas said plainly. 'John being the local school master is in charge of them. He mentioned that the boys could stay with him overnight. They meet one weekend, every second month.'

As Eliza opened her mouth to speak, Thomas interrupted. 'It's law, Eliza, we have to comply.'

Eliza put back her shoulders, lifted her skirts, and walked towards the door.

'We'll discuss this later. We had better get this load put away,' was her final word.

Men, women and children pitched in, helping to unload the supplies into the store. Jack, Matty and Sammy finished with the horses and helped Eliza sort the goods into their various places. It was several hours before they stopped, when Tan called for everyone to come and get breakfast. He had dragged a table out under the trees, loading it with damper, honey, golden syrup, jam, dripping and the big teapot full of scalding tea.

Everyone sat about, replenished, blowing on their cups of black tea. The last cow to calve, had not taken to being broken to milking; Tan still wore the bruises from her kicks.

Thomas questioned the men as to how the bores were and organised the stockman for a muster. It was shearing time again, and the shearers would be arriving in a few weeks' time. The sheep would have to be brought into Angle Paddock; it would be a long and exhausting muster. The sheep, weak from the drought, would travel slowly. He had decided to send one of the boys with each of the mustering parties so he could stay and get the shed ready. It needed repairing and he and Charlie had some work to do on it.

He also looked forward to spending time with Eliza. Bess had told him, on the way to the homestead, of the Missus not being herself for a while. Sammy also had told him of the two visitors who had threatened their peaceful existence. He was proud of the boys, and how they had taken on the responsibility of getting the women back to the homestead. He smiled as they sat talking to Charlie, questioning him about Bourke, about the railway and other things that they had heard about.

He thought to himself, *'It has been a large oversight not taking the boys sooner. They have grown. I hadn't realised how much.'*

After giving Charlie time to finish his breakfast, Matty started to pester him to go to the horse yards. He stood, hopping from one foot to the other, his spirits rising with the thought of showing Charlie how much he had done with Cedar. Suddenly he stopped and looked over his shoulder. A worried look appeared on his face and he bit at his bottom lip. His mother!

Walking over to where his father sat talking to the other men, Matty bent down and whispered in his ear.

'Could you get Mother inside, please?'

Thomas looked up in surprise at his son. 'Why is that?'

'I want to show Charlie what I have been teaching Cedar and it means getting on her.' He went on quickly, seeing his father's frown start. 'All I've done is put weight on her, just sit. I haven't walked her or anything.'

Letting out his breath, Thomas remembered what Eliza had said. Matty was growing up; they had to let him stretch his wings. Thomas would have to get Eliza over her fear of losing Matty. He was nearly a man.

'All right, son. I'll do that. You be careful though.'

'Yes, sir!' Matty said, the excitement back in his eyes.

He walked casually over to Charlie and said loudly, 'We had better go and check the horses, Charlie.'

He winked at Jack and Sammy, while he reached down and gave his hand to Charlie to help him up. Lowering his voice he said, 'C'mon, I've got something to show you.'

They walked over to the horse yards, Matty turning his head to see if his father had done as he said he would.

Matty said to Sammy, 'You keep an eye on the front door, let me know if the Missus comes out.'

Sammy smiled. 'This gonna be good, maybe you land on your backside!'

Laughing, Matty replied, 'No way, she's quiet now.'

Charlie's face started to register alarm. He shook his head. 'No, young fella. I get in big trouble with the Missus.'

'It's all right, Father knows. He took Mother inside,' Matty assured him. 'Once it's done, it'll be over with, won't it?'

Taking the rope halter that Jack handed him, he slipped through the rails. Cedar immediately trotted up to him, nuzzling at his pockets. Stroking her neck, he put the halter on, saying, 'No, this time no free tit bits. You've got to earn this one. We're gonna show Charlie how good you are.'

He led her over to where Jack had climbed through the fence and stood waiting. Taking a handful of mane and the rope with one hand, he patted her back with the other. He lifted his leg for Jack to give him a push up and slowly, he lay across her back. The mare stood quietly, unconcerned at this. Gradually, Matty swung his leg over her back and eased himself into a sitting position. He leant forward, rubbing his hand up and down her crest.

His smile was huge and there was pride in his voice, 'See, Charlie, isn't she a good horse?'

Charlie stood mute, his thoughts jumping.

'Charlie?'

The horse-breaker started to speak, the words coming slowly. 'You done good job with dis mare. The Boss, he be proud, I be proud. You bin learnin'. But what the Missus gonna say?'

'That's why I showed you. If you help me finish breaking her in, Mother won't mind.'

'No, she your horse. She no give no trouble. Sammy, git the saddle. Git the Boss's.'

Sammy hesitated and looked from Matty to Jack. Both stared at Charlie with their mouths open.

'Did ya say the Boss's, Charlie?' he asked.

'I say the Boss's. It got big knee pads. If horse buck, Matty hang on betterer,' Charlie said matter of factly. A smile lifted the corner of his mouth. 'Bin long time, eh, young fella?'

Suddenly, Matty felt nervous. It had been a long time since he had sat and watched Cedar born; now it was time to saddle her, to complete the process he had waited so long for. The mare lifted her head, feeling his body tense and shifted underneath him. Immediately, he let out his breath and relaxed; the mare stopped. Leaning down again along her neck, he slid off her back.

Stroking her forehead, he said to her, 'This isn't goin' to be easy. I've got to stay relaxed and not frighten you.' Turning to Charlie, he asked, 'Are you sure I should do this? You're the expert.'

'We mouth her, by-n'-by. Now we see what she do with the saddle.'

Sammy put the saddle across the rails, laying a blanket beside it. Charlie went into the yard and held Cedar, while Matty took the blanket and carefully laid it across the filly's back. He drew it slightly back, remembering that you had to smooth the hair down. Lifting the heavy saddle from the rails, he carried it towards Cedar. Glancing at Charlie, he took a deep breath, stepped up to Cedar's side and slid the saddle gently onto her back.

The filly's head lifted as the unaccustomed feel of the saddle settled onto her. Her skin shuddered but the strange object did not hurt. Matty reached underneath her belly and caught the girth that hung from the offside, gently pulling it up. Cedar tensed as the girth drew tight. Matty spoke softly to her, stroking her neck. Charlie nodded to him and walked out to the side of the filly, encouraging her to take a step forward. Cedar took one hesitant step then another. As one, the group let out a sigh. Jack and Sammy laughed as they realised how tense they had all been.

Charlie held out the halter rope to Matty saying, 'She all right. You take her, walk her. Tighten up girth by-'n'-by.'

Taking the rope, Matty walked around the yard, leading the filly, who followed, calmly, as if nothing untoward had happened. Stopping, Matty tightened the girth another two holes, stepped back and coaxed the filly to take another step. Cedar flinched as the girth pinched, then she lowered her head and kicked her heels high in the air. Matty quickly took a step back as the filly's body twisted sideways, then she reared, trying to dislodge this band around her girth. Just as suddenly as she had bucked, she stood still, giving in to the saddle. Matty let out his breath and reached forward, stroking her neck, talking to her.

He led her forward again and she walked quietly.

Matty looked at Charlie, raising his eyebrows. 'What do you make of that, Charlie?'

'She not bad, she just loosenin' up. She enough now. By-'n'-by we bridle her.'

Matty gave the rope to Charlie and unsaddled Cedar. Jack and Sammy climbed down from the rails, disappointed that there hadn't been a bigger show.

Thomas's voice stopped them as they headed towards the shed.

'Jack, Sammy, come back here. Matty, finish with Cedar. I have to talk to you three.'

The boys glanced at each other, then back at Thomas. Each of them thought that he didn't look angry. Jack raised his eyebrows at Matty, and

Matty replied by shrugging his shoulders.

As Matty climbed the stockyard rails, Jack and Sammy returned and stood by Thomas.

'Let's go and sit in the shed, shall we?'

The boys waited until Thomas had sat on Charlie's stool, then they sat down on the empty kerosene tins that were stored for future use.

As Thomas looked at each of the boys in turn, he said, 'I was talking to John Peters, the school master in Bourke. It appears there is a government law that escaped our attention. All boys over twelve are to be trained as Cadets in the Militia.'

'Whoo-hoo!' Matty exclaimed, jumping up from his tin seat.

'Not so fast. Do you know what this means?' Thomas asked.

Jack spoke up. 'Yes, sir. We march and practice rifle shooting.'

'And drill, I've read somewhere, they do that in armies,' added Matty.

Sammy sat back, staying quiet. He had heard of soldiers and police from his people. He wasn't keen on becoming one, if it meant doing what the stories described them doing.

'So, when do we go, Boss?' Jack asked excitedly. He turned to Sammy. 'What a turn, Sammy. We'll have a lark, won't we?'

'I dunno, Jack,' he said doubtfully. 'Me no soldier. They do bad things.'

Thomas turned abruptly and gave Sammy a long look. 'Sammy, not all soldiers do bad things. You boys won't go out on patrols or anything. It's just training,' he said gently. 'I've heard the stories, hopefully all that is past. The police are there to protect you, now. The next meeting is six weeks from now. That will mean just after shearing. We'll talk some more when it gets closer.'

Leaving the boys to dream about their trip to Bourke, Thomas rose and walked reluctantly towards the house. The hardest part was to come and that was to convince Eliza that the boys must go.

ELEVEN

The days at Mulga Plains were full of sheep, sheep and more sheep as shearing progressed. The boys fell into bed exhausted, only to rise before dawn and start the process again. The barking of the dogs, the bleating sheep and the often-colourful language turned the peaceful homestead into a moving, swirling cacophony of dust and sound. Even at night, the noise from the singing of the shearers, accompanied by a banjo, could be heard until late.

The only time Matty could spend with Cedar was Sundays, and her education went along in bits and pieces. Charlie had mouthed her for him. Now Matty was in the saddle, and under Charlie's tutelage, teaching her to turn on his leg, stop at the gentle pressure of the bit and to stand still while he mounted and dismounted. The mare took it all calmly and acceded to Matty's wishes with good grace. Until the day that Charlie thought she was ready to go for a run in Angle Paddock.

Cedar was trotting along beside Charlie's horse, her gait free and easy. Matty thought that her trot was very comfortable compared to some bone shakers he had been on. His legs tightened instinctively as Cedar suddenly slid to a halt, then reared, throwing him backwards. He reached for the pommel with his free hand and hung on grimly, saving himself from tumbling backwards out of the saddle. His body was immediately thrown forward again as the mare lifted her heels and kicked them skyward. Trembling, the mare stopped and with a loud hollow snort, she raked at the ground with her front hooves. Matty let go of the pommel and with both hands on the reins, tried to pull Cedar's head up. The mare swung her head from side to side, trying to evade the bit, then, wrenching the reins from Matty's hands, dropped her head and bucked hard.

Matty hit the ground and rolled, leaping up immediately. The ground was thankfully soft sand and, unhurt, he tried to catch his mare to calm her. Stepping around a spinifex mound, he saw the cause of her behaviour. A brown snake lay in the red sand, torn and bloody from the hooves of the mare. He looked over at her, then back at the snake, then back at Cedar, who now stood trembling and blowing heavily.

Talking quietly to Cedar, Charlie edged his horse closer to her and leaning out, he grasped the reins and held the still snorting mare.

'She no like snakes, eh, young fella?' Charlie laughed, his eyes slits in his face.

'Bloody hell, that came out of nowhere!' Matty swore, dusting the sand of his trousers.

'Lucky we weren't in Eagle Paddock with all those rocks. My backside would be broken.'

Laughing again, Charlie held Cedar's reins out to Matty. 'Git on, she right now.'

Reaching out and taking the reins, Matty led the horse away from the snake. Tightening the inside rein, he put his foot in the stirrup, swinging up quickly into the saddle; he sat waiting to see if there would be any more trouble. The mare was heaving a little from her exertions, but otherwise stood quietly. He squeezed his legs and she moved forward in a walk, then pushing her again, she trotted.

'Well, I'll have to watch out for that in future, won't I, you silly cow,' he said to his horse.

After riding for a few more minutes, Charlie suggested that they ride through into Sandy Paddock to see how she went around the cattle.

'You reckon she's ready?' Matty asked excitedly.

'Yeh, she ready,' came the short answer.

Matty took the lead and reaching the gate, spent a few moments getting Cedar to walk up to the gate sideways, so that he could lean down and open it without dismounting. She responded well to his leg movements, standing patiently while he leant down several times. The mare was a bit toey when he finally unlatched the gate and dragged it back towards her, shying a little as it touched her side. He rode her back up to it and tried again, this time she sidestepped slowly until Matty relaxed the pressure on the reins. After repeating the process on the other side of the gate, he leant down and hugged her neck, patting her.

'You are a smart girl, hey, Cedar.'

He turned to Charlie and caught the grin on his face.

'What are you smiling at, Charlie?'

Charlie shook his head. 'Nothin'. The cattle over dis way,' he said with a jerk of his head to indicate towards the bore. 'We go pick out a few. See how the mare work 'em.'

As they came upon the bore, a few weaners sprang up from their resting place under the trees. Needing no urging, Matty pushed Cedar into a canter and rode to wing them. The young cattle had a head start and Matty pushed Cedar into a gallop. She stretched out, going where Matty's hand guided. As they drew level with the weaners, the cattle turned and headed out across the sandy plain. Matty turned Cedar gently and pushed her again. The mare jumped the spinifex mounds and gradually overtook the fleeing cattle. They turned again, this time heading back to the herd. Matty pulled Cedar up and gave her a pat, pleased with her first experience with the cattle.

Riding back to Charlie, who had dismounted and sat on his heels in the shade of a tree, he asked how she had done.

'She do all right,' he said. 'You start ridin' her all time now.'

Sitting up in the saddle, Matty felt a flash of pride. He had seen his filly born and now at the end of a long process, she was ready to start work, his horse.

Charlie brought him back to earth. 'She got lot more learnin', but she be dinkum horse.'

* * * *

The end of shearing brought the trip to town closer. Eliza gave into the law of the government and wrote to Bourke, making arrangements for the boys to stay with the school master. Thomas insisted that every piece of equipment they would take with them be stripped down and thoroughly cleaned. Eliza sorted out their best clothes, finding some of Thomas's old clothes and boots for Sammy. Having never worn boots before, Sammy had blisters for a few days. Thomas declared Sammy's the shiniest as the boy worked on those boots for days.

As the days shortened and an autumn chill crept into the evenings, the moment for them to leave arrived. The boys had saddled up before first light and were impatient to leave but Eliza fussed over them, making sure that Tan had packed enough food and gave them a lecture to remember their manners.

Stockmen stood around in the dim early light of dawn, waiting to see them off, Thomas giving them instructions for the time that he would be away. As the horses became restless, Thomas mounted and led off down the track.

The women were waiting at the river crossing to say goodbye. They made a fuss of the boys and nodded wisely when Minnie said that they were men now. Thomas smiled at the proprietary air of the women; they had helped raise all three boys and felt a need to share in this moment. Taking their leave, the small party rode through the crossing and onto the Yantabulla track.

The horses stepped out eagerly, as the boys had ridden them daily, getting them as fit as possible; the horses shied playfully and looked about with interest as they covered new ground. The three boys were full of questions, driving Thomas to distraction as they asked about each part of the track they would cover, who owned what property, and what they would find in Bourke. Riding for two hours, they rested the horses for fifteen minutes and then rode on again, stopping for lunch for an hour. Pulling up just on dark near some trees, they made a fire and prepared dinner before falling into bed early.

The next day they met a drover taking cattle up to a property in Queensland. They shared lunch with him, Thomas catching up on cattle prices and other such news. Covering fifty miles a day, it was three days before they sighted Bourke in the distance and their excitement rose again.

Their heads turned from side to side as they rode down the main street of the town, the horses snorting at the strange sights and smells. People paused only briefly to watch the small party leading pack horses, walking down the street and occasionally some who recognised Thomas raised a hand in greeting.

Spying the local grocery store, Matty's mouth watered at the thought of boiled lollies, a rare indulgence at home. His father caught his glance and promised them a treat after they had settled in at the house of the school master. Thomas indicated that they turn left into a side street, and then pulled up in front of a large brick house. John, who had been watching for them, came to the front gate to meet them.

'Well, Thomas, you have arrived! No trouble on the trip in, I hope?'

Dismounting, Thomas shook the outstretched hand. 'No.'

Turning, he saw that the boys had dismounted. 'This is Jack, Matty and Sammy,' he said, gesturing to each boy in turn. 'They have been looking forward to this for weeks.'

'Hello, boys, I, ah, hope you enjoy your stay with us,' John replied. 'How about you put your horses in the yard around the back? Go up the street three houses until you see a lane. You will find it easy enough. I'd like to talk to Mr Watson.'

The two men stood at the gate, in the shade of the arch, which was covered with a climbing rose.

'That native boy looks quite smart. Did you bring him to look after the horses?' the school master asked.

Thomas stared at John. 'No, he's come to join the Cadets.'

Watching the boys lead the horses up the street, John spoke quietly. 'Thomas, we do not have any natives in the Cadets. The government doesn't recognise blacks like that.'

Taking a deep breath, thinking for a moment before he spoke, Thomas replied, 'There is always a first time, John.'

The other man looked at Thomas. 'It's just... I don't know what the other boys' fathers will say.'

'How about we ask Bert? Being the magistrate in town, he is the protector for the natives. He should be able to tell us,' Thomas suggested.

Realising that this issue was going to be a touchy one, John agreed, albeit a bit reluctantly.

'If you say so, Thomas,' he replied. 'Shall we check on the boys, then go round to the courthouse? Bert should still be there.'

Matty and Jack were rubbing down the two packhorses and Sammy was finishing cleaning the sweat off the girths as the men came around the side of the house.

'What a fine mare! Where did you get her?' John asked as he gazed admiringly at Cedar. As if on cue, the mare arched her neck and trotted up to the edge of the yard, nickering to a horse in a paddock across the lane.

'We bred her at the station. She belongs to Matty,' Thomas answered.

'Well, I'm sure you will get a few offers for her while you are here.'

Thomas laughed. 'They can offer what they like. I can tell you Matty will not part with that mare. He watched her born and he broke her in. He is very attached to her.'

Having finished putting the horses away, the boys came and stood shyly, waiting to see what would be doing next.

'Could the boys and I wash up a bit and then we might take a walk into town, John?' Thomas asked, eyeing the other man meaningfully. 'How about it, boys? Some lollies at the store?'

Matty answered for them. 'Yes, please, Father.'

Fifteen minutes later, the boys were trying to choose what sweets to buy. Thomas had given each of them some money and now they stood at the counter eyeing the jars of lollies, acting like little boys instead of half-grown men. The man behind the counter stood patiently, waiting for them to make up their minds, smiling at their dilemma in choosing just which sweets to buy.

'This your first trip to town?' he asked, wiping his hands down his apron.

Sammy nodded. 'Yes, sir. We not been off the station before. Well, Jack has, 'fore he come live with us.'

The shop keeper's face registered shock at Sammy's little speech. 'Where are you from?'

Jack and Matty's eyes snapped up from the lolly jars to the man's face at the tone of his voice. Sammy looked around, wondering what he had done wrong.

'Why?' Jack said sharply, instinct stopping him from saying more.

'Oh, it's just he speaks well, for a native,' the man spluttered, feeling the animosity from Jack.

Matty opened his mouth to speak, but feeling Jack's elbow in his side, he shut it.

'Come on, fellas, let's go wait outside for the Boss,' Jack said, giving the man a last look.

The three of them turned and left the store, walking a little way up the street.

'What did you do that for?' Matty said angrily. 'I was just gonna tell him we were mates.'

Jack apologised. 'Sorry, Shorty, but remember what the Missus said.'

'Well, I don't care. Sammy's our mate and no one's gonna treat him wrong.'

Sammy looked at the ground, drawing circles in the dust with the toe of his boot. 'I don't want be trouble for you fellas.'

Putting his arm around Sammy's shoulders, Jack said, 'You ain't no trouble, Sammy. Like Matty said, you're our cobber, and we stand by our mates.'

A shy smile appeared on Sammy's face, breaking into a grin.

'Come on, we'll go sit down on that seat and wait for the Boss,' Jack said, pointing to a garden bench in the small park.

They sat and watched the town go about its business, talking about the different sights they had seen. They were strangers in Bourke and the sight of two white boys with a well-dressed native drew more than a few looks from the townspeople.

After a few minutes, Thomas strode across the street, his face tight with anger, the school master nearly running, trying to keep up with him. The three boys remained silent. That look meant trouble.

Stopping in front of them, breathing hard, Thomas tried to compose himself.

'I've just been to the courthouse. There seems to be a problem with Sammy joining the Cadets.'

Jack and Matty jumped up from their seat, looking bewildered.

'What do you mean, Boss?'

'Yes, Father, what's the problem?'

Glancing down at Sammy, who sat hunched over on the seat, staring at the ground, Thomas explained what had happened.

'The magistrate gave his view that natives are not permitted to join the Cadets.'

'Well, if Sammy can't join the Cadets, then we aren't either, eh, Jack?' Matty stated, not looking at Jack but staring at his father, his face angry.

'I agree, Boss. Sammy does everything with us.'

Slowly, Sammy stood up. All eyes turned to him.

'Me don't want trouble. Uncle says these things happen,' he said softly, his eyes pleading with Matty.

'No, this is nonsense,' Thomas explained gently.

Turning to John, who had watched this show of united friendship with amazement, he said, 'I thank you for your offer of hospitality, but I have brought these boys up to respect a person for who he is, not the colour of his skin. We will be returning to the station today. It is unfortunate that their first trip to town has been a disappointment.'

'Why not stay the night? We may be able to go and see Bert again, talk him around?' suggested John.

'And what about the parents of the other boys and the laws?'

'You have a point, Thomas. If I can't get you to stay, at least let me give you a meal before you go.'

Thomas let out a sigh. 'I'm sorry, but the natives have been our main support out there. We would not have lasted without them.'

'Well, hopefully, things will change.'

'It's bad enough that I have to keep applying to the Government to keep them on the property. They want to put them in the missions. Our people, well, it is probably hard for you to understand...' Thomas paused, considering his next words carefully. 'Our people know our ways and we know theirs; we get along just fine. The inspector came out last year and could not find fault with us.'

'Not all people feel as you do, Thomas. Some still treat them as savages. I must admit, I have not had much to do with them,' John remarked, sensing that Thomas's feelings for the natives ran deep.

The men, continuing their conversation, walked towards the school master's street, the boys following quietly behind. The three boys glanced from side to side, staring at the shopfronts, full of many wonders and then, as they turned into the street, they looked in awe at the gardens of the houses.

'Mother would love to have a garden like this one,' Matty said, pointing to a large expanse of lawn, bordered by many different coloured roses.

'I wonder what Tan would say about it. He thinks vegetables are more important than flowers,' replied Jack.

The men in front stopped when they reached John's front gate. An awkwardness, which Thomas tried to dispel, settled on the group.

'If you can get away, why don't you come out to Mulga Plains for a stay? We'll show you around, won't we, boys?'

John smiled as the boys just nodded, not an eager display of agreement.

'Well, I'll look forward to it,' he said as he put out his hand to Thomas. Then he shook hands with the boys. 'I'll help you saddle up, if you're determined to leave now.'

'The sooner we get home, the sooner I can write to the government.'

'Go carefully, they might not like their policies questioned. It might make things difficult for you,' John advised.

'Thank you for your offer of a meal, but I want to show the boys the railway and then we'll start home.'

After saddling the horses, Thomas took the rope of the packhorse from John and turned, heading up the lane. The boys followed, eager to see the great machines they had only read about.

The railway station lay a few blocks from John's house and well before they reached it, they could hear the steam engine letting out its groans. Rounding the corner they saw men, cattle, horses and wagons, all going in different directions. Wool bales were being brought in on large drays to be sent south, while in the cattle yards, cattle bellowed as they were herded up the ramp into wagons.

A lanky, sunburnt man paused to check his paperwork and in doing so, caught sight of the group of travellers watching. He stared at them for a while, then giving instructions to an offsider, he climbed out of the yards and walked over to Thomas.

'Good day, sir,' he said, taking off his hat. 'Micky Brown's my name.'

Thomas leant down and shook the man's outstretched hand. 'Thomas Watson.'

Micky put his hat back on and walked around the group of horses, looking carefully at them. The boys looked at each other, then at Thomas, who shrugged his shoulders slightly.

On returning to the front of the group, Micky said, 'Did you breed these horses, Mr Watson?'

'Well, yes, I did,' Thomas acknowledged.

'Would you be interested in selling them? I buy remounts for the government and these horses are the type they are looking for.'

Thomas smiled at the man. 'These particular horses are not for sale but I do have others back at the station you might like. How many are you looking for? I've got about twenty that might interest you.'

'What about that chestnut mare? I'd give top price for her.'

Cedar's head flew up as Matty's hands tightened on the reins. 'She's not for sale, sir,' Matty said forcefully.

'Pity,' Micky replied. 'But if you have others like her, I'd be very interested. Could I come out and have a look at them?'

As Thomas and Micky fell to arranging a visit, the boys pushed their horses closer to the railway to have a look at the steam engine. Sammy offered to hold the horses while Jack and Matty walked up onto the platform for a better look. The horses, their bodies tense, stared at the big black monster pushing its steam out with a loud shushing noise.

A call from Thomas brought Jack and Matty back to mount up and they turned their horses for home.

TWELVE

'War… War there is to be!' were the first words out of the hawker's mouth as he tugged his horse's reins to stop the poor beast, who was pulling a heavily laden cart.

Jack and Matty rushed down the stairs, running to the fence.

'Wha'dya mean? The last lot of papers only said Britain was watching what Germany was going to do. When did this happen?'

'I hear it in Bourke seven day ago! It in the paper and on telegraph. The gov'ment, they are looking for men to fight the Hun,' replied Naveer.

'Well, I'll be.' Thomas sighed, overhearing the conversation. 'Micky will probably come early for the next lot of horses. I'll have to get Charlie moving on the breaking. You boys will have to help.'

Naveer nodded. 'The whole country, it be buying wool, guns, wagons and horses for the men to fight, Mr Watson.'

'Yes, Naveer,' Thomas replied. 'Well, well! What's it been, a fortnight since the last mail? Then it's due in the next day or two. We will be able to read about it then.'

'I take the cart around the back. Is Tan in the kitchen?' Naveer asked, thinking of the meal that Tan customarily served him on his visits.

'Yes, and the Missus will probably take a look at what you've got as well.'

Flapping the reins, the hawker urged his horse to walk and, groaning, the horse put his shoulders to the collar and heaved the heavy cart forward.

The boys had remained quiet through this exchange, but now they asked Thomas question after question.

'Boys, we will see what the papers say. The mail should be here in two days. We shall know more then,' he replied, frustrated that he did not know what was happening in his own country.

Thomas kept the station busy, mustering the horses, drafting the ones that he thought Micky might take. Charlie and the boys worked on each horse and took the rough out of them. They were by no means properly broken in. That would be finished by the horse breakers, when the horses reached their destination.

The mail arrived with a letter from Micky, asking Thomas to send whatever horses he thought suitable as soon as possible to the Bourke rail yards. He apologised for not coming in person, but, with war being declared, he was very busy arranging remounts for the new army.

Thomas on reading this letter, took himself into his small office and looked through the newspapers. Some hours later, he asked the family to sit at the dining table.

'The news is very grave,' he began.

Eliza looked fearfully at Thomas. 'You won't have to go will you, Thomas?'

'Not at the moment. Men have been lining up to enlist since before war was declared. Besides, I am older than the enlistment age and married. They should, by now, have enough.'

'But what's happened,' pleaded Matty. 'Why are we at war?'

'In Europe, countries have been fighting wars for thousands of years. You learnt about some of them in your history lessons. Gradually, different countries made agreements with each other, that if attacked, the other country would come to their aid. Nearly all Australians come from Britain. Your grandfather, Matty, came out to Australia from England. We trade with Britain and she has always been there to help protect our shores.'

Thomas paused and Matty asked, 'But why is Australia going to fight?'

'I'm getting to that. We have an allegiance to Britain, the same as New Zealand or South Africa has. Austria declared war on Serbia. That didn't mean much to Australia, at the time. But, when Germany declared war on Russia, France would, as Russia's ally, declare war on Germany. Britain and France had an agreement that if one was at war then so would the other be. So, Britain has declared war on Germany. They have sent a request to Australia for men and, as Britain is our mother country, we will go to war. If Britain is defeated, we will have no protection from any invading nation. That would be a sad day for Australia, if we did not help our mother country.'

Jack spoke up thoughtfully. 'My da, he was born in England. He came out on a ship when he was a boy. He worked on the ship for no pay to get here.'

Watching Jack's face, Eliza rushed in to stop Jack's next words.

'Don't you even think of joining up, Jack! You are far too young. They won't take you,' she said, her voice rising. 'Both of you, don't even think about it.'

Watching his wife becoming distressed at the thought of her boys going to war, Thomas interrupted. 'Now, now, Eliza. The war will be over in six months. Our men will probably not even get to fight,' he said quietly. 'By the time they organise everything and train the men, it will be over.'

Mollified by her husband's words, Eliza rose from the table. 'I don't want to hear any more about war. It is men who fight wars and die, but it is the women who lose.'

She smoothed down her dress and, with a last meaningful look at the boys, she left the room.

Matty squirmed in his chair, waiting until his mother had gone before the questions spilled forth.

'You haven't said much about Grandfather Watson, Father. Why did he come to Australia? Why don't we visit him?' He paused to look at the door. Lowering his voice, he added, 'What will happen if the war goes longer than six months?'

Thomas caught the look in Matty's eyes. The boys had studied the Boer War. He could see Matty thinking of himself, mounted on his horse, attacking the enemy.

'Your mother was right. Jack, you are only seventeen. You would not be allowed to enlist without your parents' consent. Matty, you at sixteen would not have a hope. So, both of you, put it behind you. There are other ways to help the war. Our wool will go to factories to make blankets. We'll break in more horses for Micky. That is how we will contribute. I don't want to hear any more about enlisting.'

'Yes, Boss,' both boys answered at the same time.

'Well, the two of you had better ride out to the camp and tell the boys we are mustering the horses.'

Leaving the house through the kitchen, to grab some tucker from Tan, the boys saddled up their horses, stowing their guns in the rifle buckets. Once away from the homestead, they pulled their horses back to a walk and the conversation began.

'If the war does go on, we might be old enough to join. We'll have to practise our shooting!' Matty said excitedly.

Cedar, feeling his excitement, broke into a trot. He glanced over at Jack, and seeing his face, Matty reluctantly slowed her. He wanted to gallop, to pretend they were charging a great enemy.

Jack stared between the ears of his horse, his thoughts slow in forming. 'We could go shooting rabbits more. If we can shoot a rabbit at five hundred yards, they'd have to take us. We can ride, and shoot.'

'Wait till we tell Sammy! They'll want everyone this time, so Sammy can join up with us.'

Jack glanced over at Matty. 'I don't know about that. Look what happened in Bourke. We'll have to keep this from the Missus. She'll cut up worse than that bloody snake I fished out the tank!'

They rode on for a while, the horses' hooves swishing in the sand and the creak of leather the only sounds, each with their own thoughts until Jack spoke.

'I wonder what it's really like, to go to war?'

'It would be bonzer, mate. We'd get to see the countries we've read about and have a grand time.' Matty wasn't quite sure of what he actually meant by a grand time, but it would surely be exciting.

They read every newspaper avidly, discussing the contents for days. Soon, the three of them knew every battle fought and poured over the atlas, following the whereabouts of the British Army.

Gradually, the excitement wore off. There was the breaking in of the horses and the daily running of the station to keep them busy, but the war was never far from their minds. As the days lengthened and Christmas drew nearer, they rode from tank to tank, checking that the windmills were working. Micky surprised them by arriving to pick up the remount horses shortly after New Year's Day. He told them of the rumours that were flying around in the city, that the war would take a lot longer to win than first thought. The fighting in France had been terrible and the casualty lists were growing. The boys listened, then talked about it quietly, away from the ears of the Boss and the Missus.

THIRTEEN

'Jack's gone! The begger's gone without me!' Matty yelled, as he stormed up the hallway to his parents' room.

After knocking quickly, he flung open the door. 'Father, Jack's gone to enlist. He snuck out last night.'

On hearing Matty shouting, Thomas had sat up in bed, wondering what was going on; now he knew. He looked out the window at the dawn sky and sighed.

'What are we going to do?' Eliza asked, trying to stay calm as she got out of bed and threw a shawl around her shoulders. 'We will have to get him back. He's too young to go.'

'He's gone without me, his cobber,' Matty cried out angrily. 'I don't want him to fight for me. I want to go with him.'

Thomas glanced quickly at Eliza and seeing the look of fear on her face, he spoke harshly.

'That will be enough, Matty! Is it not enough that we have this to worry about, without you carrying on?'

Matty made to protest but he thought better of it. Instead, he walked over to his father and handed him the letter.

'He left it in my boot.'

Taking the letter from Matty's outstretched hand, Thomas smoothed the paper out, crinkled from Matty's clutching it.

Matty,

I have gone to join up. I could not take you with me, you are too young. They would have sent you home anyway. I have to do this, it's something I reckon my da would have done, the way he used to talk about England.

Don't worry about me, I'll be fine. I'll give those Germans enough for the two of us.

Tell the Boss and the Missus, I am sorry. I know if I had asked them, they would not have let me. I hate to disobey them but it is something I have to do.

I will leave Nugget at the river and catch the coach to wherever I have to go. The money that the Boss gave me for Christmas will pay my way, so I will not have to rely on anyone else.

I will write when I find out where I am to be.

Till then,

Jack

'Well, he's not giving any hints as to where he is going to join up, is he?' Thomas said thoughtfully.

'Thomas, what are we going to do? How can we get him back? You will have to ride to Tinapingee and use their telephone,' Eliza asked, her mind whirling with images of Jack stranded or worse, actually fighting. 'Oh, if only we had the telephone!'

Taking a deep breath, Thomas looked at Eliza and then Matty. 'I don't think that, even if we do track him down, that he will stay here.'

Matty looked at his father wide-eyed and shook his head furiously. 'He will if you tell him.'

'No, son. Now, he has something to do, that in his mind, will make his father proud. I think we might let it be. Anyway, they will probably refuse to enlist him without consent.'

Eliza's voice shook as she said, 'We are his parents now, we should stop him!'

Thomas rose and put his hand on Matty's shoulder. 'We have to let Jack do as he will and pray that he comes back to us safely,' he said heavily. 'Go and tell Tan that there will be one less for breakfast. I want to talk to your mother.'

Matty turned and left the room, his mind screaming in anger. 'Why did he leave me behind? What's his da got to do with the war?' he muttered as he walked down the hall. He could not see why Jack would leave him behind; he could not understand how Jack's dead father meant that Jack would run away to war.

In this mood, he flung himself down at the kitchen table and poured out his anger to Tan.

The old Chinaman went about his morning rituals, breaking eggs into the frypan and cutting the bread. He paused at one stage, holding his knife up, but changed his line of thinking and continued on with his work.

Matty finally ran out of words.

Glancing down at the boy, Tan saw the frustration on his face. He walked around the table and patted Matty on the head. Matty pulled his head away.

'I tell you my story, leaving China. It not easy. I want to stay with my family, my friends. But I owe my family to do what I could. So, Jack. He honour his father this way. You angry now. You think about it hard enough, you will see.'

Matty did not want to hear this and, pushing his chair back, ran out the back door, letting it slam shut.

Tan shrugged his shoulders and returned to the stove. *He will calm down, but I don't know that he will ever forgive Jack,* he thought, as he lifted the eggs out onto the warm plates on the side of the stove.

Not knowing what to do, Matty went to the yards and called to

Cedar. The mare trotted up to him and he put his arms around her neck, hugging her tightly. The mare stood still, waiting patiently for Matty to move. Eventually, he stepped back and looked at her. His face lit up as an idea came to him. Saddling the mare quickly, he opened the yard gate and mounted, turned the mare towards the river and took off at the gallop.

He crouched low over her neck, his hands holding the reins across her mane, moving in motion with her stride. Soon enough, sense came to him and he drew her back to a trot then to a walk. He knew that damaging her would not bring Jack home. The gallop had soothed him a little but his mind still searched for answers. He sat a littler straighter in the saddle and looked ahead, alert for movement. Maybe Jack had changed his mind; maybe he was returning home along the track now. His excitement stirred the mare and she jogged, breaking into a trot that Matty did not slow. He searched ahead, hoping, but saw nothing. The miles to the river seemed to take forever. As he stopped at the river, Matty saw Nugget tied up in the shade of a tree on the other side. The horse nickered to Cedar, who answered with her own. Matty's heart sank. His mate had not changed his mind. Jack would have walked the two miles to the Hungerford Road and as fortune would have it, the daily coach came through early from Hungerford.

'An hour is all I've missed him by, girl. That's all,' Matty said sadly to Cedar.

Riding Cedar through the puddles that was once the river, he dismounted and walked over to where Nugget stood, his tail flicking at the flies. Hoping that Jack may have left another note, he went through the saddlebag. Nothing. Untying the horse, he mounted Cedar and led Nugget back to the station.

Eliza met him at the yards, her eyes red. She watched as Matty unsaddled both horses and wiped the sweat from them. As he shut the gate and she saw the loss in his face, she said hopefully, 'Your father will not change his mind. We can only pray that the people in charge won't let him enlist, son.'

'No. If he's determined to go, he'll get in. Jack never let anything beat him yet, Mother.'

Matty walked away, his head down. He wandered from place to place, his mind going through all that had happened. He ended up at the kennels and sat patting the bitch that the kangaroo had opened up. He fondled her ears and spoke to her.

'I don't understand. Why didn't I see that he might do this. I never thought he would leave us. If I follow him, Father would hunt me down, I know that.'

He stared at the windmill, watching it spin in the slight breeze. The kelpie pushed her nose into the palm of his hand when he stopped stroking her.

Glancing down, he saw her brown eyes fastened on him. 'You have no idea what I'm saying, but you know I'm down, don't you, girl?'

The dog pushed harder at his hand and he patted her again as he continued his thoughts out loud.

'You know, for as long as Jack's been with us, I suppose I never really thought that much about his father. I mean, he never talked about him and Jack was part of our family. I suppose I should have talked to him more about those things. It must have meant a lot for him to go. I just never thought about it. Pretty selfish I was, really.'

Matty gently pushed the dog away and stood up. He felt lost and alone. Always Jack had been there, not with him all the time, but Matty knew he was close. It felt like a part of him was missing. He felt the same about Sammy, but he knew Sammy hadn't left, he was still at the camp and that comforted him.

He started towards the house, muttering to himself.

'I don't know what I'd do if Sammy went too.'

Sammy came as soon as he heard that Jack had gone, and together the boys talked about him for hours. To them it was as if he had died and they grieved for their loss. They rode out to the waterhole, the far paddocks but everywhere they went reminded them of Jack.

Thomas noticed that Matty was not eating and that he came to the table every morning dark under the eyes.

He spoke gently. 'Matty, Jack's gone but you're acting as though he has died. You must get over this.'

Deep brown eyes looked up at Thomas. 'That's what I'm afraid of, Father. I am afraid that he might die in the fighting. I dream about it, bad dreams where I see him lying there, calling my name and I'm not there for him.' Matty's body shook with emotion as the words fell to a whisper. 'I'm not there for him.'

Shaking his head, Thomas could only say, 'Son, you are worrying your mother sick. Please try to get over this. Like I said before, he could be back any day.'

The days became weeks and although Matty thought about Jack every day, gradually he began returning to normal. He and Sammy continued helping Charlie break in horses for the remounts and after the horses had gone to the railway, they returned to riding the boundary, checking on stock.

The mail arrived and Matty, who had waited impatiently for the mail every week, now showed no interest until his father handed him a letter.

Staring down at Jack's handwriting, he thought not to open it, dreading what it might say, but curiosity got to him and he ripped it open.

Liverpool Camp
Sydney
6th June 1915

Dear Matty,

I am sorry I took so long to write. I wanted to every day but I knew it was better if I did not until we were leaving. I arrived in Sydney six weeks ago. I met up with some fellows on the train. They told me that I would have to get someone to sign the papers and they would help me. When we got to Sydney, they got a woman to fix up my papers. They told her I was an orphan and that I wanted to go but needed a mother put her signature down on the enlistment forms. I think they paid her. She was not like the Missus. I think she might have been what the men here call a floozy. But she signed the papers and I don't think the army really cared.

We marched from the barracks to the railway station and then got a train to the Liverpool camp. There were tents everywhere, about eight fellows sleep in one tent. The food is not near as good as Tan's cooking but it's all there is. They gave us a riding test. And a needle. It is to stop us getting sick overseas they said. They called it a vaccination.

A loud bugle sounds in the morning and then it's a rush to get dressed and onto the parade ground. Every day we do drill and other training and talk about clean gear! You'd go spare if you saw how much gear there is to clean. I'm glad the Boss got us in the habit. Some blokes take forever to strip their saddle and put it back together. And the bridles, they go back together in all different ways, it's a bit of a laugh. The horses are all fit as we work them well. We have to be getting the best horse feed in the country, shame our food's not half as good.

We have been issued with .303 rifles and practise a lot with them. They are a fair bit heavier than our .22s but I am getting used to them. Some of the horses are a bit rough and there's a few blokes with broken bones, but on the whole the horses are fine.

At night we can go into town. You should see what goes on down here.

It is noisy and there are automobiles everywhere. I've met a good bunch of blokes and we have been put in the same company so I'll be right.

I have been put in the 12th Light Horse and we are to sail tomorrow. Most of the men got leave but I decided to stay here in camp as it was only for three days.

So, tomorrow we'll be heading for overseas. We are to go around under Australia to Fremantle then across to Columbo then to Egypt. This is what the men say anyway.

I had a photograph taken and enclose it with this letter. It cost a shilling. I look pretty smart, don't you think?

I hope that the Missus got over me leaving like I did. I expected the Boss to turn up at any minute or to send a wire, but after a while I thought that he may have decided to let me go. We will be getting paid while we are over there, and I have signed a paper to send some of my pay to the Missus.

I know you will be spitting chips about me leaving you like that, but I hope that you see now why I had to do it. My memories of Da are all I have of him and I know that from the way he talked about England that he would have joined up. I never knew my mother and I don't know of any family. You are the only family I have now but I have to do this for Da and myself. It is more than just going to fight. It is doing what is right.

I have written a letter to Sammy and one to the Boss to tell him why. I wouldn't feel right going without saying goodbye after the way I left. Please write often and tell me what is happening on the station. I miss it so much already. Say hello to Tan and Charlie and the men for me and tell Tan I miss his cooking.

Well, goodbye Shorty and look after Nugget for me.

Your good mate,

Jack.

PS. You can write to me care of the Light Horse, Egypt. Just put my number and name at the top. It's all on the back of the photo.

Matty put the letter down and picked up the photograph. He stared at Jack's face, realising that his friend was no longer a boy. It was a man's face that looked at him from the photo, with his hat at a jaunty angle and the uniform snug on his wide shoulders. It made Matty wonder when had this happened; why hadn't he noticed that they had grown up.

He got up and went to his mother's desk. Taking a sheet of paper from the drawer, he sat down and tried to write what he was feeling.

Mulga Plains

Via Bourke

22nd June 1915

Dear Jack,

You mongrel. Left me here and snuck away. That's how I first felt. I missed you terribly but have got used to you not being here.

I haven't spoke to Father yet about your letter to him. He will tell me if he thinks he should. Mother took it badly, but she is doing all right now. You had better send her a letter.

I rode to the river and found Nugget. You would not have been long gone. Father said to let you go, that maybe they would send you home. He said that if you had to do it then he wouldn't be able to change your mind.

Now that I have had time to think about it, I see your reason for going. You never talked about your father and I just assumed that you felt that the Boss was your father. I never understood that you still felt so strong about your da. It was very selfish of me and not what a cobber should be like. I hope you will forgive me. Sammy and the others had a ceremony for you, to keep you safe and make you strong. I think you were supposed to be there for it, but I hope it works anyway.

Well, how is it? This letter will probably get to you in Egypt. Who would of thought that I would be writing to you overseas! The blokes that you met sound like a good crowd. Have you made new mates? Don't forget your old mates back here.

We broke the rest of the remounts and Micky took the lot. He said a few would do for the wagons, they're the ones out of the Clydesdales and the rest would go to the Light Horse. You never know, you might end up with one of our horses! Wouldn't that be a lark.

Sammy and I have been riding the boundary, we had a few stock stray onto the property next door, but we got them back right enough.

I will not be able to send this until next mail so it will be a while before you get it.

I know you will do a good job of it but keep yourself safe.

Keep writing, we all miss you.

Your mate,

Matty.

PS. Nugget is fit as a fiddle.

Matty rose from the table. He stared at the letter, realising it was the first letter he had ever written. His world had been so small, he had not had anyone to write to in the past. Mother wrote to her relatives and spoke for them all. Now, Jack was headed to the other side of the world.

Dragging out the atlas, Matty and Sammy studied the voyage that Jack had described and they read the newspaper, following the accounts of the war.

Unexpectedly, another letter reached them.

On Board Ship

Off Fremantle

19th June 1915

Dear Shorty and Sammy,

We had a bad time of it when we sailed from Sydney. A lot of the blokes were sick as dogs. That didn't leave many of us to care for the horses in the holds. The stink down there is enough to make you sick even if you weren't seasick. There's about one hundred and fifty soldiers on board this ship, which is quite a small ship.

The horses will be off loaded at Fremantle and come over on another ship. I have been keeping an eye out for the station's brand but have yet to see one of our horses.

I have written a letter to the Missus, so I hope that will help.

How are all our people going? How is old Min? Hard to think that I was scared of her that first time, what a baby I was.

The men here talk quite a bit about their families and women and things. I'm learning a lot of things that we never knew.

I'll send this from Fremantle and hope that there is a letter or two for me in Egypt.

Your mate,

Jack.

Mulga Plains

Via Bourke

3rd July 1915

Dear Jack,

Got your letter today. It sounds like you had a rough time of it.

Things have been happening here. First of all, a fellow came looking for work and Father put him on fixing the fences even though he wondered why he hadn't joined up. The bloke said he didn't have any family. But anyway, Charlie saw him beating the hell out of one of the horses and Father spoke to him about it. The fellow, his name was Lawrence, he apologised and went out to River Paddock to work. Sammy came riding in to say he was annoying the women and Father and I rode out to the paddock. He was a bit of a rum one. He had this dog, a black thing, that had skin missing off it. Apparently, he would get on the grog and belt it. Why it stayed with him, we don't know. Anyway, Father paid him and told him to leave. About five days later, the dog turned up here at the station by himself. Father thought it a bit strange so he and Charlie and Ernie went to see if they could find Lawrence. Ernie tracked him half way to Hungerford and they found him dead beside his campfire. The police came and it turns out that he was a bad case. They think that some people he had dudded caught up with him, because he had been shot. The dog has attached itself to Charlie and is like his shadow.

We killed a bullock the other day and had fresh meat for a couple of days. Tan and Mother have been salting all week.

Sammy and I went shooting and got a couple of pigs! They have been breeding up and moving out this way. Father said if we get rain then they will become a nuisance. You should have seen Cedar when Sammy and I lifted this pig on her back. The smell of the blood sent her crazy. She snorted and shook her head all over the place but she eventually settled down and we slung it across the saddle. Tan was beside himself when we got the pigs home. We had roast pork and he made this Chinese food with rice and vegetables with some of the pork. It was great.

Everyone is fine and it looks like we will get some rain. Father has sent to Bourke to get the telephone put on, that will be good.

Charlie says I should put Cedar to the stallion, but I think I'll wait a while yet. I'd like you to have her first foal.

Well, that is our news. Write soon as you can,

Your mates,
Matty and Sammy.

Egypt
6th August 1915

Dear Matty and Sammy,

It is easier to write to both of you at the same time, as I would only say the same thing to both of you.

The trip after Fremantle was quite good, except Aden, where it was as hot as we have it on our worst days at the station. But it's sultry and the air is heavy. When we crossed the Equator, we had a ceremony. That was a bit of fun. Mostly we had parades and played cards and games. Some of the men got measles and they were offloaded at Suez. Suez is a very big canal. It took ages to get through to the Mediterranean Sea. We are now at the Heliopolis Racecourse near Cairo and the sights that I've seen. The Nile River land is very fertile, the Boss would love to be able to grow crops like they grow here. There's cotton and rice and every one rides these small donkeys. There are date trees and the fruit is sweet. Most of the men have had upset stomachs, vomiting and the runs, but soon got over it. You have to be careful what you eat. The Pyramids are huge, bigger than anything you could imagine and very old. I have sent you fellows some postcards of them. We had our photograph taken in front of the Sphinx. I'll send it when I get a copy.

We spend all the time looking after the horses. It is very hot, with a wind that blows every day. The nights are cool though. The horses stood up to the journey very well. I still have not seen one of ours.

There are rumours, what they call furphies, flying around that we are to be sent to a place called The Dardanelles. Some of our blokes are already there and by all accounts had a very rough time.

There is a zoo here that takes two days to see and they have all these weird animals in it. There are palaces and markets that they call bazaars. Everything here is very dirty and there are always natives trying to sell you things. They are very poor here.

There are a lot of French people here and I had a chance to practise my French, but the poor fellow didn't understand much of what I said. I must find out what is wrong with how I speak it.

We went to a place called the Wazzer. It's full of houses where men go to get women. They pay the women to go to bed with them. The officers gave us all a lecture about these women, about how we could catch VD, but some of the men don't care. Some fellows in my company were going to pay for me, seeing I was what they call a virgin, but my mates said no. I'm glad that they stuck up for me because I didn't want to catch a disease. A few of the men have apparently got it.

You should see the camels, they use them to pull wagons and they ride them, like the Afghans back home The horses hate the camels.

So enough about my stories, what is happening at home? Have you read about Gallipoli?

How is everyone? Have you had rain?

You must write and tell me about everything at home, I miss you all terribly. How is Nugget?

Waiting for your letters,

Your mate,

Jack.

Egypt
10th August 1915

Dear Matty and Sammy,

Got the mail today. There was parcel and a letter from the Missus and the Boss and two letters from you Matty and one from Sammy. It sounds like you had a bit of excitement there. Glad to hear Nugget is doing well. Thank you for your offer of the foal. I will look forward to it. I knew you would be cut about my leaving but you seem to have worked it out. Tell the boys thank you for the ceremony.

I sent another letter a couple of days ago so I am just writing a short one now to say I got the mail. Tan's biscuits are great and everyone is trying to buy them, but I just share them with a few of my mates. Pork, you lucky thing. We have bully beef that tastes like shit and we have tea to drink. You have to boil any water you drink. You can buy fruit and things from the natives, so it's not too bad.

We have been told that we are going to the Dardanelles. We are to leave the horses behind, just when I'd got used to mine. He is a big bay, about fifteen hands and long legged. He's got a fair amount of thoroughbred in him and is a handy galloper. He blows himself up when I saddle him, so I have to remember to check the girth after a few minutes. His name is Absent, on account of his brain is always AWL. He's as dumb as a sheep but he goes along all right.

You would probably have heard by the time you get this letter about the terrible fight at Gallipoli on the 7th August. We have only heard rumours but it sounds as though it was a huge mess and a lot of men died. It is very sobering when you know that you are heading where the fighting is. We are all keen to have a go at the Turks and help out there. Well, they're calling us to parade so had better close,

Your mate,

Jack.

Mulga Plains
Via Bourke
4th August 1915

Dear Jack,

We haven't had any more letters from you yet. We are hoping that everything is all right and that it is the mail that is slow.

We have had the telephone put in and Father can now talk about his business over the line instead of writing. Mother telephoned her family up at Welaregang. They were very pleased to hear from her, as Robert is the only one to have seen her since she left. It costs a lot of money to telephone that far away, and Mother said it will only be on special occasions. She telephones other women that she knows on other nearby properties, and they all have a talk.

Cedar threw me again the other day. She shied at a snake. She can be a cow of a thing. Lucky Sammy was the only one to see and he promised not to say anything because last time the boys ribbed me about it for days. Sammy has been told that his family has picked out a girl for him to marry when he is older. I don't think he is very keen on the idea. He said to tell you that we are not getting married, that we will all stay single and mates.

We had some rain up north so the river is up a bit. The wet season up north doesn't start for a while yet, so we don't expect much more rain in the near future.

The pigs have moved on, it seems it is too dry for them here now. So we haven't had any pork for a while since I wrote last. We caught some yellow belly in the waterhole, and it made a change from the salted meat. Tan is busy in his garden and Charlie and the blacks have gone walk about. Sammy stayed here with us. His uncle wasn't happy but Father said he could.

It must be hard for Sammy, as he is just like you and me but he has to follow what his people say as well.

Hoping to hear from you soon,

Your mates,
Sammy and Matty.

Egypt
24th August 1915

Dear Matty and Sammy,

Well, we have our orders. We are leaving the horses behind and heading to Gallipoli. We march out tomorrow to board the ship.

Have still not heard from you but then the mail is very slow. Maybe it will catch me at Gallipoli.

Say hello to everyone for me. If anything should happen to me, I have left what little I own to you and Sammy. It's not much but you blokes have been like brothers to me and that's that.

I'll write to the Boss before I go and thank him and the Missus for all they've done for me. They are great people, and it is only when you get away from the station that you realise how lucky we are to have them.

Do me a favour and take a trip out to the waterhole and remember the good times we had there. How is Cedar going? Did you decide to put her in foal?

And also, if you can manage it, emu feathers. They're a big thing with the men and we are supposed to get our own. Only the Queenslanders get theirs provided.

How I miss the station! Even though I'm in with a good bunch, I miss you fellows a lot.

I'll close now and write again when we land.

Your mate,
Jack.

Mulga Plains
Via Bourke
7th September 1915

Dear Jack,

We got two letters in one mail. It sounds as though you are seeing the sights! Lucky fellow. Are the pyramids as big as they say? They look big in the photographs you sent. All those strange things you must be seeing. Have you practised your French any more? It's strange that he had trouble understanding you.

You poor thing, bully beef? I bet you'd give anything for a feed of roo now. Remember when we went on that first camp and you were worried what we would eat?

We heard a bit about the fighting at Gallipoli but it didn't sound as bad as you said. They might be keeping the bad news from us.

So, you are off to fight. Well, good luck and keep your head down. I wish I was there with you! It sounds like you have made some good friends and I hope they look after you.

Your horse sounds like a good one. It's a pity you haven't one of ours. Have you seen any yet?

Mother has done up another parcel for you. Biscuits and socks and things. You must let us know what you need so we can send it.

Sammy's uncle got a bit upset when Sammy told him he didn't want to get married, but I think Minnie had a word to him.

Minnie's been very sick lately. She says it's old age and she wants to go back to her country. Father has let a couple of the boys go so that they can take her back to where she was born. It won't be the same without Min. I gave her a big hug from you and she said to say goodbye.

Well, that's our news for now,

Sammy and Matty.

Gallipoli
18th September 1915

Dear Matty and Sammy,

Have not had any mail since landing. We sailed from Alexandria on the 25th August and reached the island of Lemnos early on the morning of the 28th. We got off the ship into small boats and we put ashore at Anzac Cove at about 0300 on the 29th. We were split up as a regiment, to reinforce other ones who have lost so many men.

Boys, it is another world here. If you go for a swim in the sea, the Turks shoot at you or send their artillery over. Many of the men don't care, they just want to be clean for a while. The 'chats' invade you within hours. Chats are lice, like you get on the sheep sometimes. They live in our clothing and it is pure torture. We sit and pick them out when there is a quiet moment. Not that it is ever quiet. There are always bombs exploding and the artillery open up at all hours. The Originals don't seem to notice it, but they are so worn out I reckon they could sleep on a bucking horse.

You cannot move on this place without something trying to take your head off. If it's not the snipers then it's shrapnel. By all accounts, it has settled down quite a bit from the first few months here. The men have told me about the various battles and horrific, they were. At the Nek, two lines of men were mown down, they say it was a right royal stuff up. The 8th and 10th Light Horse were nearly wiped out. A lot of men are very sick with dysentery and they do not have good rations, they are very weak, but most of them won't report sick as they want to be with their mates. The morning we arrived the fight for Hill 60 was going on. There were thousands of bombs thrown and we could hear it till the early hours of the morning.

The place reminds me of a rabbit warren. Cut into the hills are all these dugouts made out of corrugated iron and timber supports but higher up, it's just a hole in the dirt.

The trenches are terrible, very narrow and dead bodies poke through every now and then. There are corpses all over no-man's land and the stench must have been terrible when the weather was hotter. It is getting colder of a night now that it is autumn, but the days are still warm. The others who were here in summer said that it was hotter than hell and the flies were so bad if you didn't hold onto your tin of bully, they would fly away with it.

The little black buggers here make our blowies at home seem tame. Sometimes they're so thick that you can't see what you're eating. You have to shake it, then push it in your mouth as quick as you can. The smell from the shit pits and the dead bodies would put a man off his food, if he wasn't so hungry.

The soldiers who were here from day one have certainly proven themselves beyond all doubt. There had been talk that the Light Horse would not match up to the infantry, but the boys of the Light Horse dispelled that notion.

Boys, a lot of brave men have died on this bit of land and it is a tall order to match up to them. All us new chums can do is try to finish what they started, and hope that we can do them proud.

I am writing this to you from up on Chatham's. We have been playing catch 'em, throw 'em back with the Johnny's bombs, a bit of a game but one not to muck up. We are expecting to go over the top in the morning, but this place is full of rumours, so you really don't know what's going on until it happens.

Yesterday I was asked to go up into a possy and do some sniping. Charles, a fellow from my squadron, came with me to spot. It's quite interesting, as you get him to spot through a periscope. If you show any part of you over the sandbags, you won't have that part for long. So, he spots, and I shoot. We got two confirmed and one maybe. I'm told that's not bad for a day's shooting. It makes them keep their heads down anyway. Has it rained? Is the waterhole full? I sometimes try to put myself to sleep by imagining we are still camping by the waterhole but the noise in this place never lets you forget for more than a minute, that you are in hell.

I look forward to your letters and hope that everyone at home is safe.

Your mate,
Jack.

Mulga Plains
Via Bourke
20th September 1915

Dear Jack,

The papers are full of the war. It seems to us that the war in Gallipoli is bogged down and that there have been tremendous losses. A lot of men have had second thoughts and have joined up to go over and help out.

We still have not heard any more from you and can only hope that you are still healthy.

The horses are fit, as we have been doing a lot of work with them. Sammy has been riding Nugget to keep him in shape for when you get home.

Mother is talking about getting another worker in to help Tan, as he is slowing down a bit. He and Bess still fight, she calls him a yellow man and he calls her a debil. I think they enjoy fighting but it gets on Mother's nerves. The telephone has made a difference to Mother because she can now talk on the party line to other local women. Her and Father have been invited to a wedding in January, so that should cheer her up. I know both Mother and Father have been writing to you, but I don't ask what about. That is between you and them. I only hope that they didn't go too hard on you about enlisting.

Hopefully by now you will have got Mother's parcel and you will be eating the things that Tan made for you. Sammy has at last decided to contribute, the lazy fellow, so I will hand the pen to him.

Hello Jack,

I hope that you are well and giving the Turks plenty. You hear about them trying to marry me off, good old you know who, she stuck up for me. She died a few weeks ago and we no speak her name anymore. I miss her lots.

Matty and me, we are going to take the herd to Bourke, we get to see the trains again. I bet you have seen a lot more since your last letter to us. Tan's yelling at us to get dinner so we go now.

Mates,

Sammy and Matty.

Gallipoli

24th September 1915

Dear Sammy and Matty,

The mail is so slow. I finally received you're your letters dated 4th August and 7th September and the Missus' parcel. I was attacked from all sides when the men saw what was in it. I was offered huge sums of money for the biscuits! The socks will come in handy when the cold weather comes. I will write to her and thank her. I will also write to Tan.

The station has the telephone on, hooray. They use it here but the lines are always getting broken from the shelling.

Sammy getting married, no! He is too young. But I suppose it's their way. Poor old Sammy. I'm glad Minnie stepped in. I miss old Min. It's sad that she is sick.

You really will have to do something about Cedar's snake problem, it could be nasty one day.

From the way you write, you hadn't got my letter to say that we are at Gallipoli. Well, I expect you will have it well before this letter reaches you.

Matty, do not be in a hurry to turn eighteen so that you can enlist. War is not what we thought it was. It is dirty and bloody. There is suffering everywhere, from wounds and disease. Men walk around here like they are old and some are only twenty.

I have had time to see more about this place. There is a spot on the beach that Johnny Turk can see all the time. You have to run across it and pray that they are not looking, or they will get you. Around at North Beach it is a little safer.

We are either digging deeper dugouts or carrying supplies up to the trenches or standing on the firing line. There is no rest, even for the sick. They are being taken off the beach in huge numbers and there are no reinforcements coming, we are told. The furphies fly round here quicker than a cut snake. There is supposed to be heavy artillery coming up for the Turks, so we might get a pounding. That is why we are digging all the time. The boat that was bringing iron and timber for the dugouts got run aground in the storm we had the other night. Because of the rough seas we have not had any water from the ships. They opened up an old well but it's not enough. We get one cup of water in the morning and one at night. We haven't shaved in a while and with the uniforms getting a bit tattered, as well as the alterations the men have made to them, well, we look a mean bunch.

Two blokes from my squadron got blown up yesterday. One of the shells that come over all the time got them. They were good men. We had a service for them after we buried what was left of them. There's many a dead soldier here who will never be found, there are skeletons in clothes everywhere. Like I said before, it is very grim.

You won't like me telling you this but stay home, Shorty, please.

Your mate and brother,

Jack.

PS. Sammy, you make sure he stays home.

Mulga Plains
Via Bourke
30ᵗʰ October 1915

Dear Jack,

We still have not had any mail from you. As you said, last we heard from you, that you were heading to Gallipoli, that is where we assume you are. We sit down and read the papers as soon as they come and we follow the reports of the fighting. It's pretty bad in France as well.
What is it like? And what are you doin'? I have tried not to ask as I thought you would tell us, but we haven't heard from you. I can't wait till I'm old enough to join, Father will have to let me go, if it keeps on like this.
I will go to Sydney and ask to be put in the 12ᵗʰ so I can meet up with you. It is only another year, if the war lasts that long. We had some rain and it freshened everything up. Sammy and I went to the waterhole like you asked, but it wasn't the same without you. Sammy shot a roo and we cooked it like we used to. It was good eating. We brought back some yellow belly for Tan. He was happy with that.
Hoping to hear from you soon,

Your mates,
Matty and Sammy.

Gallipoli
1ˢᵗ December 1915

Dear Matty and Sammy,

Still no mail. Sorry about the paper I'm writing on. If you send another parcel, paper is a good idea. It is in very short supply. It's getting cold here now, nights are freezing and when the wind blows, it would make a bandicoot burrow for all he was worth. We are always on the hop, carrying ammo up to the lines or digging trenches. Those Turks keep putting shells in and wrecking what we have done, so back we go.

We just came off a few days on the firing line and it gets on your nerves, sitting there wondering if Jacko Turk's going to make a rush. The noise is always there, never a quiet moment. Although, the other day we had a bit of a talk to the Turks. They wanted condensed milk and sent a note over. They put it in a tin. You should have seen the men scatter when it landed. They thought it was a bomb. Anyway, Dick yells out, 'Milk for tobacco'. They yell back, 'We throw, you throw.' So, no one fired or anything for about an hour, just swapped rations. It is really strange sometimes, sitting there knowing that if they attack they'll do their damndest to kill you but when no one's attacking they're like us, eating and smoking. Swapping things over the trenches. Some of the trenches are only twenty yards apart and we can hear them talking. The sappers that are mining under the ground, get really close and sometimes break through into the Jacko's trenches, then it is on. Those sappers are brave men, tunnelling underground. That I couldn't do.

If I get back to Mulga Plains I will give Charlie the biggest 'whatever' he wants. We sometimes go out into No Man's Land on scouting forays. The other night, I was on one and after crawling on our bellies for ages, we were about four yards from the Turks trench laying there, listening. I felt a shiver up my spine and turned around. There was a Turk holding my mate by the neck. I froze, just like I saw Charlie do when he was hunting roo. Then, I stood up, one foot raised and my arm held like I had a spear. I only had a bayonet, but the Turk looked up and he thought I was going to throw it at him. He rolled away and let my mate go. I fell to the ground pretty quickly before the Turks in the trenches saw me, and me and my mate skedaddled back to our lines very quickly. I don't know why I did it, it just happened, but it worked.

Men are falling sick everywhere and just yesterday, one bloke reported sick, finally. The doctor asked him what was wrong. He said, 'Well, Sir, I got a pain in my shoulder and in my leg, I'm shitting water and can't hold any food down. The sores on my legs and arms are driving me crazy.'

It turns out that he had been shot twice but had stayed in the lines until his squadron had finished the fight. Then, he did not want to complain and kept on going until he could not use his right arm and so couldn't use his rifle. That is the calibre of the men here, mates.

You know how we used to go shooting and put our rifle away. Well, here we sleep with it, eat with it. When you go for a dip in the sea, you don't feel naked because you haven't got any clothes on, it's because you haven't got your rifle. That and the bayonet are your best friend here. Men spend their free time cleaning their rifle and sharpening their bayonet. We played two up yesterday, I won some money. The men here don't stay down for long. There's always a joker to make you laugh. One or two have been sent to hospital with nerves, and now it's cold there is a lot of frost bite. but mostly it's cause they're worn out.

It's a different world here and I can't wait to get home. The socks the Missus sent are coming in handy. If you can see your way clear to it, I'd appreciate a sheepskin coat. Put plenty of wool fat on the outside to waterproof it.

I have run out of paper so will say goodbye now,

Your mate and brother,

Jack.

Mulga Plains
Via Bourke
1st December 1915

Dear Jack,

We finally got another letter. It sounds exciting but as you say, very tough. What was it like shooting at other men? It sounds like you have to have eyes in the back of your head with all those bombs and snipers. The smell must be terrible with all those dead bodies around. Where do you sleep and eat? It sounds as though you are living out in the bush. The newspapers are reporting stories of the fight over there. They said about a bloke called Simpson with his donkey who rescued about forty blokes before he got it. The reporters are saying that the country there is very steep and rough. Not flat like at home.

There was a piece in September about the 8th and 10th Light Horse who got it bad in a battle, it must have been terrible.

I hope you are all right and not too hard done by.

Charlie has a new horse. He broke it in not long ago and it's a cranky begger. Bite you as soon as it looks at you. But for Charlie, this horse is like a lamb. I don't know what it is but Charlie certainly has a way with horses.

Well, must leave off now. Hoping you are safe and well,

Your mates,
Matty and Sammy.

Gallipoli
10th December 1915

Dear mates,

Well, I know what hell is now. It's here. The flies are not so bad now, but that is only because it is getting cold. It snows here. The food is not fit to feed to a dingo, he would spit it out. But it's the men who would make you cry. They are shipping the sick ones out every day, twenty, thirty, forty. Everyone is covered in lice and have the Barcoo Rot. That's not too bad, it's the Gallipoli trots that's putting them down. Frost bite is the next thing to get us. I don't care about any of it. I am sitting here in a trench with dead men, and I look at them. Yesterday they were joking about my not ever having had a girl. Now they are blown apart or, like Dick, look as though they have closed their eyes to sleep. Except for the bullet in his brain. They were my mates and I can't leave them. The CO told me to go down to the beach this morning because I got a bit of a scratch, but I told him where to go. I'll probably be charged but like I said, I don't care. Two of my mates are out in no man's land. It's about forty yards across, and I can hear them calling. We got into a stash last night and they didn't make it back. Me and Chris are going out for them tonight if they are still alive. We've had no food today and water is scarce. The men are too weak to bring it up the hill. Hill, I should say cliff. It is so steep, even a goat would have trouble.

It was all right when we were fit, but not now. The lieutenant has been a chum. He stayed with us. It's going to get a whole lot colder. What I wouldn't give for a couple of skin coats. We will try to bury our mates soon, I don't know where. They are just laying out there, falling apart, just like Dusty did. It's cruel to watch. There are so many missing, so many we can't bury.

Tomorrow we will go down to the beach, another regiment will come into the trenches. I expect we will be back to digging dugouts. One rumour says the Germans are on their way but then another furphy reckons we're getting off this hellhole. I can't even begin to imagine what it will be like to leave our mates here, some aren't even buried. It will be harder for the blokes who have been here from the start.

The men of my troop celebrated my eighteenth yesterday. They saved their issue of rum for a few days in a water bottle and passed it around last night. They're a good mob. Bluey found a spare tin of jam and some bread. Bluey is good at finding things. One of our officers stopped in and wished me happy birthday. He made a joke about how in one more year I would be enlistment age. The fellows offered him a sip from the water bottle, but he said no, enjoy it yourselves and winked. We are lucky to have some good men as our officers. Some of the others, we hear, are real dolts.

I can only write this because one of the men in my regiment found a diary on a dead man and shared out the blank pages. I have torn mine in half, so as to send another letter later, so I'm sorry about the small writing.

Still no more mail, I miss everyone back there and long to lay at the water hole on a summer's day. It would be so quiet. Hello, here are some blokes, they have bought up some rations and more ammo. They're done in from the climb.

Better leave off,

Your mate and brother,
Jack.

Mulga Plains
Via Bourke
2nd January 1916

Dear Jack,

Father has been asked to supply beef for the war effort and we will be taking the bullocks to Bourke. It should liven us up.

Sammy and I have been out mustering with the stockmen and we have about one hundred and fifty bullocks, so far. Father is drafting out the ones we will take to Bourke.

Sammy, Charlie, Ernie and I are to take them. Mother and Father are going to a wedding down near Wanaaring. Father said he owes it to Mother to go and so, we are to be entrusted with taking the cattle to Bourke. Jim is staying to look after the place.

I am hoping that if we don't hear from you before we go, we might meet the mail man along the way.

It will take us about two weeks to get to Bourke. Sammy can't wait to see the trains again. Ernie and Charlie have seen it all before and reckon town is nothing much.

We had a little rain again. It should freshen the feed a little along the track.

Cedar is as fit as a fiddle and jumping out of her skin. The ride to Bourke should settle her down. Sammy is going to ride Nugget. It will do the horse good as he has had it fairly easy since you left. We are taking a plant of about fifteen horses and Father has said to sell most of them in Bourke to Micky's man.

Your last letter said you were back in Egypt. I hope you are going well. Till next time.

Your mate,
Matty

Mulga Plains
Via Bourke
15th February 1916

Dear Jack,

I have calmed down enough to sit and write to you. I am sorry to say that Matty has let us all down badly by running away to join up. He went, knowing how much distress it would cause his mother and me. Sammy and the boys are very upset. They were afraid that I would hold them responsible, but my son has a mind of his own and the fault was not theirs. It has been everything I can do to get through to Sammy that he is not responsible.

They took the cattle to Bourke and on the morning that they left, about five miles out, Matty told the boys that he would ride back into Bourke for a few last things. He told them to wait for him at the bore. Sammy didn't like this and said so, but Matty was insistent that he would catch up. After riding awhile, Sammy became positive that Matty was up to something and asked the others to turn back. They rode into Bourke and could not find him or Cedar. Sammy showed some initiative and went to the bank. When they tried to tell him to leave, he stood his ground until the manager came. Sammy then asked the manager if Matty had been there and why. The manager told him that Matty had been in and deposited a cheque to my account that morning. He had also drawn some money out of the account that I set up for him when he was born.

Guessing Matty's intentions, Sammy then went to the railway station. The men there told him that a young man had loaded a chestnut mare with the remount horses and boarded the train. He then asked the men to ring ahead to the next station to get a message to Matty. Unfortunately, the men laughed at him and told him to get lost.

As you can imagine, I was livid when I heard this and since have made a complaint to the railway manager.

Sammy then went to the police station and asked the policeman to telephone us. I had taken Eliza to the wedding at Wanaaring. Tan came along with us for the outing. We were on our way home. Poor Sammy did not know what to do when he could not contact me. If Matty had ridden away from Bourke, the boys could have tracked him down, but the cunning little beggar knew this and hence the train. The boys were at their wits end and I dare say extremely nervous about telling me the news. They rode home in all haste and got in the day after we had returned.

As you can imagine, the Missus was beside herself and I feared she would collapse. The gins came and looked after her, while I tried to track Matty down. I rang all the stations along the line but he must have got off at Dubbo and rode to wherever he was headed.

I have written numerous letters to the Army for them to keep an eye out for him, but I don't know if this will do much good.

I do not blame you in anyway, Jack. I understand your reasons for going. If you can do anything from your end, I would appreciate it very much.

I have been following the events of the Light Horse closely and it seems, by all accounts, the Anzacs have done well. We are very proud of you and hope that you come through safe.

Please write to us if you have any news and write to Sammy. He is adrift without the two of you and is still blaming himself.

Sincerely,
Thomas Watson.

FOURTEEN

'Boss?' said Sammy, as he stood, hat in hand beside Thomas.

Thomas jumped, startled. He looked up from his papers that he had been searching through, looking for news of the war.

'Sammy,' he breathed. 'I didn't hear you come up.'

'Sorry, Boss.'

'What's up, young fellow?'

Sammy stared at the worn dusty hat in his clenched fingers. Without looking up, he said slowly, 'I bin talking to Uncle and he said I could join up.'

Thomas sat straighter and his shoulders stiffened. A frown wrinkled his forehead as he stared at the lanky boy in front of him. Crossing his leg over the other, he asked gently, 'What brought this on? I remember you saying that you didn't want to be a soldier.'

The words tumbled out. 'I know that, Boss. That was different. This army, it different to the old ways. I bin reading about the war in the papers. They need more fellas to help out over there. Maybe they take us now. No worries about me, I fit, strong, can ride and shoot. It not right I stay here, with Jack and Matty over there doin' somethin'.'

Stroking his chin, Thomas thought several things in succession: this is the longest speech I've ever heard from Sammy; if the boy wanted to go, he deserved to be helped; he did not lack courage. Indeed, it had taken a lot for him to come to me, knowing how angry I had been with Matty.

'Sammy, I'll take you to Bourke myself. I'll pay your way to Brisbane. I noticed an article saying that Brisbane has been enlisting Blacks, so I reckon you'll get fair treatment there.'

Breathing a sigh of relief, Sammy smiled. 'Yeh, Boss. But you don't have to take me.'

'You let me worry about that. I'll see at least one member of this station off to the war,' Thomas said. 'Now promise me three things. I'll give you extra money so that if you run into trouble, you can come straight home. You'll keep that money for that purpose, all right? Next, no women and no grog. In the army, there will be lots of that, and it will do you no good. You wait till you get home and marry your girl, right?'

'Yeh, Boss,' agreed Sammy, nodding his head vigorously.

'Last, be proud of yourself. You are a good boy… no, you're a man now. Don't let anyone tell you you're not. If I'd had the chance, I would have said the same to the other two boys, just so as you know.' Thomas added, as he pushed back his chair and stood up. 'You go and say goodbye to your people. I'll meet you in the morning at the river. Tell Charlie, Jim and Uncle that they can come with us. We'll take the wagon, it's nearly time to go for supplies.'

* * * *

Sammy leant out over the ship's rails, watching the throng of people on the dock as they waved and cheered at the departing ship.

A slap on the back made him turn. Blue eyes set in a sun-browned face looked at him.

'Well, we're soldiers now, off to do our bit, eh, Sammy?'

'Yeh, no worries about it, mate,' he replied. 'We goin' to France.'

A fleeting look of sadness crossed Sammy's face, and his mate picked up on it.

'I know you wanted to join the Light Horse to be with your mates, but we needed you more,' Dave said, trying to cheer him up.

Sammy had already become popular in his company. He never complained and was always quick with a smile. Mostly he was quiet, but when the men persuaded him to talk, he told them funny stories about what happened at Mulga Plains. The men in his Battalion had gained further respect when Sammy quietly took the harassment of a sergeant. Day after day, the Sarge had needled and derided Sammy about being a lazy black, good for nothing.

After a month of watching Sammy go about the menial tasks that the sergeant made up for him, the men in his company had had enough. One night, four men jumped the sergeant, who was on the way back to camp from the pub in town. Putting a bag over his head, they punched him repeatedly, all the time, telling him what a pathetic bastard he was to pick on such a good kid as Sammy.

The next morning at parade, the sergeant, obviously worse for wear, made a short speech about cowards and how he would find out who they were. Then he would give it to them.

A battalion boxing match was announced, and when the men found out that Sammy had had boxing lessons with his mates on the station, they gave him a few practice rounds. After watching Sammy spar, the men of his company got together and pooled all their money to make a bet on him.

Rank did not matter once in the ring, and Sammy came up against a few men until finally it was down to the hated Sarge.

The men were beside themselves, yelling instructions to Sammy and jeering his opponent. No matter what the big man did, he could not land a punch on Sammy. The boy from the outback danced around the canvas, laying in hard punches to the man's stomach and chest, at will.

Finally, the other man snapped, and with a roar, he came at Sammy with his arms open wide, intending to get him in a bear hug. Sammy suddenly stood still, but the Sarge, with blinding rage, did not stop. Drawing up his fist, Sammy delivered an uppercut to his opponent's chin. The big man's head snapped back and he fell to the floor, stunned.

The men went wild and lost no time in gathering in their winnings. They hoisted Sammy on their shoulders and paraded him around the ring.

The Sarge got to his feet, shaking his head. He stared at the boy he hated so much.

'Put that nigger down,' he roared. 'I'm gonna strip his fuckin' black hide offa him.'

The men put Sammy down behind them and stood, shoulder to shoulder.

Dave spoke up. 'He beat you fair an' square, Sarge. Leave him be.'

A captain, who had been watching, decided things had gone far enough and stepped in. The end result was the sergeant had been transferred to who cared where. The Army wanted men who could lead, and 'A' company had a boxing champion.

The boat ride was long and boring. The army devised training programs to keep the men fit, gave concerts and practised drill on the decks. Sammy learnt to play cards. When the men found out that he was educated and could speak French, they nicknamed him Darky. As one soldier had said, he's a dark horse in more than his colour. The name stuck and Sammy realised it was a compliment, in a funny sort of way. After passing Suez, the men disembarked at Alexandria and marched to Tel El Kebir. The sights and sounds of Egypt fascinated Sammy. He wrote to the Boss and told him what he had seen, asking that the Boss pass this on to his people. After a few weeks and an inoculation, the battalion continued on its way. They watched the shores of Mediterranean countries pass by and landed in Marseilles in July.

The first night was spent in dirty billets which they were glad to leave the next morning. They marched in high spirits to the railway station, where they found themselves loaded into horse boxes, forty men to a box. The trip was slow, thirty hours before they reached Bailleul. From here, they marched to Ootersteene, singing and smoking along the way. They stood about in the streets of the town, as they waited for their officers to sort out their billets. Some men scouted around, looking for the estaminets that served wine, beer and coffee. Young women came along, selling cups of hot coffee and cakes. The girls proved of more interest than the food. Eventually, with the billets allotted, the men fell into their blankets, thankful for a night's rest.

After leaving Ootersteene, the men marched, singing and calling out to the civilians they passed. Arriving in the town of Armentieres, the soldiers stared about at the damage the German shelling had done. Some of the men spent their free time in the estaminets, sampling the wine and beer in great quantities. Sammy walked through the streets, the smell of baking bread, sausages hanging in shop windows and varieties of cheeses assailing him. He stepped into a shop that had laces in the window. Standing at the counter, sorting through some fine white lace, stood a young woman, her hair pulled back tightly into a bun. She looked up as the door opened, saying tartly as she saw Sammy staring around the shop, 'Bonjour monsieur, que puis-je pour vous?'

Taking off his hat, he turned to her, his shy smile working for him. The young lady smiled back. Pointing to a beautifully worked lace shawl, he said hesitantly, 'Bonjour madamoiselle, ah… je voudrais acheter… de la dentelle pour la femme… ah… de mon patron.'

A look of amazement spread across her face and she looked Sammy up and down. Realising she was being rude, the woman made her way to a row of shelving and took great pains to show him the shawls in her shop, bringing him several different ones. Sammy chose one for Eliza. He asked to be shown some lace that might be added to a dress and once again, the young woman obliged. Sammy rewarded her kindness by buying quantities of both, and an elaborately embroidered postcard.

Completing his purchase, Sammy asked. 'Est-ce que vous pourriez les emballer? Ils… doivent… aller en Australie.'

She nodded and reaching for thick brown paper and string, the French woman wrapped his goods carefully.

'Quelque chose d'autre pour monsieur?'

He shook his head. 'No, merci. C'est tout. Merci beaucoup.'

'De rien. A votre service.'

Sammy placed his hat back on his head and left, his parcel under his arm. He took his treasures back to his billet and carefully wrote on the postcard.

France

Dear Boss and Missus,

I am well. The parcel is for Missus. I'll send more things later for everyone. I have had no mail. Could you pass my details to Jack and Matty, please?

Sincerely yours,
Sammy.

The battalion marched to Moolenacker, passing through country that was green and flush with spring. The people came out to greet them, waving and cheering. Sammy was in demand to translate, others made do with hand signals, which caused much merriment among old men, women, young boys and girls. The soldiers gratefully accepted offerings of wine and cheese, fresh baked bread, and noticed the lack of men. They reached their destination and began the intensive training that would prepare them for battle with the Germans.

Some of the company went for bomb training, others sniping and reconnaissance. All learnt about using gas respirators and care of the feet. The steel 'Brodie' helmets were issued, reminding them that their peaceful time would soon end. They were close enough to the battlefield to hear the guns in the distance and at night, the sky was never dark, but lit with flashes from the shells and Verey lights. Their section received passes for the night. As the men tidied themselves for a visit to town, Sammy sat at a window, looking out at the fields, alone.

'Come on, Darky. Get ready,' Dave called to him.

Shaking his head, Sammy continued to watch the fields.

Walking over to the table where Sammy sat, Dave pulled out a chair and sat down opposite Sammy.

'Hey, mate, what's up?'

Sammy looked straight at Dave. 'The Boss, he made me promise no girls, no grog. The Boss, he's been good to me. I learnt to read an' write on the verandah school with Matty an' Jack. He gave me a gun at Christmas.'

A smile came on Dave's lips. 'We don't have to tell the Boss anything.'

'No,' came the adamant reply. 'I make a promise. The Boss, he don't have to be good to me. Some blacks, they live on missions. We have a very good life on the station. The boys, they're my mates.'

Nodding his head, Dave stepped up to Sammy and put out his hand. 'Darky, you're a rare one. A man of his word. Shake on it, mate. I didn't mean to offend.'

The cheeky smile of Sammy's broke the tension as he replied, 'That all right, mate. I won't tell your wife, eh?'

'You could still come with us. There is no reason why not. There won't be any girls, not like you think, anyway.'

'Maybe other time, Dave,' Sammy replied. 'I want to write home.'

Dave gave up and when the men were ready, they left the billet, laughing and joking in expectation of a good time.

Training came to an end, when they were ordered to march to the front line. They were to relieve a British battalion that had been in the trenches for eight days. The Tommies stumbled out, hungry and worn. They had not had supplies sent up for days and the Australians gave them what they could of their own rations. Sammy's company moved into the trench and began to repair the damage. There was never any rest. If the men of the platoon were not in the trenches, then they were carrying to and from. One time it might be barbed wire for fortifications, next it might be food. Duckboards had to be laid to allow movement in the trenches, while sometimes the men were assigned to burial parties. The burial parties horrified the men unaccustomed to violent death. They soon became used to it. Some corpses had been lying out in no-man's land for weeks, a shell having buried them and then another shell turning them up. Others were fresher, but still, their wounds made them a sight that lived with the men and filled their dreams. Sometimes there was no time to bury the bodies. They lay where they were, on the parapet, in the trenches, and out in the wasteland between the two enemies.

Trench life became their only world. The dugouts in the trenches often flooded, due to the marshy ground. The soldiers fell asleep leaning against the parapets. When they did lie down, rats the size of cats, chewed at their leather belts. Often, they would extinguish the light and wait in a circle. When the scrabbling of the rats could be heard, a cry of go, would sound and the light would be turned on. The men would thump the rats to death with their entrenching tool or spear them with their bayonets.

During the day, everyone kept their heads down but at night the activity started. Sammy's native abilities were soon realised. Often picked for reconnaissance into no-man's land, his uncanny sense of direction and ability to melt into the landscapes made him an ideal scout. Night after night, the men went out into the wasteland to repair the wire and listen for enemy movements. They would tumble back into the trenches, tired and desperate for sleep, only to be woken an hour before dawn for the Stand to. This was when the danger of an attack by the Germans was the greatest, and every man stood on the fire step. Both sides let loose bombs and rifle fire. It became a daily ritual and intensified the tension of those early dark mornings.

The stretch of land between the enemy and themselves was a wasteland of wire, bodies and mud. At night, the Verey lights made shadows that moved, and men's nerves strung tight as their eyes searched every shadow and shell hole for signs of enemy raiders.

It was the bombs and the shelling that caused the men the most fear. When they exploded, the noise was deafening, and sent out concussion waves. Shrapnel flew everywhere and there was never a silence, only a roar that sometimes was low and at other times, a mind-numbing cacophony of screaming, booming and blasting.

Some men's nerves gave out; they became shivering wrecks. Their eyes rolled back in their heads and froth formed at their mouths. They could not talk and often screamed in terror. The medics removed them quickly from the frontlines, fearing the effect that they would have on the other men. The soldiers pitied these men but did not pity the ones that sheltered in the trenches, instead of standing to, the ones that found other jobs to do in the communication trenches, when enemy barrages were put over. These men were cowards and reviled by the frontline soldiers; no time was spared on them. The original platoon had dwindled; some dead, some wounded and evacuated. New reinforcements coming into the line took some time to get used to the daily grind, the constant bombardment of noise and the wet.

The captain appeared around the corner of the trench, a folded piece of paper in his hand.

'The telephone lines are out again. The poor buggers are trying to get them hooked up. The only runner I've got at the moment is knackered. I need one of you blokes to get this to the rear,' he said, holding the paper forward.

Sammy reached out and took the message. He nodded at his mates as they called out their various orders for beer, eggs and chips, or women. Smiling, he made way along the trenches, relying on memory to guide him through the maze. Coming to an area where the trenches were impassable, he climbed up onto their edge, finding wooden duckboards and ran, bullets thumping around him. Keeping one eye on the condition of the trenches, he jumped into the first that appeared to be good going and continued on his way. He breathed easier when he left the trenches behind, although artillery fire still fell this far behind the lines.

He heard the whine of a shell and ducked behind the wall of a war-torn farmhouse. The bomb exploded thirty yards away and judging it safe, Sammy turned to continue on his way. His foot kicked a grotesque mound of matted fur and flesh. As he pulled his boot away, he realised that the mound was a dog surrounded by her pups. He, a man accustomed to the sight of death, gagged violently and was about to leave when he heard a whimper. Turning the dog over with the barrel of his rifle, Sammy stared down at a shivering pup, the lone survivor. The mother had taken refuge in the nearest thing to shelter she could find, only to have the Hun's bomb take her life and all but one of her pups.

Bundling the pup into his shirt, under his tattered greatcoat, he made his way to the supply lines. The going was hazardous, as the shelling and the rain had reduced the countryside to a treacherous lake of grey mud. It stank from the corpses of men and animals that lay across it, slowly sinking into the quagmire. He stepped carefully around the horses that had bogged down in the mud, huge rats gnawing at their flesh. Men ploughed their way through, bent on the horrendous task of retrieving and trying to identify the remains of dead soldiers. Whenever Sammy came across a fallen horse that had managed to linger, he would put it out of its misery with a bullet to the forehead, not letting it wait for the vets; they had their hands full. A crime, if he was caught doing it by an officer.

After he had delivered his message from the front line and scrounged some food for the pup from the field kitchen, Sammy made his way back by the same dangerous route, to his company's position in the trenches. Finding some of the men in the dugout, he entered quietly, sitting on an ammunition box. Dave noticed a bulge under Sammy's coat.

'How's that? Darky's brought us a surprise!'

Sammy slowly looked around at each man, waiting until he had everyone's attention, then with a serious look on his face, he reached down into his coat and lifted up the pup for all to see.

'Stone the crows,' Harry yelled. 'Where the hell did you find that?'

The men crowded around, reaching out to touch the small tan and white bundle with its eyes staring about, little whimpers coming from it, a small token of innocence in a place totally surrounded by suffering and death.

After telling them how he found it Sammy, placed the pup back against his heart. The pup settled down and slept.

Dave asked, 'What are you going to call it?'

Reaching down to stroke the pup's ears, Sammy looked thoughtful. 'I never name a dog before. The Boss always name them.' He stared at the pup some more. 'It sleeps like a Joey in a pouch, how 'bout Bandaarr?'

It took the pup, which the men judged to be about six weeks old, only a few days to work out which men would give him some of their rations, and which would sit patting him. His name quickly became shortened to Bandy, and although he was friendly with everyone, it was Sammy that he slept with.

The company spent three days in the reserve trenches, then a few more in support. When he wasn't detailed to a work party, Sammy began teaching the pup its name, and to stay and come when called.

Finally, the company was sent to the rear, supposedly for a rest, but training and work parties took up most of their time. Bandy grew quickly, learning who was in his platoon then his company. Dave teased Sammy about the time he spent with the pup, but Sammy shrugged and continued to teach the dog new commands.

Sitting beside an old garden wall, out of the chill wind, Dave watched Sammy with Bandy and was amazed to see what Sammy had taught him. Sammy would tell the dog to stop and as Sammy walked away, disappearing around some buildings and returning five minutes later from a different direction, Bandy would still be sitting there, not moving, except for his ears, pricked for the sound of Sammy's voice. Then Sammy would tell the dog to go to another man, calling the man by name. Bandy would run up to the soldier, sit in front of him and then run back to Sammy.

The days grew longer and spring came to the front. By now, Bandy could carry messages between the men and would growl softly at anyone that came near their belongings. His form was maturing into what he would become, and the men passed the time arguing about what breed of dog he was.

Dave talked Sammy into accompanying them to an estaminet for a feed of eggs and chips. He promised that he wouldn't offer him grog, or anything else that would break his promise to the Boss.

The men cheered when Sammy entered, ducking under the low door.

''Bout time, Darky! And here's Bandy,' Harry called. He held out a chip for the dog, who sniffed it carefully, then dispatched the morsel, looking for more. Not many could resist his liquid brown eyes; Bandy was soon full.

The debate arose again as to his breeding. Sammy noticed an old lady, dressed in black, sitting on a stool near the fire. It seemed that her job was to keep the fire stoked, and an eye on the pot of stew that hung from the trivet.

Sammy tried to catch her eye but failed.

'Excusez-moi, madame,' he called.

The old woman looked in surprise at Sammy. 'Dis-moi, mon brave?'

He gestured at the dog that now lay at his feet. 'Ahhh... Est-ce que pouvez me dire de quelle… ah… race est ce chien?'

Rising slowly from her stool, she shuffled over to Sammy's table and peered down at the dog, her rheumy eyes squinting.

'Eh ben. Je dirais *un epagneul de Bretagne*. On avait les mêmes chiens au château ou je travaillais quand j'étais jeune.'

She looked back at Sammy to see if this was all he wanted.

'Merci beaucoup, madame,' he said, as she made her way back to her stool, shaking her head at the strangeness of these Australians.

Turning back to the men, he asked them all to name their guesses, as to which breed of dog that Bandy might be.

'How much dosh on this?' he asked.

Harry laughed. 'Well, it's not like us not to have a bet now is it, eh?' He consulted a small notebook that he took from his pocket. 'About twenty quid.'

Dave whistled. 'Looks like the winner shouts for the next week!'

Grinning mischievously, Sammy glanced around at the men, drawing out the moment.

'You all off the hook, nobody guessed right.'

The men all spoke at once, wanting to know the answer.

'Bandy's a Brittany Spaniel,' Sammy answered.

'Never heard of one of them,' Kenny said.

FIFTEEN

Jack paused a moment, wiped his forehead with the sleeve of his shirt. He bent again, shifting the weight of the horse's hoof higher up on his thigh. Taking the hoof pick up again, he scraped out the mixture of sand and manure that was imbedded in the hoof, then loosened his grip on the horse's leg, letting it return to the ground. Straightening up, he turned and gave the horse a pat on the rump.

'You're not a bad old nag, are you, Absent?' he said.

The horse flicked one ear back, while it munched contentedly on the grain in the nosebag that hung from its halter.

Looking down at the half-grown pup lying in the shade of the horse, Jack said, 'What about you, China? Are you a good pup?'

The young dog raised his head, one ear folded over as he pricked his ears on hearing his name.

Bending down, Jack ruffled the black fur that grew longer each day. China rolled over, his legs in the air, silently begging for a rub on his stomach.

'You're a con artist, aren't you? Just like that kid I got you from.'

Jack put the pick away in the horseshoe bag attached to the saddle. Breakfast would be ready soon and he still had the manure to remove from his line of horses. Some men hated stables, but Jack found it a time for doing a job that made him feel useful.

Since they had returned from Gallipoli, it seemed pointless to ride drill and parade. They had had the hard fight and now they were waiting around in camp, back in Egypt. Rumours had it that they would be off to France next, but then again, the word was that the Turks would try to seize the Suez Canal. The 1st Brigade had not had three days' rest before they were mounted and off into the desert.

As he reached for the rake, Chris came sauntering past and stopped when he saw Jack.

'You know how you put the word around to keep an eye out for a young fellow on a chestnut horse? Well, Freddy saw another one just now,' he said casually, waiting for the reaction. He was disappointed.

Thomas's letter had been waiting for Jack when he landed off the ship from Gallipoli. After reading it, Jack had stormed around for days, looking for Matty. The men of the regiment had helped him out, keeping an eye out for a chestnut horse with four white stockings and a blaze. Jack guessed that Matty would insist on bringing Cedar if he enlisted in the Light Horse. Thomas had sent another letter, telling Jack that their search in Australia had turned up no news, repeating his request for Jack to keep at look out.

Turning to Chris, Jack said, 'It won't be him. Even though you boys have been cobbers, helpin' me in my search, I'm slowly givin' up hope. He's probably been sent to France.'

'Oh, well, he may turn up eventually,' he replied, saddened by Jack's disappointment.

Chris waited until Jack finished in the horse lines. Together, they walked over to the other men who were gathering for breakfast. China got up and stretched, then shook the sand from his coat. He followed behind, sniffing at the ground as he went. The two men sat down on the sand; leaning against their saddles, they drank their mugs of tea. Already the day was hot; it was not yet seven o'clock and sweat stained their new uniforms. Their tattered uniforms had been replaced, and the fresh food that they were now receiving had done a lot to improve their health. They appeared different men from the ones that left Anzac. Their cheeks were still a little hollow, the Barcoo sores still lingered here and there, but most of the men were improving rapidly.

Coming back to their horses helped the men put the sadness of leaving Gallipoli behind them. The horses gave them something to concentrate on, a familiar friend. Back to regular meals and routine. It was a sharp contrast to what had gone before.

Gradually the talk of Gallipoli faded, but it lingered in their thoughts, in their dreams. It still angered them that they left so many men behind; not a few of them felt that they had stolen away in the night, like thieves. Oh, it had been loudly applauded, that the evacuation had been a tremendous success. The men were chuffed that no losses had occurred when it had been well expected that the evacuation could cause up to forty per cent casualties.

No, it was when they walked silently past the graves, each of them saying a last goodbye to the soldiers who had fought and died in this back of beyond battlefield, that they felt a sense of betrayal, of remorse. It was their mates that lay in that rugged windswept piece of land, and their mate's bravery had been for what? As they walked quietly past in single file, each man looked down at those graves and wondered why in heaven had they been given such an impossible task.

The hardship they took in their stride. So long as they were still breathing, they considered themselves lucky.

They remembered the laughter: Bobby putting his fingers through his sock, it was so rotten. He turned that sock into a puppet and made ribald comments about what the commanders could do with their plans. When Bluey helped himself to a bag of flour at the stores, while Snowy kept the quarter master sergeant busy, the bugger lugged it all the way up the hill, only to trip, ending up looking like a ghost. He shed white dust for days.

It was the good memories that the men stored away, the lid to be lifted on these treasures, only when there was time to reflect.

Here and now – the desert was a different theatre; one they could understand.

'I hear Meredith is to be our CO,' Chris mused as they sat in front of their bell tent, drinking their tea. 'He did all right, back there.'

'He'll whip the new chums into shape pretty quickly. We're supposed to be getting a new batch tomorrow, so says Mr—' Jack stopped as his breath caught in his throat.

He rose slowly to his feet, gazing along the lines of tents. He threw his cup down in the sand and in long strides, headed towards a group of riders approaching the lines.

His mates quickly glanced at each other. Guessing something was on, they sprang up. Following his line of sight, they saw what had taken his interest.

A squadron of mounted men was riding towards them, among them, an attractive chestnut horse with four white stockings, prancing and pulling at the bit. Its young rider sat calmly in the saddle, chatting to the soldier on his offside.

A roar from Jack attracted the young soldier's attention, a look of joy lighting up his face.

Jack pushed through the horses, making them shy away. The NCO of the troop called to him, the call turning to a yell as Jack grabbed the soldier's arm, pulling him from the saddle. Astonishment replaced the joy on the soldier's face. Struggling to regain his feet, he winced as Jack's fingers dug into his shoulders.

'I flamin' told you to stay home, you idiot. I told you it wasn't bloody worth it,' Jack shouted into Matty's face. 'You've hurt your parents, no end, you spoilt little shit. I told you—'

He got no further. Soldiers from the squadron jumped from their horses, wrestling Jack away. More noise ensued when Jack's mates entered the fray. The pup had followed Jack and now jumped about, barking excitedly.

'What the hell is going on here? Stand away!' a voice demanded. The owner of the voice pushed his horse in amongst the men, who fell back, leaving Jack and Matty facing each other, both breathing heavily.

The men of Matty's troop stood waiting, curious as to why Jack had attacked Matty. He had told them all how anxious he was to find Jack.

Looking up at the horse now nearly on top of him, Jack stood to attention.

'I repeat, Henderson, what is going on?' Captain Brown asked, not so loudly this time.

Ignoring Matty, Jack spoke straight at the officer.

'This, sir, is my mate I grew up with. My little brother, you might say,' Jack replied. 'I told him not to join up until, well, I told him not to come, but he did. I was angry, sir. He's upset his parents badly.'

'All right, men, a family squabble, we'll call it. Now, back to what you were doing. Except you two. I want a word with both of you,' the captain said, pointing at Jack and Matty.

Matty's sergeant called to the captain. 'Sir, what do you want to do about this?' he asked.

The captain looked down at Jack. He saw a seasoned soldier, a boy who had become a man at Gallipoli; his eyes still carried the shadows. He felt the anger in him and understood it. If he had had a brother, he would have cautioned him against coming, after what they had been through at Anzac.

He then turned to Matty, noticing the bewilderment and hurt on his face. This was still a boy, innocent and fresh. The captain wondered if he was underage. *More than likely,* he thought, given Jack's reaction. Well, if the army had enlisted him, and the parents hadn't objected, it was done.

'I think we will let it pass, as I said, a family argument. Now, get about your business,' he replied before turning his horse and leaving the small group.

'You two will have plenty of time to catch up later. Go and put your horse away,' demanded the sergeant. He turned to Jack. 'Henderson, is it?'

'Yeah, Sarge.'

'Are you with the 12th?'

'Yeah, that's us over there.' Jack pointed towards the tents and horse lines of his regiment.

'Well, we're your reinforcements, so you'll have no worries about keeping an eye on your mate, will you?' the Sarge said with a smile. 'Mind you, he has been a good recruit. Eager, a little too eager sometimes. He has not stopped talking about you.'

Jack brushed away a fly, then said slowly, 'Yeah, he's got lots to learn.'

He dipped his head to the Sarge as he left. As he watched Matty unsaddle Cedar at the lines, Jack wondered what the hell he was going to tell Thomas in his next letter.

The new reinforcements were mingling with the seasoned soldiers, introductions being made. The soldiers settled down to morning routine duty, Jack staying away from Matty until he calmed down. He caught up with him as they broke for the midday meal, the pup at his heels.

'Have you wrote to the Boss?' he asked.

Matty stared at Jack. This was not the boy who had left Mulga Plains. This man was nearly a stranger. There were lines of weariness about his face and he had grown another inch. His eyes had always been guarded, but now they were impenetrable and cold. Matty felt unnerved by it. There was a suggestion of laziness in Jack's stance, his movements relaxed and slow.

'What did you mean by havin' a go at me like that?' he asked, then added, 'Yes, I wrote to them when we left Fremantle. I told them I'd joined up and got put in the 12th so I could find you.'

'Have you had a letter from your father yet? You've got a lot of apologisin' to do,' Jack replied, getting angry again. 'And how the hell do you think Sammy feels? I don't know, Matty. You always think of you. Sometimes you're the best mate ever. Then other times you're a spoilt little shit.'

Matty winced at these words. They stung deeply coming from Jack. He couldn't speak, he just stared, his hurt in his eyes.

Realising how his words had cut Matty, Jack's voice softened. 'I don't know, Shorty. Maybe it's because your mother was too clingy. You'll have to grow up here. You got to look out for your mates, not think of yourself. After what I saw over there, war ain't what we thought it was. It's a dirty mean thing that eats away at you.'

'I had to come; don't you see? You and the others, over here, fightin' for us. I used to have these dreams that you were dyin' and I couldn't get to you,' Matty said quietly. 'I know I've hurt Mother. But I had to come. She would've cut up bad even if I was eighteen.'

'You'd better write to Sammy. Your father wrote to me, when you left. He said Sammy is pretty low, blames himself.'

Matty nodded. 'I'll do that first chance. The boys would have tried to stop me, that's why I caught the train.'

'So, how did you avoid the Boss?'

'I changed my last name when I enlisted. I did like you did. Got a woman to say she was my mother. I paid her,' Matty answered. 'I got off the train at Dubbo and rode to Sydney. Cedar nearly had a fit when I rode her past all the automobiles in the streets. She settled down pretty quick though.'

Matty looked up at Jack, his eyes searching his mates face. 'Don't you see, Jack? I had to come.'

'What name did you use?'

'Matty Thiri.'

Jack burst out laughing. 'And they believed you?'

'Well, the fella behind the desk looked at me strange and asked was I sure that was my name. It was all I could think of at the time. He asked me again if that was my name before he wrote it down. I think he spelt it a bit weird. Everyone has trouble sayin' it.'

'Poor Willie Wagtail, havin' you take his name. Well, we'll see the captain about getting your real name put on the books, eh?'

The laughter had softened Jack's anger and he wrapped his arms around Matty, giving him a slap on the back.

'It is good to see you, Shorty. Got a bit pissed off that you came, but glad you're here.'

Smiling up at Jack, Matty replied, 'Well, whatever happens, we're mates together again.'

'So, how'd you get Cedar over here?'

Matty's eyes crinkled, and he glanced over to where Cedar stood in the horse lines. She was nosing the horse beside her, squealing, getting acquainted.

'I got onto Micky. He had a mate in the remount section. He's always liked Cedar. I promised Micky a foal by Longman, one out of Dusty's sister, if he could make a deal that I was to draw her when we got over here. The foal would be as close in bloodlines as you could get to Cedar, so he came through.'

Jack shook his head. 'You'd better let Charlie know to put the mare to the stallion then.'

'He already has. You get that one, and Micky gets the next one,' he replied, smiling. He pointed at the pup. 'Where did you get the dog?'

'That's China. When we were in Lemnos on the way home from Anzac, I traded him from a kid.'

'Traded?'

Reaching down to pat China, Jack replied, 'The kid was a street kid, no food. He was carrying this little skinny pup around, trying to sell it, crying 'cause he said he didn't want to get rid of it. I gave the kid some money but said I didn't want the dog. He took the money, dumped the dog and bolted. I found out later he had got enough money out of the soldiers to last a month. He had a few different tricks. I was the only one that got caught with a dog.'

'So how come you kept it?'

'It followed me. No one would take it, so I thought, the other regiments have mascots, so this little fella could be ours. He was as skinny and rough-looking as what we looked like when we came off Gallipoli.'

'What's the Brass say about him?'

'Full of questions, ain't you?' Jack laughed. 'They don't mind so long as he's kept out of the way. He stays with the cooks on the wagons when we ride or when Big Brass is around.' Jerking his thumb towards the tents, he added, 'Come meet the boys. I'll show you the pup's tricks later.'

Jack led him over to the tents and introduced his troop to Matty. Tactical drill took up the greater part of the day, so it wasn't till later in the night that Matty got a chance to sit down and talk to Jack about Gallipoli. The new chums crowded around, eager to hear the first-hand accounts of the soldiers. The night grew chilly and at lights out, the men went to their tents.

At dawn, the horses moving restlessly in the horse lines woke Matty. He crawled out of the crowded tent where men still slept and snored. Going to his saddle in front of the tent, he drew out a notebook and pencil from his kit.

Egypt
2nd April 1916

Dear Sammy,

I am in Egypt. You needn't blame yourself, old mate, I had to come and there was no way anyone could stop me.

I thought Jack was going to punch my lights out when he first saw me, but he settled down.

I hope everything is going well back at the station and everyone is all right. I will write to Father and Mother. I bet the Boss was wild, but like I said, I had to do it.

The boat ride over was smooth and all but three of the horses made it. Cedar took it like a gem. We did stables in the morning then walked the horses around the deck for hours. This was so their legs didn't swell. When we offloaded, it took a few days for them to recover but after about seven days we just gave them some gentle work and they are coming along just fine.

The desert is just like home but no bush. Lots of sand and warm during the day. It gets cold overnight, though. It is spring here now and they say summer is very hot, so we will have to see how we go.

I am in the 12th Light Horse with Jack and there was some talk that the 12th would be sent to France. They sent some of the 4th instead, but that was back in February and it looks like the 12th will stay in Egypt. Please write back and tell me you forgive me for doing such a rum thing to a mate.

Your mate,

Matty.

Matty put the letter in an envelope, Jack's words ringing in his ears.

'I didn't mean to be selfish,' he said quietly to himself. 'I thought Sammy would understand. I knew Mother'd be upset, but then I was goin' when I turned eighteen anyway. I'll just have to prove to Jack I'm not selfish.'

A tap on the shoulder made him jump. Turning, he saw Jack with a mug of tea.

'Here, Shorty, get this into you. The camp'll be up in a minute and we're on stables.'

As Jack spoke, reveille sounded, men stumbling out of tents in all states of dress. Some headed for the latrines, while others did as Jack had done and went to cadge a cuppa from the cooks.

The day was filled with cleaning up the camp and drill, the men chaffed at the repetition and boredom. In the afternoon, they rode out into the desert, having a sham fight with the infantry. It proved a bit of an exercise when one squadron got lost in the dunes but eventually found their way back.

Matty had been to the staff tent to see the adjutant to have his name changed back to Watson. The captain had berated him for causing more paperwork, but as the recruitment office back in Sydney had passed Matty, probably knowing he was underage, he did not take it any further.

The next morning before breakfast, Jack saw Matty sitting in front of a blank sheet of paper. He squatted down beside his mate, flicking his cigarette away.

'You have to do it sometime, Matty.'

Matty nodded. 'I know. I just don't know how to start it.'

'Well, an apology to the Missus would be a good start,' said Jack, rising to his feet. 'Just start with Dear Mother and Father, then apologise.'

Taking the pencil up again, Matty began the hardest letter of his life.

Egypt
3rd April 1916

Dear Father and Mother,

I am in Egypt with Jack.

I am very sorry that I ran away like I did, but it was something that I had to do. I know that you would have tried to stop me and I couldn't bear to be at home when all our boys were over here doing the fighting for our country. I couldn't stand the dreams anymore.

Cedar came through the journey very well and Jack is mostly recovered from his time on Gallipoli. Jack was very angry when he saw me but he has settled down now. He has changed. From all the stories I have heard, our regiment did well over there.

I shall write again soon,

Please forgive me,

Your loving son,
Matty.

A weight fell from his shoulders as he placed the letter in an envelope and put it with Sammy's to hand in to the censor. He looked about him, taking in the lines of tents stretching across the desert. Behind him in the distance, rose the ancient buildings of Heliopolis. He felt the heat starting to rise and remembered the early summer mornings of home.

I've put myself in, this time, he thought. *I'll prove myself to Jack and Father.*

He rose and went to the horse lines. He started shovelling the manure that the horses had dropped during the night.

In the background, he heard the camp stir and soon Jack and the other men joined him in his work.

The news that greeted the men that day caused a stir in the ranks. They were to hand in their horses! They would be infantry! Again! The Turks had been raiding near the Suez Canal and the men were to march in two days.

Knowing that Matty was not going to like giving up Cedar, Jack had a quiet word to the farrier of the regiment.

Gareth was a small man, burnt brown from the sun, his pipe never out of his mouth. He knew every horse in the regiment and his eyes lit up when Jack explained his problem.

'No, you won't get her.' Jack laughed, as he saw Gareth's face. 'I just need you to put her out, lame.'

The man reared back, indignant. 'I don't bloody well do that. It's not allowed.'

'Be buggered you don't. I know how you got your present horse. A little matter of a stone jammed into the frog of the hoof. That's a fine horse for a farrier to be riding. Wasn't that horse drawn in the 8th's draft of horses?'

Gareth snorted and looked over to a bay horse, mostly thoroughbred, standing in the lines.

'The mug that drew him had no idea. Would have ruined a fine horse like that in a week.'

Jack let the man talk.

'He brought him to me 'cause their farrier was sick. So, I saved the horse, you might say.' The little man grinned.

'Well, I want you to save another horse. Follow? We don't know how long it'll be before we get horses again, but I need you to keep this mare in the 12th's draft of horses.'

Gareth looked slyly at Jack. 'What's it worth?'

'I'll decide that when we get back, see what condition she's in. But I'll make it worth your while.'

The farrier nodded his agreement and as Jack turned to leave, he said, 'Didn't anyone tell the little fool not to bring his horse? It belongs to the army now.'

Turning back, Jack replied, 'Yeah, he's got a lot to learn. This mare means everything to him. I'd like to see him keep her.'

'All right, mate. I'll do what I can.'

Returning to his squadron, Jack explained to Matty what he had done. Grateful, Matty thanked him and made his way to the horse lines. Brushing her, talking to her, he tried hard not to give way to the wrenching sadness he felt. When the mare nibbled at his pockets looking for a treat, tears crept into his eyes, and he brushed them away.

'You'll be right, girl. I'll be back in no time. That bloke, he said he'd look after you.'

Matty heard the order for the men to sort their kit out. He gave her one last pat, turned on his heel and went towards the tents, stopping for a second, when the mare nickered to him. He clenched his teeth and kept walking.

The men'll think I'm a sissy, getting upset over a horse, he thought. He ignored the impulse to go back for one last pat; instead, he went to pack his kit.

They marched to Tel-el-Kebir, the experience not welcomed by men used to riding horses. They crossed the Suez Canal to Kantara. The heat was more than most of the regiment had ever experienced. The mercury climbed, and they were ordered to remain in their tents as the temperature went over one hundred and thirty degrees. Work was carried out at night; the furnace of daylight, too much.

Word came that the Turks had attacked the Royal Scottish Fusiliers at Dueidar. The regiment was called out at two in the morning, marched the ten miles in the soft sand to relieve them. By ten am, men were straggling into Dueidar, desperate for shade, mates half-carrying, half-dragging each other.

In the searing heat, the regiment dug redoubts, stringing barbed wire around the edges, waiting for an attack that never came.

Billy, ever on the lookout for fun, organised a scorpion race. No one joined him in the hunt for these creatures, but most of the regiment, when they could steal a moment away, dropped in to have a bet.

Orders came to return to No. 2 Oasis camp. As every step of the march led them closer to their horses, the men of the 12th could feel their legs itching to be astride again.

Their squadron were to be mounted and ride guard on the railway and water pipeline that was making its way from Kantara to Katia. The men had had enough of being poor bloody infantry; stables were done with gusto, more than one horse getting a bit extra in their nosebags. The little brown farrier was dismayed at the news; he had already made plans for the chestnut mare. He walked away, mumbling foul sentences about officers and their orders.

The mail caught up with them and men read eagerly the news from home. Jack received only one letter.

Mulga Plains
Via Bourke
15th March 1916

Dear Jack,

Have you had any word from Matty? We just had a letter from him marked Fremantle saying he was in the 12th Light Horse. Sammy came to me and asked for permission to enlist. I let him go. He feels like he is not doing his bit. He wrote to us and told us that the Light Horse would not take him, so he joined the infantry. He thought that they were headed for Egypt.

The country is dry and we have had to cut mulga for the stock. Eliza is still very upset and has her bad days. If only Matty would write. If he is there, I won't insist that he come home. He made a decision that he will have to live by.

I know that you will let us know as soon as you can if you hear anything.

Yours sincerely,
Thomas Watson.

Showing the letter to Matty, Jack said, 'We'll have to send a telegram. Your letter will take too long. Stop 'em worryin'.'

'Sammy's enlisted!' Matty exclaimed. He looked at Jack. 'It's my fault, isn't it? If I'd have stayed, he wouldn't have gone. He didn't want to be a soldier.'

'Ah, who knows. Maybe given more time, you two would've gone together, anyway. But, what's done's done. Now, go see about that telegram.'

Lines of horse made their way into the barren landscape, each horse loaded with extra ammunition, three days rations for horse and rider, blanket, spare horseshoes, firewood, billy, mess tins, saddle and rider, a load that would become their daily burden, in the months to come. Now and then when a German plane was heard, the horses became restless, throwing their heads and prancing. They had learnt that these strange birds meant trouble.

China spent his days on the wagons, at night he stayed by Jack's side. Sitting around outside the tent with the men one evening, Jack showed Matty what he meant by China's tricks.

'Matty, get my water bottle off me saddle, will you, mate?'

Matty looked at him, raising his eyebrows.

'Humour me, mate,' Jack said.

Getting up, Matty walked over to the line of saddles and leant over Jack's. He had just touched the buckle on the strap holding the water bottle when a set of teeth grabbed his hand.

Springing back, shaking his hand, Matty swore at the growling dog. 'You bloody mongrel, I'll...'

Hearing laughter, he turned around and saw Jack smiling.

'Don't worry, you're not the first,' he said. 'He doesn't break the skin, not yet anyway.'

Matty, with memories of Brownie in his mind, walked around the pup, who sat by the saddle still growling.

'Bloody hell, Jack, that's a mean trick to pull.'

'He's got attached to me, and me things. It's good actually, 'cause we get Bedouins that come in the night and take anything not nailed down. Since China's been with us, we haven't had that problem. Not our troop, anyway.'

Matty checked his hand. There was no broken skin and to show he had forgiven the dog, he called him over. China came cautiously, crawling along the ground, not knowing what to expect. Soon, he was lying on his back, Matty rubbing his belly.

'China, you gonna learn to look after my gear too, hey?' Matty said to the dog. Then he asked Jack, 'How old do you reckon he is?'

'I guess about eight, maybe ten months old. He's pretty intelligent too. He knows when it's time to go to the wagons and when to stay with me. Don't have to tell him. And he's starting to protect more than just us. The wagons and the horses are checked by him too.'

The men fell to talking about dogs they had owned, and the talk died away as they fell to thinking about home.

The weeks of daily patrols and guarding the railway were relieved for a few short days when the Brigade marched to Romani, where men and horses swam in the sea after the morning regimental exercises, the salt air fresh in their nostrils.

A games afternoon had been arranged to break the monotony. The regiments each nominated their teams and to the surprise of the Brigade, the 12th nominated Matty and Cedar in the mile race along the wet sand of the beach.

'Wots in hell is that little mare gonna beat?' came one derisive cry. 'A tortoise?'

Jack had put forward Cedar's name, and, letting his squadron know he had done so, the troops decided to back her. The favourite was a tall, rangy bay, belonging to Lt. Johnson of the 4th Light Horse. Coming a close second in the betting was the grey gelding of Captain Adams from the 11th.

Some men of Matty's troop had second thoughts, as the horses rode to the start, far down the beach. They quietly put a bet down on the favourite to cover themselves both ways.

'Are you sure about this mare?' Bluey asked Jack nervously. 'I've put two week's pay on this mare.'

Jack's lips curled into a knowing smile. He looked at the worried faces around him, nodding his head slowly.

'I'll say three things about the mare. She was bred and raised in the desert Mulga country. She's by a stallion with a Caulfield Cup winner in his blood lines. And, she's as game as Ned Kelly – she won't quit.'

Bluey studied Jack carefully. 'You've always been a dinkum fellow, Jack. So, here, hold me chits, I'm gonna put some more on her.'

The excitement in the troop rose as they saw the horses wheel into line. One of the horses reared, nearly throwing its rider.

Matty felt Cedar's muscles tight beneath him. She knew this was a race. They had raced many times at home, away from the eyes of the homestead. The sand along the water's edge was hard packed, unlike the soft sandy soil at home.

If I can keep her on that we'll be fine, he thought.

In front of him, he saw the vast expanse of sand dunes on his right, the rippling blue of the sea on his left, with the racecourse marked by flags up the middle. At the far end, he saw the khaki mass of men lining the sand dunes, spilling down to the course, waiting excitedly for the start.

The grey horse next to him became excited and spun around, crashing into Cedar, knocking her off balance. The rider of the grey grinned and muttered an apology as he lined his horse up in the place Cedar had been. Matty sighed in dismay as he saw that he was now on the outer edge of the course, out in the drier, deeper sand. He glared at the other man, but held his tongue, as the other man was a captain.

The warning shout came from the starter and then the flag fell.

Matty held Cedar back as the rest jumped. They had three strides on the mare before he let her go. She flew forward, but to the left, as he guided her towards the water. Looking ahead, he could see the five horses in front, racing in a line across the beach. He urged her on, sitting quietly in the saddle. She pulled at the reins, anxious to catch and pass the horses in front. As she caught up with them, he tucked her in behind them, fighting with her to stay there. Two hundred yards flew by, then three. The horses in front were slowing, the riders realising that it was a long way to go. One horse dropped back noticeably, running beside Cedar.

Glancing up ahead, Matty judged his timing. Guiding her with his right leg and left rein, he urged her towards the water's edge. He saw the horse in front drift towards the right; in that moment, he let go of the reins and slapped the mare's shoulder.

That was all Cedar needed. She stretched out her neck and lunged forward, lengthening her stride, gaining ground on the horses in front. Captain Adams, sensing a horse coming up on the inside, glanced across. Astonishment crossed his face when he saw the little mare. He urged his own horse on, but it was starting to labour and slowly dropped back.

Now there were three of them racing for the finish.

Bluey was screaming at the top of his voice, while Billy had climbed on Doug's back for a better look. Jack stood quietly; the only give away to his tension were his tightly clenched hands.

Come on, Matty, she can do it. I've told the men; the mare can do it. They've put a lot on this, he thought, watching the mare's hooves flick up sand as she raced. *Ask her now. Now, Shorty!'*

As if he had heard Jack, Matty sat deeper in the saddle, his hands on her neck, moving with her stride. He spoke to her softly, 'C'mon, girl, you can do it. This is nothing to back home.'

Cedar flicked her ears back, listening to his voice, then flicked them forward again. The horse immediately on her right put in another effort and drew slightly ahead. Cedar's spirit rose; she was not going to give in. Her head dropped a little and her stride increased again, reeling in the horse in front. Matty felt her heart pounding and his throat tightened with pride. He stayed still, letting the mare run her own race. With a hundred yards to go, the horse in front veered suddenly into her path. Cedar's head flew up, her pace checked. It was then that Cedar's heart began to tell of her breeding. Matty blinked, then smiled when he felt the mare unbelievably change leg and draw to the outside. As the finish line came closer, the mare lifted again, her body straining with every stride. He glanced across at the bay horse beside them. They were neck and neck as they crossed the line.

It was then he heard the roar of the crowd. Easing her into a slow canter, then a trot, he rubbed her neck, telling her, 'What a horse you are, girl. What a mare.' He turned and rode back to the finish line. The soldiers of his troop gathered around them, cheering, laughing and bragging about their winnings.

They dragged Matty from the saddle and hoisted him on their shoulders, while others argued for the privilege of leading Cedar around to cool off. Jack settled that argument by stripping off the saddle and leading the sweat-lathered mare himself.

A roar of anger rose in the desert air; Lt. Johnson had been declared the winner. Soldiers shouted their disbelief, some calling for a rematch; others threatened bodily harm. The men suddenly quietened as Jack strode up to the group of officials who had run the race.

'Sir, I'd ask you to reconsider that call. I'm entering a protest on behalf of the 12th's entry,' he addressed the sergeant who had made the call. 'Everyone saw there was interference to the mare and we reckon it was a dead heat. You gotta do what's fair, sir.'

The sergeant looked at Jack, at the determination in his face, then, he glanced at the faces of the soldiers. Realising that this could turn ugly, he replied, 'I'll confer with the other officials, soldier. Go back to your troop.'

As the officials conferred, Jack went back to the men who stood dumbfounded.

'They gotta give it to her,' Billy said angrily. 'It ain't got nothin' to do with the money. It's what's right, that counts.'

Bluey thumped him on the back. 'That's well said, Billy boy. That mare would've won outright if that horse hadn't come across in front of her. I'm not saying it was deliberate, but it happened, didn't it?'

The rumblings of the men grew louder. It took a bit of whistling to get them quiet enough to hear the verdict.

'On further deliberation, it has been ascertained that that the race was a dead heat,' the sergeant called out.

Men rushed to collect their winnings, others stood around, discussing the outcome and cursing the judgement of officers to put NCOs in as officials. There was a hush when Lt. Col. McIntosh, Commander of the 12th, came to congratulate Matty. The Lt. Col. asked Matty about Cedar.

Matty replied shyly, 'She's by Jack's thoroughbred stallion, Longman. Her dam was a station horse, sir.'

'I should put your troop on report for not letting me in on this little secret of yours. What do you think, men?' the Lt. Col. said with a smile and only half-jokingly.

Cries of 'we didn't know till the last minute' and 'we won't make that mistake again, sir' came from amongst the men of the troop.

'I'm sure you won't.' the Lt. Col. laughed, then winking, he added, 'And I think we'll choose our officials a bit more carefully next time. Might do it myself.'

The CO stepped back as Jack handed Cedar's reins to Matty. Cedar lowered her head and butted against Matty's pockets. He opened the flap and drew forth a little packet of paper. The men looked on in astonishment as Matty tipped a small mound of sugar into the palm of his hand and fed it to the mare.

'Where on Earth did you get that sugar from, Watson?' the Lt. Col. asked, incredulously. 'We haven't had any for weeks, not since the supply ship ran aground.'

Matty's face reddened as he realised he had been caught out. 'I… well, sir,' he stammered. Taking a deep breath, he looked at the 12th's commander, and said defiantly, 'I brought some with me in my kit when I came over. When that ran out, I traded some kangaroo feathers with a Tommy from the Yeomanry for some sugar. I didn't ask him where he got it.'

The Lt. Col. put back his head and laughed loudly. 'Some poor Tommy officer will be going without sugar in his tea for a while. You little begger, Watson. And, what's this about plumes?'

'When Jack wrote home, he said that the regiments have to provide their own. Sammy and I went out and shot a bird, old it was. We figured it would die soon any way. We plucked it and I brought the feathers over in my kit as well. I gave some to our blokes. I've been swapping stuff for them from men from the other regiments.'

'And managed to keep a few spare for necessities, I see,' the CO finished for him. 'Well, boys, well done. Watson, you look after that mare.'

The men breathed a sigh of relief as their CO made his way back to the other officers, still laughing quietly to himself.

Bluey whistled. 'I thought you was gonna cop it then, Matty. Lucky he's one of ours and not a Tommy officer. They don't understand.'

Matty felt someone staring at him; turning, he saw Jack's frowning face.

'You took those feathers with you when you left the station. When did you first plan to go?'

'Oh, c'mon, mate, let's not go over that. Let's celebrate. How much did you win?'

SIXTEEN

Sammy's battalion left behind them the small creature comforts of their last billet. A large, cold barn – full of the ripe rich smells of rural animals and complete with mice – had been their last resting place. As they made their way up the road, towards the maze of trenches that would eventually lead them to their new billet, the front line, they looked about at the green fields dancing to the tune of a soft breeze. The poppies lifted their fiery red petals to the sun, spread like a blanket laid for a picnic, catching the eye of Dave. He leant over and picked a single bloom, placing it in his hat.

An old woman dressed in black leant over a gate that hung precariously on one hinge. She grinned a toothless smile and nodded at each soldier that called a greeting. Her eyes were vacant and her smile a little vague. A few of the passing men wondered if she had suffered one too many losses.

All too soon, they were in the narrow confines of the trenches, a different landscape. Silent, they passed men returning from the frontline, haggard and grey-faced. Their guide took them through trenches twisting this way and that, signage with familiar names, at each new turn: Piccadilly, New London, names from far away given to these lanes of wet muddy earth, dug by human hand. Men of every description jostled and cursed as the fading light made the going more difficult. The stench of war invaded their nostrils. The smell of unwashed bodies, cordite, decomposing flesh, rotten earth and cooking food mingled to become a hated aroma. The dread of the front line was overtaken by weariness, their tread becoming slower, their limbs heavier as they battled through the trenches that remained sodden because of the flat marshy ground that they had been dug into.

Now they had to flatten themselves against the wall of the trenches as exhausted stretcher bearers manhandled their sad loads past. Some soldiers looked at the men laid upon these canvases, and thought, 'But for the grace of God…'

Now and then, one of the injured would call out 'good luck, boys' or 'give Fritz one for me' but mostly, they lay quiet and stoic, with only a tight smile hiding their pain.

The darkness fell softly, unbelievably softly. They didn't notice. The lightning of the Verey lights and the thunder of the guns made them think that they were in a nightmare, where nature consisted of churned, blackened earth and stark sticks that were once trees. One by one, they settled down in their positions, resigned to their fate, sharing silently, the horror of war.

Behind them, on the floor of a trench a few hundred yards back lay Dave's poppy, one blood red petal untouched beside its trampled, torn sisters.

The guide went to leave them but slid to a stop, turning back to the men.

'I'll give you a tip. There's going to be a big bang soon. I heard about it at HQ. The sappers have been working on a heap of tunnels under the Huns for months. They've packed them full of high explosive. They reckon it'll be heard in—'

A distant rumble, like thunder on the horizon came to their ears. The ground began to tremble. As some men dived for the bottom of the trench, an explosion of noise greater than anything they had ever heard before coming to this wretched gutted piece of France, hit them. The roar intensified into a rolling wave, Sammy, quickly followed by Dave, jumped up on to the fire step in time to see a long line of fiery orange pillars streaking skyward. Dust and dirt brought up from under the mud, spewed and roiled in the air above the flames. The glow lit up the battlefield. As they watched, the blast hit and they were thrown backwards. Getting up quickly, they went again to the edge of the trench, fascination drawing them back. In awe, they watched as earth, timber, iron and other debris drifted back to earth. Silence followed.

'Those poor bastards,' Dave said, shaking his head. 'Those poor bloody bastards.'

* * * *

'I've had a gutful of being their target practice,' Dave exploded one morning. 'Darky, you're the best shot. I'm going to build you a possie like you've never seen before and you're going to keep those bastards busy. All right, cobber?'

Sammy shrugged his shoulders. To dig or to shoot. If it finished the war quicker, he would do anything Dave asked.

Together they levelled a section of the parapet, thirty yards from where the men were working. They filled sandbags and piled them up, two deep in a continuous line. In one section, Dave put a long, narrow bottomless ammunition box. Then, he piled another layer of sandbags on top. Sammy leaned against the trench wall and cleaned his gun the best he could with a sodden wad.

One of the new reinforcements pushed past Dave, on his way to the other men.

Shaking his head, Dave bawled at him.

'Keep your bleedin' head down, you mug. You new chums are the dizzy limit.'

Sammy paused, glancing up at the startled man. 'The Boche, they like new chums, they make easier target practice,' he said with a smile.

The soldier's back bent and he scuttled along the trench, chastened and wiser.

Looking at Dave, Sammy loaded a round into the chamber and pushed home the bolt.

'I never told you much about the Missus. 'Cept she was good to me.'

His mate stared at him, mute, wondering what had brought this on.

'Chances are gettin' smaller that I see my people again,' continued Sammy. 'You been a mate.'

Dave did not know what to say. He stared at the sandbags that hid their view of no-man's land. He looked at the ground, and then turned his eyes on Sammy.

'It works both ways, Sammy. You've been a dinkum mate to all of us.'

'Everythin' I got, goes to the Missus. She'll do right by my people.'

There was nothing for Dave to say but 'no worries, mate'.

Sammy's affairs were now in Dave's hands. It's what a mate did, this was understood. It puzzled Dave for the next few minutes, why Sammy had mentioned this now, but a shell landing close by drove those thoughts out of his mind.

'I'll scope, Darky. You shoot.'

The men who were working near them made themselves scarce. With calls of 'good luck', they moved away from Dave and Sammy. Bandy curled up against the wall of the trench, his nose tucked into his tail.

Stepping up onto the fire step, Sammy settled the .303 onto the folded piece of blanket that Dave had put in the box as a gun rest. He nestled the butt of the rifle well into his shoulder, leant over and looked up the sights, out across no-man's land. Dave, below him, in the trench, raised the periscope and turned it slowly along the German lines.

It was half an hour before Dave said slowly and evenly, 'Twelve o'clock, to the left of that stump. He's moving up and down. Probably an officer, telling off his men.'

Sammy swung the rifle in the direction Dave had given him, his eye staying with the barrel until the bobbing helmet of the enemy came in line within his sights. Very slowly, his finger tightened on the trigger. He breathed out and when he got to the end of his breath, he paused. The helmet came up just that little bit further, exposing the side of the man's face. Sammy pulled the trigger. The helmet dropped.

'You pukka bastard, Darky. One more and we'll change position.'

It was another hour before a fool in the other lines got careless and decided to lean over his parapet to have a shot at the British trenches. In seconds, he was dead.

'Let's get out of here,' Dave said to his Sammy as rifle fire poured into the sandbags above their heads. 'They'll be following that lot with the heavy stuff.'

As they moved further down the trench, shells rained down around the place they had just vacated.

Harry greeted them on their return to work. 'That kept their heads down for a while. It let us get some work done.'

'Seventeen days we've been doing this and going out there of a night,' said Dave, jerking his thumb in the direction of no-man's land. 'Anyone would think we committed some bloody crime to get lumped with this.'

The men nodded their heads in agreement.

'If it wasn't for those babbling brooks making sure we get one hot meal a day, I'd reckon a bloke would be a bit poorer off,' Harry remarked, as he tried to light his pipe. 'Bloody tobacco's wet. Anyways, I reckon those blokes that get our tucker up here are bloody saints.'

Dave scratched at his belly. 'I don't know who's hungrier, me, or them bloody chats that are eating me.'

Pushing Bandy away from his kit, Sammy scrounged around in it, finally drawing out a small tin. He leant forward, offering the tin to Harry.

'Here, Harry. My bacca's dry.'

Harry reached out, taking the tin from Sammy. 'Ta, Darky. It's lucky I got a mate that don't smoke. I'll do enough for both of us.'

'If they giving it, I'll keep it for you fellas, eh?' Sammy smiled.

'Darky, I think you're a saint as well,' Harry replied, adding under his breath, 'You've got the smile of a saint, leastways.'

Runners carrying food in blanket-enclosed kerosene tins arrived, making the men scramble for their mess tins. Bandy went from man to man, waiting for the titbit that was sure to be offered.

The mail came up with the runners and Sammy was happy, receiving two letters. He tucked them away to read later.

The daylight was fading. In expectation of more raids that night, the men went into the dugout and tried to get some sleep, but the Germans decided to have a hate attack, opening up with every gun they had. Despite the noise, Dave closed his eyes and nodded off, snoring loudly enough to be heard in the few seconds of quiet that occurred every now and then. Most of the other men, tired as they were, could do no more than shut their eyes, trying to will themselves to sleep.

Above the dugout, the clouds slowly cleared, letting the rising moon bathe the battlefield in light. Guards scanned the shadows of shell holes and tree stumps for movement, stamping their cold feet, wishing they were below with the others. Shortly before midnight, the captain came up from Battalion HQ and made his way down into the dugout. Bandy growled softly, quietening only when he saw it was the captain.

Sammy prodded Dave awake, gesturing at the captain as Dave opened his eyes.

'Bloody hell, I was just dreaming of a blonde serving me beer on a sunny day in Paris,' he joked as he sat up, putting his kit behind him as a back rest. 'What are we doing tonight, Captain?'

The men respected this captain, he had earned his first stripes at Lone

Pine. He had been transferred to their battalion two months ago, when their previous captain had been blown to bits by a whizz-bang.

The officer leant against a timber support, his foot up on an upturned box.

''A" Company will be going out at three, the barrage will be set down at three fifteen. We'll do it just like in training. HQ want anything you can get out of the Boches trenches to the east of number two pill box. The badges you got last time, showed that reinforcements from northern sector have been moved into the lines.'

Clearing his throat, he finished his orders. 'Dave, you, Darky, Harry and Kenny, you will go out at one thirty and clear a path through the wires. I've got some tape being brought up shortly, not that we'll need it to guide us. It's so bloody bright out there. When we go, we'll veer to the east. If anything goes wrong, get back here best you can. Password tonight is Dubbo,' the captain said, nodding to emphasise his point. Turning to go, he stopped. 'One more thing, pray for some cloud cover.'

The men talked for a bit, they smoked and slowly quietened down, each to his own thoughts as they settled back to wait for the zero hour to arrive. Sammy took his two letters and opened the one from the Boss, written months ago, but only just arrived. He leant back against the dugout wall, under the wavering lamp, and smoothed out the crinkled pages.

He read the one from Thomas first, then one from the boys in Palestine. Sighing, he folded up the letters and tucked them into his breast pocket.

'Not sad news, cobber?' Dave's voice was hard to hear over the barrage that raged above the dirt roof of the dugout.

'No, a letter from the Boss. He says it rained. And one from my mates in the desert.'

Dave scratched at his whiskers, saying, 'My wife mentioned, last letter, that the winter was very mild this time, but she's in Sydney with her mother.'

'Why'd you join up if you married, Dave?' Sammy asked.

The direct question caused Dave to sit up a bit straighter. Sammy and he had never discussed this, not really. 'I really don't know, Darky,' he answered slowly. 'The honest truth is, I was away shearing and all the boys were talking about it. Some of them got liquored up one night, jumped on the train and headed for Brisbane. I was a bit older than them and married. I stewed about it a bit more and thought I'd better go with them, look after them.'

Sammy stared at Dave, noticing the scattering of grey whiskers amongst the black ones that hadn't been there six months ago.

'What did your missus say?'

'I telephoned her from Brisbane. She was as mad as hell.' Dave's mouth turned up at the corners in memory of that conversation. 'We had a bit put aside and she moved in with her mother. So, she won't be doing it hard. We've got no kids, so that wasn't a worry.'

Dave paused a moment, wondering what the hell had got into Sammy. He never asked many questions, let alone private ones.

Another one came. 'Where are the fellas that you joined with?'

'Well, there's another story. They hit Brisbane all liquored up and got themselves put in the clink. When they sobered up, they changed their mind. In the meantime, I ran into Harry. I had known him when we were at Longreach, so we joined up anyway. The poor buggers had had a hard time at Gallipoli and needed reinforcements, so we enlisted. By the time we got on board ship, Gallipoli had been evacuated and you know the rest.'

Nodding, Sammy said, 'That's why I join up. Matty and Jack, they join up. I told you that,' he said. 'But I didn't say the rest.'

He stopped, his eyes wandering over the men. He sighed and stared down at his hands, spreading them out on his legs.

'The Boss and the Missus, they treat us different. I see how fellas think of blacks. They say we should be on missions. They don't pay blacks. I work, I work hard, but I don't get paid. Not till I join up. My people at the station, we like the Boss. When his boy go to join up, I go to look after him, just like Charlie looked after us fellas when we young. But, in Brissy, one fella, he don't like darkies, the other fellas did. They say I could join up, but the captain, he say no. So, I joined up anyway. Not the Light Horse. I join the Infantry.'

'Well, I'm glad you did, Darky,' Dave said, a lump in his throat. 'Hey, cobber, you know we call you Darky because you're special, not because you're a black. I don't know many men that can speak French, box like a champion and to top it off, you don't drink.'

In the wavering candlelight, Dave saw the smile on Sammy's face. 'That's better, mate. As Harry says, you have the smile of a saint.'

Harry rolled over and sat up. 'I couldn't help but hear you blokes. While the questions are goin', what I want to know is, how come you speak so educated, Dave?'

'Ah, so you have noticed my breeding, have you, squire?' He laughed. 'I'm the bastard of a judge, who secretly paid for my education!'

Loud shouts of laughter rose around the dugout. A voice from near the door sung out, 'Aye, and I be a leprechaun!'

Dave picked up an empty sandbag and threw it at the man.

'Irish, that will be enough out of you, sir! No, I'll tell the truth, it is even stranger. My mother married a squatter, a bloke that came out from England with some money. He was doing pretty well, but he decided that there was more money in mining, so he went out to the Kimberleys to investigate some mines. He never came back. They found him by the side of a track. They reckon he ran out of water.'

Dave paused a moment, then, with urging from the men, he continued.

'I was only a year old, so I never knew him. Mother packed me up and moved to Sydney. The relatives in England didn't want anything to do with us, so my mother set about bringing me up as a gentleman.'

More shouts of laughter drowned out Dave's voice.

'Boy's a dear,' cried Irish. 'I been sharin' me sumptuous quarters 'ere with an Englishman.' Winking at Sammy, Irish proclaimed, 'It be just as well I like the beggar.'

'I was born in Australia, that makes me an Australian. Where did you hail from?'

Irish laughed and spread his arms wide. 'I've been all over.' He added more seriously, 'But, me hometown was Ballymena. Me ma's still there, weepin' in church for her errant son.'

A silence descended on the group at the mention of family. Trying to recapture the light mood, Harry asked, 'Well, Dave, how'd ya end up a shearer?'

'That is another story. It's time boys,' Dave said, checking his watch.

Sammy stood and began to load up. First, he placed two Mills grenades in his bomb bag. He took from his kit a long-bladed knife, held securely in a pouch and attached it to his belt. Extra rounds of ammunition went into his spare magazine, which he tucked into his breast pocket.

Picking up his rifle, he clicked his bayonet into the end of the barrel, slung it across his back and, taking the wire cutters that were held out to him, he followed Dave up the roughly hewn stairs, into the trench. Not a word had been spoken between the men; there was no need.

They sat along the fire step, their faces blackened with burnt cork, waiting for the order to go.

Catching Sammy looking curiously at his bulging bomb bag, Dave grinned.

'That pill box is annoying me. I reckon we might give it a bit of redecorating on the inside.'

Sammy nodded his agreement. Kenny looked dubiously at them.

'The captain'll never go for it,' he said.

'He don't have to know,' Harry replied quickly. 'Anyway, we can hang back a bit till everyone's nearly home.'

'Oh, I suppose so. You blokes are crazy.'

Dave cleared his throat as he saw the captain come around the corner.

Checking his watch, the officer nodded his head to them. Sammy spoke to Bandy, ordering him to stop. The dog lay down, his head on his paws, sorrowful eyes staring at Sammy.

'I'll watch him, Darky. He has become more than a mascot to our company, hasn't he?' the captain said, leaning over to fondle Bandy's ears. The dog's eyes never moved from Sammy's face.

With wire cutters in hand and rifles slung, the small group slid over the edge of the parapet, hugging the greasy mud as they slowly snipped a path through the rows of barbed wire in front of the trenches.

As they waited for the others in the lie up possie, Sammy turned on his back, looking up at the stars. Verey lights going up now and then made them fade, and shells of different shapes crossed over above him. For just a few minutes though, the shells stopped, and no flares lit up. He stared up, thinking that the stars here were all jumbled compared to home. It was fitting that they were jumbled over this part of the world, as down here, the world was a hell of a jumble. He noticed clouds obscuring some of the stars, and sent a silent wish to them, asking them to cover the moon.

Dave's boot in his ribs caught his attention. He saw that the lieutenant and the other men were sliding towards them. A screaming sound forewarned of the barrage. Next, the sky above was rent with the 3rd Division's artillery pouring out all the shells they could feed into their guns. A nod from their officer got the men moving. They jumped to their feet and unslung their rifles. Keeping behind the barrage as best they could, yard by yard, they picked out the firmer ground and made their way towards their objective. In and around shell craters, over slimy ground strewn with rubble and dead bodies, the men ran, trudged and crawled. Sammy smiled to himself as the moonlight dimmed. Glancing up, he saw a large cloud begin to blanket the moon. The artillery kept the barrage pouring into the German trenches.

Nearing the enemy trench, the men with the wire cutters went forward, kneeling down to cut the thick belts of wire that the barrage had not cut. Machine gun fire opened up on their left. Kenny, with a few of the others, charged the gun post, killing one of the enemy and taking three prisoner. With the wire cut, the soldiers waited impatiently for the barrage to move onto the German lines. In a few minutes, the artillery lifted the barrage. The men ran the rest of the way, jumping into the enemy trench. Its inhabitants would not fight back. The Germans lay in tattered uniforms, bits of bodies blasted into the walls of the trench. A shell had done its job. Sammy and Dave searched what was left of the enemy for documents, tearing off the badges and insignia that were still intact.

Other men guarded each corner of the trench, grenades ready, expecting the enemy to rush in to fill the void. Following their training, the men with the goods left the trench first, followed by the others who covered their backs. Moving as fast as they could in the heavy going, most of them headed back to their own lines. But not fast enough. The Germans opened up with their artillery, pounding shells and mortars into the earth around them. Men were flung into the air, others disappeared. Machine guns opened up and spat a hail of bullets at the raiders. As men who made it back threw themselves over the parapet, others dived into craters, making themselves as small as possible. They huddled in the greasy water and prayed that no shell would have their name on it.

Sammy, Dave and Harry did not return with the others. Veering off to the west, they crept up behind the pill box that overlooked their trench. Sammy slithered up from a shell crater and observing no movement of soldiers outside the box, motioned for Dave and Harry to come forward. Each taking a Mills grenade from their bag, they pulled the pins, waited a few seconds and threw them into the firing slit. A series of muffled explosions followed by screams of pain and confusion told them of the damage. Sammy drew another Mills from his pack and crawled around behind the pill box, calling down into it, 'Kamerad?'

Not receiving an answer, Sammy pulled the pin and threw the grenade down into the pill box, rolling back from the doorway as it exploded. Taking the torch from his belt, he carefully shone it around inside, the beam playing over the torn remains of five soldiers and the twisted wreckage of the machine gun.

The noise drew the attention of the Germans. Bullets flew around them as they made their way back to their own trench, until, thinking it prudent to take cover, they dived into a shell crater. Slowly, the Germans realised that it wasn't a second attack, and the intensity of the shelling slowed. Those men who had been caught out from their trenches when the Germans opened fire dragged themselves towards their own trenches. Others, who were badly wounded, lay in their misery in no-man's land, praying for the stretcher bearers to find them. Sammy was the first one to move, the others following him. Because they were coming in from a different direction, Dave and Harry were counting on Sammy to find the way back through the wire.

Passing a shell hole, Sammy stopped, listening. He crawled over the edge and slid to the bottom. His mates followed, wondering what he was up to. At the bottom of the crater, half submerged, lay their lieutenant. He managed a wry smile when he saw who had joined him.

'I don't seem to be able to make it back, boys,' he said between clenched teeth, gesturing towards his legs. 'Fritz has a good aim.'

Sammy got behind his head and grabbing the lieutenant under the armpits, pulled him out of the water. A slight moan came from the officer before he fainted.

'Jesus wept,' Dave murmured.

They had seen it all before, soldiers blown to bits, mates with holes the size of a fist in them. But somehow, this was more shocking, more personal, down in the bowels of the earth with their officer.

They stared down at the stumps that had been his legs, blood spurting in rhythmic jets from their ends, growing weaker as they watched. Dave moved first. He pulled the field dressing from his bag and held it hard against one of the ruined legs. Harry followed his action, while Sammy strapped the tapes tightly around each of the dressings.

Taking Harry's other tape, he sliced it in two with his knife and wound it around each of the lieutenant's legs, just below the groin, pulling them tight.

'We gotta get back quick,' he said, as he stood and hoisted the captain over his shoulder. Sammy slipped, finding it hard going. Dave and Harry helped him up the side of the shell hole. Step by laborious step, he gained the top and set off for the trenches. Dawn spread its fingers across the sky, while on the battlefield a fog formed, cloaking them from the sight of the Germans. Shells exploded around the small party of men, showering them with mud, as they dragged themselves through the debris of no-man's land. As they entered the wire, a soldier challenged them.

'Bloody Dubbo, you bloody Queenslander,' Dave shot back.

Dave took the officer from Sammy's shoulders and lowered him into the trench before tumbling in himself.

'Get a medic, now,' demanded Dave as Kenny came to help.

Kenny lent over the lieutenant and stood up slowly, regret in his words. 'He's gone west. Sorry, mate.'

Dave turned to tell Sammy he had done a good job, but Sammy had gone.

'Where's Harry? Where's Darky? Where'd that black bastard go?' he asked, panic in his voice.

Bandy paced up and down, looking for Sammy. With a large leap, he sprang up and over the edge of the trench. He stopped, belly to the ground, sniffing the air, whining softly.

Dave leapt up on to the parapet, imagining Sammy or Harry hit. He called softly for Bandy to come back into the trench.

Kenny and the tall, muscular soldier who had challenged Dave grabbed at him, pulling him back.

'Nah, Darky's gone back out. Maybe he saw somethin',' Kenny said.

His shoulders slumped; Dave leant against the wall. The sentry stared at Dave before slowly asking, 'How'd ya know I'm from Queensland?'

Dave glared at him. 'Oh, sod off.'

He climbed onto the step again, his eyes trying to pierce the fog, looking for his mates.

In the insipid light of the dawn, Sammy lay beside his mate's broken, distorted body, knowing that all he could do was hold his hand and make promises that he might not be able to keep. To move him would be to send him before his time. Around them, the dead of the past few nights lay in disarray. Sammy stared about, the men's grey bloated faces, the dull muddy khaki of the uniforms and the greasy black mud. The only colour in all this was the spurting bright blood from Harry's neck. It slowly lowered to a trickle as Harry's heart stopped beating. Then, Sammy knew, it would turn black, like everything else in this place, the bowels of Hell.

SEVENTEEN

'Damn, you're a blighter of a horse!' Matty growled as he struggled to control Cedar.

Suddenly there was the 'crack-thump' of gun fire and the soldier spun the horse on her haunches as bullets thumped into the sand around him. Given a free rein, she raced along the narrow valley between the wind-swept ridges before climbing out over a steep dune. As the mare struggled up the slope, her hooves sinking in the burning sand, Matty threw the reins over her head and leapt from the saddle to lighten the floundering horse's load. Once safe on the other side, Matty turned to his horse.

'You're the worst damn neddy I've ever ridden! Try that again and I'll slice you up for China's tucker!' he whispered savagely.

The mare's large liquid eyes looked at the soldier, one ear forward, one back.

'Don't you look at me like that. Should've named you Meathead. Better still I should've left you the first day I laid eyes on you!'

The horse lowered her graceful head and gently nuzzled at the pockets of her master's uniform. He snapped the reins back over her head and vaulted into the saddle, his continued cursing not affecting the mare, or shifting the look of calm from her eyes.

The horse trotted on through the desert sand, surrounded by the massive dunes, neither vegetation nor rock in sight. The only sound came from the muffled swish of the mare's hooves and the occasional metallic rattle of the bit, when she tossed her head at the sticky black flies that swarmed about her. Mounting another dune, a welcome sight met their eyes. In the shimmering haze, between orange-gold sand and blue sky, there appeared the dirty white of army tents in lines under the scattered date palms that surrounded an oasis. The mare knew that water and grain would be waiting for her at the horse lines. She pulled at the bit impatiently.

A loud barking hit the air. From amongst the tents, a huge black dog hurtled straight at the mare. Running low and straight, the dog pulled up just short of crashing into the mare's legs. The horse lowered her head and sniffed his fuzzy fur, while he tried to lick her face. Matty dismounted and patted the excited dog.

'Yeah, China, we're back mate. Only just, no thanks to this cow!'

Jack had followed the dog and stood watching the reunion.

'You got a fag, Jack?' Matty asked wearily. 'This cow nearly got me done today!'

Jack rolled and lit a cigarette, then passed it to his mate, his blue eyes smiling. 'Why's that? What'd she do this time?'

Matty leaned back against his horse, a rolly hanging from the corner of his mouth.

'While you were pulling piquet duty, Billy and me went out on patrol, Bill's horse pulled a shoe, so he turned back. I reckon I should've too, but Cedar was jumpin' out of her skin, so I reckoned I'd stretch her legs a bit. Anyways, I was comin' back when Cedar here,' Matty said as he jerked his thumb towards the mare, 'jumps back, then lets go with a beauty. Blanky fool of a thing saw a snake. One of them asp things Billy collects.'

Jack grinned.

'So,' Matty continued, 'off she went, squealin' an' hoppin' round.

Damn if the Turks hadn't set up an outpost on the other side of the dune behind us. Them Turks must've heard the racket and poked their heads over the dune. They lets go at us. The sound the bitch was makin', I reckon they thought it was ten horses comin'!'

Jack burst into laughter.

'You insisted on bringin' her, Matty.' He chuckled. 'Reckoned she was the best thing ever born.'

'Yep, I said that,' he agreed, stroking her neck. 'It's true, but she's still a damn cow when she wants.'

'That mare troubling you, Watson?'

The two men stood to attention; it was the captain's voice. Matty glanced at Jack, who stood red-faced, trying to control his mirth.

'No, sir,' he answered.

The officer inspected Matty. He saw the dusty sweat-stained clothes.

'I thought you went out with Thompson on a patrol?' the officer said as he cast his eye over the mare, noticing the sweat on her flanks. 'He came back two hours ago.'

Matty looked his captain straight in the eye. 'Yes, sir. His horse threw a shoe. I had a bit of a look around, sir. There's Turks nor' west, 'bout eight miles out. Not much in the way of guns. I'd say they've set up an outpost.'

'Mmm. Our flying blokes said the Turks were getting cheeky,' the officer mused.

The captain decided against disciplining Matty about being AWL for the past two hours. 'Better get your horse bedded down. You know better than leaving a patrol. I'll not report you this time, Watson, but you're on notice!'

'Yes, sir,' Matty replied, feeling lucky, twice in one day.

The patrols into the desert continued. There were skirmishes with the Turks; hit and miss affairs. As soon as the Light Horse fired on and pursued them, the Turks turned and bolted back to their lines. The dunes rolled on endlessly, while the wind whipped sand into every crease of the body. They ate sand with their meals, they slept in it. The horses became conditioned to the hard feed, the long miles and the shortage of water. Even though the men never had a spare moment, not one of them envied the infantry. For although infantry soldiers could fall down at the end of a march and feed only themselves, the lives of the Light Horse soldier revolved around their horses. Clean the piquet lines and feed up before the soldiers ate. Grooming and watering, after breakfast. Saddle up and patrol in the hot dusty sand dunes, back to camp to repeat the watering and feeding. Then there was horse line duty of a night, making sure no horses got loose or tangled in the lines. Men in charge of Hotchkiss guns had an extra horse to care for, and then there were the packhorses to attend to as well. The men of the Light Horse grumbled about the heat and the flies, but they would never swap their positions with the infantry.

The YMCA tents that set up behind the lines provided fresh fruit and chocolates; the men rode miles to assuage their cravings for sweets. The Light Horse still found time for sports days and games of two up. To give the soldiers a break in their daily routines, the Yeomanry challenged the Light Horse to a game of cricket. The pitch was a stretch of sand, dampened and with tibben stamped in. The Yeomanry team, all officers, walked onto the ground in spotless flannels. The Australians whistled and bellowed at the sight. The Australians won the toss and batted first. The Light Horsemen batsmen filed out onto the ground, dressed in shirts, and riding breeches; their leather boots stirred up small puffs of dust as they set themselves in front of their stumps.

'Where the hell do they carry those whites?' Blue asked no one in particular.

Billy answered, 'Their batmen probably starched 'em as well. I'd like to see the colour of their trousers if I put one of my pets out there!'

'You just leave your pets wherever you've hidden them, Billy. Tibby'll colour their trousers for 'em.' Jack laughed, giving Billy a warning glance.

The men cheered every run and as usual, the betting was ebbing and flowing between them.

As Lt. Col. McIntosh walked up, the men quietened, and imperceptibly straightened up. He passed a coin to Jack and asked him to put it on the Aussies. 'That Cotter boy will sort this lot out. Put this on for the regiment.'

Jack's jaw dropped, then he nodded. 'Yes, sir! Should get good odds from the Tommies, they fancy 'em selves, sir. '

'No matter, just get me good odds. You boys divide the winnings amongst yourselves. I don't know where you will get to spend it, but it is yours,' Lt. Col. said with a wry smile as he walked away.

Jack looked around. 'Here, Blue! Go and see if any of them Tommies will have a bet.'

He held out the gold sovereign.

Blue's eyes opened wide and he whistled. 'He's keen!'

'Well, the CO said to, so? He's a good bloke, that one,' Jack replied.

Blue was back shortly with a chit, just as the Australians were thirty-eight runs for five wickets.

The word spread quickly of the Lt Col's gesture and the cheering from the regiment rose. They now had a bit more riding on the outcome.

The heat was stifling and the men out on the pitch wiped their faces with their handkerchiefs after every run. At fifty-seven, the last wicket fell.

After a short break, two Yeomanry officers took the crease. Clapping and cheering broke out as Tibby Cotter took the ball to open the bowling. He started his run up, his stride lengthening until the final step when his arm went up and the ball left his hand. The officer at the other end swung wildly, but the cracking of wood told the worse. As he left the crease shaking his head, another teammate strode confidently to the wicket. He watched as the umpires hammered in a new stump.

He swung and missed. Crack, another stump flew. He cursed on the way back to his team. 'How could I not see the ball?'

Another bowler began his run in from the other end of the pitch. The men started to cheer but fell to murmuring when the batsman hit a single out into the gully. The batsman played carefully, tapping the ball away, waiting for a ball he could drive. One run for the over. Tibby took the ball from the fielder. The crowd noise rose. Tibby began his run up, the crowd cheering. Stumps flew through the air. The batsman stood there, staring at the bowler. He shook his head, then looked at the umpire. The umpire pointed at the broken stump that lay on the ground. The shocked man tucked his bat under his arm and walked off the ground.

The Australians were jubilant. The Yeomanry made only four runs including one bye. They paraded Tibby around on their shoulders, singing *For He's a Jolly Good Fellow*.

Blue collected their winnings from a very disgruntled Tommy and gave Jack the Lt Colonel's money to look after.

'Matty's got Cedar entered in the second race later. We should put it all on her and make a killin'.' He grinned.

Taking the money, Jack swore. 'Bloody hell! I forgot to tell the CO. He said last time, we were to let him know next time she raced.'

Jamming his hat on, he sprinted over to where the Lt Col sat talking to other officers.

Throwing a salute to the Lt Col, Jack said smartly, 'Sir, I took care of that bus'ness and It had a good outcome. I'd also like to mention, sir, that your horse has been taken care of and is in fine condition.'

Staring at Jack as if the boy had gone mad, the Lt Col saw Jack's head swing slightly to the left, his eye drooping almost in a wink. Following the line of Jack's gesture, he saw the men of his troop gathered around a liver chestnut mare.

'Ah, yes! Thank you, Henderson. That's good to hear,' he said gruffly, a nod dismissing Jack.

Walking away from the officers, Jack smiled as he heard the Lt Col. ask, 'Now, gentlemen, the races are starting. I don't fancy any in the first but would any one care to have a wager on the second race? I fancy that little chestnut mare. Any takers?'

'I'll take you, Geoffrey. I believe that was just luck when she ran at Romani,' came a reply.

The men lined the edge of a hurriedly prepared racetrack, cheering their men on. Cedar flew the colours for the 12th and again proved her breeding, beating the field by a head.

The short relief from war was over and the 12th Regiment received orders to prepare to march. They had heard the reports of the failure after the first battle of Gaza, and now they were to be thrown into the cauldron, their first major engagement in the desert war. The reinforcements who had not fought at Gallipoli were excited at the prospect of battle, in contrast to the dinkums, who shook their heads, knowing that war was something to be endured.

The miles of sand left behind them, the regiment crossed low hilled country that carried grass on their approach to Khanyunia. They could barely keep the horses moving as the beasts snatched at the greenery beneath their feet.

The troops went out on patrols morning and night. Bedouins, hidden from sight, harassed them with rifle fire, then disappeared into the land when pursued. Orders came down from Command for the Gaza stunt. Officers shook their heads as they handed down their orders, not impressed by the battle plans. Leaving Khanyunia, they cut their equipment down to the bare minimum and took on rations for each man and horse. Men and horses were constantly on the move for three days, no sleep, no time for rest. The horses suffered, as they remained saddled twenty-four hours a day. As they stopped for the ten-minute halt in every hour of the march, a few of the men would lie down, stretched out on the ground. Some horses would lie down beside them. Other soldiers slept in the saddle, trusting their horse to stay in formation. The horses seemed to know when the ten-minute break finished, and would begin to get restless.

Matty had not thought it possible to become any more attached to Cedar than he already was, but the long marches and the trust that his mare gave to him made him realise how lucky he was to have her. Some men spent their days complaining about ill-mannered horses, or their mounts that bucked every morning, no matter how tired they were. But, when the firing started, the horses knew it was time to be on their best behaviour. Bullets from enemy scouting parties would sing around them, but the horses obeyed the reins. It seemed to the men that the horses had taken their sixth sense to a new level, knowing an enemy plane from a friendly one. At the sound of a taube, they trembled and were ready for when the order came to scatter, whereas a friendly plane did not affect them.

He watched as Jack's horse, Absent, plodded along, his ears waving back and forwards in time with the walk. Billy's horse jerked at the reins, jogging, his rider constantly growling about the rough ride. Cedar walked well enough, but with her ears pricked, feeling like a wound-up spring between Matty's legs, ready to go at any time.

The march began in darkness with only compass bearings to guide them. The horses trotted, eagerly snatching at the bit. The men talked quietly but obeyed the no smoking rule. Tiredness vanished; they sensed battle time. Riders tensed, conveying their feelings to the horses. The yards flew beneath the hooves of the regiment, drawing them closer to their objective: Gaza. A plain without grass caused clouds of choking dust to rise, smothering the horses. The men cursed the land they rode across. The ground beneath gave steeply into a gully, the Wadi Ghuzzi. The men reined in their excited horses, throwing the reins to the third man, three horses to every handler. He grabbed at the flying leather, wheeled his horse and led the horses back out of the Wadi, taking the horses to the rear lines.

The dismounted men unslung their rifles and moved forward, their objective, the Atawineh redoubt, two and half miles away. Climbing out of the wadi, they moved across the open rocky plain, their feet kicking up puffs of dust. The rising sun showed small ridges, which the dark line of men snaked up and over. The Turkish guns began raining down shrapnel. Men fell, but the regiment moved forward. As they crested a rise, a crop of barley swayed in the breeze, the creamy heads bent with their own weight. Yellow buttercups and red poppies studded the swaying crop, splashes of colour on a golden canvas. The men moved out into field; the dew, which had been heavy during the night, soaking their trousers. So few men, for the task they had been set.

On their left, the British Infantry advanced behind tanks on open ground. Shells in their hundreds fell amongst them, most missing the tanks, falling among the men. Soldiers of the 12th watched helplessly, praying for the allied artillery to open up, but it remained mute.

The Turkish guns found their range on Matty's regiment and shells began to find their mark. Machine gun fire swept the crop, forcing the men to dive to the ground, their only cover the barley. The soldiers fired their rifles when they could see a target. A marker stood out in front of them: they realised it was a range finder for the Turkish batteries. As the men crept closer to the marker, the Turkish artillery opened up, eight guns sending in high explosive rounds, each round set to explode just above the ground. Men grunted and screamed as shrapnel pelted the regiment. Soldier after soldier was hit. Cries for stretcher bearers filled the air.

The men crawled their way to the edge of the barley, looking out over bare ground to the Turkish trenches, five hundred yards in front on a rise. Jack and Matty lay five yards apart, each wondering why the allied artillery had not opened up. Blue made his way towards them, dragging himself along on his elbows as he held his rifle. Matty scanned the

Turkish trenches in front, searching for a target. He shuddered as a shell exploded very close, the shock wave rolling over him. He looked back over his shoulder and gaped as he saw Bluey rolling in agony, his legs torn from his body. As he made to move towards his mate, machine gun fire raked the barley above his head, sending down showers of ripening seed. He turned to Jack, shouting at him.

'Jack, Bluey's hit. We gotta help him.'

Jack took no notice, his hand working the bolt of his rifle as he shot towards the Turkish lines.

'Jack!' Matty screamed. 'Bluey.'

Shaking his head, Matty slung his rifle and crawled to where Bluey was writhing in agony, screaming for his mother, his hands reaching for the bloody stumps of his legs. Grabbing him around the shoulders, Matty forced him to be still, yelling for the stretcher bearers. He pulled out a field dressing, a small dull green package, containing a bandage, with ties. He ripped it open and using the ties as a tourniquet, wrapped it around one of Bluey's bleeding legs. He reached into his tunic pocket, his hands bloody, dragging out his last field dressing.

Lt Col McIntosh came up beside Matty and tapped him on the shoulder.

'Trooper, we're digging in. Send the word along.'

Turning to the CO, Matty stared at him in bewilderment.

'Finish the other leg,' the Lt Col yelled at him over the noise of the guns. 'The stretcher bearers will come for him.'

Matty let Bluey's body gently to the ground. 'We'll be back for you, mate. The boys'll be along soon for you.'

He wriggled his way back to Jack, wincing every time a shell whizzed overhead.

'We're diggin' in, mate,' he shouted at Jack, scratching at the earth with his bayonet. Men around did the same; some were lucky to have a shell hole, which they set about deepening.

Continuing to look down the barrel of his rifle, Jack showed no sign of hearing Matty. He jumped when Matty threw a handful of dirt at him. Swinging around, his mouth open in exclamation, Jack stared at Matty.

Matty screamed at him, 'We are digging in!'

A look of incomprehension clouded Jack's face.

It hit Matty. Jack couldn't hear him. He was deaf from the bomb blast.

Matty made digging movements in the hard clay ground with his hands. Jack nodded in acknowledgement.

It continued, the artillery fire, the shrapnel, the rifle fire. Man after man, killed, wounded. Word passed up and down the thin body of men that held the line. 'Hold on, arty fire will start any minute… We are retreating… The captain said dig in.'

It was confusion, it was death.

But men laughed and joked, in the barley fields. Men died.

They could hear General Royston shouting, 'There's a gap to the right, Captain, send for the 8th.'

They could not see him but knew that he would be riding his horse recklessly up and down the front, looking for problems, encouraging the men.

Matty lay prone, sighting his rifle on the trenches of the Turks. His rifle followed the line of his eye, looking for a target. Seeing movement, he squeezed off a shot.

A shuddering of Jack's body, felt but not seen, alerted him to his mate's trouble. Keeping his head low, Matty pulled himself on his elbows, over to Jack. Blood seeped through Jack's sleeve; a hand lay useless on his rifle.

Matty's mind rejected the idea that Jack could be hurt. He stared at the blood.

'The bastard's hit me!' Cursing, Jack gripped his upper arm. 'The bloody bastard!'

Bits of buttercup, barley and poppy dropped around them like confetti as a burst of Turkish machine gun fire swept their position. The men pushed their heads into the dirt.

A movement from Jack caused Matty to snap out of his bewilderment.

'You'll have to make your way back,' Matty shouted at him.

'What?'

Realising Jack's hearing was still not working, Matty pointed to Jack, then jerked his thumb in the direction behind them.

'Nah, I'll just shoot with my left,' Jack yelled. 'Here, strap me arm up, will ya?'

Passing Matty his package of dressing, he held out his arm along the ground. Matty tore open the packet, shaking his head.

At least this will stop the bleeding, he thought. *Stubborn bastard.*

The sun rose and the men in the field felt their lips burning. The sweat mingled with the dust on their faces, and ran in their eyes. They scratched at the hard earth with their bayonets and hands, as the shrapnel took more men from the line. Their picks and shovels were miles behind them on the horses. All morning they fired at the Turks, waiting for the allied artillery. The 8th Light Horse came up on their right to fill the gap that had opened when the 9th Regiment were ordered to draw back and join up with the Yeomanry.

Looking to his left beyond the 11th Regiment, Matty saw the Camel Corps moving up. A shell landed and two camels disappeared in a second, the guns they were carrying flying high in the air. He returned his gaze to the Turkish trenches, a few hundred yards in front.

Now I know what Jack meant, about war being a bastard, he thought as his eyes scanned the Turkish trenches five hundred yards in front of him.

A head, covered by a woollen cap moved slightly. Matty's finger pulled the trigger of his rifle instinctively. The head dropped.

'Shit, it's like you're shootin' bloody rabbits. See and fire,' he muttered. 'But that was a man I hit.'

Matty shook his head, clearing the shambled thoughts.

'My first kill, an' I'm wonderin'. Christ, you idiot, look what they done to Bluey,' he said to himself.

A whizzing caused him to lay his cheek flat against the ground, his body tense. The explosion came twenty yards behind him. A scream and then men calling for the stretcher bearers.

He scratched the grit out of his eye and stared at the trenches again.

Something in him had awakened.

The world was no longer a happy carefree place. He'd heard the stories the men told of Anzac Cove, Lone Pine, but they had been stories. This was reality. Any piece of shrapnel, any bullet could snuff out your life in a split second. All his schooling, all that the Aboriginals had taught him, meant nothing, right here, right now. What mattered now was that if he was lucky, a bullet did not find him, and that he could shoot straight.

His hands trembled; his stomach tightened into knots. Deep inside, Matty acknowledged he was afraid. Afraid of dying, afraid of seeing his mates blown to bits. Bile rose in his throat, burning and choking. He spat it out. He continued to stare at the trenches.

A movement from his left caught his eye. The Lt Col was lifting a whistle to his mouth. Matty heard the whining of a shell, then watched in horror as it landed near the Lt Col. Blood spurted out from pellet wounds in his neck and shoulders. Another soldier went to his aid.

The Turks rose and attacked the allied lines. The men who could hold a weapon fired into the masses of troops that ran at them. Light Horse machine gun fire rattled incessantly, accompanied by the rifle bullets whistling their way towards the Turkish lines. Matty opened another pouch on his bandolier, took out a clip and rammed it into his magazine. He shifted his feet slightly, allowing his body to flatten, giving his arm a better position to hold the rifle.

His finger pulled the trigger, then worked the bolt. His first shot had been wide, his next hit a Turkish soldier, throwing the man backwards.

His mind shut off. All he could see was a wall of Turks coming, men who would kill. His hand worked the trigger, then the bolt. A new clip. The barrel of the gun grew hot. Puffs of dust rose from the ground as enemy bullets rained into the barley field. The Turkish guns laid in the artillery fire. Men screamed. Matty's mind stayed blank.

The resistance was too much, the counterattack failed. The Turks retreated to their trenches, their dead and wounded littering the ground. Silence reigned for a minute; the artillery began again, the cries for the stretcher bearers, the rifle fire.

Matty jumped as Jack shouted in his ear.

'Now you know why I told you to stay home, Shorty. War's not pretty, is it? This time we beat them.'

Swinging his head, he looked at Jack. A gleam of self-righteousness faded quickly from Jack's eyes, replaced by concern.

'You all right, mate?'

Matty nodded. 'Yeah, I think so.' He took a deep breath and let it out slowly, feeling his body loosen up. 'Yep, I'm fine. How about you?'

'Well, I can't hear with this ear.' Jack gestured at his right ear with his uninjured arm. 'But me shoulder's startin' to play up.'

'Don't be a stubborn bastard then. You'll have to go back,' Matty yelled at him.

Laughing, Jack said, 'And who'd keep an eye on you?'

Matty shook his head, his face drawn. 'Jack, I don't need lookin' after anymore. Not after that.'

He pointed towards the Turkish trenches.

Jack realised that something in Matty had shifted. He had lost his innocence. His eyes held a soldier's look now, knowing, deep, inward.

He closed his eyes for a moment, regretting that this boy, whom he loved as a brother, would never be the same. 'I can't go back, Shorty. There wasn't enough of us in the first place; now, we are worse off.'

Matty took the cork from his water bottle and offered Jack a sip. The water was hot and brackish and did not slake their thirst.

'The bloody officers knew this was a screwed-up plan from the beginning. Well, two of them have paid already. It's bloody murder,' Jack said angrily, passing back the water bottle.

The afternoon dragged on, the sun punishing the remaining men. The wounded lay in agony, dying slowly. The stretcher bearers risked their lives, bringing in the wounded; the casualty toll mounted.

As the sun faded into dusk, the word came for a withdrawal. The men dragged themselves and the wounded back to a Wadi, where in the darkness of night, they dug a trench with the picks and shovels brought up on their horses, which had been kept well back behind the lines. The men joked that from all the night work they had been doing, they must have developed owl eyes. The trench, dug in the dark, followed the lines mapped out by the officers, nearly perfectly.

Morning found the men weary and sunburnt. They had not slept for four days, and the scorching sun had caused blistered lips. A well nearby provided water and little fires sprung up to boil billies for a mug of cocoa. The men waited for a Turkish assault that never came and were happy when they were given the order to retire to Khan Yunis.

Anxiously, Matty waited on news of Jack and Bluey. Water was two miles away and the soldiers had to take the horses to it twice a day. The heat and dust drove the men to distraction, and they managed to go for a swim in the sea. On arriving back, they heard the news that Lt Col McIntosh had died from his wounds. This hit the men hard, as they were fond of him. Worse information arrived with the mail. Bluey was dead. He died on a camel's back during the long trek to a field hospital. A letter from Jack eased Matty's mind.

Field Hospital

2nd May 1917

Dear Matty,

Can you write to the Boss and the Missus? Tell them I'm all right. Don't bother writing to me here because I'll be back to the regiment before I get your letter.

The shoulder wound was through the muscle and clean. Didn't hit any bone. It is healing quickly. Stayed mum about my ear. It will get better on its own. The nurses here make life so good. Just looking at them makes you better. They are good sports too and tough. They work hard. There are many poor beggars here that need more than a nurse. Some won't even make it home. They have terrible wounds. The fellow in the bed next to me, he got a blighty. Lost a few fingers, but he can't wait to see England.
Well, hope you are looking after China and Absent for me. I will be back soon.

Yours sincerely,
Jack.

EIGHTEEN

In the early morning light, Sammy sat on an ammunition box by the stream, dangling his battered hat between his knees, watching the dirty water eddying around some rocks. He felt someone sit down beside him. Bandy raised his head, saw who it was, then lay his muzzle on his paws, his eyes on Sammy.

'Three days ago, we were in trenches, now we're resting here. They call this place Jesus Farm. Cause of the big crucifix over there?' Dave said softly as he handed Sammy a mug of tea.

Placing his hat on the ground, Sammy took the offering, blowing gently across the scalding brew. He rested his elbows on his knees, still staring into the water.

'When a fella dies at home, our mob, we don't say his name again, but we remember him,' Sammy said in a sing-song voice as he lifted his head and looked towards the west where the noise of the battlefields could be heard sixteen miles away. 'Here, so many die, it's hard to remember when they die. They all one big mob. When a fella tries to remember them, they get all mixed up.'

He sighed and returned his eyes to the water, taking a sip from his mug.

'It's 'cause we're knackered, Darky. Sometimes I can't think straight, I'm that tired. It'll sort itself out eventually. They'll come back to you.'

'Are you gonna write to Harry's mother? The captain'll write; maybe one of us should too.'

Dave stared at his mate's black curly hair, sensing that something was going on in the mind under it, something that he would never understand. They had lost so many of their platoon, but you got on with it. *If there is a God,* Dave thought, *and we get out of this, then we'll have time to remember. It's better not to think about it now.*

'I'll write, Darky. The poor woman, one boy dead, one with no legs.'

Sammy leant over to pick up his hat, glancing at Dave.

'That Queenslander bloke, he still scratchin' his head about how you knew,' he said, the start of a smile on his lips. 'You'd better tell him.'

They went back to their tents, tidied up and got ready for parade.

Standing in the warm sun, they stood at attention while the sergeant called the roll.

'Hey, laddie,' Dave whispered to the big, tall Queenslander. 'I know you're a Queenslander 'cause you're so bloody big. They breed 'em big up there.'

Sammy tried hard to suppress a laugh but failed. It came out as a snort. The lieutenant scowled at them.

Dismissed, they broke ranks, the object of Dave's teasing following them to breakfast.

'Are ya havin' a go at me?' he asked, menace in his voice.

Stopping, Dave turned around to face him.

'Well, I might have took the piss a bit. But I'm not having a go. Shearing's my game. I've travelled all over the country. Sometimes you can pick a man's state by the way he talks. You talk like a Queenslander. Everyone in our battalion, except for Darky and I, are from Queensland. I was shearing at Warwick when I enlisted.'

'Ah, I see,' the man said doubtfully.

Dave smiled at him and stuck out his hand. 'You're new, aren't you, cobber? Came in with the last reinforcements. What's your name?'

The big man hesitated, but only for a second. He took Dave's outstretched hand and shook it firmly. 'Clarry.'

'Clarry, I'm Dave and this is Darky.' Dave gestured towards Sammy. 'Well, Sammy, really, but his got so many tricks up his sleeve, we call him Darky.'

Clarry nodded in Sammy's direction. 'We got blokes like you back home. Good blokes.'

Sammy took that as a compliment and shook hands. 'Where's home?'

'Charleville.'

Dave laughed. 'That would make you near neighbours then. Darky's from west of the Paroo, just under Hungerford.'

Clarry nodded.

'That was your first time out, back there, wasn't it?' Dave asked him.

'Yeah, we got here the day before.'

'I didn't think I'd seen you before. Well, now you know what it's all about,' Dave said, adding thoughtfully, 'We got a long way to go yet.'

Sammy stared at Dave, his black eyes remote. 'Longa way, mate. Longa way.'

Dave shivered and looked away, wishing that Sammy had stayed the happy smiling boy he had first met.

'Come on, I'm hungry.'

They found Kenny holding a place in the line at the dixie pots. As each man filled his mess tin, he entered the tent, sitting on the long bench seats.

Clarry joined them at breakfast, asking Dave about his travels.

Sammy sat back, saying nothing until Clarry started talking about their last time in the line.

'That Warneton place, we did good there, didn't we?'

'Yeah, we did good,' Sammy agreed. 'You new fellas, you learn quick.'

Dave glanced up from his mess tin, regarding Clarry carefully.

'You know, big fella, I saw you out there, the last night we were in the line, when we raided the western section. I thought you were a goner at that second pill box when that shell dropped near you,' he said slowly. 'I said to myself, another new chum gone. But what gets me is how you got through the mud. You're bigger and heavier than anyone here, and yet you just waltzed through it.'

Clarry beamed at the praise, reddening slightly. 'I dunno. Just always been good on me feet, played a lot of football.'

'And when you jumped in those trenches, and all the Fritz put up their hands, I thought you were going to shoot them.'

'I couldn't understand what they was sayin'. I reckoned they might be trickin'. I was going to shoot 'em, but Darky here, he yells, "No, they givin' up",' Clarry replied, still beaming. 'Boy, we took some prisoners that night.'

Kenny put his hands across his mouth, pretending to yawn, but could not hide the laughter in his eyes.

He turned towards Sammy. 'And how about you, Darky? I thought you'd gone mad when you broke off and headed for that crater.'

'I saw a machine gun gettin' into our blokes.' He shrugged.

'So, you take yourself over there, kill three of them and get yourself four prisoners. You'll get a mention for that.'

Again, Sammy shrugged.

A quiet descended on the men as an officer came in, looking around at them. Spotting who he was looking for, he made his way through the crowded tent.

The lieutenant stopped at their table, leaning on it in front of Dave.

'Congratulations, Dave. You've just got yourself a stripe,' he said, smiling as he watched Dave's reaction.

'What? No, sir. I don't want a stripe. These bastards'll never listen to me,' he replied, a look of alarm on his face. 'What happened to Smithy, anyway?'

'Corporal Smith got transferred to HQ. Bugger had kept quiet about his real career before the war. Seems he was a clerk in one of the banks. HQ is getting short on clerks and, well, Smith was getting a bit jittery.'

The lieutenant stood back up, placing his hands behind his back. Glancing from Sammy to Clarry, then back at Dave, he commented, 'These men already listen to you, Dave.'

'Yeah, but now I got to be above them and I don't like that,' Dave muttered. Quickly, he looked up. 'No offence, mate.'

The officer laughed. 'None taken. But get used it. You're the CO's choice for Corporal and Corporal you'll be.'

When he left, the men swarmed around Dave, congratulating him.

'If the lieutenant hadn't been such a good cobber when he was a sarge, I wouldn't give him the time of day. He'll go far, that one. If he doesn't get killed first,' Dave said to no one in particular.

The men ribbed Dave about his promotion for a few days, but then they settled back into routine.

The news came through that their stay at Jesus Farm was at an end. They entrained at Bailleul, then dismounting from the train, marched to village of Remilly-Werquin. The platoon shifted into barns that became their home for the next three weeks. Dave tried to get Sammy to go to the nearby town of St Omers to visit the estaminets, but Sammy just shook his head and stayed in the village. Later that night, he was woken by the return of his platoon, singing and talking loudly about the good brawl they had had.

Getting up, he guided his drunken mates to their beds, smiling to himself when Dave said, 'You should've come, Darky. What a biffo we had with some other blokes. You would have cleaned them up.'.'

Sammy patted his mate's shoulder.

'You be lucky not to get charged. Where were the guards?'

'We told them that there was more blokes causing trouble back on the road, so they took after them, eh. Didn't worry about us being late.'

The men turned out in the morning, a little worse for wear, but by mid-afternoon, the effects of last night's carousing began to tell.

'We're supposed to be here for a rest.' Irish moaned, as they ran up the field, their rifles at their hip, ready to stick the bayonet into a straw dummy.

'I'd like a quid for every time we've done this,' Dave growled.

The training was hard, and long hours of it tired the men. The visits to town became less frequent. The battalion turned out for parade and there, they received their new orders from the brigade commander.

'Now we're for it! I'll bet there's a big push coming on,' Dave said as they were dismissed. 'Come on, boys, let's go see what the major's got to say.'

The battalion's rest had come to an end.

Marching over cobblestones, through various towns over a period of days, the men were glad to board a train that would take them to Ypres. The weather had been warm, and the roads dusty. To be able to ride instead of marching with full kit, was a luxury to the troops. Sammy took the time to write to the boys in the desert.

France

27th August 1917

Dear mates,

We somewhere in the Ypres sector. Not allowed to say where. Censor will mark it out. We have been in more fighting. The weather, it all right but they think it might rain soon. I hope not. It makes the trenches too wet. The shells tear up where we have to advance, makes it hard going. The Missus sent me a parcel. I shared the tucker with the fellas but kept the socks. They are good ones.

I've had a dog for a while. A lot of men have mascots, little terrier sorts, cats, birds. Mine is a Brittany Spaniel, a gun dog. I call him Bandaarr, Bandy for short. He's good at carrying messages and lets us know if any enemy are close to the trench. He doesn't bark, just growls soft. He stays in the trenches when we go out on raids or on a push, but behind the lines, he is with me all the time. The men all give him food and treat him good. Kenny got a gas mask from the Tommies for him. They have their own special trained messenger dogs. Write and tell me about what's happening over there.

Your mate,
Sammy.

The weather turned, rain and cold chasing away the warmer days. At ten o'clock at night, the battalion made its approach march to the frontline. Zero hour was five fifteen a.m. and they pushed through the sodden, sticky mud of the trenches until they came to their jump-off point.

Their artillery opened up and shells screamed over on their flight to the German trenches. It pounded the very inner fibre of their bodies, hour after hour, until not only were their ears were hurting, but their whole being felt shocked, numb. The ground roiled, trembled and spewed forth all its buried secrets then buried them again, over and over.

Sammy leant against the parapet, his shoulder wedged against Dave's arm. The voice of their captain echoed in their ears. 'Stand to, boys, at the walk, we'll go. On the whistle.'

The knot in Sammy's gut twisted and wrenched until it was alive, raging in his body. He closed his eyes and saw the river at home. It was replaced by old Minnie's black face, but it was blurred. He tried to see but it kept fading. He saw a haze of red soil. The harsh outback sun glaring out of the vivid blue sky, swirling, bouncing around in his head.

He saw Charlie, silent and stealthy as he stalked a roo.

Opening his eyes, he stared at Dave and watched as his mate turned to him. He was astounded by the thought that Dave was seeing his own images of home; it showed in his eyes, in his face. He leant closer to him.

'We see it again, mate. Buggered if we don't,' Sammy shouted, trying to be heard above the pounding of the artillery.

Dave nodded and rested his hand on Sammy's shoulder. 'Too right, cobber, I reckon we will.'

The smoke from the shells lay over them, hiding no-man's land and what was left of the waiting enemy. Sammy shuddered as he sensed the tension rise in the men around him. He felt as though he could reach out and with his fingers, grasp strands of the nerve stretching substance as it lifted from the soldiers.

This was the moment in which some men pissed themselves with fear, or their hands shook and their muscles strung so tight that they felt as though they couldn't take that leap up over the wall. Some sat and cried, while others just seemed to retreat inwards; each man had his own reaction to the thought of going over the top.

The shriek of the whistle cut through the air. Men scrabbled and crawled up and over the parapet, walking forward, bending into the fog, their rifles held at the hip. Looking about him, Sammy wondered at the sanity of what they were doing. It seemed that the soldiers waded through the mud as though they were detached from the living world, a group of men trudging through a black wasteland, in a wet grey shroud, knowing that death was ahead of them, theirs or their mates'. Yet it didn't deter them from what they had been ordered to do. He shrugged and forced himself to think of nothing but the enemy, waiting in their trenches. And avoiding the shell craters, full of the dead and grey, slimy water.

Mud dragged at his feet as he pulled one leg then the other through the stinking morass. The barrage was a warning of attack and German artillery threw all it could at no-man's land, knowing that out in front of them, allied soldiers were coming at them across the narrow piece of ground that separated the two armies. The German machine guns on the flanks opened up, their deadly fire dropping soldiers as the bullets swept the battlefield. A descending shrill sound caused an instinctive tightening in Sammy's movements. A shell hit the ground close to the platoon's line, the deafening roar pounded their senses. Earth, corpses and sizzling shards of metal punched them. As one, the men were blown off their feet, sinking into the clammy reeking muck. Those that could, got to their feet and continued forward, dazed and mostly deaf. Sammy reached down and pulled a man up by his collar. He had a large piece of shrapnel in his leg and Sammy turned him back towards the trenches, giving him a gentle shove. He didn't see the soldier hold his stomach with his filthy hands, as loops of grey intestine escaped through the torn cloth of his coat. The soldier staggered slowly and uncomprehendingly, towards his own line for a few feet before his legs folded underneath him and he crumpled to the ground.

Glancing to his right, Sammy saw Norry crouched low, his rifle held in both hands across his chest, as though he was not sure whether to pull it up and aim it or thrust it out in front, bayonet towards the German line.

Sammy prodded him in the ribs, yelling into his ear, 'Hey, mate, let's get these bastards, eh?'

Norry turned his head slowly to look at Sammy.

'Shit,' Sammy whispered. His jaw clamped hard, his mind stopping any more words.

The left side of Norry's handsome face was shorn of skin and a thick dark bloody rope ran from under his hair over the silvery blue muscles of his face. His eyes, glassy and senseless, stared through Sammy into the fog that enveloped the men. Slinging his rifle over his shoulder, Sammy grabbed Norry's elbow and dragged him to ground. Pushing his shoulders down, he leant over the man, and with his lips brushing his ear, shouted, 'Mate, down, stay down. The bearers'll pick you up.'

Norry lay still, his grimy hands still gripping the rifle to his chest, his vacant eyes staring upwards through the grey fog. Sammy stood up and looked at Dave.

'It like rabbit shootin'. A waste of—' His bitter outburst was drowned by the roar of another close explosion. Neither man ducked; there was no point. A rifle barrel prodded Sammy in the ribs and swinging around, he saw a sergeant, his face glaring with anger.

'You ain't a bleeding Salvo, you nigger, you're a bleedin' soldier. Now move it,' he roared.

Sammy opened his mouth to reply but the rifle rose to rest under his chin. He turned and moved forward again, his mind cursing at not being able to help his fallen mates. They were here to advance at the walk, to the enemy's trenches and advance they would, with men falling all about them, some screaming, others sliding silently into the slime. There was no escaping, no cowering. The alternative was to shelter in a trench, littered with refuse and body parts, waiting to be buried by an avalanche of rank earth caused by a barrage of shells, to be forever labelled a coward.

He was not a coward. He would go with his mates.

'Bugger 'em. They yell, swear at us in drill so we'll walk past dying men. They're our mates, for hell's sake,' his mind screamed in frustration.

As the smoke swirled, thinned, the ground beneath them shuddered under the impact of shell after shell, surge after surge of shock waves. Debris assailed them, blind and random. Shrapnel flew out, indiscriminate in its murderous path.

Rory was twenty yards in front, then gone, dispersed into fragments of flesh and bone. Boy'o fell backwards, laid straight and stiff with a shard of sizzling metal in his forehead.

As he tramped forward, Sammy's eyes glazed and his mind became a silent empty place, his legs moving without conscious effort.

Dave glanced sideways at Sammy and his gut shrivelled at the look on his mate's face. Reaching out and grabbing his friend's arm, Dave pulled his friend to him. Sammy showed no reaction as Dave shook his arm, or as Dave's arm went around his shoulders. Dave shouted into Sammy's ear, fear making his arm tighten into a stranglehold around Sammy.

On the third attempt, Dave's hoarse voice started to seep through.

'Don't… in on me… not now… too far.'

Sammy stared into the red-rimmed eyes of his mate and heard again the hellish noise hammer him. He felt the cold vapour of night on his face. He shook his head, trying to recall the past few minutes. Dave's arm stayed tight around him for a second more, then dropped away.

'Those bastards are still waiting. Come on,' Dave yelled as he jerked his rifle towards the German lines.

The lines of soldiers, once shoulder to shoulder, were now scattered individuals, advancing relentlessly over the dead and wounded, stepping through and around the scattered remnants of the barbed-wire fortifications that their own artillery had shredded. The smell of decay rose again as corpses were churned up by the shelling.

They could see the German trenches. The smoke that had hidden them from the enemy's sight now cleared and with a guttural roar, the Australians charged at the trench, screaming with rage and determination, firing into the trenches, following their mates into the hail of bullets let loose by the waiting foe.

Those that remained of A Company jumped, stumbled and fell into the trench, hacking and thrusting with their bayonets. Their captain stood with his back to the firewall, making every shot of his revolver count until it fell from his lifeless hand. Sammy fired his rifle at point blank range, obliterating the face of the German who was too slow in pulling the trigger of his own gun. Another grey uniform took his place; Sammy worked the bolt, loading another cartridge and pulled the trigger. Side by side, in the confined space of the trench, no room to lift their rifles, they kept feeding in cartridges, the rifles jerking in their hands, not lifting to aim, but firing from the hip. When the clip ran out, they used the bayonet, watching the fear in the enemy's eyes as they went to work with the long blade.

The Germans retreated up the trench, falling over the perished and maimed lying on the floor. As more and more men of the battalion came over the parapets, the enemy threw up their hands, not wishing to be slaughtered in a flooded, stinking hole in France. Instead, they would take their chances as prisoners of war.

As the order came along to the exhausted men – 'secure the trench' – Sammy stood very still, his hands loading and unloading his rifle. He stared at the water running down the greasy edge of the trench wall. His eyes shifted to the death masks of the dead soldiers that lay in the trench, his look jerking from one to another. Their scattered forms led his eyes upwards to the parapet, where grotesque figures lay in a state of putrefaction, their faces missing, eaten by the rats. It was not a new sight to Sammy. There were bodies all over no-man's land, bodies that each army had not had time to bury, or the chance. His hands stilled as his brown eyes bulged and his jaw tightened into a grimace.

Dave slung his rifle and took Sammy's face in his hands. He jerked Sammy's head up and looked into his eyes.

'Are you with me, Darky?' he demanded. 'Get yourself together.'

Tears dribbled slowly down Sammy's face. Dropping his gun, he reached out and gripped Dave's forearms as his body convulsed with sobs. He tried to keep them inside, but they burst out and turned into a raging incomprehensible rambling. His legs melted and he sank to the ground, dragging Dave with him.

'The bastards, them behind the lines. They murder us,' he screamed at Dave, his face inches from his mate's face. 'We made it… but them, our mates, they dead!'

Dave prised Sammy's fingers from around his arms and slowly got to his feet. He stared down at his friend lying in the filth on the floor of the trench, a shivering wreck of the boy he had known since the camp near Brisbane. Without any conscious thought as to why, Dave bent over Sammy and grabbing him by the shirt, pulled him up. As Sammy swung limply at the end of Dave's grip, Dave drew back his arm and with a swift punch, gave Sammy the gift of unconsciousness.

Dave leant over and pulled him into a sitting position. The soldiers around them watched wordlessly. Dave lifted his mate over his shoulder and carried him down the trench to a dugout, where he laid him gently down. As he wiped the foul crud from Sammy's face, he muttered angrily, 'We aren't goin' to be parted like this, Darky. You're a good bloke. Too good for here.'

A stern voice made Dave look up.

'Soldier, I spoke to you! If that man's injured, he'll have to go back.'

Dave's eyes were cold as he stood up in the small space, coming very close with the officer who had addressed him. Dave was the taller and with his face tight, he looked down at a captain he had not seen before.

'He just took a hit to the head,' Dave replied, his voice level. 'He'll be all right in a mo'.'

The captain felt the emotion pulsating from the soldier in front of him. He wondered if they had come from the same town.

'Soldier,' he said gently, 'we are to be relieved as soon as our flanks consolidate their positions. When that happens, you get this man back to the rear trenches.'

'What do you think I'd do with him? Leave him here?'

'No, but I know why he's not awake. I'll ignore it for now, but if he's not with us when he comes round, you get him to the rear. They'll find something for him to do there.'

The officer spoke slowly and clearly. Dave got the message. His body relaxed a little and he nodded his head at the captain.

'Yes, sir.'

Taking the corner of his shirt from inside his trousers, the only part of it not covered in muck, he finished wiping the mud from Sammy's face. Dave pulled him up by the shoulders, shook him gently and leaning into his ear, he called to Sammy.

'C'mon, mate, wake up. Come back to me.'

He raised his head to look at Sammy; he saw his eyelids start to tremble. Slowly they opened and Dave was relieved to see comprehension in them. They stared at each other, lost in a cocoon of their own making while around them, the fury of war raged. Sammy opened his mouth to speak and felt pain along his jaw. He raised his hand and felt it, expecting to find a wound.

'Sorry, mate, but you went a bit maggoty on me. I outed you for a while,' Dave said. 'Been a long time since I got a good one on you, eh?'

'I can't remember leavin' our possy, Dave. What the hell happened?'

'Like I said, you got the wind up a bit, but you're all right now. C'mon, the suicide club'll be along in a mo'.'

Sammy looked up and saw the stretcher bearers arriving to pick up the badly wounded.

'They're already here, mate. Let's get out of their way.'

Standing up, Sammy felt a slight dizziness. He put out a hand to steady himself, pulling it back quickly as his hand sunk into the wound of a dead soldier.

'It's no bloody wonder a fella'd go nuts in this place,' he muttered to himself as he wiped the gore off his fingers onto the dead man's uniform.

NINETEEN

'Get the dog out of sight. Allied High Command are due in tonight!'

Matty acknowledged the captain with a quick salute and led his mare forward; the dog immediately rose and fell into stride beside Cedar.

The captain resumed his daily walk around the camp but then turned back to the men.

'Boys! Reveille 0500. Inspection and drill at 0600,' he announced with a wink.

The soldiers grinned, nodded their head in thanks and continued towards the horse piquets.

'Bloody Mitchell, he's a good bloke,' Matty mumbled to Jack. 'He never lets us down.'

Jack nodded in agreement. 'He's a cobber, all right! The Brass reckons to surprise us, eh? Bugger 'em. Mitchell fixed that for us.'

'You tell the others an' I'll put Cedar away,' Matty said with a grin.

'All right. C'mon, China.'

The dog looked at Jack, then back at the mare as she was led away, his face a study of torn loyalty. Jack shrugged and gestured towards the horse.

'Go with yer mate, dog.'

China wagged his tail and scampered after the horse. As Jack watched him frolicking in front of the mare, he thought back to the first time he saw China wrapped in the arms of the dirty young street boy.

'What are ya' doin', Jack? Stone the crows! Daydreamin' won't get our gear cleaned!'

Jack's mind snapped back to the present. 'Just thinkin' about when I got China. Funny, how animals mean so much to us.'

'Yeah,' Matty said thoughtfully. 'You know, maybe that's why Cedar and China are mates.'

'Yeah, maybe,' Jack said and patted China, who had followed the men as they went into their tent. Matty had already spread the word about the inspection while Jack had been daydreaming. While they cleaned their gear, the talk amongst the men fell into the usual vein of trying to work out what their next move would be. One soldier had overheard Captain Mitchell telling their sergeant that to retake Gaza, they would first have to take Beersheba, then drive the Turks back towards Jerusalem.

Other men would drop in from time to time, and the word spread quickly to men in other units that something big was about to break. An undercurrent of excitement rippled through the camp. Some men wrote letters home, some cleaned their equipment, while others boiled their billies of tea and sat about in their tents, smoking and talking till lights out.

The heat from the early morning sun slowly replaced the chill of the desert's night air. Horses nickered and stamped about impatiently as they heard the men stirring. They knew a grooming and feed were near.

When the order came for inspection, the men were ready and waiting. They lined up in their regiments, each soldier at his horse's head. Each squadron had its own sergeant major, captain and major who stood slightly in front of their troops.

The 'Big Brass', as the lesser ranked men called their superiors, walked along the lines then returned to their field headquarters. The soldiers sensed that they had been right about another offensive, for amongst the usual officers was General Chauvel, the commanding General of the Desert Mounted Corps.

The quietness of the desert was broken by the order to mount, immediately followed by the sounds of creaking leather, snorting horses and the clinking of metal as men rode through various drills and formations under the instruction of their sergeants. The captains were receiving their orders from the staff tent. As Captain Mitchell prepared to re-join his squadron, a British major, who had been with General Chauvel, intercepted him.

'I noticed, Captain, that your soldiers were not up to standard in dress regulations and yet, the horses and equipment were spotless. Have they no personal pride, Captain?' he queried.

Captain Mitchell studied the major, realising he must be straight out from England. Seasoned English officers never would have asked; they already knew.

'Sir, my men have been fighting for the past two years. A fair few of them fought at Gallipoli. Our last affair was Gaza and before that El Arish. My men are not your "regulation" soldiers, sir. I would not swap any one of my men for a whole British Division,' came the proud reply from the offended captain.

Smiling inwardly at the captain's fierce loyalty towards the men under his command, the major decided to soothe the captain's ruffled feathers.

'I must admit, though, your Walers are holding up to the conditions better than any other type of horse out here. You Australians know your horseflesh!'

'Yes, sir! Our horses are the best, and there is no other soldier in any other army that treats his horse better than our boys do,' stated the captain. He paused and looked out over the mounted soldiers. Almost too quietly for the major to hear, the captain murmured, 'He'd hang his captain before he'd let anything happen to his horse!'

Suddenly, a commotion broke out amid the parading horses and a loud cheering rose in the air. Men were reining in their mounts and waving their hats jubilantly. Amongst the sea of soldiers, horses and red dust, a lone horse was involved in a spirited display of bucking.

'Well, I never! Those men should never break rank. Ever!' spluttered the major.

The way he was gasping and waving his arm at the cheering soldiers, Captain Mitchell thought that the officer beside him was about to choke.

'That's Cedar, sir. Everyone here knows her. She has a phobia about snakes. You can bet a snake started that,' he said knowingly.

The major stared at the captain in disbelief. 'A snake?'

'Yes. Watson told me a grey mulga snake landed on her when she was a yearling. He had her in a yard near the homestead and happened to see the whole thing. Ever since then, she goes off whenever she sees one.' Mitchell paused and turned to the major. 'That mare—'

'Should be put down! She is unsafe and has no place at the front line,' interrupted the major.

'No, sir! That mare is the fastest horse in the regiment. She's won every race the men have had,' the captain said. 'I've seen that mare stay beside Watson, of her own accord, under enemy fire. When her rider is on scout duty, she'll do double the miles of other horses and look fresher. She does not buck out of meanness; she has a great temperament, has never put a foot wrong on march.'

The captain conveniently forgot to tell the major that some of the reconnaissance was not always official.

'Excuse me, sir. I had better get these boys ready to move out,' said Captain Mitchell as he mounted his own horse.

Matty had calmed Cedar by this time and the men had resumed their positions. Billy candidly admitted to his captain that he had dropped the asp in front of Cedar to settle a bet with another section about how good a rider Matty was. He was promptly put on suspended field punishment. The captain reprimanded the men, telling them if they wanted to be galahs, to do it other than when on parade and not in front of visiting officers.

The officer, having vented his anger, gave an outline of the forthcoming action. A loud cheer rose when the captain told his men to prepare to march. They packed the tents on the supply wagons. They would sleep on their groundsheets from now on and these were carried tied to the saddles, along with iron rations for both the horse and rider.

A tangible air of tension hung over the Light Horse regiments as they formed into their sections. At the walk, they proceeded east from Tell el Fara along the southern side of the Wadi Ghuzzi, a large column that stretched for one and a half miles, a dark strand that broke the barrenness of the landscape. When they were out of sight of the visiting officers, Jack made his way to the supply wagons to get China. The dog lunged about, straining at the rope that held him.

'Settle down, mate. Now don't go makin' a fuss,' Jack said as he leant from the saddle and untied the dog. The dog raced ahead to Cedar. A quick lick to her face assured the dog that the mare was quite well.

The column halted just past Esani. The men set up camp and fed the horses. They were relieved to find pools of water, the only water since leaving Tell el Fara. After only a few hours' sleep, they received their orders, watered the horses and began to make preparations for the next move. Hearing the guns over towards Gaza caused excitement to flicker through the regiment. Mounted up again with only fighting rations and the order 'no smoking', the regiment headed for Khelasa. The Anzac engineers had repaired the wells that the Turks had blown. This was to be their last water until Beersheba. As well as being a crucial point in the allied offensive, the soldiers knew it was essential to capture Beersheba before the Turks could blow the wells there. To get to Beersheba meant a rigorous forty-mile ride through the night, then a hard fight to secure the town.

While men rested at the feet of their horses in whatever shade could be found or made, General Chauvel and his staff was completing plans for the night march to Beersheba. Allied troops had been shelling Gaza for the past few days, hoping to delude the Turks into sending troops to the west, while the allied forces marched towards Beersheba in the east. It was critical to allied plans that Beersheba fell on the first day of attack. Arab spies had been telling the Turks about the allied movements, but the enemy was hesitant to believe them.

Matty lay with his back against a thin palm tree, which afforded hardly any shade in the sweltering heat; flies buzzed about annoyingly in great numbers. He reached up and stroked Cedar's soft muzzle, feeling a touch of guilt about bringing her to this cruel land. He could not believe his luck that neither of them had been hurt, when more than one hundred men and horses of their regiment had been wounded or killed.

The desert sun began its descent on the horizon as the order came and soldiers rose and organised themselves. The water carts were empty. All the water the soldiers had was in their water bottle. They set about checking their horses' feet, grooming out the sweat marks before saddling and making sure their gear was tightly secured. They knew that the order to mount would come shortly; night in the desert fell quickly.

Matty felt a restlessness. He checked Cedar's girth again and lifted her feet to examine her shoes. He could feel a gnawing inside him and though he could not explain it, he needed action to dispel it. Matty decided to meet any trouble that may be coming his way head on. After telling Jack what he was up to, he found his captain and waited until his captain turned to him.

'Yes, Watson?'

Matty, not used to asking permission for such things, fumbled with his reins and then taking a deep breath, looked straight at the captain. 'Sir, I'd like to be in the screen guard for this march.'

Matty glanced at Jack, missing the fleeting look of amazement that crossed the captain's face.

'I suppose you are going to make the same request, Henderson?'

Jack looked at his captain, as if to say, 'Need you ask?'

The captain looked back at Matty, a smile touching his eyes. 'Strange that you ask first. Usually, you two just disappear and do it. Are you looking for Valhalla?'

'Valhalla? What's that?' asked Matty.

'It is a place in Viking legend. Warriors who died as heroes in battle went there,' explained the captain.

The two soldiers not only had the reputation for being the owners of the regiment's liveliest animals but had also proven their scouting ability. The officer nodded and outlined plans for the march to the two men, then left them to carry on. The regiment was ready, waiting for the order to move out. The command 'forward, at the walk' echoed down the column.

The Australian Light Horse were on their way to Beersheba.

A full moon, rising on the horizon, threw its ghostly illumination across the stony ground, creating voids of light and dark. As it climbed higher, the shadows slowly receded until the landscape glowed in gentle pearly light. One hundred yards ahead of the marching army, Matty and Jack rode screen guard, eyes flickering from up ahead, then to the earth as they looked for sign of enemy movement. Growing up on the outback station, tracking lost stock in the mulga country, this assignment was second nature to them.

Cedar stepped out eagerly, refreshed by the cool night air. She could feel the alertness in Matty's body and nearly unseated him when he pushed her into a trot. The regiment would trot for forty minutes, walk for ten, then dismount and lead their horses for ten. The scout horses had to bear the twenty stone loads of their rider and his equipment, for a full hour at a time. They would halt sometimes to allow the regiment to gain ground, but the scouts would remain mounted at the halt.

The regiment were to reach the appointed place at dawn. As they drew closer to their objective, they could hear the artillery shelling Beersheba to soften up the defence of the enemy.

A low resonance of thousands of hooves filled the air as three divisions marched towards the rendezvous. When Cedar saw the large body of horses far to the right, she ground the bit and jerked the reins impatiently.

'You silly cow! Haven't you worn out yet?'

Jack chuckled and gestured to his plodding horse. 'Absent's got the idea. He doesn't reckon on wastin' energy.'

The 12th Regiment were not needed as yet, so Brigadier Grant gave orders for them to spread out, so as not to make a target for the enemy to shell. Grant then made his way to General Chauvel's headquarters to receive his orders.

The men dismounted, glad to give the horses a well-earned break, although the men themselves were eager for action now they had arrived. The sound of the guns – from Field Marshall Chetwode's bombardment of the Turkish advance defences to the southwest – had added to their excitement. The 12th Regiment sat in the shade of their horses, waiting for news. They watched as the 7th Regiment broke away towards the east, and Ryrie's regiment moved to the northeast.

The hours passed, and while 'he 12th Regiment waited, the fierce sun rose higher, driving some horses to lie beside their masters. Captain Mitchell walked amongst his men, telling them of the progress on the different fronts as news came to hand. He came across Matty lying against Cedar's side, for the mare had also lain down to rest. As the captain approached, Cedar raised her head, but on hearing Matty's voice, she relaxed and waited for Matty to move before gathering her legs under her. Contented to stay in that position, the mare closed her eyes to the flies and the harsh glare of the sun.

'We've been hearin' the guns. What's been happenin', sir?' asked Matty as he stroked the mare's ears. 'We're ready to go, me an' Cedar.'

The captain smiled at the words 'we're ready'.

He answered, 'The infantry has managed to get hold of the objective in the south. That will stop the Turks from flanking us. The En Zeds and some of our boys from the second and third have moved on Tel El Saba in the north. That is from where the Turks will bring reinforcements. Apparently, they are putting up quite a fight over there. When that has been taken, the main attack on Beersheba can start.'

Matty raised his eyebrows and nodded. 'How 'bout us, Captain? When do we go in?'

'I'm not sure. The Brigadier is up at HQ now. We'll know soon.'

'Too right!' hooted Matty, slapping his thigh in excitement.

'Don't get too worked up, Watson,' warned Captain Mitchell.

'It's goin' to have to happen soon. There's only about three hours of daylight left!' replied Matty.

A messenger galloped up to the captain, his horse throwing flurries of sand into the air. Cedar to jump to her feet in alarm. The mounted soldier threw a salute at the captain and relayed his message.

Matty, overhearing the orders, tightened the mare's girth and went to find Jack. Searching among the soldiers, he found his mate playing cards with other men from their troop.

'It's on fellas!' he whooped. 'We're goin' in! The 4th and us.'

'Trust you to be the first to hear. You're the luckiest devil I know,' a soldier called to Matty.

Matty poured the last of his water into the crown of his hat and offering it to Cedar, said, 'This is all there is, girl.'

The horses had now been without water for nearly forty hours.

The mare lowered her head to the water, and in three sips, she had finished it. Matty scooped up the small amount that the mare had not been able to get out of the creases, and wiped his wet hand over her eyes, then over his own face. All around him, soldiers were repeating the same process with their own mounts. Jack shared his water with both his horse and China, who quickly finished his and gazed at Jack, looking for more.

'Sorry, China Plate, me old mate.' Jack sighed. 'We've gotta chase them Turks out before any of us get more. You'll have stay with the wagons.'

Dust rose as the regiment formed under the orders of the officers but because the men had been dispersed over such a wide area, it took some time to regroup – precious time.

General Chauvel had decided on a cavalry charge and had chosen the Light Horse over Fitzgerald's Mounted Yeomanry. The Yeomanry had swords for a charge, but the Light Horse were closer to Beersheba. Four miles from it. The Light Horse normally galloped up to within a few hundred yards of the enemy, dismounted and proceeded with the attack on foot. This would not be the case today. It was to be a mounted charge across open ground against a heavily fortified enemy; rifles slung, bayonet in hand.

As the word spread, voices rose in excitement. This was every mounted soldier's dream. Then a quietness descended as the men took in the enormity of what was before them. A charge into gun and artillery fire.

Matty rubbed Cedar's neck, trying to calm her; it was her sixth sense working again. The mare was dancing up and down on the spot, tossing her head with impatience.

'You're ready, aren't you, Cedar?' he said.

'There's not a man here who wouldn't bet on Cedar being at the front when we hit them Turks. We all know she's the best,' Jack said. It was his way of saying good luck.

Matty stroked Cedar's muzzle as he prepared himself for the attack. His stomach tightened as he felt the tension rising. The command came to mount. As he swung his leg over and settled into the saddle, he looked about, feeling confident here in the desert, so like his home.

The regiments moved forward, led by Grant and his officers, who would later fall back and direct the battle from the rear. They broke into a trot and started up the rise. The ground became hard, stones flicking up from the horses' hooves. Then, still in line, the leading companies spread out and surged forward into a gallop. Two regiments of Light Horse, over six-hundred men, thousands of hooves pounding the hard earth, in an all-out assault on the ancient town that lay at the foot of the Judean hills.

Matty crouched low over Cedar's neck as he tried to hold her back with the other horses; she was eager for the gallop. Her mouth was open, trying to evade the bit, her ears flat against her head. As one, the horses galloped to the rise that was before them, then over it, a huge sea of men and horses, streaming down the long bare slopes that led to the enemy, now only three miles away.

They were in sight of the Turks now and the reaction was immediate. Shells shrieked overhead, exploding amongst the charging ranks. Horses screamed as pieces of metal tore into them. They crashed to the ground with their riders. Other horses leapt to avoid the bodies underfoot while never slowing their stride, their mouths foaming, sucking air in gulps; they stretched their necks out and raced for the enemy. They passed through the falling shells into heavy gunfire. The frontline fell almost as one but the ranks kept pushing forward.

Matty had lost sight of Jack. Cedar's flying pace had swept them forward and Matty, in his exultation, did not try to hold her back. Her mane flew, whipping his face, and her tail streamed behind her as she jumped the injured that lay fallen. The hail of bullets continued to bring down those around her and still she galloped forward, her breath coming in agonising gulps.

The machine guns ceased firing. The Essex Battery had found their range and silenced them.

Cedar groaned; her stride faltered. Matty glanced down but could not see if she had been hit. The mare raised her head and quickened pace again. They were in the front line now, nothing ahead but bare ground and the enemy trenches. Surprised at the sudden lull in gunfire, the men of the Australian Light Horse urged their horses on, bayonets aimed at the trenches.

Cedar was giving her all and Matty knew it. He felt her courage with every stride, every lunge of her body, her heart pounding beneath his leg, the rise and fall of straining muscles. The mare gathered herself to leap the first trench and Matty leant forward in the saddle, helping her balance. As they landed, she tore the reins from his hands and raced forward. The next trench was much wider, filled with Turks aiming their rifles at the mighty Walers as they leapt over. Horses had their stomachs slashed by swords and bayonets. They fell, screaming, into the trenches. Some troopers pulled their horses up and using their rifles as clubs, fought the Turks in the trench.

As Matty's mind tried to absorb what was happening, his face went slack, then his eyes narrowed. Anger exploded in him; riding without reins, he slashed at the Turks as he raced past. Again, the mare collected herself. She tucked her forelegs under and hurled herself over the last trench with her final reserve of strength.

Matty felt a shudder pass through Cedar's body as she landed on the other side. He wrenched her to a halt, just managing to avoid crashing into the tents that blocked the way. A Turkish soldier came at them with his sword raised, yelling wildly.

Matty unslung his rifle and fired down on the man. Missing with his first bullet, his hand quickly worked the bolt, loading another cartridge. He pulled the trigger and the Turk fell, his sword skating along in the dust. Jumping from the saddle, Matty landed in a crouch, firing at a second ragged soldier who rushed at him, intent on killing. Matty had no time to think. From his right, a soldier screaming in Turkish rushed at him. With his magazine empty, Matty took a grip on the barrel of his rifle and swung the butt upwards, catching the Turk under the jaw. The man fell in a heap at his feet. Matty slung his rifle and pulled out his bayonet.

Everywhere men struggled in hand-to-hand combat. The fighting from the Australians was hard and furious. Rage swirled in Matty's mind. Friends lay in the desert sand, maimed, dead. The screams of the horses echoed in his ears as he raised his bayonet at yet another Turk. He could still feel Cedar's heaving body as she had given him every ounce of her strength. He thrust the cold steel harder and watched the man's face as the Turk's body slumped slowly down to the ground, a trickle of blood leaking out as he pulled the bayonet out. Matty shook his head, trying to clear the noise that echoed around in it.

The main fight was over in a short time. The Turks believed that they were fighting mad men, so fierce was the Australian attack. Cries of surrender filled the air. Troopers searched alleys and the buildings, looking for hidden soldiers; some troopers pursued the enemy beyond the town. Gradually the clash of steel and the sound of gunshots ceased; dust hung thick in the air. Matty heard the moans of the dying; anguished cries of the wounded calling for their mates.

He gazed about, taking in the carnage. All around him men were trying to water their horses, some had their heads in the well beside the horses' muzzles, such was their thirst. His heart pounding, he searched desperately for Jack and Cedar. Pushing his way through the confusion of men and horses, he found them.

Jack stood at her head, holding her reins, unashamedly wiping tears from his cheeks. Matty's throat went dry. His stomach constricted as his eyes fell upon his gallant mare.

Her head hung towards the ground as she desperately tried to gulp air into her tortured lungs. Her beautifully coloured coat was a mess of dust and sweat, the muscles beneath shivering from the effort asked of them. Blood streamed from a bullet wound to her shoulder. Large strands of flesh hung from her heaving stomach where Turkish swords had slashed as she had jumped that last trench.

Matty now knew what had caused her to shudder. He walked to her side. Taking his bayonet, he cut the girth, so as not to cause her further pain getting the saddle off. He then went to her head, and gently removed her bridle. She would not move; she could not, he thought. Matty ripped the hat from his head and turned towards an undamaged well. Men were three deep at its side, trying to get water. He pushed through and scooped cool water into the crown of his hat. Soldiers who knew him drew back when they saw his face; their eyes followed him as he turned back to his horse.

Matty halted, his body rigid, his heart tortured. Mouth open, his eyes wide, Matty watched in awe as his mare took one painful step at a time, making her way toward him. Cedar lifted her weary head in anticipation of the cool liquid that he carried. She nickered softly. Her legs collapsed beneath her and she fell heavily to the ground, a groan of pain rising from deep within her. Matty ran to her, sloshing water as he sank down beside her and lifted her head into his lap. Gently, with his fingers, he wiped the water over her parched tongue, trying to give her the water she had gone without for so many hours. Now, Cedar was beyond needing water. Although her defiant spirit made her fight for life, her body could not – the mare had lost too much blood.

He would have to put an end to her suffering. He knew he should wait for the vets, but he could not let her linger. She was his mare, a part of him from her birth. He stroked the soft skin of her muzzle, her deep liquid eyes gazing at him, full of pain and yet, there was something else in them: a shared love, a memory for all that had been.

'How you ever made it this far, I'll never know...' Matty's voice broke and he laid his head on her neck, his tears mingling with the mare's sweat. 'You're the best damn mate a bloke ever had.'

He stood up, wiping his eyes with his sleeve. Picking up his rifle, Matty took a clip from his bandolier, loaded it and fed a round into the chamber. He took a step back and lifted it towards her forehead.

'Go to Valhalla, Cedar.' A whisper on his lips as he pulled the trigger. The shot echoed in his head, closing a part of his heart forever.

That part would remain in this ancient land, buried beneath the drifting desert sands, with the little mare that had been the pride of the 12th Light Horse Regiment and an extension of his own being.

TWENTY

It was left unsaid, what had happened that night. Sammy could not remember, and Dave did not remind him.

Sammy sent a letter to the boys in the desert, a short note, but it said all he needed.

France

25th September 1917

Dear Matty and Jack,

The fellas I am in with, they are good men. We have seen lots of fighting. It snows here in winter. It is nice in summer, not hot like home. Green grass. Flowers. We go back behind the lines and then it is all right. There are villages where we stay. I hope you are both all right and not doing too much.

Your friend,

Sammy.

There was a buzz in the air as rumours flew. For the first time in the war, four Australian divisions were to fight side by side at the front line, each division given the task to advance 1500 yards on a 1000-yard front. The 7th British were on their right, the New Zealanders on their left, both, proven fighters. Dave advised caution when Clarry became excited at the news that the Australians and New Zealanders would at last fight together on the Western Front.

'The NZs will have their own battle, but I agree to have us all together, instead of strung out amongst the Tommies… Well, it should mean something.'

'Whadya mean, Dave?' Clarry asked.

'Well, it stands to rights that we'll do better together.'

The battalion were relieved the next day, spending one day resting before moving to Ypres sector.

The water-logged ground proved a death trap for any that left the route or duckboards. Soldiers marched along a road to the frontline that was littered with the debris of war. Smashed and broken wagons, vehicles and bodies made progress nearly impossible. The stark blackened remains of trees stood lonely in the wasteland beyond the road. The enemy shelled the choked thoroughfare ceaselessly. There was no other way to the front. The men trudged and stopped, waiting, watching, hoping that a shell did not land amongst them. They noticed the mangled bodies of the horses and mules that lay strewn along the road and its edges but that was all, they were used to such sights now. Wounded men, blown from the ambulances, lay waiting for help. Those casualties that could walk stumbled along, helping each other get to the rear lines. Sammy watched as the heavy horses strained every muscle to pull the gun limbers through the morass, their hides dark with sweat. The drivers yelled and cursed at them, but never touched the whip to them.

Daylight faded and the Verey lights took over. As they headed for their position in the lines, the way became more and more crowded until the brigades were massed tightly in the confinement of the narrow trenches, nowhere to go but forward. The enemy artillery found their range and dropped shell after shell into the allied lines, one man here, ten there, blown to pieces, the wounded trying to crawl out of the path of soldiers moving forward, the dead stepped over or trampled underfoot, no time to move them, nowhere to put them.

They reached the jump-off point; a quarter of the men who started out from the billet lay dead or wounded behind them. There was no turning back; the plans had been made.

The barrage began at 0515, the noise deafening, as the men sat huddled, cold and wet in the trenches, gas masks at the ready. They had been told of the battle plan and each man knew what to expect. There would be a forty-minute barrage, then attack. Reaching the appointed place on the map, they would mop up and wait, regroup while another forty-minute barrage would descend on the next line of German trenches. They were to attack one thousand yards forward, then another five hundred over a thousand-yard front until they reached the final objective. At 0600 hours, the captain gave his company the command to go over the parapet and lay up at the jump off point. As men rose and struggled through the slime, rifle fire and shells dropped the soldiers indiscriminately.

The barrage began to move forward, the crump of artillery fire punctuated with rifle fire and shrapnel. The captain checked his watch; he had his orders.

Dawn was a misty grey haze on the horizon as they charged, bayonets fixed, rifles loaded. The shells landed; pieces of rock, globs of mud and human remains flew about them. Their faces were set, their eyes glassy. Battle hardened, they knew their objective. It would be theirs. The Australians had their sister battalions beside them, behind them. They would see this through.

Greyness surrounded the soldiers. Dave and Sammy were in the front, struggling to go forward, sinking in the mire. Gaining a bit of higher ground where the mud was not as deep, the company rushed forward, their gutteral roars heard between the artillery overhead. Machine guns from the German lines poured enfilade fire into the Australian flanks. Men dropped, screams of pain coming from those who still lived. Cries for stretcher bearers went out, officers yelled orders and guns roared.

Glancing to his right, in the dim light, Sammy saw Germans hidden in brush behind a low bank. It was the movement of the gunner, struggling to clear an obstruction from the machine gun that caught his eye. He swung to his right, crashing into Clarry, who cursed, then questioned.

'What's goin' on, Darky?'

'MG, over behind that bank. If they get goin', they'll wipe out our flank,' he shouted.

Their lieutenant heard Sammy and, signalling to him, Dave, Irish and Clarry to follow, he led them in a charge at the Germans. Rifle fire thumped about them, one bullet glancing off Sammy's rifle stock; wood splinters gouged into his hand. Swearing, he shook it and continued towards the low bank.

With a yell, they charged up and over the bank, firing into the sunken lane that ran behind the bank. The Germans that survived raised their arms in surrender. Resisting meant death. One man made to raise his rifle. Irish raised his gun and took aim at the German. Irish's head snapped back, he stood rigid for a second, then sank slowly to the ground, blood pouring from his eye where a bullet had entered. His mates instantly squatted and raised their rifles, scanning the prisoners and beyond for the gun that had killed Irish. As the German soldiers cringed in fear, expecting to be punished for the stray bullet that had killed the Australian, the men lowered their guns; they could not find the weapon that had killed Irish.

There was nothing they could do for him. They would bury him later. The captain sent two men from the company to escort the captured machine gun and prisoners behind the lines, while the remaining soldiers moved forward to their appointed place.

Sammy could see the Germans clearly now. He halted. The mist cold on his face, he felt his wet clammy tunic sticking to him. He shivered. Raising the butt to his shoulder, he picked his target. His finger squeezed the trigger. The German hit the ground, a bullet through his skull. Sammy swung the rifle, sighting the next soldier. The shot went low, catching the man in the stomach. He fell to his knees, then using his rifle as support, he tried to rise again.

Grimacing, Sammy loaded and fired again, this time into the soldier's heart.

'Him take days to die, this way he won't suffer,' he muttered to himself, justifying the second shot.

Their voices grew louder until they were a running screaming horde, scrambling for the German line, their rifles firing as fast as they could work the bolt. The enemy broke and ran, desperately trying to reach their trenches. Those Germans who had had enough, raised their arms in surrender. Their rifles stripped from them, they were pushed towards the rear, now prisoners.

The Australians went forward, shells and rifle fire thinning their lines.

A hard thump against his chest caused Sammy to grunt. Glancing down, he saw a ragged hole in his tunic. He tried to lift his rifle, only to find his arms had no strength. His chest felt numb. He tried to take a breath and coughed. Tasting the sickly sweetness of blood, he stared in confusion at the ground in front of him, the rifle hanging heavy in his hands.

Dave looked across at Sammy, recognising his figure outlined against the dawn. He wondered why his mate stood still. Spotting a German in the trenches raising his pistol, aiming at Sammy, Dave fired. The German fell back against the beams of a dugout. Glancing towards Sammy again, Dave's eyes widened. His mouth opened in a voiceless shout as he saw his mate pushed backwards by a bullet hitting his shoulder, spraying blood and bone into the grey air. Sammy tried to keep his feet, but another hit him in the leg. He crumpled slowly into the mud.

The Australians carried the assault. With the enemy trench cleared, the soldiers began to mop up. Lookouts posted; men began to relax as well as they could in the frontline. The artillery fire lessened to a few desultory shells. Dave looked wildly back to where he had last seen Sammy.

A familiar muddy shape showed him where Sammy lay. Dave's breath came in ragged gulps as he struggled through the sticky mass that tried to slow him. A pain rose from his stomach to his chest, constricting it as he looked down at his mate.

Sammy lay on his side, blood pouring from his wounds. A gaping hole in the back of his tunic told the worst. The bullet had entered his chest and glancing off bone, exploded out of his back. His leg hung at the knee, nearly severed, the foot twitching. Bandy lay beside Sammy, his nose gently nudging Sammy's neck, whimpers coming from his throat.

Dave sank to his knees, his rifle sliding slowly from his hand, splashing into the slop in which Sammy lay. Gently, he rolled Sammy over, lifting the boy's head into his lap. He wiped the mud from the dark face, startled to see the eyelashes flutter.

'Country… back…' The words were slow, choked.

Dave gasped and bit his lip. Staring down at Sammy, he watched the blood trickle from his mate's lips, the lips that had warmed so many hearts with its smile. Dark eyes searched Dave's face.

The words came slowly, hoarse. 'Mate… country… go back to country. Bandy… he know I'm goin' west.'

Sammy coughed, blood drowning his lungs.

The dog lay beside Sammy and as Dave watched, Bandy crept forward to lick Sammy's face. The dog that stayed behind when the men went forward, the dog that obeyed his master's every command, now lay beside his master out in no-man's land. He had known.

Men of the platoon stood close, ragged, exhausted and silent, not wanting to leave their quiet mate, who had won the respect of so many of them.

Struggling for his voice, Dave answered Sammy. 'Darky, I promise I'll take you home somehow.'

Opening his dark eyes, Sammy stared up at Dave. 'If you can't… take something of me… back to country…'

'You are one brave bastard, Sammy. Your people will know how brave you are.' Dave's voice broke, his head bowed.

Time stood still for Dave and the men as Sammy took slower gurgling gasps for air until his chest did not move again.

Bandy raised his nose and howled, sending shivers up the spines of the soldiers gathered around.

The stretcher bearers came and, realising Sammy was dead, went in search of wounded. Without a word, Clarry shrugged out of his tunic and lay it on the ground. Bending over, he lifted Sammy from Dave's legs and placed the body on the dirty cloth. Each man took a corner and slowly, they carried Sammy's body back to the trench. There, they placed their mate gently down. Bandy crept forward, laying his head on Sammy's chest. Dave came up slowly, carrying Sammy's rifle. He turned the rifle upside down and thrust it, bayonet first, into the ground.

'Give me your knife, Clarry,' Dave said, holding out his hand.

Taking the offered knife, Dave twisted a lock of Sammy's black curly hair around his finger, pulling it taunt. The blade sliced through easily, releasing a springy curl into Dave's palm.

A hand came forward with an empty tobacco tin. Placing the lock of hair into the tin, and shutting the lid shut, Dave placed it in his tunic pocket. He looked up at the men.

'Which ever one of us gets out of this hell hole alive, he takes this to Sammy's people.'

The men nodded, accepting the duty, if it should fall to them.

TWENTY-ONE

Matty leant his head against the grimy window of the train carriage. The flat red plains of the western country held no interest for him as his mind wandered. Memories flashed in and out of focus. The gaiety aboard the ship coming into Sydney Heads quietening, as the men realised that it would soon be time to say goodbye. They had swapped addresses, promising to keep in touch. Their faces reflected the long years that they had been away, the hardship and the sorrow showed in the lines and creases.

He glanced at Jack, noting that although his eyes were closed, as he leant back against the seat, his fingers were tapping a tune on his leg. Turning back to the scene outside the window, he remembered the day that Jack was wounded at Gaza. The feeling of losing a mate, like when Jack had been sent to hospital, and the joy of his return six weeks later. He sighed, remembering the loss of Cedar, long gone now. He had been reported for shooting her, she was army property. It was up to the vets to put her down. Their captain had wanted to let it slide as Matty had owned and bred her, but some clerk had already forwarded the paperwork and he received two weeks field punishment.

The shock of the telegram from some bloke in Sammy's battalion informing them that Sammy was dead. He'd died the same month as Cedar. That always caused Matty a shivery tingle up his spine.

The night they received the telegram, both he and Jack had sat and wrote home, trying to explain to the Boss the loss they felt and asking him to tell Sammy's people how brave Sammy had been. After they finished writing, the boys talked of the days on the property, those carefree days, when the hardest thing they had to do was chase cattle or fix a bore. The laughter and the stories came back to them, but their dreams that night had been of Sammy in France.

Several letters from Sammy's platoon mates followed the telegram some weeks later. The most moving one was from Dave, telling of Sammy's compassion for his wounded and dying mates, of his fearlessness in attacking the Germans. Matty had forwarded these onto his father so that Bess and Big Jim knew of their son's war. He didn't know how his father would approach the telling as he couldn't mention Sammy's name.

The train pulled into Byrock station, the hissing of the steam and the grunting of the train snapped Matty out of his reverie. He watched as people bade goodbye to each other or greeted new arrivals. The thoughts of what he would say to his mother when he finally got home, crashed in on him. He felt as though he was five again and had been caught being naughty. He had apologies to make, but he was not sorry he had gone. The friends he had made, the countries he had seen.

He pushed the hard times to the back of his mind and instead, he tried to picture his father and Charlie, but the images of the desert, the dust, the screams, crowded in. He heard the compartment door slide open and he turned his head to stare at the intruder.

The man, dressed in a suit and tie, stepped back as the feeling in the tiny compartment hit him. He glanced at Jack, slouched in the corner of the seat, his long legs stretched, who stared back at him with a detached uninterested look. The man glanced at Matty and saw a weary, sad face. He closed the compartment door, moving off down the aisle to find another compartment, one that might hold more congenial travellers.

Jack's eyes closed again. Before long, faint snores came drifting across to Matty. He envied Jack's ability to sleep at any time. He smiled.

Then again, he thought, *Jack has always liked his sleep.*

They hadn't got much of that in the war. Riding night and day, an hour's sleep here and there. The times when you didn't take your boots off for a week or more and when you did, skin came away in layers. The nightmares after burial parties, that was the worst. He'd been on four burial parties and could remember the sound of the swishing noise the bodies had made, like parchment rustling. The dead had been out in the sun and wind of the desert for days, their bodies drying out quickly in the Jordan Valley. What a hell hole that had been. The heat was the worst any of them had ever felt. Men went down with sunstroke and burns. The malaria had taken a lot of blokes, dysentery a few more. The worst was having to check every time you sat down or got your blanket out. Spiders, scorpions, wasps and vipers would hide in equipment and blankets, just waiting. Billy would have loved those vipers, but he didn't get to the Jordan Valley. Billy copped a Turkish bullet at Third Gaza.

He remembered the look on the sergeant's face when he went through Billy's things after he died. Matty's mouth stretched into a smile. He could still hear the yell the sergeant gave when he opened the bag holding Billy's pets. The men reckoned that the sergeant couldn't hold a mug of tea steady for a week and dreamt of snakes for months.

Then he remembered the cold. You wouldn't have thought that it could get so cold in the Middle East, but when they went to relieve the Scots Fusiliers in the Judean Hills, it was cold. Their orders had been to leave all their gear except weapons on the horses and go forward without the horses. It was only supposed to be for one night, but it was five weeks before they got out of there. No shelter, no spare clothes, rain and blizzards for two weeks. It even snowed a few miles away. Soaked to the skin, some men got frost bite and were evacuated. He remembered the men's satisfaction when they were issued with swords and began training in cavalry tactics. They had used the swords in their victory at Samakh, proving them an effective addition to the Light Horse weapons.

The battles, the men, the dust storms, the hunger. Each element attached to the other played constantly through Matty's mind as he sat on the hard train seat, wishing he could sleep.

Noticing that they had reached Maroona, Matty called to Jack to wake him up.

'Not long now, mate. Bourke in half an hour.'

Jack didn't open his eyes, but said, 'Tell me when we're five mile out, eh, Shorty?'

Matty smiled and shook his head. 'You'll have plenty of time to sleep now we're home.'

'Mmm, that's what I'm lookin' forward to,' Jack replied. 'That and the longest soak in the waterhole.'

Looking out the window again, Matty saw cattle standing in the shade of some mulga, and immediately his mind went back to the day they had come across some stray cattle in the desert. Some quick work with a knife and the regiment ate beef that night. They paid for it the next day, their stomachs not used to the rich fresh meat. There had been a bit of commotion when a Bedouin arrived claiming that the men had stolen all his cattle, but a lieutenant had given the man a chit and told him to take it to the British HQ, who would pay him compensation. Seeing that the lieutenant had shared the beef on offer, nothing more was said about the incident.

'Hey, Jack, I hope Father got that telegram we sent, telling him we're on our way. It'll be a big shock when we turn up if they didn't get it.'

'Mmmm.'

'C'mon. We're here,' Matty said, throwing Jack's kitbag at him.

The train slowed, grunting, its brakes squealing along the track, steam swirling as it pulled into the Bourke station. They opened the compartment door and, hitching their kits over their shoulders, stepped down onto the platform.

Immediately there were Aboriginals all around them, crying and calling out. Matty laughed as one young fellow jumped up and down, yelling at the top of his voice, 'Missus, they home, they home.'

Looking in the direction that the young boy was pointing, Matty saw his mother. She was smaller than he remembered; the dress she was wearing emphasised her loss of weight. Tears streamed down her face as she opened her arms, waiting for Matty to come to her. He dropped his kit and with three strides enveloped her in a hug, lifting her from the ground.

Jack followed and shook hands with Thomas, who hurriedly thrust his handkerchief away, tears still lingering in the corner of his eye.

Eliza pushed her son away, looking him up and down. 'Well, you are still whole and how tall you have grown, Matty.'

Turning to Jack, she gave him a hug, repeating, 'I can't believe how much you boys have changed.'

Thomas coughed, clearing his throat, although his voice was still husky when he said, 'That's because they're not boys anymore. They have come home as men.'

Matty felt his mother's eyes on him and he raised his head to speak.

'Mother, I—'

'Matty, we won't talk about any of that now. Let's just be glad that you are both home and in one piece.' Eliza interrupted him.

'Jack's deaf in one ear and his shoulder plays up now and then, but other than that, yeah, we're fine.'

'It looks like the whole station has come to town, Boss,' Jack observed as he watched the children gawking at the train. 'Who's left at home?'

'We thought that they might like a treat. The women have been shopping for clothes with the Missus and the men and I have been looking at some bulls I'm thinking about buying,' Thomas replied.

'We've been staying at the Carriers Arms and the natives are camped down at the river.'

Matty glanced around, searching for someone. 'Where's Tan? Is he here?'

'No. Tan's starting to feel his age. He has a touch of rheumatism now. He said he would wait at home and prepare a big feast,' Eliza explained. 'Bess and Big Jim stayed home to keep an eye on things.'

Matty and Jack looked at each other, their sadness tangible at the thought of Sammy's parents.

Thomas noticed the look. 'We'll talk about him later.'

Matty said impatiently, 'Well, let's go. I can't wait to get home!'

'It is too late to start out now, Matty. We'll stay at the hotel tonight and leave early in the morning,' Thomas remarked.

Charlie stepped forward and asked, 'Boss, we take supply wagon, start off now? That way we get head start. Then you an' Missus come in morning with the boys. Catch us up?'

'Sick of town already are you, Charlie?' Thomas laughed. 'All right, if you like, get everyone together and I'll see you off.'

Matty and Jack hugged the women and shook hands with the men as they left the platform. Charlie promised them a camping trip when they got home and the children jumped around, begging to be allowed to go.

After a long bath, the boys went down to dinner. They sat at the white-clothed table, napkins rolled in rings and felt uncomfortable. They stared about them, realising just how far they had been from 'civilisation' in the past four years.

Noticing their discomfit, Thomas started to tell them of what had been happening on the station in the four years that Matty and Jack had been away. Soon, the boys relaxed and asked lots of questions.

They finally ran out of things to talk about and Matty knew it was time.

'Mother, I want to apologise for running off. I know it hurt you deeply,' Matty started.

Eliza nodded. 'Yes, Matty. It took me a long while to get over it. But then, with all the reports that came through in the newspapers, I realised that you would have had to go sooner or later. As I said before, I am just glad to have you both home.'

'Boss, Missus, while we're saying thanks, I'd like to thank you both for your letters and things you sent me at Gallipoli. They helped me get through that.'

'Jack,' Eliza replied. 'We think of you as our son now. You have been through a bad time and now you're home.'

'We won't talk of the war here,' Thomas said quietly. 'We'll sit down at home one day and you can both tell me of your adventures, eh, boys?'

Next morning, they were up early and out to the paddock behind the hotel to get the horses that Charlie had brought for them to ride. Nugget stood waiting patiently, flicking his tail at the flies. Beside him, a gelding who looked vaguely familiar to Matty snuffled at the ground.

'I know he won't ever replace her, but this is Cedar's half-brother,' Thomas' voice spoke from behind them. 'Charlie broke him in six months ago when we knew you would be coming home. He is still a bit green, but he shouldn't give you too many worries.'

'This is the horse you promised that bloke for getting Cedar back when you got to Egypt.' Jack laughed. 'Did you ever find that bloke again?'

Shaking his head, Matty said, 'No, last I heard he ended up in France as a driver. I'd better make some inquiries.'

Catching the horses, Matty took a closer look at the gelding.

'What did Charlie call him, Father?'

'He said he wouldn't give him a name. That was for you to do.'

Although he was a liver chestnut, the horse had only one white stocking and no blaze on his face. His build was similar to Cedar's but he was maybe a half a hand taller.

'I'll have to think about it on the way home,' Matty mused. 'Can't have a horse with no name.'

Matty and Jack revelled in being back in their home territory. Old familiar sights were looked at with fondness, and the sight of a kangaroo or eagle made them smile.

A shadow rode alongside them. If he had lived, Sammy would have been with them, so in their minds, a tall black man rode beside them, a cheeky grin on his face, sharing in their joy at being home.

Tan had been looking out for them for hours and as he saw the dust rising further up the track, the old man became young again and started flinging out orders to Bess and Big Jim.

'Missy and Boss, bring home the boys. We get dinna cooking. Big Jim, get fire stoking!'

Jack and Matty laughed as Tan came up to them, chattering away in Chinese in his excitement to see them again.

After they calmed him down, they went in search of Bess and Big Jim.

It was hard to explain their sorrow to his parents. Their law did not allow Sammy's name to be spoken, but Matty, who had been with the Aboriginals since he was born, overcame the problem.

'That fella that I used to play with when we were little, he went away because of me. I'm sorry he did that. It was my fault. But, that fella, he was a brave warrior. He fought many fights. He saved many lives. We will never forget him.'

Big Jim bowed his head, saying, 'It not your fault, Matty. Him make up his mind. Boss told us what he did. He hero in our people. Boss tell us about the war, we proud.'

* * * *

Life settled down into the normal station routine, helping Jack and Matty to put the war behind them. Days were full of hard physical work, food was again plentiful and nights were spent, not in a saddle or on the ground, but in a bed. The strangeness of sleeping in a bed soon wore off and Jack always had to be called twice to get him up. They kept thinking about a trip to the waterhole but work kept them on the other side of the property. When Thomas said that they would have to muster the water hole paddock in the next week or two, they were happy.

Sunday lunch was still heavy in their stomachs as the men sat on the verandah, smoking and enjoying a beer. Matty shaded his eyes as a whirl of dust rose out along the track, coming closer. The sound of an engine broke the silence of the hot afternoon. A flock of cockatoos flew up from a tree, adding their squawking to the noise.

A motor car swung through the gate and pulled up with a rattle in front of the house. The three men on the verandah watched in amazement as a short, stocky man, clad in goggles and a collarless shirt, climbed out over the door, leant over the back seat and lifted out a dog, a leash dangling from the dog's neck. They had not expected any visitors and assumed that this man must be lost. With their curiosity aroused, they walked down and opened the front gate.

Placing the dog on the ground, the man pulled the goggles of his head and threw them onto the front seat. Squaring his shoulders, he tugged at the lead, saying, 'Here, fella.'

The dog looked at him questioningly, then proceeded to lift his leg and relieve himself on a tyre of the car.

Matty and Jack laughed, Jack calling out, 'He must have been bustin'. How far have you come, mate?'

The man looked at the boys, then at Thomas. 'I've come a long way to find you boys.'

The boys flicked a glance at each other, both shrugging their shoulders.

The man stepped forward and taking Thomas' proffered hand, shook it.

'You must be the Boss, and these two would be Matty and Jack,' he stated.

The boys shook his hand and stepped back, unsure of what was to come. Their minds were frantically searching their memories to see if there was anything there about this man.

'My name's Dave and I was with Sammy in France,' he said quietly. 'I've bought Bandy home. It was a wish of Sammy's.'

The two boys reeled back as if struck. Thomas put a hand on each of their shoulders and steadied them.

'I'm sorry if I've given you a bit of a shock, but I didn't know how to tell you what I was bringing home, so I just came.'

Jack recovered first and gesturing towards the verandah, asked Dave to come in.

The dog stayed beside Dave's leg all the way up the path, settling himself beside the chair that Dave sat in.

'Dave, would you care for a cup of tea or a beer?'

Laughing, Dave replied, 'After all the dust I've swallowed since Bourke, a beer would be just the thing, thanks.'

Once a plate of food and a beer had been organised for the visitor, Thomas introduced Eliza.

'Ah, the Missus.'

Eliza raised her eyebrows and looked at Dave.

'I won't beat about the bush. I've a story to tell you. I've come to tell you about Sammy.'

Jack and Matty sat forward, eager to hear what this man could tell them about their friend.

Suddenly jumping up, Matty asked Dave to wait a moment. Running out to the kitchen, he told Bess about Dave. Bess called out to Jim who was stacking wood at the back of the kitchen.

'I understand if you don't want to listen to him, but you're welcome to come and hear what he has to say about that boy who was my mate.'

Bess gestured towards the door. 'You go listen, Jim. We part of white man's ways now. The elders, we tell 'em by-'n'-by. You tell me by-'n'-by.'

Dave stood up to shake Big Jim's hand. 'Your son was my best mate in France, Jim. I brought his dog home for him. It's what he would have wanted.'

Jim looked Dave up and down, then his eyes settled uncomprehendingly on the dog.

'He found him on the battlefield as a pup in a shelled farmhouse. He taught him all sorts of things. The government banned the return of animals last year, so a mate in England kept him till early this year and got papers made up to say he was a show dog. The boys in the battalion all threw in to get the dog into quarantine in England, so as we could bring him home. The customs passed it,' Dave said. 'Many of those boys owed their lives to your son.'

Dave reached down and picked up the dog's lead, holding it out for Jim to take.

'The dog is a Brittany Spaniel. His name is Bandaarr, although we called him Bandy.'

Jim glanced at Thomas and after seeing Thomas nod, Jim took the lead from Dave's hand. He sat down against the verandah rail and called to Bandy. The dog lifted its head, pricking his ears. Jim spoke softly in his own language to the dog. Bandy got up and went straight to Jim, licking his hand.

Eliza gave a sniff as tears sprung to her eyes, while the men looked elsewhere for a moment, blinking rapidly.

Settling himself down in his seat, Dave sat back and began his story.

'First, Thomas, I would like you to know that Sammy kept his promise to you. He never touched a drop of alcohol while he was in the army. For this, the other men were grateful as Darky – sorry, that's what we called him. But I'm getting ahead of myself. Sammy would always give his rum ration to the bloke he felt needed it most. Likewise, his tobacco ration. He never touched a woman, either.' Dave stopped and glanced at Eliza. 'Excuse me, Missus.'

Eliza smiled at Dave's manners. 'It's all right. I understand.'

'He was popular with the French girls because he could speak French. He could translate between them and the soldiers. He had plenty of offers, but he kept his promise to you, sir.'

'I knew he would,' Thomas replied. 'He always did as he was asked.'

'Now, the reason he was called Darky was nothing to do with his colour. It was because he was a bit of a dark horse. It seemed as if there was nothing he couldn't do. I don't know if he told you in his letters about boxing?' Dave looked about at the group, noticing the shaking of heads. 'I thought as much. Sammy was our battalion champion. There was an NCO that gave him a hard time. Sammy beat him with skill and class. Then, there was his speaking French. That came out of the blue. As I said, it came in very useful for the rest of us.'

Leaning back, Dave sighed quietly. He took another sip of his beer and placed the glass on the table.

The others did not move, so intent were they on Dave's words.

'Sammy could march further than any of us. He would go for days with little or no sleep, but always, he'd have his wits about him. He dragged in wounded during the night. He would just sneak out and get them. The officers thought he was the best scout as well, because he brought back information that he could only have got by getting right up to the German lines. No easy thing, mind you.'

Here he took a pause, his face reflecting the memories in his mind. He gave a sad smile.

'The thing that we all remembered about Sammy afterwards was his smile. One bloke, Harry. Sammy sat with Harry, out in no-man's land while Harry died. He said it first. Sammy had the smile of a saint. He was as brave a man as I ever met, and generous, but he had something else, something special.'

Dave's voice grew husky and he remained silent for a while.

Matty and Jack sat still, knowing war, knowing what Dave was saying.

'You boys had a different war out in the desert. I've heard a lot about it since I got back. You Light Horse did a great job. But on the Western Front, it was different. We never covered the ground you blokes did. We fought over a couple of hundred yards at a time and lost thousands of blokes for every square mile that we fought in. When I remember back, I remember the mud, the blokes and Bandy here. Maybe we'll talk a bit more later, about the war,' Dave said. 'I came to tell you about Sammy and I have. But there's just one more thing.'

Reaching into his trouser pocket, Dave removed a tobacco tin.

'At Passchendaele, that hell on earth where Sammy went west, we made a pact that whoever survived would bring this home. You see, after he got hit, he knew he wouldn't make it. So, he asked me to send something of his "back to country". Sammy never talked much about being a blackfella; in fact, we never thought about it, but I figured that "back to country" had something to do with his people's traditions, so we took a lock of his hair and put it in here.'

Dave opened his hand, the scratched dented tin sitting in his palm. He looked about at the stunned gathering. Thomas, after noticing Jim's expression, reached forward and took the tin from Dave.

'I'll take care of it until Sammy's uncle gets back. He is away on blackfella business. He will know what to do with it.'

Seeing the puzzled expression on Dave's face, Matty explained. 'When an Aboriginal boy gets to a certain age, his uncle takes over and teaches him all the Aboriginal ways. When Sammy went to enlist, he had to ask his uncle.'

'Ah, I see. I hope I haven't upset anything,' Dave said.

'No, no,' Thomas said forcefully. 'We appreciate you going to all this trouble to come and tell us about Sammy. To carry out his wishes. You are a good man for doing it.'

'Yes, sir,' Matty added. 'You've filled in the gaps for us. Sammy only wrote us a couple of letters. And you've told us what we felt. That our mate was a dinkum.'

Dave nodded his head. 'He should have got a medal several times over, but the first time, there were no officers left that could bear witness to his actions and the second time, the officer that could have put it forward, he died before he finished putting the paperwork together.'

Eliza rose and turning to Dave, asked, 'What are your plans? We would like you to stay for a few days or more if you wish. I am sure there are things that you and the boys could talk about.'

'Mrs Watson, I would appreciate that very much. Sammy told us so many stories about this station, I feel as though I know it already. I liked his story about the snake in the tank the best.'

The look on Eliza's face caused Jack and Matty to stare at the ground, waiting for the outburst.

'What snake? In what tank?' Eliza demanded.

Dave realised that he had let slip a secret. Stammering, he said, 'Well, it was—'

Matty interrupted him. 'Mother, it happened years ago when we were playing. No one got hurt – no one else knew about it except Sammy, Jack and me.'

Eliza took a deep breath, calming herself down. 'After all that has happened since, I suppose it's a little silly to get upset over a snake, isn't it?' she asked. 'I'd better go and see what plans Tan has for supper.'

As they watched Eliza walk away, Dave apologised for letting out the childhood secret.

'I don't think the boys will hold that against you. I think the boys had better tell us the story later.' Thomas grinned.

Their eyes were drawn to Big Jim as he stood up, holding Bandy's leash tightly in his hand.

'You… you bring my boy back, Mister,' he whispered.

He offered his hand to Dave, who leapt up from his chair up to shake it.

'I'm sorry for your loss, Jim. I was proud to have served with such a fine, brave boy. He will always be with me.'

Jim looked into Dave's eyes, meeting him man to man. 'Thank you.'

Looking down at the dog, Jim spoke softly to it. Bandy looked at Dave then at Jim. He was confused, not knowing quite what he was supposed to do. Dave had looked after him when Sammy had gone; now there was a new man, but a man very similar to Sammy.

Dave helped the situation. 'Go, Bandy, you go along.'

The dog rose and, guided by the leash, went with Jim as the big man went to tell his wife the news of their son.

Settling back into his chair, Dave said, 'That dog was Sammy's pride and joy. I'm pretty sure he'll be happy knowing Bandy's back here.' He shook his head as if to clear the memories. 'Now, you blokes were going to tell your father about a snake?'

Matty and Jack took turns in telling Thomas about the snake in the tank, drifting on to other stories about Sammy and their childhood adventures.

Over supper, the group asked Dave about his wife and his plans for the future.

'Can you ride a horse, Dave?' Matty asked.

'Well enough to stay on.'

Jack had understood Matty's question straight away.

'We're goin' out to the waterhole paddock to muster. A few scrub bulls got in from the next-door property. We've got to get 'em out and send 'em back.'

'Yeah, and we were thinkin' about campin' at the hole for a day or two. We haven't been out there since we got back. Been meanin' to, but been busy on the other side of the place,' Matty added.

Sitting back in his chair, Thomas looked at Jack. 'That waterhole meant a lot to you, didn't it?'

'Yes, Boss. There were days when I thought that I'd never see it again. 'Specially at Anzac. I'd close my eyes and see it, all peaceful, and I'd feel better.'

'Well, I'm up for that. When are we going?' Dave answered.

Matty raised an eyebrow at Jack. 'Get the gear and horses ready tomorrow? Set off next day?'

'Sounds good to me.'

TWENTY-TWO

Dave shivered as he waited for Matty and Jack to finish organising the men. He stared out over the tops of the mulga trees, watching the darkness fade as the sun bit through. He remembered the dawns that he had spent wet and cold in the bottom of a trench, not able to stick his head up to admire the rising sun, and then the mornings he spent behind the lines, soaking up the warmth of the new sun in spring, greenery and flowers all around them, a stark contrast to their winter experiences in the trenches.

'Hey, mate,' Jack's call broke his reverie.

He looked at Jack with blank eyes.

'I know, mate. You get drawn back by all sorts of things,' Jack said gently.

'How did you know what I was thinking?'

Leaning back against his horse, Jack put the finishing touches to a rollie. He said, 'It's on your face. I've seen it a hundred times. Most of all on the ship coming home. Little things set you remembering.'

'I suppose so. I saw it myself.'

Jack gave a sad grin. 'C'mon, let's get goin'.'

The boys had given Dave a quiet old roan, one that Charlie had semi-retired. Patting it on the neck, Dave pulled himself into the saddle and found his stirrups.

'He is like an old rocking horse, Dave,' said Thomas as he came out to see them off. 'He will do you no wrong.'

'I more afraid I'll do him a wrong.'

Matty laughed. 'Nah, just sit back and enjoy the ride.'

Charlie led out with the pack horse, the dogs running to and fro excitedly while Jack and Matty said goodbye to Thomas.

'Don't forget to fix the fence when you put those bulls through, will you?' Thomas called.

'Jesus, Father, we know that.' Matty smiled. 'And to brand the cleanskins, and to pull out the old cows and to get our count right for the books.'

Throwing back his head, Thomas let out a loud laugh. 'I should know by now, you two know all you need to know! But Charlie will keep you on the straight and narrow.'

The group laughed as they swung their horses' heads down the track, waving a final goodbye to Thomas.

The day became warm, a clear blue sky allowing the sun to heat the land. The boys pointed out features in the landscape to Dave and told him some more stories of their upbringing. Slowly, the group fell silent. All of them could feel the shadow of Sammy riding with them.

Charlie broke the silence, calling softly to Matty. The ringer was pointing at a small roo, who stood still, watching them, ready for flight. With one easy motion, Matty pulled his rifle from its bucket, rammed the bolt home and fired.

Trotting over to the dead animal, Charlie grinned at Matty. 'Got him through the head, Boss. Good tucker tonight.'

Swinging down of his horse, Matty helped Charlie lift the roo onto the rump of Charlie's horse.

Dave had watched in silence, but now he spoke up. 'I've eaten some rum things in the past four years. I think I'm going to enjoy this. Dark – Sammy told us about educating Jack, here, in the ways of bush tucker.

When we were sitting around in a dugout with only army biscuits to eat, we would have given anything for a roo steak, he made it sound so good!'

Charlie laughed. 'That Jack, him proper big smoke boy when he first come. Now he one of us, hey, Boss?'

Jack laughed to cover the rising emotion that swelled at Charlie's words. 'You one proper teacher, Charlie.'

Excitement rose in the boys as they neared the waterhole. For the first time in nearly five years, they would see the place that had meant so much to them as children.

With no warning but a whoop, Matty and Jack leapt out of their saddles and raced to the water, hopping on one foot as they pulled first one boot off, then the other.

They ignored the sand burning their feet, the twigs and pebbles that dug in. They were eight years old, racing to be the first in the water. Jack beat Matty by a whisker to the water's edge, but Matty outswam him to reach the lignum bush out in the lagoon.

They looked at each other, breathless, then looked back at Dave and Charlie, who were laughing at two grown men acting like children.

Slowly, the boys swam back. Stripping out of their wet clothes, they hung them on the branches of the coolabah tree to dry, then set about gathering wood to get the fire going.

Once the kangaroo was on the coals, Dave stripped down and joined the boys as they went back in for another swim. Dave stared about, taking in the misty green of the lignum, the yellow-brown water and the pendulous shady branches of the yapunyah. He cocked his head listening, hearing nothing but the gentle swish of the water as he moved his arms through it, and an occasional call of a bird.

'I understand why you would think of this place while you were over there,' he said to them. 'It certainly is peaceful.'

'Yeah, except when the cockies come down to drink at dusk and dawn. You won't get a sleep in here in the morning,' Jack warned him.

Charlie had unsaddled the horses, putting them in the small horse yard after watering them. Calling the dogs, he tied them at intervals along the yards wherever there was shade. Squatting by the fire, he watched as the others swam, enjoying the water. When the meat was cooked to his liking, he called to them, indicating that it was ready.

Slowly, they dragged themselves out of the water, regretting the need to come back to land.

Slicing chunks of meat off, Charlie placed it on a worn enamel plate for all to share. He lifted the billy from the coals and poured out mugs of tea.

'Thanks for takin' care of the horses and cookin', Charlie. That water was just too much temptation,' Matty said through a mouthful of meat.

'Charlie, you don't know how much I missed this. Thank you,' Jack said softly as Charlie sat beside him.

'No worries, Boss.'

'You gotta stop calling us Boss, Charlie. There's only one Boss – that's Father,' Matty said with a grin.

'I know that, young fella. But you boys, you bin away. You done things. You all grow up. You soldiers, like guba ra, now.'

Jack and Matty both blushed, shifting uncomfortably at Charlies simple words, while Dave acknowledged the Aboriginal man's words.

'You have to remember that you two left here as boys and came back as blooded men. From the little I have picked up, it is like a rite of passage in Charlie's culture. You have earned his respect.'

Matty shook his head. 'There's no way Charlie can call me Boss. He helped raise me, didn't you, Charlie?'

Charlie nodded. 'You no trouble, long as we didn't tell Missus anything.'

Turning back to Dave, Matty explained. 'My mother lost a brother in a riding accident. She was terrified of me riding horses. And 'cause I nearly died from snake bite, she had a horror of snakes. You saw her reaction the other day. So, Charlie here kept us on the straight and narrow. Didn't he, Jack?'

'Most of the time, eh, Charlie?' Jack agreed.

Sitting back, Matty sighed. 'I reckon we had the best childhood, here on this property. Shame we had to grow up.'

The sun slid gently down the horizon, throwing out its last rays, turning the few clouds fiery red and orange.

'Reminds me of the Verey lights, but there's no noise. That's what used to get us, the constant noise,' Dave observed as he watched nature at work.

Lying down on his side, stretching his legs out, he looked at the two boys, catching their eyes.

'Did you two have trouble talking about it when you came back?'

'Didn't talk about it. No one out here would understand,' Jack said hesitantly, his fingers stripping a piece of bark.

'What about you, Matty?'

'Well, we told Father a few things, but there are things that you can't talk about. Like when we fought at Beersheba. Stickin' a bayonet through a man. We told them about seeing Jerusalem and things like that. But, like when Bluey lost his legs, dyin' in agony. You can't talk about it to them.'

Dave rolled over on his back, staring at the stars as they emerged in the darkening sky.

'That's the trouble. You boys are lucky, you both know what each other went through. I had a cobber that put a gun in his mouth and blew himself away. I only heard about it when I got back from England. Seems his wife couldn't get used to him having one leg and waking up with nightmares. She left him and took the kids. So he took himself west.'

'Shit, Dave,' Jack swore.

'There's blokes all over, having problems with coming home. Most of us have just got on with it, kept it to ourselves. You and I are lucky, we've got a life to get on with.'

The lonely call of a mopoke caused them to fall silent, all of them lost in their own thoughts. After a while, Matty slowly rose and brushed the sand off his backside. He picked up what was left of the now cold kangaroo and took it over to the dogs. He washed his hands at the edge of the waterhole and went over to the pack saddles. Digging down to the bottom, he drew out a bottle, raising it to the darkening sky to check it hadn't leaked. Walking back over to the fire, he sat down and pulled out the cork.

Looking at Charlie, he said, 'Charlie, we gonna toast the dead. I know it's not black man's ways, but you're our mate. I think you understand.'

'Yeah, Bo – young fella. You fellas gotta do it your way.'

Matty turned to Dave. 'Just as you did, we lost a lot of mates We all lost our best mate, Sammy. Even though he never drank, I want to share a drink to him – a drink with his best mates.'

Dave and Jack lifted their mugs for Matty to splash the rum in. After he had filled his own cup, Jack raised his up. 'Our mate, Sammy.'

The other two men nodded, and all three took a sip.

'Jesus, Matty, where did ya get this? This is camel's piss.' Jack choked.

'I pinched it out of Tan's pantry. I think Naveer gave it to him years ago.'

A quiet chuckling caused them to look at Charlie. 'You fellas, you no learn!'

Dave took another sip, smacked his lips together. 'Well, beggars can't be choosers, and I reckon by the next mug full, it will taste as smooth as silk.'

'We'll call it Sammy's Revenge. Here's to you, Sammy,' Jack said as he raised the glass again.

As the fire died down, the talk between the men swung from Palestine to France and back again as they shared their war experiences. Soft snores let them know that Charlie had fallen asleep.

Eventually, the long day and the rum got the better of them, and they rolled themselves in their ground sheets and fell asleep, sad but contented.

TWENTY-THREE

Jack's prediction of a loud awakening in the morning came to fruition as a huge flock of cockatoos descended at dawn to drink at the waterhole, their squawking piercing the silence. Dave sat bolt upright, his eyes wide and staring. He shook his head as if to clear it and looked out over the waterhole. Everywhere were white birds in all manner of poses. Some sat high in the trees; others sat on the lignum bushes, the thin branches swaying under the birds' weight.

He smiled to himself and stood up, stretching tight muscles.

From under his swag, Jack said, 'Told you they are loud. Bloody noisy buggers they are.'

Charlie rolled out of his swag, his bones cracking as he knelt beside his bed. He rolled the swag up, tied an old rope around it and carried it over to the tree near the yards. He tipped out a measure of grain for each horse, giving the old roan a flick with a branch when it tried to pinch another horse's feed. Dave, after washing his face in the tepid water of the lagoon, gathered some wood and started a fire.

By the time the coals were ready, Matty and Jack had made a damper and filled the billy. While the bread mixture was cooking, the four men brushed their horses and saddled up.

'At least here, there's no NCO bawling at you to do this, do that,' Jack said. 'Sometimes we'd be called out at two or three in the mornin'. We'd sleep in our clothes and be saddled ready to go in five minutes of the warnin'. Pack horses, rations and all.'

Matty dug him in the ribs. 'Remember when we reckoned we had a day's rest next day and tied Billy's legs together? Then the bastards called us out. Billy went face first into the sand. We copped a bollockin' for that.'

'Yeah, but he got us back. I'll never forget that hiss when you lifted your ground sheet up when we were outside Damascus. The look on your face.'

'Billy and his pets!' Matty laughed. He glanced at Dave, explaining, 'One of our mates, Billy, used to collect snakes in the desert. He kept 'em in a ration bag, lettin' 'em go when he found a more interestin' one. No one ever went near his things.'

Jack shook his head. 'Billy got it at Gaza, the third time that place was attacked. We lost Bluey at second Gaza.'

'Sammy said you had a dog as well, Jack. What happened to it?' Dave asked.

'I left China with a nurse in Cairo. She was engaged to an English officer and said they'd take it back to England with them. Poor ol' China, he wanted to come with us.'

Sipping at his tea, Dave nodded his head. 'Dogs have a way of getting under your skin, don't they? When Sammy brought that little pup into the dugout, most of us nearly had a tear in our eye. He was such a little tyke. So innocent in a mad world. Every man in our battalion knew that dog. He carried messages to HQ and back. He did everything Sammy told him. It was like he read Sammy's mind.'

'It was Cedar with me. My first horse. I was stupid enough to take her to Egypt. She was a bit of a character,' Matty said, staring at the ground, images of Cedar in his mind. 'Cedar had a thing about snakes. I was lucky she didn't get me in trouble. But she proved herself over and over. In the end, she… well… she died doin' what the horses were there for. Helpin' us win.'

He shrugged and reaching forward, raked the coals off the camp oven. He turned the damper out onto a piece of bark, pulling it apart to cool. Jack retrieved some jam from the pack saddle, spreading it liberally over the damper. The men ate, washing the bread down with the last of the tea.

'All right, time to go,' Matty said, a touch regretfully. They straightened up the camp site, dousing the fire.

'I'll take Dave and ride down towards the bore, if you an' Charlie want to take the wing. That way we can push the cattle up to the corner yards.'

The sun had just spread its rays out over the land as they set off, each pair with their own dogs. The early morning light soon gave way to a glaring brightness, the heat rising steadily until sweat trickled down their backs and coated the horses' flanks.

Quietness gave way to the lowing of cattle and the higher pitched bawling of calves as the men and dogs searched out the pockets of cattle among the mulga, forcing them into a larger mob. Dust swirled and coated everything, whips cracked, while dogs yipped and barked at the heels of the cows, harrying them forward.

By late afternoon, the men were content with the sixty head they had rounded up for that day. They secured the yards and made their way back to camp, leaving the branding for the cool of the next morning.

The boys unsaddled the horses, taking them into the water to wash the sweat from their coats. After putting the horses into the yards and feeding them, the boys went back over to where Charlie had started another fire.

'Hey, Charlie?' Matty said suddenly, his face thoughtful.

Charlie looked up inquisitively at Matty, knowing that tone of voice. 'No snakes.'

'No.' Matty laughed. 'But how about takin' Dave on a hunt? We could get some lizard an' maybe another roo for dinner? Otherwise, it's tinned beef an' the three of us never ever want to eat that shit again, eh, fellas?'

Dave watched in awe as he followed Charlie, admiring his grace and tracking abilities. Within half an hour, Charlie had brought down a small grey kangaroo and caught two goannas.

'Not bad, considerin' how much we stirred up the area today,' said Jack. 'Tan packed some onions an' carrots an' spuds. We got flour, so we got ourselves roo stew.'

Charlie busied himself cooking the goanna and when it was done, offered the steaming cooked flesh to Dave.

'Him sweet, here.'

'I'm up for anything that doesn't come out of a tin,' Dave said wryly as he took a piece of the meat. He chewed and swallowed. Licking his lips, he reached for some more. 'You boys must have missed all this?'

'Sure did, 'specially when all we had to eat for days on Gallipoli was those rocks they called biscuits,' replied Jack.

They fell to discussing army food while the stew cooked in the camp oven.

With the stars as a ceiling, and the ground as a bed, the men did not stay awake for long after their day's work.

The next day dawned overcast, but the heat still rose, muggy and thick. Charlie looked at the sky, muttering about storms and rain, just when there was work to do.

They rode back to the yards, tied the horses up and set about the process of drafting off the calves; marking and branding them. It was hot, tiring work, the noise of the bawling calves ringing in their ears.

By mid-morning, they had finished. They left the cattle in the yard and cut the fence in the corner of the paddock, peeling back the wire to make a clear fifteen-foot gateway. After mounting the waiting horses, they rode out to find the micky bulls from the neighbouring property. Jack had seen a couple over in the corner yesterday but had been too intent on getting the cows and calves to do anything about them. The bulls had made themselves scarce at the scent of the men and left the cows to hide in the mulga. The dogs raced ahead in excitement, a blue-speckled dog being the first to get the scent of cattle. He raced into a stand of mulga. The hiding bulls charged out, heading for the next stand of trees. The pack of dogs raced after them, fanning out to try and turn the cattle back towards the riders. Matty and Jack rode hard, galloping their horses, trying to get around in front of the beasts. The bulls broke cover again, racing for open country, kicking at the dogs that nipped at their heels.

Swinging their whips, cracking the snaking leather over the backs of the bulls, the boys gained on the tiring animals and turned the thundering beasts towards the fence line, careful to avoid the long, wicked horns. The pace settled into a walk as the bulls blew heavily from the mad race. Their tongues lolled out of their mouths as they drooled ropes of saliva in their exhaustion. Charlie and Dave took up positions behind the small herd, while Jack and Matty flanked the cattle to stop any breakaways.

Jack turned his horse towards the mob, waiting for Matty to push the cattle up to him.

Matty's horse pricked its ears towards a stand of trees to the left, then two of the dogs raced away, barking excitedly. A red bull broke from the bush, its head high, tail lifted. Matty watched in horror as the bull gained speed, making straight for Jack's horse.

Digging his spurs into his horse's sides, Matty yelled at Jack, who had his bad ear to him, and although he could see Matty coming towards him at the gallop, could not understand what he was yelling.

Matty sat down further into the saddle, his spurs raking the horse cruelly. He lifted his arm, pointing at the bull bearing down on Jack behind him, out of Jack's line of sight. Matty's actions woke Jack's instincts and he spun his horse around to see what had Matty so anxious.

The bull's horns caught the horse in the ribs, ripping up viciously, flipping the horse on its side. Jack was thrown clear, the air forced out of him as he hit the ground. He tried to draw breath into his lungs, his head swimming. He heard Matty scream as a white-hot pain ripped into his stomach. He felt his body lifted into the air, his hands searching for something to hold onto. His eyes opened and he stared into the maddened face of a scrub bull. Somewhere in his mind, beyond the pain, Jack knew he was suspended on the horn of the bull, but his body had no strength; he could not get his arms to push himself away from the horn that held him.

The crack of a rifle echoed in his head as he felt the beast stagger, then stumble. He felt the horn tearing at his guts as the bull somersaulted over, flinging him to the ground.

'Jack, Jack…'

Jack brought his hands up to his stomach, feeling the slippery ropes of his intestines. He smelt the hot, woozy smell of his own shit. Staring at the clouds, he wondered why the pain had gone. His body felt numb. Then he remembered.

A shadow passed over his face. Matty was there, his arms around Jack's neck, lifting him up.

'Jack. Oh sweet fucking Jesus, Jack.'

'It's all right, mate. I can't feel anythin'. It must look pretty bad. I think he's gutted me.'

Matty stared down at Jack face, his eyes unwilling to look at his mate's torn and bleeding stomach. He stripped his shirt off and tore it into strips to pack the wound, then he tried to pull Jack's shirt back together to keep the flies off.

He heard hoof beats in the sand as Dave and Charlie rode up.

'You just lay there, mate. I'll get Bess, she'll fix you up.'

Matty lowered Jack's head gently to the ground. He stood up, turning to Charlie.

'Go get Bess, Charlie. I don't care if you kill that horse, just get Bess back as fast as you fuckin' can!' Matty's voice rose as fear crept in. 'Get Father to bring the wagon.'

Charlie spun his horse on its haunches and booted it to a gallop, its hooves sending spurts of sand out behind it.

Dave jumped off his horse and gathering up the reins of Matty's horse, tied them both to a tree.

Seeing that there was nothing he could do, Dave took Matty's gun from the rifle bucket on the saddle. He walked over to Jack's horse that had managed to stand, head down, its body trembling, teeth gnashing as it groaned in pain. Dave took aim and fired, shooting through the forehead, down the spine. The horse collapsed, shuddered, and was still.

Ejecting the spent cartridge, Dave made his way over to the bull. He looked at the hole in its side, just behind the foreleg. Matty had shot it straight through the heart. Dave looked over at Matty, then back at the bull, wondering at the risk Matty had taken to save his mate. He could have just as easily hit Jack, Dave thought. That was a very good piece of shooting, under the circumstances.

He went back to where Jack lay, his head in Matty's lap. Dave couldn't help but grimace. He had seen wounds like this before – not from a bull, but from shells. Torn skin, the frayed jagged edges of intestine, leaking blood and faeces everywhere, poisoning the body. He knew there was nothing he could say. Matty had retrieved a water bottle and was wiping Jack's lips with the water. Matty looked up at Dave, his eyes full of despair. Jack coughed, making his stomach ripple under the shirt which was red with blood.

'Mate, I'm not gonna make it out of this one. You know that,' Jack gasped out.

'No, Bess will fix you up. She learnt off Minnie and Minnie could fix anything!' Matty insisted, shaking his head in denial.

'No, Shorty. We've seen blokes like this. Anyway, I think it's more than my gut. I can't feel nothin' past me chest. I felt a crack when I landed on the ground, when the bull fell. I think me back's broke. That's why I can't feel anything.'

Dave came around and knelt beside Jack's legs. He reached out and pinched the soft inner of Jack's thigh. Jack did not respond. Dave's eyes flicked up to Matty and then to Jack. He nodded his head.

Jack lifted his bloodied hand and grabbed Matty's chin. He turned Matty's face until he could stare into his eyes.

'You and me, we've been through a lot. We both seen gut shot men before. I don't want to linger for days.'

Matty pulled his face back from Jack's hand, shaking his head violently. 'No. Bess'll fix you up.'

'Shorty, she can't.'

Matty's shoulders sagged. He knew Jack was telling the truth. He took a deep breath and closed his eyes. 'I'll do it.'

'No, mate. I'll do that. If you and Dave just leave the gun, go for a walk.'

Matty stared into Jack's eyes. 'After all we've been through, you still don't think I'm up to it?'

'Matty, you shot the bull, knowin' if you missed, you'd get me. I don't want the shot to be in your head for the rest of your life, like it is with Cedar. No man can ask another man to do that. I'll do it, but I'd like to see the waterhole one more time.'

Matty pushed himself up off the ground. He went to Jack's dead horse. Unsaddling it, he stripped the surcingle and stirrup leathers from the saddle and grabbed the blanket. He lay the blanket on the ground and together, Dave and Matty lifted Jack onto it. Dave caught onto Matty's idea and broke some saplings from the stand of trees from where the bull had charged. Forming a stretcher with the leather and saplings, the two men lifted the blanket on which Jack lay onto the makeshift stretcher. Matty went to Jack's horse and took his spare shirt from the saddlebag. He packed it into Jack's stomach, trying to stop the blood. His nose wrinkled at the pungent smell leaking from the wound.

Taking an end each, they lifted it up and began the long walk back to the waterhole. Matty knew that Charlie would be able to follow their tracks. He left the horses tied to the tree.

Jack made not a sound as the men carried him. They stumbled now and then as they grew tired, sweat darkening their shirts. Dave noticed blood dripping from the stretcher to the ground. He wondered at Jack's bravery in facing death. His mind wandered back to Sammy's death. How similar, in a way, the two men were.

Matty stopped. 'Put him down, Dave.'

He took the water bottle from around his neck, pulled out the cork, and splashed water into his hands. Wiping his wet hands over Jack's face, he brushed the hair out of his mate's eyes.

Matty offered Dave a drink from the water bottle. Gratefully, Dave swished the water around his dry mouth. As they lifted the stretcher to continue their trek, Dave saw the sand beneath it soaked in blood.

A high screeching whistle made Matty look up. A pair of wedge-tailed eagles glided on the heated air currents, watching the green parrots winging their way from tree to tree. He saw the horse yards and beyond them, the waterhole. His legs felt leaden as he trudged through the sand.

As they placed the stretcher down in the shade of the tree, near the water, Jack tried to turn his head. His face was pale from the shock and the blood that he had lost. Matty sat down, his back against the tree and lifted him, cradling him in his arms. Gazing out across the water, Jack's cheeks were wet with tears. He murmured, 'Shorty, thank the Boss and the Missus for their kindness to me.'

'Bess is comin'.'

The corners of Jack's mouth curled in a smile. 'Shorty, you always hope, don't you?'

Dave could sense the pain of these two men: one who would lose a brother, the other at having his life cut short after surviving the war. He shrugged; there was nothing he could say about the unfairness of it. Slowly, he wandered off, leaving the two of them alone.

After an hour had passed, he came back and gently lifted Jack from Matty's lap. He closed Jack's staring eyes and placed his head on the ground, covering him with the saddle blanket. Matty sat, covered in his mate's blood, his back against the tree, his own eyes staring, not seeing, not hearing.

TWENTY-FOUR

Time passed slowly as Dave sat beside Matty, watching and waiting. Matty hadn't moved, but Dave saw tears dropping down his cheeks. He heard the voices of Charlie and Thomas, the jingle of a bit. Standing, he stretched his legs and walked out to meet them.

Thomas took in the still body at the base of the tree and his son. He looked down at Dave, who shook his head.

Thomas' face stiffened and he gave a loud gasp as if he had been punched. Charlie glanced at him, then dismounted. He walked over to take Thomas' horse, his eyes on the older man's face.

'Boss?'

'I'm all right, Charlie. We had better see to Jack.'

Thomas walked slowly over to where Jack's body lay under the blanket. He knelt down and lifted the blanket from Jack's face. Staring down at the man whom he had raised, Thomas wept. Wiping his nose on his sleeve, he turned his eyes towards his son. Matty had not moved, had not seen his father. Thomas stood up wearily, the fast pace they had set playing havoc on his ageing body.

'Matty,' he said softly. 'Matty, we have to take care of Jack.'

There was no response.

'Matty,' Thomas said a little louder.

Matty's head rolled towards his father. Brown eyes blinked, moving down to stare at the body under the blanket. He shuddered, drawing up his legs. His gaze returned to the water and he said in a whisper, 'Why, Father, why?'

'Son, I don't have an answer for you. He was good boy and grew to be a good man. We will have to take care of him now.'

Nodding slowly, Matty said, 'We'll bury him here. He loved this place.'

Gradually, Matty stood up. His body felt like it had been dragged through the desert. He swayed and caught hold of the tree.

Thomas reached out to steady him, but Matty waved him away. Looking down at the dried blood covering his chest, he stroked it with his fingers.

'He didn't want to take days, Father. He knew.' Matty spoke softly, slowly. 'Is the wagon comin'? Is Mother comin'? I'd better get cleaned up; it will upset her.'

Thomas felt his stomach twist. His son was in a place he couldn't reach. He knew it was the shock; he searched for words of comfort for his son's loss. Thomas placed his hand on Matty's shoulder and squeezed it.

'You boys went through a hell of a lot together. Only you know how much. But Matty, you have to pull yourself together. Yes, your mother is coming. And you are right, you had better get cleaned up.'

Matty walked to the water's edge and scooped water over his face. Straightening up, he turned and looked at the others. He took a deep breath and let it out. He felt empty. His mind took in the scene, but he wondered why he felt so empty. He shook his head, wanting to clear it, to feel something. Walking over to the pack saddles, he took a short, handled shovel from it and looked about. A picture rose in his mind. Three children playing at the water's edge, Charlie and Annie laughing at them. His gaze went to where Jack's body lay under the tree.

'I'll lay you there, Jack, where you can see what we saw as kids.'

Dave and Thomas lifted Jack's body to the side, making room for Matty to dig where he wanted to bury Jack.

Matty drove the shovel into the sand. Gripping it hard, he lifted a shovel full and threw it to the side. He stabbed at the ground, his rage building until he was working furiously, sweat pouring from his body. Charlie put out his hand to take the shovel, but Thomas shook his head. He realised that Matty was working out his grief, his anger at his mate's pointless death. After he threw the last bit of sand to the side, Matty sank down, exhausted. Dave offered him a water bottle, but he shook his head.

The creaking of wood alerted the group to the coming of the wagon, bringing Eliza and Bess closer to them. Thomas walked out to meet them, to tell them of Jack's dying.

Matty heard his mother's sobs. He knew he should go to her, but his body refused to move, so he sat there, his legs in the grave. A picture of Jack leaning against Absent, a rollie hanging from his smiling face, floated through his mind. It was pushed away by another image, then another until it seemed as if a silent movie starring Jack was rolling through his head. Sammy, Jack and him, playing, fighting, laughing, all mixed up.

He sensed rather than saw his mother's approach. He felt her arms around his neck, heard her soft whimpers as she struggled to keep control of her grief. Matty looked up at her. She stared into his eyes. He turned away, not being able to answer the questions he saw there.

Thomas cleared his throat. 'We best not wait for a minister. Not in this heat. We will bury him ourselves. What do you say, son?'

'Jack would like that.' Matty's voice was stronger. 'He said to thank you, to you and Mother for your kindness. He wouldn't want anyone else.'

Eliza knelt down beside Jack and lifted the blanket from his face. Great racking sobs shook her body as she stroked his hair. As her sobs subsided, she told him how much he had come to mean to them. Bending over, she kissed his forehead, her tears falling onto his pale face.

Wrapping Jack in the horse blanket, Matty and Dave lowered him into the sandy grave. Thomas searched his memory for lessons from the scriptures he had learnt in church, all those years ago. Cockatoos screeched in the background and horses stamped at the flies, their bridles jingling. Slowly, Matty shovelled sand back into the grave. As Thomas helped Eliza back to the wagon, Matty began to gather stones. He placed each stone carefully on the mound that lay in the shade of the Yapunyah tree. Dave and Charlie looked at each other, but Charlie shook his head. It was something Matty had to do.

Looking up, Matty saw them.

'I'll be along. You go home with Father.'

'Yer horse, him over there in the yards, young fella.'

Nodding, Matty returned to his task. He heard the wagon move off, Charlie calling the dogs. Slowly the mound of rocks grew, until he was searching further and further out. Finally, he was satisfied with his cairn over Jack. He wiped the sweat from his forehead with the back of his arm, staring at the grave.

'I never expected to bury you, mate. We got through over there,' he whispered. 'Why, is what I'd like to know. After all you've been through, I... I just don't know, mate.'

Instinctively, from habit, he unsaddled the chestnut. He poured out some grain from the feed bag, patting the horse, an unconscious movement, as he turned back to the waterhole.

The dusk settled around him as he sat down beside Jack. His skin shivered as the cool night air touched him.

The last glow of day faded, taken over by the soft light of the stars. Matty lay down, his arms cradling his head. He heard the night birds calling, the soft rustle of animals as they foraged in the darkness. None of it held any fear for him, it was natural, right. Rolling over, he stared at the cairn.

'Sammy is here with us, Jack. He would have come back to country.

This is his country. Somewhere you two must have met up by now.' Matty smiled at his own words. 'You two will have a lot of catchin' up to do.'

He felt the need to talk, to hear a voice rather than the bush.

'What am I supposed to do without both of you? It was hard enough losin' Sammy. I've never told you fellas how much you meant to me. You probably know now. They reckon you see everything, up where you blokes are now.'

The words ran out, but his mind kept replaying the images of their childhood, the war. He was vaguely aware of a sliver of a moon rising, spreading its faint glow over the water. His eyes grew heavy. He shook his head, trying to stay awake, to keep vigil over Jack. Slowly, he faded into sleep, his body exhausted.

The first thing to greet him as he opened his eyes was the cairn. The pain rushed back in, the unbelievable truth. He lay there, his mind screaming out at the futility of it all. As full consciousness came to him, he forced himself to steady his thoughts.

He raised himself up and went to the water hole. After washing his face, he looked at the rising sun.

'I can't stay here. Not on the property. Not for now.'

Turning back to the tree that shaded Jack, he gave a nod. 'You understand, don't you? You always reckoned I lived in a dream world. Well, I wish I was dreamin', but I'm not. You two are gone. Gone like our mates over there.'

He walked a step at a time closer to the grave until he looked down at it. 'You said I had to grow up. Well, I thought I had. Maybe I have to get away from here, go do some things. Might go find Grandfather. Might head down to Uncle Robert's.'

Kneeling, he shifted a stone, placing it at the very top.

'I'll come back. I'll bring two headstones, carved, saying what my two mates did, who they were.'

Matty stood up and threw a short salute at Jack's grave. 'Bye Jack, bye Sammy.'

* * * *

He stayed long enough at the homestead to pack clothing and rations. Matty spoke to Thomas, telling him that he couldn't stay for now, but would return. Eliza held her tongue. She craved to cradle her son, to take away his pain, but she realised that only time could do that. Dave spoke of his wish to visit Clarrie in Charleville and left, giving his condolences to the family.

At dawn, two days after Jack's death, Matty left Mulga Plains.

TWENTY-FIVE

The train groaned its way to a halt, clanking and groaning, steam bellowing out from under its huge black body. Matty stood up and dragged his kit down from the brass luggage rack. He stepped out onto the platform, idly marvelling at its length. Somewhere he had read that the Albury station was the longest train platform in Australia, maybe even the world. Two governments could not agree on the gauge of the tracks, and so the platform came into being to accept two trains at once. He made his way through the crowd, passing through the large waiting room and out onto the vast parking area. New cars sat waiting, while horses and wagons eddied around them. He asked a grizzled wagon driver for the name of a good hotel and where he could buy a few horses. Matty had decided during the long train journey to ride up the mountain instead of catching a coach. That way he could please himself; he would not have to pass idle talk with passengers. It was easy enough on the train. He just pretended to be asleep. If the other passengers got too nosey, he would leave the compartment until they had nodded off. You could not do that in a horse-drawn coach.

The old man gave him directions to Soden's Australia Hotel, telling him that they had stables and that the groom there should be able to find him some suitable horses. Matty threw his kit over his shoulder and started up the wide dirt road that the driver had indicated.

Matty paid for his room, put his kit on the bed and went looking for the stables. The smell of fresh straw and manure drew him out to the back of the hotel. There, a row of loose boxes was being cleaned out, two horses tied to a rail that ran along the front of the boxes. The sound of cursing led him to the end stable where a bearded man, short in stature, was trying to put a halter on a tall thoroughbred. The horse simply stood there with his head held high, turning it away whenever the man reached up with the halter. Matty smiled as the fellow walked towards the feed bin and rattled it. The horse came immediately to the bin and lowered his head, allowing the groom to slip the head collar on.

Turning to lead the horse from the box, the groom looked surprised to see Matty.

'Didn't see you there, mate.'

Matty grinned. 'Stubborn beggar, is he?'

The groom smiled and jerked his thumb at the horse. 'This one's not too bad. He's a bit of a character. Some of them that comes here are just plain mad.' Tying the horse to the rail, the man turned and introduced himself. 'Me name's Fred. Can I helps you?'

'Matty. I'm lookin' for a couple of horses to buy. One for ridin' and another for a pack horse. I need them with gear as well. Fella at the railway station said you might be able to help.'

'All I've got here is the horses going to the Melbourne races. They stop here to give 'em a rest from the train.' He pulled at his whiskers, thinking. 'The saddler in Dean Street, he mentioned getting a few horses in from a property out at Culcairn. I'll just finish the boxes and take you down.'

The saddler showed Matty six horses in a yard at the back of the shop. Throwing a saddle on one that looked promising, he took it out for a short ride. Satisfied with the horse, he took the saddler's word about a pack horse and purchased some gear. Fred then took him to the general store where Matty purchased cooking utensils and rations for his trip to his uncle's station.

Fred helped him settle the horses in yards attached to the hotel stables and showed him where to store the saddles. The groom, intrigued by this quiet young man, had tried to engage him in conversation and invited him for a beer, but Matty pleaded tiredness from the journey and after having an early dinner, went to bed.

Faint streaks of light were in the east when Matty went down to feed his new horses. Using brushes he found in the tack room, he gave them a thorough grooming and returned to his room. It only took a few minutes for him to have a shave and pack his kit before he went down to the dining room. The cook was startled to see someone down for breakfast so early, but quickly produced a plate of eggs and bacon for the departing guest.

Matty was just finishing saddling when Fred turned up, looking a little worse for wear.

'Just as well you didn't come out last night,' he mumbled. 'You wouldn't be lookin' so fit this morning.'

Nodding, Matty tightened the girth and turned to the groom. Shaking his hand, he thanked Fred for his help and gave him a handful of coin.

'No need for that, but I thank you for it,' he muttered. 'Well, you'd better get on your way.'

Swinging up into the saddle, Matty reached down and untied the pack horse's lead rope. He gave Fred a bit of a wave and rode out onto the main road.

Following the river, Matty took his time. He had sent a telegram to his uncle, giving him an approximate arrival date and therefore felt no need to hurry. Shadows rode with him, and he caught himself thinking about the what ifs.

He shook his head, trying to take his mind off Jack and Sammy. He started to make up names for his newly acquired horses. Occasionally he passed other horse riders and more rarely, a motor vehicle. As the sun started its climb down behind the hills, he sought a place on the riverbank to camp. He didn't need to think; after the years in the desert, the unsaddling, feeding and preparing a quick bite to eat were instinct.

Glad that he had chosen to ride, Matty studied the country he was passing through. Green river flats rising to large, granite rocked hills fascinated him. The country looked lush; fat cattle grazing proved it so.

Three days later he passed a stockman at some cattle yards beside the road.

'Excuse me, mate. How far is Myora Station?' he asked.

The tall, lean man wiped sweat from his forehead with his arm and looked at the stranger. He took in the horses at a glance, well bred, worth a bit. Running his eyes over the pack horse, he noted the load was well-balanced and tight.

'Lookin' fer work?'

Matty shook his head. 'No, relatives.'

'Five mile'll see ya there. Can't miss it. Big white gates.'

'Thanks.'

The shortness of Matty's words made the man wonder. Most people stopped and talked about the weather, the state of cattle prices. He sighed as he turned back to his work. *You never know these days,* he thought to himself.

The afternoon heat was rising as Matty looked down at the winding river below him.

'What Father would give to have a river like that runnin' through our place, eh, Freddie?' he asked his horse.

The land wound deep into a horseshoe bend in the river and Matty saw Hereford bullocks resting in the shade of large river red gums. To his left, the hills climbed up and up, heavily timbered at their tops, granite outcrops strewn across the slopes. Here and there, he could see sheep grazing, newborn lambs cavorted around their mothers, trying their new life out of the womb.

He came to the white gates and pulled his horse up. Pillars made from rocks sat either side of a five-barred wooden gate, all painted white. The name of the station was painted in copperplate in the middle of the gate.

'So, this is Uncle Robert's,' he mused. His eyes scanned up the long driveway, either side were golden poplars. He tugged at the lead of the pack horse and nudged his horse forward. This would be home for a while. How long, he didn't know.

The homestead was quiet as he rode up. A dog barked half-heartedly, bringing an old man to see what had disturbed it.

He limped as he walked slowly towards Matty, flicking crumbs from his long beard.

'Bread just come out,' he said in way of explanation. 'Can't beat fresh hot bread and drippin'.'

His mouth was lost in his beard, but Matty saw a tooth and assumed it was a smile. Dismounting, he put his hand about. 'Matty Watson.'

The old man wiped his hand on his trousers and shook Matty's hand hard, surprising Matty with its strength.

'I be called Ol' Tom. I ain't that old. Harry over the way, he's risin' eighty, I'm only seventy-five, but anyways, that's what they call me,' he prattled. 'You be Mr Robert's nephew. We heard all about your place up there. What do ya think of this place?'

Matty's mind was not so much on the property as on the rapid deliverance of so much information.

'Eh, yeah. Looks good,' he replied. 'Got somewhere I can put my horses?'

Ol' Tom looked him up and down, thinking, 'This young man is a man of few words. Maybe he's just shy.'

'I'll put 'em away for you, young fella,' he offered, taking a step towards the horses.

Matty drew back his hand holding the reins; the old man to look at him strangely.

'No, if you just show me, I'll take care of them,' he said brusquely. Realising by the look on Ol' Tom's face that he had sounded short, he added, 'Habit. I like to see to them myself.'

Ol' Tom turned and hobbled towards a set of high-railed yards, Matty following him, flashes of memory flitting through his mind. The lessons of Charlie, the horse piquets in the desert, Cedar nickering to him as he went to her in the morning. He closed his eyes for a second, telling himself to forget. He tied the horses to a rail and after unsaddling them, he took out a brush from the pack saddle. As he brushed the dust and sweat from their coats, Tom leaned against the fence and kept up a running commentary on what Matty would find here.

'Oh,' the old man said suddenly. 'You must be wondering where your uncle is!'

Matty didn't answer, just gave a nod.

'The family, they've all gone over to Tintaldra. That's across the river,' Tom explained, waving his hand towards the south. 'There was a Gymkhana today and Mr Robert took some horses over to see how they'd go. They'll be along directly.'

Matty untied the horses and led them through a gate. Once free of their bridles, the two horses looked about, then headed towards a water trough. Shutting the gate, Matty asked where he could store his gear.

'The tack room's behind the hayshed there,' Tom told him. 'We'll put your gear away, then I'll introduce you to the housekeeper, Mrs Nealle. She'll know where you're to bed down.'

The smell of hot bread preceded them as Tom took him up to the homestead. A carriage way encircled the house. A wide verandah looked south, giving views towards the river and the snow-capped mountains. Matty could not help but be impressed. An idea came to him. His mother had sat on this very verandah as a young woman while his father had come to court her.

He realised that Tom was taking him to the front door.

'Where's the back door, Ol' Tom? I need to wash up before I go inside.'

Tom halted, looking startled. He had formed the impression that this young man would be used to the rules.

Matty watched as these thoughts flitted across the old man's face.

'We don't stand on ceremony where I come from, Tom,' he said with the ghost of a smile on his lips. 'Show me where the back door is, eh?'

As they walked towards the back of the house, Tom showed Matty the large oven that was used for cooking bread and large roasts. A cast iron door hung open and Matty could feel the heat from it.

'In there's the meat room, that's where we cut up the kill.'

Matty looked through the wire mesh covered door. A well-scrubbed large wooden table stood in the centre of the room, while above it hung butcher's hooks, knives and saws.

They entered onto a small porch where Tom indicated a room for Matty to have a wash. He placed the saddle packs down against the wall and filled a basin with water.

Hearing the noise, the housekeeper came to see who had arrived.

'You would be young Matty, Eliza's boy,' she said warmly. 'I've turned out your mother's old room for you. Come along, we'll put your things in there, and then how about a cup of tea?'

Matty wondered if everyone here spoke so much. He let himself be shown to his room and after unpacking his clothes, he went in search of Mrs Nealle.

'I've just filled the teapot, so you sit yourself down and have some bread that I just baked,' Mrs Nealle offered when she saw him in the doorway of the kitchen. 'The cook will be in later to do the dinner, but I like to cook the bread.'

He pulled out a chair from the table and sat down, feeling like a child again with this woman. He guessed she was about sixty years old, small and bent, with her grey hair swept up into a bun.

'Now, let me look at you. Yes, you have Eliza's eyes. I came here when she was ten. A right little miss, she was. And, what a wedding the old Mr Robert gave her. Your father was so handsome. But here I am, rattling on.' She laughed as she placed a plate of thickly buttered bread in front of him, quickly followed by a cup of tea.

Letting her words wash over him, Matty thought of the grandfather he had never met. He had died while Jack and Matty where in the Jordan Valley. His mother's letters showed her grief.

'Sorry, Mrs Nealle, what did you say?' Matty realised that the housekeeper had stopped talking.

'Oh, nothing really. You must be tired. Why don't you go and sit in the library, have a rest till your uncle gets home?'

'Thank you, but I'm all right. I might go for a walk around the garden. Mother used to tell me all about the flowers down here. She couldn't grow them at Mulga Plains. It was too dry and hot. Tan tried to, but they wouldn't grow.'

Matty realised that was the most he had said to anyone in days. He shook his head; he really had to get on with things.

He wandered about, noticing the green shoots of bulbs poking through the soil. He looked at the fruit trees in bud. The jasmine along the verandah rail. Soon, this garden would be full of colour. Pinks, white, reds, yellows and magentas. Home was red soil, green bush, blue sky. Here, everything would have bright colours.

The noise of the carriage pulling up broke into his thoughts and he walked to the front of the house. Robert came towards him, his face slightly puzzled, then it cleared.

'Matty, how you have grown! Annette, this is my nephew Matty,' he called to his wife.

'Pleased to finally meet you. I knew your mother when she lived here,'

Annette said warmly. 'How is she lately? I haven't heard from her for a while.'

Matty looked at his uncle then at Annette. 'Father hasn't telephoned you?'

Concern flitted across Robert's face. 'What has happened, Matty? I only know that you sent me a telegram to say that you would be coming to stay for a while. I thought it a bit strange that you would come so soon and without Jack.'

'Jack's dead,' Matty said bluntly. 'He was killed a week ago.'

He watched as his aunt raised her hand to her mouth, seemingly in slow motion. Robert absorbed the shock more quickly. He took in the anger in Matty's voice and decided to ask questions later.

'I am very sorry; I know how close you were to Jack. We'll talk about it later, shall we?' he said. 'The telephone lines must be down somewhere for your parents not to have rung. We shall send them a telegram tomorrow from the post office at Tintaldra.'

His aunt took his arm, chatting about inconsequential things, asking him had he met Tom and Mrs Nealle. He answered in short words; not rudely, but he could not make himself string long sentences together.

At dinner Robert told him something of how the property worked and about the people in the district.

Sitting quietly, Matty listened, his thoughts going back to how curt he had been when his aunt and uncle had greeted him. He tried to apologise, but his uncle replied, 'You have been through a hell of a lot in your short life, Matty. It will take you a while to get over it. We have all the time in the world here. So, don't you worry too much about it.'

Robert showed him about the property over the next few days and seeing Matty was willing to get into the work, allowed him to go ahead and help the men. The workers accepted the quiet, reticent man as not only the Boss's nephew, but a good worker.

They offered to take him to the pub on the first Saturday afternoon, but he declined the offer. Matty wore himself out working during the day, hoping that it would make him too tired to have nightmares at night. But the house was often woken by him calling out to Sammy or Jack, depending on which nightmare he was having.

Weeks went by and he helped Robert prepare his best thoroughbred for the upcoming races at the Tintaldra Picnic races. They came up quickly. His aunt organised Mrs Nealle and the cook to prepare food for the outing. Tom packed the table and chairs into the wagon.

As they rode over – leading Highpoint, the horse that would be racing – Robert explained why he did not have a car. It seemed that Annette could not abide the new contraptions and so, to keep the peace, Robert refrained from purchasing one.

Other people had set up tables laden with food and a refreshment tent was off to one side. The racetrack was a wooden rail, curving around a large paddock. The scene was gay, with ladies wearing bright-coloured dresses and large hats, and men in their best suits. Here and there, a woman wore black, showing that she was still mourning a loss in the war.

Standing by his uncle, Matty was astounded by a short, fat gentleman who kept glaring at him. He turned slightly to avoid having to look at the man but he could still feel his eyes on him.

Robert noticed Matty's discomfort and murmured, 'That is Mr Halpin. He lost two sons in the war.'

Unfortunately, the man in question overheard Robert and said meanly, 'I see some families did not send their sons to war, unlike others.'

Anger surged through Matty and he trembled as he tried to control his reply. Robert forestalled him by placing an arm around his shoulders, digging his fingers into his nephew's shoulders.

'Mr Halpin, this is my nephew Matty. He served in the Middle East along with Jack, his brother. We also lost a family member, Sammy, at Passchendaele. I know that you lost your boys and we are sorry for your sacrifice.'

The man looked taken aback for a second but then he looked Matty up and down. 'Not a scratch on him. Must have had a desk job, somewhere safe. Everyone came home wounded.'

Under his hand, Robert could feel the anger in Matty, in his tensing muscles, his heavy breathing. Fearing that his nephew would take this man to task for his words, Robert pushed Matty towards the horses behind them, saying loudly as he turned himself, 'Mr Halpin, you should watch your words.'

As they drew up beside the wagon where Highpoint was tied, Matty rounded on his uncle.

'I can speak for myself, Robert. I fought a god forsaken fuckin' war, you know. Killed men that I never knew. How dare that bastard have a go at me!' Matty paced up and down, his hands shaking. 'How dare he belittle Sammy's death.' Stopping in mid stride, Matty stared at his uncle. 'I just realised what you said. You said… a member of our family.'

'When I came to your property all those years ago, I learnt many things. One of which was how close you were to Sammy and Jack. Then with all the letters from your mother in the years after my visit and when you boys were fighting, what struck me was how Eliza herself had come to think of Sammy and Jack as her boys. That makes them our family.'

The breath went out of Matty. He leant against the wagon; his head bowed. 'Thank you, Robert. That means a great deal to me.'

Robert slapped him on the arm. 'Now, that man was a mean-mouthed man before his sons went to the war and if the truth be known, they probably went to get away from him – not that I like to wish the man or the dead ill. What I am trying to say is his opinion is not worth listening to. He may be grieving but he has no right to cast aspersions on you. You know what you have done and you should be proud of yourself.'

With that, Robert turned and went over to Annette, who had been trying to attract his attention.

TWENTY-SIX

Matty put his anger aside as he stood by the wagon, stroking Highpoint's neck, calming the excited animal as it watched the racing horses. Matty heard the rise in the voice of the crowd. He could hear the rhythm of hooves, feel the ground beneath his feet trembling, as the horses pounded the hard earth of the straight. He closed his eyes, screwing them shut, his teeth clenched. When would the memories fade to a bearable level? He could not stop the flow. The mass of horses galloping in the dust of the desert. The strength of Cedar as she gave everything in her last race. Her lunging, gasping strides, her pounding heart.

The roar of the crowd faded as the vibrations of the racing horses permeated his body. His legs trembled, feeling the rise and fall of Cedar's ribs as they lunged towards the last trench. The flash of steel in the sinking sun of Beersheba; the dust... he could smell it all again.

'Excuse me, are you all right?'

Matty opened his eyes, staring at his hands that had become tangled in Highpoint's mane. He tried to stop them shaking, rubbing them down his trouser legs.

'You are Matty? Robert's nephew?' a female voice insisted.

Turning slowly towards the voice, he took a deep breath, trying to appear calm.

The eyes that finally focused on the woman were remote, staring;

watery from tears that hung suspended on the bottom lashes. It was the stare of a man that had seen too much pain and suffering, one who had performed deeds that no man should be asked to, who had given all that he had and left behind part of himself with those that had not survived. She knew those eyes – she had seen them too many times to remember; they haunted her and would forever.

She watched as Matty fought to bring himself under control. She reached out and stroked the horse's nose, murmuring softly to the horse that was sweating from excitement.

'You know what is happening, don't you, boy? I believe you are in the next race. If you keep this up, you'll have run your race before you get out on the track.'

Clearing his throat, Matty said, 'He'll do all right. He's fit as a fiddle.'

The woman looked again at Matty, elegantly offering her gloved hand to him.

'My name is Sarah. And you would be Matty,' she said quietly.

Matty shook her hand carefully, embarrassment reddening his face. He nodded his head, cursing his inexperience with females.

Sarah's eyes followed her hand back to the horse's neck. 'I saw you the other day, by the yards over at Myora station. You were branding cattle.'

'Yes, ma'am.'

'Your uncle Robert is a well-liked man around here,' she continued, keeping her eyes on the horse. 'He has put a lot of time and money into our little community.'

'I've not been here long, ma'am. I'm just hearin' about it all.'

Sarah tried again. This time her eyes flicked up at Matty, noticing that his pallor had returned to normal and his eyes had softened.

'You may think me a bit forward, but I have learnt to be. I am the district's only nurse.'

Matty reddened again under her look. He picked up a piece of blanket and began to wipe the sweat from Highpoint's neck and back.

'Uncle did say that when we saw you ride past,' he mumbled.

'Oh, so you did see me. Yes, I was on my way down to Ournie to help Mrs Bridie deliver. A boy, another one. That makes eight.'

Matty stopped and looked up at Sarah. 'Eight!'

'Yes, she has her hands full. And that's with running the farm. Her husband lost his legs in France.'

She saw the cloud come across his eyes again before his head dropped. Sarah had to strain to hear his next words.

'I lost a good mate in France.'

'We lost a lot of good men in France,' she replied. 'We lost most of a generation in the war.'

At the anger in her voice, he raised his head to look at her face.

'I nursed them over there,' Sarah said.

Comprehension dawned on Matty. His body lost a little of its tightness.

'So, you do know how it was.'

'Oh, yes, I do at that.' Her laugh was bitter.

His brown eyes filled again with emotion.

Reaching forward, Sarah lay her hand on his shoulder, feeling him tense.

'Matty, I do understand, even if they do not,' she said, nodding her head towards the crowd of people that had drifted back towards the tables for something to eat. 'They sat out the war here, reading it in the papers. Yes, some of them suffered too. Mr Halpin over there, he lost two boys. That's why he was so short with you. It is hard for those whose sons and husbands came back injured or didn't come home at all,' she explained softly. 'They look at you and see you whole; they don't see how injured you are on the inside.'

Matty just stared at this woman. She knew. No one but those who had fought with him or had been there could know. Jack and Dave were the only ones that he had felt comfortable with.

'I shouldn't have let it get to me but I just can't stop remembering.'

A sense of relief began to rise in him. He leant back against the wagon, looking at his hands. They had stopped trembling.

Sarah moved to him and taking his hand, lifted it over her arm.

'Walk with me.' It was not a question.

Matty responded to the tone of her voice, only belatedly feeling nervous to be so close to a woman. They walked slowly, her skirt brushing his legs occasionally, while in the background, the crowd noise receded. Her head came to his shoulder and he glanced down it, noting the darkness of her hair. A fallen log under a huge red gum tree provided a place to sit. As Sarah arranged her skirts after sitting down, Matty leant against the tree, his hand nervously running over the bark. He glanced at Sarah, noticing her green eyes fringed by long dark lashes. Her cheeks were blushed, blending with her creamy skin.

Staring out over the paddocks, lined with wooden rails and barbed wire, she began to speak.

'We are like a club. The soldiers who have returned cannot speak of it to anyone that wasn't there. It is the same with me. My father was a doctor here in Tintaldra. That was fifteen years ago. When my mother died, he could not stay here. My sister was engaged to be married to a local man when we left. I am much younger than she; I was a late baby. When I was eight, my father moved down to Albury. As he got older, he relied on me to help him, so I learnt a lot. It seemed I was destined to become a nurse, so I did my three years training at the hospital there. When war was declared, I enlisted. There were a great many nurses applying, and I believed my youth would tell against me. I believe it was because of my attitude that I was one of the sisters picked. I had seen a lot in my life in the way of accident and sickness, and death, from a very young age, and knew that it would not be a romantic stint overseas. Matron McDonald who interviewed me was appalled at my upbringing. Although she did say that it had given me a look at the reality of nursing. She was a good old stick though. She was in charge on the boat going over and had an eye for those who were serious or those that had come on an adventure. She knocked the rough out of me pretty quickly.'

Sarah paused, smiling at the memory of the old dragon she had come to respect.

Matty leaned slightly forward, wanting her to continue her story. Her voice was soothing.

Sarah patted the log beside her. 'Come and sit down, here, beside me.'

He drew back a moment, shy, then squaring his shoulders, he sat where she had indicated, stretching his long legs out in front of him.

'What do you mean rough?' he asked. 'You don't seem rough.'

Sarah laughed. 'By rough, I meant that I was not a meek, servile girl. I had been helping father for so long, or it seemed a long time, that I'd grown a bit bossy and used to doing things my way. In service you had to be very obedient and do as you were told. It caused me problems at the hospital. I was always in trouble. Luckily, they thought that I would make a good nurse, but I was the cause of many headaches to that Matron. Matron McDonald was very patient with me, but strict. I began to see that it was part of being in the army. I had to learn not to give my opinion unless asked. God forgive if we contradicted a doctor! They found me very useful in the theatre. What horrible theatres we had!'

'Did you help your father with things like that?' Matty asked, feeling more comfortable.

'Yes, and everyone was scandalised. You see, he taught me and knew he could rely on me. Unusual for then, but...' Her voice trailed off.

He looked sideways at her, noticing how her long dark hair had escaped its bun, curling down her neck. He felt a warm feeling spreading out from his loins, warming him, confusing him.

'My training put me in good stead for what was to come,' Sarah continued, feeling his eyes on her. She smiled inwardly, knowing that Matty had started to relax and in doing so, had begun to feel again. The smile spread to her face as she acknowledged the effect she was having on this man, who she assumed had not had much to do with women.

'I left Australia on the "Ascanius". We were sent to Egypt. The hospitals took some setting up. And the heat. It was stifling. The boys were starting to come back from Gallipoli. They called for volunteers to go on the hospital ships. I felt that I could be of use, so I volunteered. My ship was the Dunbar Castle. What a nightmare. Not enough of anything; cots, bandages, food. Men that had lain out for days on the beach or in the hills were coming onto the ship. Their wounds were flyblown, rotten. But they never whinged. Night was the worst. In the dark, you could hear them trying not to moan, not to cry. We would do as much as we could, but sometimes you just wanted to close your eyes and have it all go away. What could you do but go on?'

Matty could not take his eyes of Sarah's profile. She knew; she had seen. He felt a calmness descend on him. He hadn't felt like that since he had got home to the station with Jack with it all behind them. He felt confused. It was her understanding that made him feel this way or was it the woman herself? He certainly felt more relaxed but there was a small knot of something in him. He turned and stared at the ground in front of him.

He heard himself ask, 'How did you cope?'

Sarah shrugged her shoulders. 'You just did. The nurses who couldn't, they were swiftly transferred. Sometimes when you were close to the shore picking up men, bombs would land in the water near the ship. How the men stood the noise up in those hills? It was bad enough out on the boat. We did not get a day off in five months, not till after the evacuation. Backwards and forwards that ship went. Sometimes it was quite nerve racking when there was a torpedo alert. But it was the men who made it worthwhile. I became friendly with a Tommy.' She heard Matty's intake of breath and considered what she had said. 'Not friendly as in walking out. God, the man was badly wounded!'

His face reddened again at her words. She amazed him with her candour. The few girls that he had met were simpering, playful fillies, not forthright as this woman was.

'No, it started when I sat with him one night. He was feverish, he called for his mates. We had no time to wash the men. All we did was cut off their uniforms and dress their wounds. A few orderlies would feed them, but they were covered in lice, some had dysentery. It was a fearful mess. We were only supposed to carry four hundred and fifty men, but sometimes there would be up to nine hundred and no room for them. Those that were not so badly wounded were put up on deck, out in all weathers. When his fever passed, he started to speak of his home. They all did that. Never about the war. They might call for their mother or talk of where they came from. Anyway, he had been a groom at Grange Mill, near Linslade, in Bedfordshire. He told me of the green hills, the woods. Of the beautiful horses he had looked after. I told him about Tintaldra and Australia. When we got to Egypt, he asked could he write to me. Having listened to his wonderful descriptions, he made it sound like I was there myself. I selfishly thought that it would be a welcome relief to get letters from him. He never looked at things from a bad side, always a good side and I needed that. And… I had found him attractive.'

Again, she paused, her thoughts drifting back. Sarah remained silent for a while and Matty sat very still, not wanting to disturb her. He felt embarrassed by her frankness but did not want her to stop. The races continued on behind them and Matty had half a notion that his uncle may be missing him. Matty could not go back just yet. He sensed that Sarah needed to talk and in doing so, she was helping him.

She gave a little shiver and continued. 'I was transferred to Mena. The hours on the ship and the poor food knocked us about. Some nights you would finish dressings at two in the morning and start again at five thirty. A lot of sisters got sick. Spencer continued to write. He was at another hospital. When we finally got two days leave, two sisters and I went to Cairo. Egypt! What a land of contrasts. So dirty and poor, yet there were some beautiful houses and palaces.'

'I loved the Sphinx,' Matty offered. 'It sat there, so proud. Looked like a big dog, sitting, ready, waiting to go to work.'

Sarah turned to him, a look of surprise on her face. 'I never thought about it like that, but you are right.'

'We got leave to go there not long after I got to Egypt. Jack and I,' Matty faltered, his voice dropping. He sat a bit straighter and cleared his throat. 'We often got day passes when we were in camp at Heliopolis. Jack and I visited the markets and got some things to send home. Then we went and climbed the Pyramids, did all the photos of soldiers on camel shots. Father laughed when he saw those, so Mother wrote. Jack had already been there heaps of times, so he knew all the good places. We'd get warnings from the CO about places to stay away from – you know... brothels and that – but quite a few of the men ignored the rules. They paid for it later.' Matty looked away as he mumbled the last few sentences, his faced flushed. 'Jack... told me he'd take me apart if he caught me in a place like that.'

Sarah sensed that he was struggling with a strong emotion. She gently asked, 'Who was Jack?'

Matty did not move. Who was Jack, what was Jack? He thought he had always known. Now, looking back, it was too easy to say, he was my mate. He raised his arm and wiped his forehead, trailing his hand down over his eyes. This woman, so calm and beautiful, raised feelings in him that he had not experienced before. Her closeness made his blood pound in his head and her words shook him, but at the same time did not hurt him.

He spoke slowly. 'I was an only child for eight years. Sammy, he was a black kid – he and I were mates, grew up together. Then, one day there was a thunderstorm. The river flooded and killed Jack's father. They were going to another property to work. Jack came to live with us.'

The words, started so slowly, now poured from him. 'Jack was a town kid, but he soon got to know our way of living. Now that I have seen different places and how people treat each other, I know that what I had growin' up was very special. Our blacks helped us and we looked after them. Sammy and Jack were my mates, my brothers. Mother let Sammy learn school with us. We got a pretty good education compared to some. We ran wild till we started work. Well, as wild as Mother would let me. You see, Mother had lost a few babies and her baby brother died young, so she was very protective of me. I think Jack was always waiting for me to grow up. Jack was always the older brother. I went to war very naïve, but he helped me through it. We heard Sammy died in France and it cut us both in two. It was like we lost part of ourselves. Jack never complained; he was always tough. He went to war 'cause his father was English and he felt he owed it to his da. He survived Gallipoli. He got wounded at 2nd Gaza.'

He felt Sarah flinch when he mentioned Gaza, but he couldn't stop the words, they just kept coming. His voice got angrier, but no louder. He nearly whispered.

'We survived Beersheba. I killed my horse there. We got through the Jordan Valley. We won the bloody war and Jack comes home and gets killed by a bull. That's who Jack was.'

Sarah reached across and wiped the tear that ran down his cheek. She let her hand trail down his arm until it rested on his hand. Squeezing it gently, she said, 'You never get over losing the ones you love. Time helps to make it hurt not so bad, but it is always there.'

Matty made no reply. He sat there, feeling her hand on his, trying to push away his anger.

'You mentioned 2nd Gaza. That is where Spencer got wounded again. By this time, we had been writing to each other for over a year. He had told me so much about his life in England that it was like I had known him forever. He said it was the same for him with me. When I heard he was wounded again, I tried to get leave, but with all the injured that were coming in from that battle, there was not a hope in hell of Matron letting me go. We nurses were not supposed to have relationships and definitely not get married. Thousands got wounded at Gaza and it was a long time before the hospitals were cleared of them. As soon as I could, I got leave to England. Spencer had got a "Blighty". He was in a convalescent home. He wrote to say that he was nearly well and that he would be going home on leave soon.'

Sarah continued to stroke Matty's hand, feeling his anger dissipating as his muscles loosened.

'I travelled to London with some other sisters. They were just out to have a good time and try to forget the war; not that you could with uniforms everywhere and food rationing. We had finally been paid, after three months, so having a bit of money, I took myself off on the train to Leighton Buzzard. I didn't tell anyone what I was doing. We were not supposed to go about unchaperoned. When I got to Bedfordshire, I stopped and thought about it. Spencer may not like me just turning up. It seemed so forward and his parents might not appreciate it. So, I stayed at a boarding house for women and sent him a letter. Over there, the mail goes three times a day. Next morning, the landlady came huffing and puffing and carrying on about a man wanting to see me. I think she was quite put out, seeing I had just arrived.'

She smiled at the memory of the small spinster, with her airs and graces, muttering, 'This will never do, it just will not do.'

Sarah shook her head and continued, 'It was awkward at first. I had seen him in his all together when I nursed him on the boat, but that was a different situation. Now, he was whole again. A bit pale but still very handsome. He said that he had been overjoyed to get my letter and came straight away. He borrowed his neighbour's pony trap and was on pins and needles all the way there. It is only a few miles from Leighton

Buzzard to Heath and Reach. It is a funny name for a town, isn't it?'

All Matty could do was nod. Her voice was washing over him, soothing him. He knew that there would be a sad end to this story but he needed her to go on, to share her grief with him. No one had done that before except Dave. But that was different.

'June in England is so pretty. The fields are always green and where we were, the land was full of gentle hills and woods. The woods in England are nothing like our forests. Spencer had spoken to the landlord of the hotel in Reach. Heath is at the top of the hill, but they call it all Heath and Reach. The hotel was a quaint English pub called the Duke's Head. I never found out why it was called so. It was quite old and had a thatched roof. The ceilings were very low. All the houses, except the halls and manors, had low ceilings, not like our high ones here in Australia. The publican's wife made a fuss of me and put me in a beautiful room that overlooked the green. A green is sort of like a park here. There is a small chapel on it, it's very striking. Spencer had ordered some lunch. What heaven it was to eat fresh bread and cheese after the poor food we had had in Egypt. I even had some English ale, but it was not to my liking. We talked about the war. He told me he would be going to France. I must have had a look on my face – I knew how bad it was there – because he said, "Cheer up, I've made it this far." After lunch, Spencer took me around to his parents' place in Lanes End. It was a narrow lane and on either side were these little thatched cottages, just like you see in paintings. They were mixed in between taller houses. His parents were very nice but I think that they were a bit shocked that a woman would travel alone. They asked me all about Australia and my nursing. I kept it as nice as I could. People don't really want to hear about the horror of it.'

Taking a deep breath, Sarah lifted his hand, shaking it slightly. 'That is why it is so easy to talk to you. You understand. I have not had any one to talk to about it. I tried to tell my sister but she is worn out with her children and her work. She just doesn't care, now that I'm home safely.'

'Where does your sister work? Have I seen her?'

'If you have been to the Tintaldra Hotel, you would have.'

Matty shook his head. 'No, I haven't, not yet.'

'I look after my nieces and nephews when Alice is at work. The oldest boy works on the Tintaldra Station. My sister does the kitchen at the hotel and some work behind the bar during the day. The mongrel she married, he took off and left her. When I get called out, Mrs Davis, from up on the hill, keeps an eye on the children.'

There was a silence between them for a moment until Matty asked Sarah to continue her story.

'His mother was very kind, offering me a cup of tea and cake she had made. As I said before, it was good to eat nice food. I think Spencer was a bit amazed by my capacity to eat. After we left his parents' cottage, he walked me up the hill to show me where he had worked as a groom. He told me that the school master wanted him to stay in school and go on, but he loved the horses and when a job came up at the Grange, he left school. He was fifteen. At the top of the hill, which was rather steep, you could look out over the fields and about three quarter of a mile away, you could see the big house. He said that in winter, his boss – or master, they called them in England – would lend him a pony to ride, so that he didn't have to walk through the snow drifts. He spoke very well of his employers. Dusk hangs around for a long time in England and after dinner, we sat on the green. People stared at us, wondering who the strange girl was. They are very reticent over there. Some people gave Spencer a nod.' Sarah cleared her throat.

Springing up, Matty asked her would she like a drink, apologising for not offering earlier.

'No, I'm fine.' She smiled. 'It is doing me some good, sitting here with you, talking. We will get something soon, shall we?'

'Please, go on,' he said, as he sat back down, a little closer this time.

'The landlady could not believe the breakfast I ate. I had eggs and kidney, a sausage, toast and two cups of tea with fresh milk. All the food comes off the nearby farms and was just so full of freshness and taste. Spencer turned up, saying sorry he was late. He went over to the Grange stables early and got caught up talking to the old man who was left there. Spencer was very upset as all the beautiful horses he had cared for were gone to the war. The owner's sons joined the Yeomanry and took the horses. He suggested another walk, this time taking me down a hill to a wood. On the way down, he showed me the big sandpit where his father used to work. They used the sand to make glass. He was full of stories about all the different people, and the history of the place. He was really sweet. He had his mother pack a picnic basket and after we looked over the sandpits and walked through the woods, he took me to a beautiful glen. We sat and talked for ages, then had a wonderful lunch.'

Sarah stopped talking.

'If it's too much, don't go on,' he said, gently.

'No, I'm just wondering how it is that I felt such about Spencer and now…' She broke off, for once shyly hanging her head. 'I don't know you. Yes, we have shared some common horrors, but…'

Not knowing what to say, Matty sat quietly, waiting for her to make up her mind.

She started slowly. 'As you can probably guess, I am very headstrong. When Spencer proposed to me in the woods, he said that he liked me being such an independent "lass". I made up my mind not to wait. I became a woman in that glen, with the sun filtering down through the leaves and the sound of water in the brook, bubbling past. He knew that I would have to resign if I got married and he knew how much nursing meant to me. We took that moment. It was what you did, you didn't know what was going to happen in a week or a month. We spent the next week together.'

This time, it was Matty that reached out and took her hand. 'I can guess what happened. Why you are here now and not in England.'

'He survived Gallipoli, Egypt and then within three weeks of getting to France, he was gone. Literally gone. A round hit the trenches and there was nothing left of him to bury.'

Her strength gave way and she sobbed into her hands. He timidly put his arm around her shoulders, drawing her to him. Sarah lay her head on his chest and sobbed quietly, feeling safe in his embrace.

Stroking the hair back from her face, Matty thought about this woman, who sounded so strong, so sure of herself and yet was now showing her vulnerability, in such an open, honest way, to him, a stranger. She had intimated that she felt a connection. His feelings were confused. He knew something was happening to him but did not know what. The men had laughed and joked about women, some had whinged about them, but none of them had ever been so candid about how a woman feels, not the depth of which Sarah had just shared.

Pulling herself up, Sarah wiped at her face with a handkerchief she took out of her small purse. She looked at him ruefully, her eyes still watery.

'I am so sorry to have let all that down on you. It just kept coming out. I needed it to come out.' She paused, nodded her head and then continued. 'You need to let yours out as well. Maybe not now or here, but if you keep it all bottled up inside you, you will go mad.'

'Dave told us of a bloke that shot himself. I don't feel like doin' that. I'm just tryin' to work out why. Why did Sammy have to die? He was a good person. Same as Jack. I know why we went to war, all the army stuff. I just don't know why so many died.'

'As Matron said to me when we disembarked, "No sense in thinking about it. You just have to get on with it." I've tried to do that and, in a sense, I have come to peace about it all. My work helps me, and you, by listening and understanding, has helped a lot.'

She threw back her head and gave a wry smile. 'I'm sorry if I embarrassed you with my confession of being a "loose woman",' she said cheekily, watching his face redden. Then she said more seriously, 'Know that I loved him and there in that wood, I knew that the chances of me seeing him again would be very slim. The death rate on the Western Front was unbelievable. I gave him something of me before it was too late.'

The sun was falling in the west as they made their way back to the others. The air had become chill, the last of the winter cold seeping down the valley. Robert made no mention of his absence and smiled politely to Sarah. He noticed a slight change in Matty's demeanour and looked at Sarah, wondering. She gave nothing away as she agreed to meet Matty for lunch at the coffee palace the following Sunday. Matty's eyes followed her slender body as she joined another group of people, his thoughts confused but a sense of peace now rested on him.

TWENTY-SEVEN

The week dragged for Matty. His aunt and uncle watched him carefully, pleased to see his mood was a little lighter, smiling indulgently as they saw him going through the first throes of love. They may have recognised it for what it was, but Matty was simply confused. He had no close friend to discuss it with and felt embarrassed to talk to his uncle. He remembered a book by Jane Austen that his mother had made them read. They had giggled behind their hands and most of it had washed over their heads. But he now realised that his mother had tried to show them another way at looking at life – that it wasn't all horses and cattle. He thought back to what the men had talked about when they discussed women until it slowly dawned on him that he had fallen in love.

That brought its own confusion. Surely, he had no right to feel happy about meeting Sarah when his mates had never had the opportunity to experience such an emotion. He wavered between guilt and happiness for the rest of the week until he met Sarah on Sunday. She sat on the verandah, waiting for him. He swung down off his horse, standing there for a moment, taking in the sight of her, his stomach tightening as she turned her eyes towards him. He laughed to himself, thinking, 'Yep, definitely been bitten, and not by chats.'

Sarah watched Matty's face break into a smile and felt relief. She had seen too many boys turned into sad, melancholy men in the four years of war. Worse still had been the shell shock patients. They had driven some of the nurses to tears. One young man had been reduced to a child-like state and nothing could be done to bring him back. She pushed those memories away, rejoicing in the sight of this man striding up the path.

He suddenly turned shy again as he stood at the table, his hands on the back of the chair.

'Well, are you going to join me or stand there like a scarecrow?' Sarah chided him.

Swiftly, he drew out the chair and sat down, her challenge emboldening him to compliment her.

'You look really nice today.'

If Sarah was anything, it was not vain. She laughed. 'I've been up all night, delivering Sally Andrews boy over at Junction Meadows. I've only just got back and look a fright.'

The waitress interrupted them, saving Matty from trying to think of a reply. He felt very tongue tied all of a sudden.

When they ordered, Sarah sat back and took a deep breath. Her hair moved silkily, from where it had escaped her bun, as she looked about at the mountains, still capped with snow.

'I've had dinners and lunches in all parts of the world now... Egypt, France, England. But you know something? I believe that this is the prettiest scene I have ever eaten in front of.' She glanced at him and noticing his stare, smiled.

'I've eaten in some very horrible places, never mind the good ones,' Matty replied. 'I agree, this is definitely the best place, because of you.'

She took the compliment gracefully, then asked, 'So what have you been doing in the past week?'

'Uncle Robert is organising the cattle to go up to the snow leases. He reckons another three weeks will be about right.'

'And you are going?'

He stumbled over his next words. 'Well, at first, I was keen, but now I...'

She smiled, feeling happy. It had been a long time since she had felt so carefree and young. The smile went to her eyes.

'You may meet another girl on the way up there,' she teased.

The waitress plonked their food down in front of them, rattling the cutlery across the table. Sarah raised her eyebrows at the girl's behaviour but said nothing.

They ate in silence, savouring the view and each other's company. Matty marvelled at how happy he felt. They did not speak of the war, but of farming and nursing, here in the mountains. After arranging to meet again the following Saturday evening at the hotel, Matty said goodbye and rode home.

When that Saturday came, he told his aunt not to expect him for dinner. Annette had written to Eliza, telling them of Matty's new interest and how much brighter he had been lately. His aunt was just happy to see him lose some of the burden he had been carrying and waved him goodbye as he rode down the driveway.

A message awaited him at the hotel, saying that Sarah had been called out, but wouldn't be long. The publican bought him a beer, asking him about the land up north. One beer became two, then three. Matty had not drunk much at all during the war and he had not had a drink since the waterhole. The beer began to taste sour in his mouth, so he bought a rum. By the time Sarah rode up to the verandah of the pub, Matty was already half cut. He rose from his stool and nearly tripped over his own feet. He grinned up at her sheepishly, her face dark in the lamplight.

'I'm sorry I am late, it took longer than I expected,' she said.

He heard the sharpness in her voice and tried to explain. 'I don't usually drink, I got talking and well...'

He stood there, his hands playing up and down the verandah post.

'We've missed dinner, but we could go for a walk down to the river,' Matty said, carefully speaking his words. 'Honest, I don't usually drink. I'm sorry.'

Sarah dismounted, flinging the reins over her horse's head. She stood close to him, staring into his eyes. 'I've seen too many good men ruined by drink. My sister's husband is a drunk.'

Her words filtered through to his brain. 'I am sorry.'

She softened and taking his arm, walked down to the river, steadying him as he swayed. The way was lit by a three-quarter moon, its light strong enough to show the way clearly as they passed the smithy and headed down stream.

He tried to take the horse's reins from her to tie it to a tree, but she just pushed him away and did it herself. A horse's hooves clattered as a rider rode across the wooden bridge. Matty looked over his shoulder in the direction of the noise. He swayed backwards, nearly falling.

'I think you had better sit down, Matthew.'

'It's Matty. My people call me Matty,' he said, his voice sinking as he remembered who it was that had called him by that name. 'Jack called me Shorty, mostly. Cause he was taller than me.'

Sarah sensed his mood was sliding and taking his hand, led him over to the riverbank. She sat down, her legs over the edge. Turning slightly, she reached her hand up to him and beckoned for him to sit down. Carefully, so as not to fall in the water, he slowly sank to the ground.

'It hasn't rained for a while so the river is down. Has your uncle told you of the stories from years ago when they used to take the cattle down stream to cross, so as they wouldn't have to pay customs tax?' she said lightly, trying to lift his mood.

Matty just stared at the water reflecting the moonlight. He seemed entranced by it and made no sign that he had heard her.

'Matty?'

Getting no response, Sarah reached out and placed her hand on his shoulder, shaking him gently.

He turned his face slowly towards her, showing half his face in light, while the other remained in darkness. The utter sadness that showed there brought tears to her eyes. He may have come through the war without a physical wound but the wounds on his soul made her weep.

She drew him to her, wrapping her arms around him. Drawing his head down on her shoulder, Sarah gently stroked his hair, feeling him shudder with emotion as he quietly sobbed.

She felt a feather light stroking across her face as she struggled to open her eyes. The ground beneath her felt hard and as awareness came to her, she realised that she had fallen asleep, holding Matty. Now she lay on her side, her head resting on her arm. Matty lay beside her, his fingers tracing her eyebrows. The moon had sunk low on the horizon and its light showed her the face of a more sober man.

'Thank you,' he whispered. 'For being here with me.'

Her voice was husky from sleep as she answered him. 'Whatever will people say?'

Sarah laughed and sitting up, raked her fingers through her hair.

Matty stood and went down to the water, bent down and wet his handkerchief. Coming back up to her, he sat down beside her again, passing the piece of cloth to Sarah.

'I've been in for a swim while you were sleeping. It certainly fixed me up. Here, wipe your face with this.'

She had noticed that he was shirtless and barefooted; now she understood. 'I don't think I'll go in for a dip. The river is still very cold at this time of year.'

'But very refreshing.' Matty laughed. 'After the Jordan Valley, nothing is cold.'

'But the desert was hot?' Sarah said. 'I know the nights can get cold, but not that cold. Well, that's what I remember. The heat.'

'Until we went there, I didn't think it could get that cold. We were only supposed to be out for a day or two. We never took coats or blankets. We were there for five weeks. It snowed about six miles away.'

Sarah made a hu-hu sound, her eyes drawn to Matty's bare chest.

Matty reached out again, sweeping her hair back from her face.

'You are a beautiful woman, Sarah. Not just your face, but inside.'

His light touch awoke memories of Spence; she pushed them back.

He drew back his hand, looking away.

'You've never had a girl, have you?' she asked.

He dropped his head, staring at the river. 'No.'

'You have a very gentle touch, Matty,' Sarah murmured as she reached out and took his hand.

Drawing it up to her cheek, she rubbed it lightly across her lips, feeling Matty tense. She kissed his hand and drew him towards her.

Matty turned to look at Sarah. Her eyes were dark in the moonlight, her skin white. A strand of hair had fallen down over her face, he reached out to push it back. In doing so, his weight took him closer to her and she reached behind his head, drawing his face towards her, her lips touching his. He felt alive, every nerve tingling. He froze; one part of him wanted to explore this beautiful feeling, the other held him back.

Sarah made up his mind for him. Pushing him back towards the ground, she leant over, dropping light kisses over his face before kissing him deeply on the lips.

A myriad of feelings pulsated through Matty's body. His mind tried to comprehend that such a wonderful feeling could arise from simple human contact. His hands went to her hair and he drew his fingers through its heavy silky mass. His lips explored hers, taking their cue from Sarah's. He brought his hands around and put them on her cheeks, pushing her chin gently upwards so he could see her. Sarah's hair hung down, forming a shield around him, keeping her face in shadow.

'Are you sure, Sarah?'

She nodded and bent her head to him again.

Wrapping his arms around her, he rolled Sarah over until she was beneath him. Now, in the moonlight, he could see her face. Her arms reached up to him, asking for more. He raised himself on his hands, so as to take his weight from her, but she reached for him again and drew him down. He could feel his excitement growing, but he still was not sure of what she expected.

Sarah smiled, realising Matty's confusion. She pushed him onto his side, keeping her hand behind his head. Her other hand trailed down his chest towards his trousers. At the sudden intake of his breath, Sarah smiled again. Trailing her fingers up his chest, she drew feather light circles around his nipple before dipping her hand down again, towards his stomach.

Feeling his groin swelling, it was all Matty could do to remain still. He wanted to throw her back and find release. *But, it's not right,* the thought drifted into his mind. She was the teacher, let her teach.

Sarah gave a little sigh, as if realising that Matty was waiting for her. Her hand went to the buttons of his fly; one by one, she popped them. Lying back, Sarah drew his head down towards her again, her mouth reaching for his.

Matty drew her lips into his, then dropped butterfly kisses down her chin, tracking the throbbing pulse of her neck to her breast. Her body rose, arching her back, thrusting her breasts towards him. He reached around and undid the buttons of her dress, letting her breasts spring free from their restricting garment. He buried his head in the creamy soft fold of them and sucked at the hard nipples.

Sarah let out a low moan, her head turning slowly from side to side. Deep inside her, a warm throbbing rose, making her hips move in an ancient rhythm. Suddenly she sat up, pulling her bodice down to her hips, showing him her naked form. Matty sat back in wonderment, his fingers reaching out to trace the form of her shoulders, trailing down and around her breasts.

Pushing her hands under her, Sarah stood up. Reaching behind her back, she deftly loosened her dress till it slid to the ground. Her dark hair snaked down her shoulders, keeping her face in darkness as she looked down at him.

His throat tight, Matty took a deep sigh and lifting his hands, gently pulled down Sarah's undergarments. He stared at that which has entranced man for eons. Her stomach was flat, her hips rounded. His eyes strayed down to the dark patch of hair between her legs, then to her creamy thighs. He sat back on his heels and raised his eyes to her face.

Sarah saw the wonderment there, his face clear in the moonlight. She felt a surge of power, in that her body could cause a man to be in awe. She reached forward and took his hand, drawing him up to his feet. He quickly stepped out of his trousers.

They stood facing each other, their hands exploring each other's bodies until Matty took the initiative and spread Sarah's dress out on the grass. Together they sank down onto the soft material, Matty asking once more, 'Are you sure?'

Sarah nodded.

* * * *

It was time to take the cattle up to the snow leases. The past weeks had been a hive of activity, purchasing stores, running in the pack horses. They had been out for six months and were very fresh. Matty found time to ride over to Tintaldra as often as he could, visiting Sarah, their relationship growing more trusting and intimate. The day before he was to leave for the mountains, Matty rode over to say goodbye. He found out at the post office that she had gone down the river to nurse an expectant mother who was having difficulties. As she was not expected back for a few weeks, she had left him a note to say that she would miss him.

Matty pushed aside his disappointment and threw himself into his work. He could still feel her touch and the scent of lavender made him remember.

The branding and marking of the calves had been finished weeks before. They bellowed as the men pushed them out the gate and onto the road. The movements were the same, Matty thought, but the people and the countryside different. He accepted now that the shadows of Jack and Sammy would always ride with him. He found himself talking to them every now and then. His fellow workers looked at him strangely; he didn't care.

Ol' Tom drove the wagon that carried supplies and cooking utensils. He would come as far as the head of the river, then turn back, leaving the men to carry on with the pack horses. They covered nine miles the first day, letting the cattle graze as they went. The men were happy to camp near the Tooma Hotel the first night, enjoying the change of drinking hole.

Gradually they drew closer to the start of the climb up the mountain, leaving the valley behind.

The country was very different from what Matty had been brought up in and he marvelled at the tall mountain ash stretching their heads a hundred feet in to the sky. Small grey kangaroos, so small compared to the large reds, bounded away as the noise of the passing cattle scared them from their grazing. The bush opened up into clearings of snow grass and the twisted, beautifully coloured snow gums that grew here and there. The cattle were allowed to spread out now; this would be their paddock for the next five months. The men unpacked the supplies into the hut and making sure that the two stockman who would stay here were settled in, the others began the trip home.

TWENTY-EIGHT

The disappointment showed in Matty's face as he stood at the front door of Alice's house, listening to Sarah's sister telling him that Sarah had gone.

'She wrote you a note, anyways,' Alice added, taking an envelope from the mantle.

He thanked her and turned from the verandah door, slowly walking down the stairs. Catching up the reins of his horse, he wandered towards the river, instinctively heading for the place that meant so much to him.

Sitting down where they had made love, Matty opened the envelope, drawing out the thin page covered in copperplate writing.

Dearest Matty,

I am sorry that I could not wait until you returned from the mountains. An old friend of my father's telegrammed to tell me of his wife's illness. He asked that I come to stay with them, to look after her. Mrs Fletcher is very old and frail, so I must do everything for her. I do not expect to see you for some time, but I will write often.

Matty hands fell to his lap, crushing the paper they held. He felt numb. He had just begun to believe life was worth going on with, then this. His eyes went to the letter again and he forced himself to read on.

I will miss you so very much. Please do not let your memories overpower you so as to lead you to drinking too much.

I believe that you and I share a bond that is more than the war. I gave myself to you that night, knowing that I loved you. I could not say those words, you were not ready to hear them.

You have your own memories to sort out, and when you have done so, then the time will be right for us to move on with our lives.

You said I was a very forward girl, and this is true. If you read between the lines, you will see my point.

Unfortunately, they don't have a telephone on out there, so until I return, I will write you,

Always yours,
Sarah.

It took a moment for her words to sink in, but when they did, Matty jumped up whooping. His horse pulled back as he waved his arms around, his body not knowing which way to move in his excitement. Steadying the horse, he swung up into the saddle, dug his heels in and raced home.

His aunt heard him running through the house and fearing trouble, called to him. 'I am in here, Matty. In the drawing room.'

The man who came through the door was not the one who had arrived at the property four months ago. His hair was wild from his ride and his face was lit from within with a radiance that Annette immediately guessed at.

'I'm getting married, Aunt!' he shouted, the letter still clutched in his hand.

'And when will this be?' she said calmly, a smile on her lips.

'Well, I haven't proposed yet. She sort of did. But it won't be for a while, 'cause she had to go away.'

'I think you had better calm down and tell me about it.'

Matty sat down, realising he had not spoken to his aunt about Sarah. He suddenly went shy, realising that he couldn't tell his aunt everything.

'Sarah has helped me a lot since I came here, and we care for each other,' he started. 'Her letter sort of says that if I proposed to her, she would accept. But we can't until she finishes nursing an old lady down in Ballarat.'

'I see. Well, your parents will be very happy. Sarah is a lovely girl. Her father, Dr Francey, was very well-respected when he was at Tintaldra. He was an Irishman, trained at Queen's, apparently. A beautiful speaker. He sometimes led our church services when the minister could not come up from Yackandandah.'

Matty nodded, then as soon as Annette had paused, he jumped up. 'I was wonderin' if I could borrow some writing paper, to write back?'

'Over there in my desk, on the left-hand side, you will find some,' said Annette, already composing in her mind the letter she would send to Eliza.

Matty wrote every day to Sarah, describing his daily work and telling her how much he missed her. He was disappointed if he did not get a letter daily, but was happy when she wrote a long letter, telling him that she had been busy, and so caught up her news with a lengthy one.

Word reached the station that the two stockmen up at the hut on the lease had fallen ill, and a party was sent out to bring them in. Robert asked Matty to stay there with the cattle until it was time for them to come down to the river flats again.

Disappointed, but knowing he had a responsibility to help his uncle, Matty wrote a last letter to Sarah, explaining that she would not hear from him for a while. Asking for Annette's promise to keep her letters for him, Matty set off with the other men.

Taking more supplies, Matty and the others found the two men very pale and weak. They did not know why they were so ill, barely able to sit in the saddle as they left the hut the next morning to return to the station.

As Matty watched them ride away, he felt the isolation of the small slab building standing in the small clearing, a creek running past some hundred yards below it. The cattle were up higher, where the bush stopped and the high plains began. He mounted his horse again and swung its head towards where the cattle should be. The air was cool and the sun glinted off a small stream that ran between banks of alpine flowers. He noted the billy buttons, small yellow balls on a straight stem and the white everlasting daisies that felt like paper. He would bring Sarah up here when he returned to the station. Next summer, when they were married, they could ride up here together, just the two of them.

It took Matty all day to ride around the cattle as they had wandered far. He still did not get a complete count and determined to ride lower into the forests the next day to see if he could find the rest of them.

It was still dark when he rose, stirring the coals in the fireplace made of stone and corrugated iron. He dressed and went outside to feed the horses. The horse that the men had left as a spare for him trotted over in expectation, while Matty's horse nickered and walked quietly to him. After pouring out some grain into the two cut down kerosene tins, he went to get some wood.

He never thought that salted meat would ever taste good to him again, but the corned meat he now heated on a frying pan over the coals was fresh and the smell made his stomach grumble. He put the kettle on the fire, then reached for the bread that Mrs Nealle packed for him, tearing off a piece to have with the beef. He banked up the fire to have some coals left when he returned.

After washing the pan and rinsing his cup, Matty saddled his horse, feeling sorry for the other horse who raced around his yard, whinnying, eager to come. He headed east, riding in and out of clearings, looking for signs of cattle having grazed these areas. Faintly he heard the call of a calf to its mother and he turned his horse's head in its direction.

Down in a small valley, the forest opened up into a large clear area, bisected by a small creek. Several cattle lay in the sun, chewing their cud, while others moved about snatching at the grass. Stopping his mount, he counted twenty-one head, still short fifteen. Pushing the horse into a walk again, he headed up a steep incline back towards the hut. He would stop in, have some lunch and change horses.

A lyrebird, who had stood still at the approach of the horse, suddenly ran across the track, its long tail jiggling behind it. The horse threw his head up and shied sideways. Matty, not expecting it, lost his balance and fell from the saddle, his leg under him as he hit the ground. He heard a sharp crack before rolling down the steep hill. Trees and bush picked at him as he tumbled before he came to a stop, his head against a rock.

He lay there; he made no sound. His head on the cool snowgrass, his eyes wide open, staring at the tall stark white ghost gums dancing above him. A rosella flew low, skimming, and he heard the beat of its wings. He smelt the damp decay of the forest floor. The sky pressed down on him with its crispness. He felt the earth cold beneath him and still he made no sound.

Is this how they felt when they lay dying? Did they see the sky, did they feel the earth beneath them? Did they feel no pain? Suddenly a surge of agony stabbed at his leg and he screamed, his mouth opened wide, teeth bared. His scream echoed in the hills and came back to him. Birds flew up from the trees and small animals scurried away from the sound.

The burning pain subsided to a dull ache and now he could feel the throbbing in his head. He reached behind and pushed himself up. Pain and nausea hit him as the movement shifted the broken bone in his leg. He stiffened, biting down on his lip. Pulling up his trouser leg, he looked at his leg – not a blemish, only a slight swelling to show what caused the pain. He stared at it, wondering, why? Why? Was this all it was? He raised his head and screamed in anger at the trees.

'Jack… Sammy… I thought I'd joined you. Why do I live? Am I meant to marry Sarah? Why'd they have to die, all our mates? Why did you have to die?'

Then he cried. Great sobs of anguish broke the stillness of the bush as the tears rolled unheeded down his face. Moments passed until he had no more tears. He lay down again, on the springy snowgrass and closed his eyes.

An hour passed and the air grew chill. His eyelids flickered and opened slowly. He stared at the sky, its azure fading into pearl as the sun faded. Rising slowly, grimacing at the pain in his leg, he looked around him. His horse had gone, either to return to the hut or join the brumbies. It was no help to him, either way. Dragging himself up, he hopped on one leg, from one tree to another, cursing as each jolting move sent pain stabbing through his leg. He looked around him for a fallen piece of timber that he could make into a crutch. Nothing. It was all small twigs and thin branches. His vision blurred and feeling giddy, he slid back to the ground. Slowly, one hand after the other he pulled himself on his stomach, up the hill, using his good leg to propel himself forward, dragging the damaged one. Once he reached the ridge, he could see the hut, far away in a clearing, its chimney leaking wisps of smoke into the darkening sky. Matty lowered his face into the tufts of snowgrass, a thumping band of pain across his forehead.

'I bloody told you we'd be mates to the end, Jack. I just don't understand. You lived through all that hell could throw at us and you had to die at home, so easy, so wastefully. If I stay here, I'll join you, I know that. I wouldn't mind. I haven't been alive since you and Sammy went, not till I met Sarah. But, what about the others? Are they waiting for me? Should we've died with them?' he raged.

Matty turned over, staring at the darkening sky. The coldness crept into him and he drew his knees up, grimacing as the pain flared again.

You spoke of nearly freezing to death over there, on Gallipoli. Is this how it will be for me? he thought. Images of the desert came to his scattered mind. *I reckoned we'd finish our days outback, at home, with the warmth and the memories. But, no, that all-knowing bastard up there, he took you.*

Matty shivered as he felt the cold from the ground leach into him. Time passed as his mind wandered, staring at the night sky, lit with a thousand stars. There was a comfort to it, a huge deep blackness, lit with blue, white grains. They swirled and then spiralled down at him, each with its own voice.

'Here I am, Shorty. I'm the one on the left of the saucepan.'

'How about me, Matty? Remember me. Bluey, I was with you at Beersheba. I'm here.'

The voices kept coming as the stars fell towards him.

'Now, look here. You pulled me out of that scrap at Gaza, but it was too late. I'm here too. I'm part of the Centaur. Christopher, old mate.'

Raising his palms to his temples, he gripped the sides of his face and screamed, tears cold on his cheeks.

'What am I supposed to do? I don't know why I lived. Why am I still here… I should be with you blokes. Why are you dead? Why did I live? What made the difference? I was shot at. Why did the bullets miss me, take you instead?'

Vibrations entered his body through the ground. It came to his consciousness slowly. Matty relaxed, letting it flow into his hurting. Suddenly, he knew them for what they were – the pounding of hooves upon the ground. He sat up. It was like the charge; it was horses galloping.

Before him, in the light of the rising moon, through watery eyes, he saw ten – no, twelve brumbies, racing through the trees. The shadows played along their bodies, making them into dreams. A young horse, lagging behind, was given a swift nip on the rump by the stallion bringing up the rear.

Taking a deep breath, Matty wiped his eyes and stared at the young horse. In the silvery light, it appeared nearly black but the four white stockings and white blaze stood out as if a torch shone on them.

'Cedar. Oh, my god. Do you now haunt me too?' he moaned.

The herd passed, leaving silence in its wake. Like an animal, Matty crawled up close to a fallen log. He pushed up against it, shivering in the cooling night and from the pain of his broken leg. He closed his eyes with the smell of damp earthy decay in his nostrils.

The night sounds did not penetrate his consciousness. He slept as though he had joined the dead. The dew fell and glistened in the moonlight, while the tall ghost gums, starkly white, stood sentinel over him. A mopoke broke the quietness with its lonely cry. A wombat trundled by, his nose to the ground. It smelt the human smell, looked about, before continuing quickly on his way. The moon passed overhead, washing out the stars with its brightness. And still, Matty slept.

The dew turned to frost as the temperature dropped. His body began to shiver again. The pain that had subsided flared again. He opened his eyes, feeling the sleep grit in them. A pair of wallabies sat staring at him, their brown eyes unblinking, their front paws dangling.

He raised a hand to wipe the scum from his eyes and the wallabies fled, their bounding crashing through the scrub. Pushing himself into a sitting position, he grabbed his broken leg under the thigh and manoeuvred it around in front of him, grunts of pain rattling in his throat.

Matty stared about him, seeing the glittering frost, marvelling at its purity. He saw the gums, their whiteness. All about him, bathed in moonlight, was an ancient forest, cradling all forms of life. He put back his head and looked up at the trees, so tall, so straight, and beyond them, the moon, starting its path down toward the horizon.

'It stays here, doesn't it, Jack? While we go off and kill each other, the land stays the same. It may burn or it may thirst, but it comes back to life. The animals return and they go on. They don't know any different.

Is this what I am supposed to learn? Is this why I fell? I've been so pissed off since you died. Felt cheated. Maybe, there is a reason I'm still here,' he whispered to the moon. 'I wish I knew what it was?'

He felt calm, calmer than he had felt since the war. He let his mind wander to places it hadn't been for a long while. The memories were not of death, but of smiling faces and proud horses. He saw them standing beside their horses, waiting for the call to mount. He saw them clustered around the two-up circle, laughing and joking. Billy, sitting backwards on a donkey, playing the fool. Bluey, getting yelled at by the sergeant, for talking on parade. What a bunch of mates they had been.

Was he going to cop out now, after all they had done to help keep him alive back then? He pulled himself up onto the log, pausing for a moment to let the pain settle.

Leaning forward carefully, he searched through the litter of the trees until he found two straight sticks. Using his knife, he slit his trouser leg up the seam. Then, tearing off the bottom of his shirt, he splinted his leg, crudely, but tightly. He sat up, breathing heavily.

'Should have done this before. Now, if I take it steady, I should be able to make it to that tree over there,' he said to the still cold air. 'It's the shock that made me think those things. I've got Sarah now.'

He stood up on one leg. Feeling faint, he wobbled for a moment, but then his head cleared. Lifting his injured leg, he took a first hop, nothing more than a shuffle, really, but the pain shot up his leg. He stopped and leant against a tree, gingerly putting his foot down. Lifting his head, he saw the hut. There, he knew, was warmth and food. That would be a start.

With the help of a branch he used as a crutch, it took him several hours to reach the hut where he sat down gratefully on the chair in front of the fire. The horse that remained in the yard called earnestly, hungry. Matty drank heavily from the kettle that sat on the now cold fire. He was exhausted from the effort of getting back to the hut, but he knew that he needed to get the fire going and to eat. Gritting his teeth, he put his weight on the branch and made his way outside. He considered hobbling the horse and letting it out to graze, but decided it might stray and so far, the other horse had not returned, so he fed it some grain, checked it still had water and left, promising it that he would try to get out later and let it graze from a rope. He carried two pieces of wood into the hut, then went back out for some kindling. His frustration at his inability to move freely, and at the pain in his leg, caused him to curse frequently.

He dragged the chair close to the fire where he could sit with his injured leg straight out in front of him and get the fire going. This achieved, Matty hobbled to the meat safe and brought out the last of the bread. He tore off a chunk, eating it as it was, not bothering to put jam on it.

He glanced at the cot in the corner enviously, but he knew he had to get in more wood and have a look at his leg. Slowly, resting between each load, his leg throbbing, Matty brought in one piece at a time until he had enough to see him through the night. He untied the laces of his boot, feeling instant relief as the choking boot released the pressure on his swollen ankle. Unwrapping the material from the sticks on either side of his leg, Matty stared at his lower leg. From his ankle to his toes was black with bruising, while streaks of blue and purple made their way up towards his knee. His looked at his leg critically, trying to see if it was crooked at any point. Happy that it appeared to be a clean break, Matty replaced the splint, took off his other boot and made his way over to the cot.

He slept for a couple of hours, his body worn out from the pain and exertion it had endured. He dreamt of Sarah, stirring only when the horse outside whinnied loudly and he heard hoof beats heading towards the hut. He put one boot on and seeing the swelling in his other leg had hardly gone down, Matty put only a sock on that foot. Reaching for his crutch, he slipped, his injured leg hitting the ground hard. A muffled scream came from him and tears sprung into his eyes. Sitting back down, he took deep breaths, trying to get the pain under control. Gradually, it died down to a bearable level and he again reached for his crutch, this time being successful. It took him some minutes to hobble to the door and out around to the horse yard. There, the cause of his accident stood, minus the bridle, but with the saddle still firmly on. The returned horse was exchanging snorts and nickers over the fence with the bay and eagerly entered the gate that Matty opened. Putting a scoop of grain in each of the feed bins, Matty undid the girth, dragging the saddle across onto the fence. Now that the grey was back, he could possibly hobble one horse at a time and allow it to graze, sure that it would not wander far from its mate.

The days passed slowly for Matty. He learnt just how much he could do before his leg started to swell, then he would rest it, keeping it propped up in front of him on an old packing case. He hobbled each horse alternatively and let them out to graze for a few hours. They would return to the yard when he called, eager for some oats.

Taking his rifle, he made his way a distance from the hut and sat patiently, hoping for a roo to come down to water. Just as the sun was setting, he shot a male and sitting on the grass, he skun it there. Slicing the meat off the bone, he placed it in the flour bag he brought with him, enjoying the thought of fresh meat that night. The rest he would salt down in the small barrel kept for that purpose. He was grateful that his uncle kept the hut well-stocked. He would not run out of much before the men were due to return for the muster in three more weeks. Trips to the creek for water, and making damper kept him occupied, as well as the slow trips into the forest for fallen branches that he could hack into pieces short enough for the fire.

It often occurred to him what a body could manage when a part of it was injured. All he had was a broken leg. Others had lost a leg or legs, or an arm, and they seemed to have adapted. His thoughts went often to Jack and Sammy and his Light Horse mates. The grief had been packed away, but the memories remained. He knew that this was thanks to having Sarah to talk to, to understand and to look forward to the future with.

TWENTY-NINE

A packet of letters from Sarah waited for him in his room. After his aunt has fussed over him and Robert made sure that he was recovering well from his accident, Matty went to his room and opened them. He started with the latest one.

Dearest Matty,

I have not heard from you for some time, not since your letter saying that you were going to get some men from the hut. I worried and so I wrote to your aunt. She assured me that you would write as soon as you returned from the mountains.

I have some news and there is no way to tell you but straight.

I am carrying your child. I was certain of this when I left Tintaldra but knew that you were not ready for a burden of this kind. Your letters over the past months have shown me that you have not lost your love for me and that you have started to deal with your grief.

I don't know if you will still want me or how your relatives will feel. The doctor has been very kind to me and would like me to stay here till the child is born but I am nearly due and wish to come home to have the child.

Please write to me as soon as you get this to tell me of your feelings.

Your loving Sarah.

Matty sat dumbfounded, thoughts racing through his mind. How dare she presume not to tell him. He was going to be a father. She loved him enough to know he needed time. Suddenly the full realisation hit him. Sarah had written this three weeks ago. She said she was nearly due.

Grasping the letter, he went to find his uncle. He was candid as he laid his problem before Robert. He watched as a myriad of expressions crossed his uncle's face, finally settling into thoughtfulness.

'You obviously still wish to marry the girl?'

'Yes, Uncle. The child is mine and I love Sarah. I'll leave first thing in the morning, ride to Cudgewa and catch the train to Albury. From there I'll take the train to Ballarat. I have her address.'

'She might have told you a bit sooner,' his uncle suggested.

Matty shook his head. 'That's what is so great about her, Robert. She wasn't thinking of herself. She wanted me to start getting over… before she laid this on me.'

'Well, what's done is done. Have you enough money?'

They broke the news to Annette at the dinner table. She took it calmly, her mind already making future.

'Where do you want to get married? Here in the garden would be very pretty,' she asked.

Matty shrugged. 'That will be up to Sarah. She may want to wait until after the baby is born.'

That comment made his aunt raise her eyebrows. 'The child would be born out of wedlock! No, I think it had better be sooner than later.'

Robert cleared his throat. 'We shall see when these two get together and work it out.'

Barking dogs, followed by a pounding on the back door, brought the conversation to a stop. Mrs Nealle came fluttering into the dining room, a yellow telegram envelope in her hand.

'It's for Matty,' she said worryingly. Telegrams were not usually good news at this time of night; the telephone was more often used nowadays.

Matty reached out and took the envelope from the housekeeper, his mind searching for a reason. His parents, some problem at Mulga Plains? He tore it open, hastily reading the few short lines it contained.

As his aunt and uncle watched, Matty's face turned grey and he threw the message on the table. Scraping back his chair violently, he leapt up. 'I must go to her. I'll take a lantern… no… the moon is full.'

Robert stood, reaching out to catch Matty's arm. 'What has happened, Matty? Tell us.'

Annette had leant over and read the piece of paper. She stared up at her nephew. Her thoughts jumped around. 'How could such a young man have so much trouble in his young life?'

Speaking softly but clearly, she said, 'Robert, Sarah went into labour on the way home. She is in Albury hospital. There are complications. She wishes to see Matty urgently.'

The words galvanised Robert into action. 'I'll come with you. You'll need someone to make sure you don't kill yourself or the horse. We will take the two thoroughbreds, they're the fittest. Mrs Nealle, while we saddle up, will you pack a flask of tea and a couple of sandwiches? And someone had better tell her sister.'

'We haven't got time,' Matty yelled.

'Matty, stop and think. It will do Sarah no good if you exhaust yourself before we get there. We will need food and will have to have rest stops for the horses, so calm down and start to think, man.'

Matty nodded his head in agreement. 'I am sorry, Uncle. All I know is, I need to get to Sarah.'

He turned to Annette. 'Aunt, could you send a telegram to the hospital in the morning? Tell Sarah we are on our way,' he asked. 'And… please… tell her I love her.'

His throat worked at the last words and striding out of the room, he went to saddle the horses.

It was only ten minutes before they were cantering down the

driveway, saddlebags packed with food and drink.

Common sense had returned to Matty. He explained to Robert how they used to travel long distances in the desert. 'We would trot for twenty minutes, canter for twenty minutes, walk for ten minutes and halt for ten. These horses are not as fit as those what were in the war. No horse here today is as tough and fit as ours were.'

It occurred to Robert that this was the first time Matty had volunteered anything about his time overseas. 'That sounds just the thing. If the horses get too knocked up, we'll stop and have an hour's rest, all right?'

At times Robert fell asleep in the saddle, his aging body not as fit as Matty's, but they kept going until faint light showed over the hills to the east. After unsaddling the horses, the men watered them at the river, then sat down to eat the sandwiches. While Robert slept, Matty sat thinking about Sarah. He tried to close his eyes and sleep, but every moment since he met her went through his mind. His anxiety made him get up after an hour and saddle up the horses. Gently he woke Robert, who looked worn out.

'Uncle, I'll ride on and you can catch me up at the hospital,' Matty suggested.

'No, no… I'll be fine.'

'I know that you're fit, Robert, but you're not a spring chicken anymore. Please, Aunt will never forgive me if you have an accident or anything.'

Robert saw the concern in his nephew's face and as much as he did not want to admit it, his body was aging, much against his will, and his bones did ache.

'All right. You should make it there by midday. I'll meet you at the hospital. If we had gone down the other side of the river, we could have caught the new train at Cudgewa.'

'But it only runs to Albury three times a week,' said Matty. 'At least this way, I know I'll be there by lunchtime.'

Matty mounted his horse and trotted down the road, leaving his uncle to rest a bit longer before climbing into the saddle.

The hours passed slowly, Matty's mind alternating between the worst of thoughts and hope that all would be fine when he got to the hospital. He wished that he had Cedar beneath him; she would have felt his need. She would have gone that bit harder than the horse he rode now.

By the time Matty rode up Dean Street in Albury, the thoroughbred was lathered in sweat and its flanks heaving. He spotted the saddler who had sold him his first two horses when he got to Albury all those months ago. Dismounting, he called to the man he could see bent over, stitching a bridle.

'I need to find the hospital,' he said as the old man came out.

'I remember you, sold you a couple of horses.'

Matty tried to hold his impatience. 'Yes, I did buy them, but now I've to get to the hospital. Could tell me where it is?'

'You're nearly there, young man. It's next block down, round the corner.'

Matty looked in the direction that the saddler pointed. Turning back to him, he said, 'I can walk from here. Could you look after my horse? I've ridden him hard, and he needs a rub down and a feed.'

'I can see that. He's a bloody mess. But I'll do him for you.'

With that, Matty passed him the reins and ran awkwardly down the street, his healing leg stiff and sore.

THIRTY

The main door of the building led into a long corridor, its quietness broken only by the soft tread of a nurse going about her duties. Matty looked about wildly for a desk or office where he could get some information.

Before he could move, a matron came up the corridor towards him, her long dress rustling as she walked straight-backed.

'Are you in need of help, young man?' she asked, looking him up and down.

Matty suddenly took stock of how he must look, no sleep, having not washed, his clothes dirty and travel-worn.

'No, Miss, I'm fine. I've come about Sarah Francey. She's to be my wife. She sent me a telegram. She is having a baby.' The words tumbled out anxiously.

The matron's face remained impassive. She nodded thoughtfully, turning as she did so.

'I am Matron Abott. Will you come with me?'

Confused, Matty followed the woman into a room off to one side of the corridor. She gestured for him to be seated in a large, winged chair by the fireplace. As he looked around, Matty saw a portrait of a nurse with medals on her chest. He noticed the settee and wondered if this was a waiting room. The matron sat down stiffly in the chair opposite him. She looked him over again, noticing his tired confused eyes.

'I believe that Miss Francey has a sister in Tintaldra? She made mention of her.'

'Yes, but I haven't seen her. We left last night, on horseback. My uncle is coming behind me. I'll contact Alice when I find out how Sarah is. How is she?'

The matron paused, considering her answer.

'There is no way to tell you other than to speak plainly,' Matron Abott said slowly. 'Miss Francey died at ten-thirty this morning.'

She was not ready for the reaction her words caused. Matty slumped in the chair, his eyelids flickering. The woman bent over the chair, calling to him, trying to get a response. He lay back, his head lolling against the headrest of the chair. Quickly, she rose and flung open the door.

Catching sight of a nurse passing by, she gave orders that the doctor be found immediately and brought to the waiting room. Turning back to Matty, the matron once again knelt by his side, slapping his face. Of all the reactions she had expected, it was not this.

In the two nights she had sat with Sarah, as the girl struggled in pain, the matron learnt of Sarah's nursing and her war service. Sarah had also spoken of Matty and his struggle to come to terms with the loss of his friends. Matron Abott recognised bravery when she saw it. She had shared Sarah's war experiences herself and her heart had gone out to the girl, and now to this young man, who again must cope with tragedy.

The doctor arrived, an old bespectacled man, his knees creaking as he lowered himself down to examine Matty.

'I've seen this before, Matron, as I am sure you have.'

The matron nodded. 'This is the young man I was waiting for. Miss Francey's intended. I fear the news has been too much. They went through so much in the war, these poor boys, and now this one… he must cope with this, on top of everyone he has lost.'

'Ah, it is a sad case, is it not? The poor girl, I knew her father when he was here. A fine man.' The doctor shook his head. He leant on the chair to help himself up. 'Call the orderlies and we will get him onto a bed. The shock has tipped him. We will have to be careful when he regains consciousness.'

A few hours later, Matty felt the bed hard beneath him, a cool wet sponge drawn across his face. He stared up into the eyes of the woman who had told him something bad. He couldn't remember what it was.

He struggled to sit up; he had to find Sarah.

'What am I doing here? Where's Sarah?' he demanded.

The matron thought carefully before she replied. 'You passed out from your long ride. I'll just get the doctor to have a look at you, shall I?'

Matty made to get off the bed, but the matron pushed him back. 'Nurse Brown, will you please fetch Doctor Felman? Tell him Mr Watson is awake.'

A small, blonde woman whom Matty hadn't noticed left the room, returning quickly with the old doctor.

'He doesn't remember, Doctor.' Matron's words were brief.

'Remember what? Where's Sarah?' Matty's voice rose in anger.

The doctor came to stand by the bed, glancing at the matron before speaking. 'We have some bad news for you, Mr Watson. The matron told you before and you collapsed.'

The matron came to stand by him, taking his hand in hers.

'I sat with Sarah for the last few days, Mr Watson. She spoke of her time in the war, but mostly she spoke of you and her love for you. I am sorry to tell you… Sarah died at ten-thirty this morning. She left…'

Matty's face contorted, his hands clutching the sheets. The previous words of the matron now flooded back. 'No… not Sarah. No…' Matty sobbed. He held his head; it felt like it would burst. His heart raced, throbbing, and he swung his head from side to side. He stopped and stared at the matron. 'How, why?'

'Sarah started to haemorrhage; there was nothing that could be done.

She was very brave. Her last words were for you.'

Matty sunk his face into his hands.

'Sarah said to tell you she loved you and that you must get on with your life, not to live in the past.'

He covered his ears and rocked back and forth as he gave way to his grief. Matron Abott glanced at the doctor, who shook his head.

Drawing her aside, he whispered, 'I will give him a sleeping draught. At least he has taken it in this time.'

The matron's eyes flicked towards Matty, then looked back at the doctor. Squaring her shoulders, she made a suggestion.

'Highly irregular, madam, but it may help,' the doctor said, peering down his nose at the matron.

She nodded, and with Matty's anguished sobbing ringing in her ears, the matron left the room.

Matty slid down, rolling onto his side. He drew his knees up and put his arms over his head, trying to shut it all out: the hospital, the doctor, the truth.

'Oh, Sarah. Why didn't you tell me sooner?' he moaned. 'I was too late. Should have known.'

Within minutes the door to the ward opened. The matron, followed by Nurse Brown, walked briskly up to the bed where Matty lay with his face to the wall. As Matron Abott looked down at the man on the bed, her usually stern face was compassionate.

She reached over him and placed her hands on his shoulders. He tried to shrug them off, but her abrupt words stopped him.

'Sit up, Mr Watson.'

With her arm behind his back, Matty allowed her to pull him forward, his head still turned to the wall, his hands loose by his sides. The nurse stepped forward, placing the bundle she carried in his lap as Matron Abott put her head close to Matty's.

'Hold your daughter, Matty,' she said. 'She is Sarah's legacy to you.'

As her words penetrated his thoughts, Matty's head snapped up. He could feel a weight on his legs and he looked down. There, swaddled tightly in a small white blanket, lay a baby. He stared, transfixed by the small face with her eyes screwed shut, her mouth opening in a yawn. Instinctively, his arms went around the baby, bringing her close to his chest.

Tears rolled down his cheeks, splashing onto the child's creamy skin. The baby opened her eyes, and although unfocused, they seemed to be staring up at him.

His grief at Sarah's death receded for a moment as a love like no other he had ever felt rose from his soul. He and Sarah had created this tiny being. Amazement and joy flooded through him.

Matron Abott watched Matty's face and wiped her own eyes before leaning towards him once more. 'As Sarah grew weaker, she made me promise to tell you this.'

Her words brought back his grief and he looked up at her, his eyes dark with emotion.

'Sarah said… "Matty, the war is over. Let our daughter be free of our sorrow. You couldn't understand why you survived, while your friends died. Our child is your answer."'

His eyes dropped to the face of his daughter.

He now knew why.

ACKNOWLEDGEMENTS

This story took me many years to get to this point, and without making this a novel of its own, I would like to thank those that helped.

In 2007, my family sent me on a trip to the WW1 battlefields – thank you, Jasmine and Kevin.

I was accompanied by the most wonderful group of friends, who understood my tears, my moods, and my need to explore. Andrew, Heather, Jeff, Sigrid and Tim.

Special thanks to Maija Wilson for initial editing and encouragement; Heather Ford (Frev), my first reader, researcher and shoulder to lean on; Jeff Pickerd for his many hours of help; Dr Honor Auchinleck, for encouragement and knowledge, Rebecca Whitehead for editing and encouragement, and Sonya Kurnof, for believing.

This story is one that relies heavily on historical research. In today's modern internet age, the help I received for this research came from all around the world.

Some people went above and beyond in providing historical documents, advice and hometown knowledge.

Steve Becker, Steve Fuller, Lt Col Glyn Llanwarne OAM, Andrew Pittaway OAM, Tim Lycett, Brig. Chris Roberts AM, CSC (Rtd), David Lam MD (Rtd), Christopher Walsh, Graeme Hosken, Pat Gavan, Eric Goossens, Kenen Celik, Prof Dr Haluk Oral, Rob Thomas, Grant Roff,

Sabine Declercq, Allie Toledo, Richard Crispin, Gal Shaine, Bruce and Julie Hearn, Fiona Boers and Janice Newnham.

Members of the Light Horse and Great War Forums, with special thanks to those of the Great War Forum's Art and Skindles sections, who gave encouragement and support.

www.greatwarforum.org

John Marsden and the Tye Estate.

The National Archives of Australia.

The Australian War Memorial.

Alana Lambert, Katrina Burge, and Steve Williams for support, editing and design.

For never-ending support and love, Jasmine and Samuel.

If I have left someone out, I do apologise.

Cheers

Kim

Web: kimwinter.com

Email: hello@kimwinter.com

Facebook/Instagram @kimwinterauthor